Suddenly, her eyes snapped open and Haylee froze. These eyes did not belong to the woman she once knew; they held a feral madness.

The fierceness projected from her mother's eyes forced Haylee back, but something clamped around her wrist. She looked down and saw her mother's good hand gripping her with incredible strength. Haylee stifled a cry as panic swept through her. She struggled to break free, but the woman's grip was too strong. The partially paralyzed arm was also in motion, pawing at Haylee's face, seeking to tear at her eyes.

"Witch," the woman hissed.

The claw jabbed out. Haylee managed to turn her head so the fingers missed her eye. Instead, they tore away skin from her cheek.

"Momma, stop," Haylee cried, grabbing her mother's wrist before she could do more damage.

"You wasn't as smart as you thought, was you, Petweenus?" The pressure on Haylee's wrist increased. Haylee bit her lip from the pain. "It's me that's got *you* now."

"Momma, it's me, Haylee."

The woman, partially erect, turned to the side, and began forcing Haylee to the floor.

"Momma, please." Haylee cried again.

# PETWEENUS

a novel

by

## Ronald Polizzi

PETWEENUS is published by:
Deer Hawk Publishing, an imprint of Deer Hawk Enterprises
www.deerhawkpublications.com

Copyright © 2011 by Ronald Polizzi
www.ronaldpolizzi.com

This is a work of fiction. Names, characters, places, brands,
media and incidents portrayed in this book are either the
product of the author's imagination or are used fictitiously.
Any resemblance to actual persons, living or dead, events or
locales is entirely coincidental.

Cover design by:
Ray Polizzi

Layout by:
Aurelia Sands

Library of Congress Control Number:
2012932307

Printed in the United States of America

In loving memory of Ruby Marie Leytham

First I'd like to thank my wife Susan for bravely reading through the creepy parts of the manuscript after each edit something she found uncomfortable and unable to sleep afterwards. Thanks to my brother Ray, Granny Fairy, my *adopted* sister Edrina and to my fans. I couldn't do it without you.

A special thanks to Aurelia Sands the most patient editor in the world.

## Slaughter County
## March 30, 2008

When Riddle stepped out of the cool interior of the patrol car, the heat hit him like a fist. Though still early March, the temperature hovered in the 90s and threatened triple digits in the upcoming months. Not only was it hot, but the mosquitoes were out. Riddle swatted at the mosquito buzzing around his head, cursing Field Agent Coleman with each swat. The ATF agent, dressed in a three-piece suit, stood a little distance away and showed no sign of discomfort in the heat or from the bugs. He motioned Riddle over.

"We got a clever one, Sheriff," he said.

Riddle slapped another mosquito on his left upper arm. Lifting his hand, he smiled at the tiny trace of blood.

The agent glared at the tall sheriff who paid no attention to him. "You with me Riddle?" Coleman asked, his voice sharp.

"It's hot today." Riddle fired back, wiping his hand on his pants leg. "And my damn car's covered with red clay from following your ass down this damn road. I spent all day yesterday waxing the thing."

"Well, I'm sorry about your car, but we got a job to do."

Coleman sighed. Why the hell did they always saddle him with these sorry excuses for law enforcement officers?

1

"I said, we got a clever one."

"What's that?" Riddle asked.

"I'm talking about the blockader, Riddle." Coleman growled, "That's why we come, remember?"

"What about him?"

"Most fellers would either go directly from the road, or they'd tromp across level ground a hundred yards into the woods, then cut over to pick up the trail to their still. This one is different."

Coleman paused to point to a tangle of brush high on the ridge where a few tall pines stretched against a cloudless blue sky. "He approaches his still from above. He circles up the ridge, and then doubles back down to the trail."

Riddle raised his eyelids slightly and Coleman thought he caught a flash of interest.

"How you figure that?" the sheriff asked, lowering his eyelids.

Coleman grinned. *He's trying to hide the fact I piqued his curious bone, but I saw him start.*

"Our feller snagged a bag of sugar when he was getting it out of the trunk. He left a trail of it leading up the ridge. Too bad you missed it, Sheriff.

"Yeah, poor me."

"Well, enough of this jawin'," Coleman pointed at the trees with the ax he'd gotten out of his trunk, "I say, let's go get ourselves a blockader."

Coleman gave a shout and charged headlong into a mass of briers and tangled limbs, swinging the ax like a berserker. The axe sliced easily through the tangle of kudzu and berry vines. Riddle followed behind.

"I been thinking," Riddle said as they climbed the ridge, "That maybe we shouldn't be traipsing through these woods. Strange stuff happens up here. There's a witch lives here with a bunch of demons. I've had to collect three bodies on this ridge just this year. The shiners feel the same as I do about this place. I doubt we'll find anything."

Coleman stopped, letting his axe fall beside his leg. He turned his head in a deliberate motion to face Riddle.

"Sheriff, I expect you to discharge your duties as specified by your office without no more bellyachin'."

Riddle's face reddened. The two men faced each other eye to eye. Coleman wondered if the big law officer was going to swing at him. Riddle opened his mouth, then closed it again. His eyes burned into Coleman's. After a moment, the fiery stare subsided as Riddle's demeanor cooled.

"Lead on, Mr. Coleman," he said, finally, "You find the still and I promise I'll carry out my part."

"I'm glad we understand each other," said Coleman.

Coleman started forward again, carving the trail with his axe. This section of the ridge proved to be tough. Roots tugged at their boots and shoes, and briers snagged their pant legs. Several times, they were forced to stop and untangle themselves from low-hanging kudzu vines. Finally, Coleman called a halt.

"Here's the spot," Coleman said, making a sort of U-turn onto a thin ribbon of trail snaking into the brush. The trail widened into a footpath as it angled down. Coleman rested the axe in the crook of his arm.

Fifteen minutes later, Coleman found the first signs of real evidence. Dropping to one knee, he jabbed a finger excitedly at a spot near his foot.

"See here," he cackled, "Mule tracks. Looks to me like two mules, each one led by a feller."

Riddle eyed the misshapen depression surrounded by scuffmarks, but said nothing.

"I figure it can't be far off." Coleman continued, rising to his feet.

He brushed off his knees and examined the underbrush. Suddenly, Coleman gave a cry of excitement and rushed into the scrub.

"Riddle, come here!" Coleman yelled. "I want to show you something."

Riddle ducked under the low branches bordering the trail and worked his way through the scrub to Coleman.

"These are all hardwood," Coleman said, pointing to half a dozen medium-sized stumps with the axe handle. "Our blockaders needed fuel to fire their still, so they cut down these oak saplings--not too big to fit the furnace, but large enough to burn steady for a time."

Coleman circled the stumps to a long, thin rut that stretched across the ground like a scar. Brushing away the leafy carpet covering much of the mark, he revealed another shallow trench.

"Here's where they dragged the logs." said Coleman. "More than likely, they used the mules to move them. They did a poor job of covering up the tracks, though." Coleman motioned with his axe. "Come on, it's got to be close."

Coleman followed the trench until it played out over a hard patch of ground filled with watermelon-sized boulders and gravel-sized pebbles. He paused.

"It's going to be hide and seek from here on out," he said. "Our blockader's still's somewhere down there, in the brush," he pointed where the land fell away in a gentle downward slope. "If we continue in that direction, I figure we'll be close."

The two men worked their way down the slope while Coleman continued to rant. "I figure our man set up his equipment near water. I understand there's a creek somewhere at the bottom of this here grade. I'll bet my twenty-five years of service that's where we'll find our target."

They reached the place where the ground leveled off when Coleman noticed an uncomfortable pressure building in his bladder--a need that could not be ignored for long.

Coleman called a halt.

"You check over there," he said to Riddle. Doing his best to hide his discomfort from the

5

sheriff, he pointed to a thick clump of scrub to his right.

"I'll go in this direction. No point in both of us searching the same spot."

Coleman watched the tall man move toward the trees. A moment later, the brush swallowed Riddle up. When Riddle disappeared, Coleman grabbed his crotch and did a hop-like dance in the opposite direction. He prayed he wouldn't pee his pants before he put a satisfactory distance between himself and the sheriff.

Less than twenty feet into the brush, Coleman heard the gurgle of moving water.

"By Gawd, that's the creek!" he muttered.

*You deserve a pat on the back, Coleman. This is the water you were looking for, that still's got to be close.*

Pushing through a patch of leggy, young growth, he parted the greenery, revealing sparkling, clear water. For a moment, he forgot all about his urge to empty his bladder. Sunlight danced on the surface of the creek as the water churned its way along. The sandy bottom tinted the water and looked as if a liquid ribbon of gold, kissed on each side by a thin, sandy bank of purest white, flowed past him.

"Why, this is Goddamn beautiful," Coleman muttered just as his bladder contracted, reminding him of his need. He turned his back to the creek--it would be a sin to piss into something this pure--and fumbled with the clasp of his zipper. A rustling from the direction Riddle had taken stopped him.

*Don't tell me that damn Riddle got turned around and is coming my way. I knew that bastard was incompetent, but how did he get across the creek? Well, no matter, this time I'm going to set him straight.*

Coleman spun around, mouth open, ready to give Riddle both barrels, as his late father was fond of saying. Then, his jaw went slack. Standing on the opposite bank was a girl dressed in a shift made of flour sacks. Her toes brushed the water. Her hair was a tangle of brown knots, her large eyes solid white, lacking pupils.

*She's blind!*

Even as the realization that the girl was sightless hit him, he felt her cold stare stretch across the narrow creek almost as if she saw him.

Coleman's mind flooded with every childhood fear he'd known.

"It's the goddamn witch!" he cried, tearing through the brush at a run, and wetting himself in the process.

He crashed blindly through the trees and headfirst into the still.

*** 

Managing to collect a little of his lost dignity from being spooked, Coleman stood, hands on hips, gazing at the find. A squat, metal drum sat inside a circular stone fireplace. The drum, crowned with a conical top, a pipe jutted to a right angle that

7

pointed downward at its end and into an oak barrel. A shorter pipe connected a second oak barrel to the first. A number of other barrels, not attached to the still, stood a short distance away, each one covered with canvas and sealed with rope tightly wrapped under the lip.

"I don't blame you for being scared," said Riddle after Coleman's recounting of events. Riddle had appeared shortly after Coleman's collision with the still, saying it was Coleman's frightened cries that led him to the spot. "You seen the witch alright," the sheriff continued, "And that ain't a good thing. You're a marked man."

"I don't believe in witches and I wasn't scared. That thing just took me by surprise, that's all. After I finish here, I plan to go back and see what that was."

*If a horse throws you, you got to get back on. That's what Daddy said. But Daddy never saw what I saw. If he had...* he let the thought trail away.

Focusing on the job at hand to rid himself of that horrible image, he examined the bricks the boiler rested on, then walked around checking the other sections of the still.

"My guess is, they was preparing to do a first run. The furnace looks like it's never seen a fire and all this other is shiny new, probably less than a week old. Too bad. When they come back, all they're gonna find is a bare piece of ground."

Coleman pointed his axe handle to the barrels standing to the side.

"That's got to be where they was fermenting the mash," he said. "Let's see what kind of mash they was working with."

Together, the two men managed to loosen the rope of the first barrel and pull away the tarp. Coleman was assaulted with the smell of something gone bad. Noticing Riddle looking on and wearing a smirk, he dipped his finger into the liquid and tasted it.

"Gwaddamn," he swore, spitting profusely, "That don't taste like no mash I ever sampled. That's vinegar in that barrel."

Coleman peered into the barrel.

"Riddle, there's something in here, hairy like an animal," he said.

"What's that?" Riddle shuffled over.

Coleman pointed to the strands of long hair drifting in the liquid.

"Take my axe and lever it up to the top where we can see it better," the agent said.

Riddle took the axe and prodded the hair. "Whatever it is, it's big. We're going to have to tip the barrel over," said Riddle, "Come on, give me a hand."

The two men got behind the open barrel and shoved. The first attempt only rocked the barrel slightly.

"You're gonna have to do better than that," said Riddle.

Coleman dug his feet into the ground and pushed with all his might. The barrel rocked and teetered, threatening to land back on its base, then tipped completely over.

The vinegar gushed out. As the liquid drained away, Coleman found himself looking at a human arm extending from the barrel.

"What the hell?" he hurried around to the opening and peered inside, but could make out little about the unfortunate soul. "I'm gonna have to drag the poor bastard out of the barrel to get an I.D."

He suppressed a shudder. Coleman grabbed the arm and tugged. The body slid partially out of the barrel face down. Flipping the corpse onto its back, he stepped away with a gasp. Laying half out of the barrel was ATF Agent Darrell Taylor, who'd gone missing a week before.

"What the shit?" he said, turning toward Riddle.

At that moment, Agent Coleman met the business end of his axe as it connected with his skull, launching ATF Agent Horace Coleman to the Promised Land.

**-1-**
**Ghost**

Haylee followed the nun's white habit past plaster-gray walls of the dimly lit hall. The woman moved so silently, Haylee imagined she followed a ghost. As fanciful as the thought was, it did nothing to relieve the nervousness crawling over her skin like a million tiny insects. She had never been comfortable in hospitals, and today was no exception.

***

She was squeezing in an early lunch between classes with her roommate, Jen, when the hospital called. Jen had insisted they sit where the plate glass window overlooked Tulane Campus, in case Mike Turner happened by. If he passed, she planned to signal him to join them. Haylee would have preferred a more private table, but this morning, she felt generous. They'd just taken their seats when her cell phone rang.

"It's Paul," she laughed, digging the phone from her purse. "He wants to remind me we're having dinner at Toni's."

Jen, with hamburger poised for a first bite, smiled. "Bitch, you always get treated to the best places."

"Don't hate," Haylee laughed, flipping up the cover, and placing the phone to her ear.

"Hello."

Jen watched Haylee's face draw into a mask. "Who is it?" she mouthed.

Haylee shook her head, continuing to listen. "Thank you."

She closed the cover and replaced the phone in her purse. Her face was ashen.

"My mother's in the hospital. They said she had a stroke and think she might be dying. They want me to come right away." Haylee's voice was flat.

"Gawd!" Jen stared at her friend, her burger forgotten. "Are you for real?"

"I don't know what to do." Haylee said, looking out at nothing.

"What are you talking about?" Jen asked.

"I mean, should I go?"

"Haylee, she's your *mother*."

"Yeah…I guess you're right. It's just…it's been so long…I…" She let the sentence trail away. Plucking a napkin from the dispenser, she tore away bits with nervous fingers until she picked it apart.

"Haylee, I know you and your mom didn't get along, but you need to do this." Jen said.

"If she were here in the city, I might could, but she's in the hospital in Mobile. How am I supposed to get there?"

Jen bit her lip, then plunged a hand into her pants pocket, "Here, take my car." She shoved the keys into Haylee's hand.

Haylee eyed the keys, then her friend. "Jen, are you sure? Your car's brand new. You bought it last week! What if…"Jen reached toward Haylee's open palm and gently closed her friend's fingers around the keys.

"Go take care of your mom."

***

Leaving the city, Haylee concentrated on the traffic. New Orleans drivers were famous for erratic lane changes while racing bumper-to-bumper with speeds reaching 80 miles per hour. The erratic driving was the foremost reason she never bought a car. Instead, she rode with Jen or took the streetcar or bus. Forced into the role of driver stressed Haylee more than she liked, but prevented her from dwelling on the more unpleasant thought of her mother.

At the Ponchartrain Causeway, the bulk of the traffic veered onto off ramps. She lowered the window and allowed the lake smell, that peculiar mix of salt and fresh water, to fill the car. The odor reminded her of those times she visited the Gulf with her mother.

Though they lived less than an hour from the beach, Haylee could count the number of trips they made on one hand. She treasured the memories as precious times of freedom, offering the opportunity to leave the crowded apartment the two shared with her mother's creepy boyfriends: Men her mother garnered from alleys and backroom bars. Some of the men were specimens worthy of pity; downtrodden souls who moved with hesitant steps and trembling hands. Others were rough-mannered thugs or sneak thieves peering from beneath hooded

13

eyes. They came during the night--an endless parade of freaks, some staying a day or two, others for months. Haylee locked herself in her bedroom, emerging from her sanctuary only after the sun hovered high enough over the treetops that the vermin, seeking shelter from its purifying rays, were driven back to the sewers and alleys that spawned them.

The memories, now unpleasant, swarmed in her head like flies around rotted fruit. She pressed the button on the padded armrest. The window rose on its track, closing with a soft thump, shutting off the smells and the unpleasant thoughts.

Moments later, Lake Ponchartrain fell away into the distance and Slidell appeared ahead. She whizzed past the Exxon stations and fast food signs. On the other side of Pearl River, she passed a big, blue sign, sporting a bud of cotton, and welcoming her to Mississippi.

When she reached Biloxi, it began to rain. The big drops pelted her windshield, cutting visibility until she only had the glowing taillights of the car ahead to guide her. As she inched along, traffic slowed to a crawl beneath the thick, black clouds.

The question of *why* things played out like they had floated before her like a hollow specter, a ghost of a ghost.

*** 

Three hours later, an hour longer than the trip should have taken, Haylee guided Jen's Toyota

Camry across the cracked asphalt of Charity Hospital's parking lot. Like the parking area, the multi-story hospital building was a study of neglect. Designated as the place for the uninsured and welfare patients, the hospital operated with only a small stipend from the state—a fraction of the amount for-profit hospitals received. As a consequence, it provided a minimal level of care.

A dour-faced woman issued Haylee a visitor's badge at the front desk before phoning the fifth floor to inform them of her arrival.

"Take the elevator on the left," she said, pointing toward the back of the lobby, "The one on the right don't work."

The functioning elevator was not much better than the other. It rattled to the point the cage vibrated, stalling twice on the way up. Haylee gave a long sigh when the doors opened.

The nun was waiting for her as she stepped out of the car. She introduced herself as Sister Mary Dugan.

"You must be Haylee Woods," she smiled, "I'll take you to your mother's room."

Now, the ghostly figure led her down the dim corridor past dark rooms occupied by shadowy figures and strange machines. Moans and sighs, like the creaks of worn out furniture, assaulted her ears as a stark reminder of where she was and why she was here.

They reached an intersection and the nun angled to the right. Haylee was grateful for the silence as they passed several vacant rooms.

At the far end of the corridor, a puddle of light spilled into hallway. The nun led the way to the open door and stood aside, allowing Haylee to look in.

A woman lay in a hospital bed surrounded by machines. Their lighted dials bathed her in a greenish glow. Someone had adjusted the bed, positioning the woman partially upright. One arm, unnaturally rigid, lay on top of the thin sheet covering her; the hand bent sharply at the wrist, frozen into a claw.

Sister Dugan motioned Haylee inside and closed the door. The woman on the bed did not react to their presence.

"She's resting now," said the nun, "There is a sedative and pain killer in the IV."

Haylee studied the deep wrinkles of the woman's face. She judged the woman to be somewhere in her seventies, perhaps older.

"You've made a mistake," she said, "This is not my mother. This is an old woman."

"Of course she's your mother," the nun said. "She asked for you before she lost consciousness. She told us how to find you."

Haylee searched the woman's face. Yes, there was the peculiar arch of the eyebrows and scar on her chin where the drunken Serb struck her mother with a whiskey bottle. Haylee was twelve when it happened. The cut bled profusely and took nearly an hour before the wound clotted. This *was* her mother, but she looked so ancient. How could a person age so quickly?

"What happened to her?" Haylee asked, "She looks like she's aged forty years. She never had a wrinkle in her life. People took her for my sister. How could she have changed this much in the time I was away?"

"She's suffered a stroke, dear, and it's taken a toll on her body. She appears to age more as her organs fail. The apartment manager found her unconscious on the floor this morning. She might have lain there for days."

Images of the apartment rose in Haylee's mind like something undead from a grave. She saw the tiny bedroom, her refuge from the filthy foreigners who smelled of death and courted her mother. When her mother was passed out drunk, they banged on the bedroom door, calling to her with offers of candy, if she would let them in to touch her privates. She shuddered, clutching her arms around herself.

"This must be very hard for you," said the nun.

Haylee turned away from the sick bed to face the nun.

"My mother and I were never close," she said. "She preferred alcohol to parenting. I left home as soon as I was old enough. I haven't spoken to her in years."

"But when the paramedics brought her in, she asked for you. And when the hospital called, you drove all the way from New Orleans. You must feel some love for each other."

Haylee's smile was bitter. "If it were your mother, wouldn't you have made the drive? It has nothing to do with how I feel about her. She's my mother. I didn't have a choice."

"I think you care for her more than you're willing to admit," the nun said. "I hope we can continue this conversation later, but for now, I'm expected at vespers. I'll have Dr. Osmani come around. He can tell you more about your mother's condition."

Haylee followed the nun to the door, then watched the ghostly figure continue down the hall.

The atmosphere in the room shifted from depressing to disturbing with the nun's departure.

*It's like she took the warmth with her*, Haylee thought. She clasped her arms around herself against the imagined chill. Her mother lay unmoving in the green spotlight cast by machines whose wires wrapped the woman's thin arms like spider web.

There was an air of creepiness about the room that threatened to unleash memories of a childhood best left behind locked doors. Maybe the doctor would arrive soon and she could leave.

*I should have more compassion*, she thought. *She's my mother. But how can I feel sympathy for someone who never showed an interest in anything I did? Someone who forgot my birthdays and Christmases, who left me lying in bed, hungry and alone, while she entertained whatever man she happened to pick up that night in the other room, with their cries of passion and raucous laughter bleeding though the thin walls.*

"It's your fault," she muttered in a low voice at the still figure across the room. "I hated you then and I hate you now. I hate you for dragging me here to watch you die."

Spotting a chair, Haylee moved it as far from the dying woman as the room allowed before sitting down. It would be easy to just leave. The halls were empty. She hadn't seen a nurse anywhere since her arrival, only the nun. Reaching into her purse, she found Jen's keys. Rising to her feet, she circled the room once, prancing with nervous steps, in the hopes of summoning enough courage to walk away for a final time. As she neared the door, something drew her back. She returned to the chair to wait. *I'm in this to the end,* she realized. *I can't leave her to die alone, no matter what happened in the past.*

Several religious prints hung on the wall. Haylee named the ones she recognized from art history class. There was Leonardo's *The Virgin of the Rocks*, Caravaggio's *The Ecstasy of St. Francis* with the angel--whose name she'd forgotten--gently supporting the unconscious monk's head. Mixed in with the others was her favorite: Bellini's *St. Christopher*. In this painting, the good saint bore the

Christ Child on his back. All of them gazed back at her like familiar friends and she found comfort in their presence. One picture stood out from the others, a depiction of Jesus in a way she'd never seen. In this painting, Christ wore his traditional robe, but drew the top half apart to bare his chest, revealing a blazing heart. Thorns entwined the heart, piercing it in half a dozen places. Blood flowed from the wounds in long, thin rivulets. The Savior wore an expression of sorrow.

*He understands what it's like to be hurt and abandoned.*

She crossed to the bed, unable to help herself. Her mother's eyes were closed, and her features were relaxed, as if she enjoyed a restful sleep. Haylee brushed the woman's cheek with her hand. Her skin felt surprising warm. Suddenly, her eyes snapped open and Haylee froze. These eyes did not belong to the woman she once knew; they held a feral madness.

The fierceness projected from her mother's eyes forced Haylee back, but something clamped around her wrist. She looked down and saw her mother's good hand gripping her with incredible strength. Haylee stifled a cry as panic swept through her. She struggled to break free, but the woman's grip was too strong. The partially paralyzed arm was also in motion, pawing at Haylee's face, seeking to tear at her eyes.

"Witch," the woman hissed.

The claw jabbed out. Haylee managed to turn her head so the fingers missed her eye. Instead, they tore away skin from her cheek.

"Momma, stop," Haylee cried, grabbing her mother's wrist before she could do more damage.

"You wasn't as smart as you thought, was you, Petweenus?" The pressure on Haylee's wrist increased. Haylee bit her lip from the pain. "It's me that's got *you* now."

"Momma, it's me, Haylee."

The woman, partially erect, turned to the side, and began forcing Haylee to the floor.

"Momma, please." Haylee cried again. She heard her heart pound in her ears.

The woman's face bore down on her until Haylee smelled fetid breath. "I know you came to take me back, but I won't go," said the woman. "You won't get her either. I chased her away and I made her hate me so she'd never come back. She's in a place where you'll never find her. Now, I intend to drag you to hell with me so there'll be no more. NO MORE!"

The woman bared her teeth. Her head jutted forward, her jaw snapped an inch from Haylee's ear. Haylee twisted away hard, breaking the grip on her wrist. Free now, she raced into the hall. Behind her, her mother began to scream.

Haylee clamped her hands over her ears as she ran from the nightmarish sounds that echoed through the hall.

Two burly men accompanied by a nurse and a stocky man wearing a stethoscope, bounded around the corner. Haylee ran toward them.

"My mother, she's hysterical!"

The orderlies and nurse rushed past. Haylee followed. When she reached the room, the stocky man, who she later learned was Dr. Osmani, leaned over the woman, now lying prone on the floor.

The doctor, noticing Haylee, said something in a low voice to the nurse, who walked over to Haylee and motioned her out. The nurse returned to the room, closing the door behind her.

Haylee was staring at the closed door when a wave of nausea swept over her and her knees almost gave way. Wobbling drunkenly down the hall to the ladies room, she stumbled into the nearest stall where her stomach gave up its contents. She continued to hover over the toilet bowl for several minutes after the sickness passed before stumbling to the basin to wash her face. The cold water eased her sickness until she was finally able to stand without the dizziness.

On her way back to her mother's room, she questioned what happened. Her mother's attack, the woman's strength and ferocity, seemed surreal. A pair of orderlies stood guard outside the door. One looked at her with kind eyes.

"I'm afraid no one is allowed in." he said, "The doctor is still with her. If you'll wait in the waiting room, I promise someone will let you know when you can visit her again."

He gave Haylee directions to the waiting room. "There are phones there in case you want to call someone," he added. "Along with a snack and drink machines."

The waiting room was softly lit, offering an atmosphere of peace and restfulness. A drink machine that also dispensed hot coffee stood against one wall. A second machine next to it, offered potato chips and other snacks.

Haylee dropped several quarters in the coffee dispenser and pressed the button for coffee with cream and sugar.

A paper cup dropped into the opening and filled with liquid. When it finished, Haylee lifted the cup free and tasted the brew. Deciding it was drinkable, she took the coffee to one of the several empty tables scattered about, and dialed Paul's number on her cell phone. She heard a faint ringing on the other end, then a voice said "You have reached Paul Carter. I'm unavailable at the moment. Leave a message at the sound of the tone and I will return your call promptly."

"Well, that's just great." she muttered, looking at her watch. Paul was probably waiting for her at Toni's, so why wasn't he answering his phone? *More than likely he turned it off during class and forgot to turn it back on.* If she was right, it might be hours before he noticed she called.

She sighed. This was just one more aggravation that added to the ever-increasing load weighing her down. Her portfolio was due in two weeks at semester's end, and the content was sadly lacking. It contained exactly three shots of Audubon Park she took on a foggy morning at the beginning of the year. Her professors were less than taken with the photos when she asked for opinions and even less pleased with her lack of motivation. The promising photography student was proving to be a let down.

Her scholarship required she keep a "B" average, and she had the first year. Their lackluster reactions to her work suggested a much lower grade this time around. She'd toyed with the idea of dropping out of school, or at least taking time off to land a job with a commercial photographer. The experience would stand her in good stead later. Now, with this new crisis adding to her already building depression, the last remnants of her desire to do anything faded.

Two elderly ladies entered the break room and settled at a back table. One woman held a rosary and Haylee watched as the woman mouthed silent prayers while her hands shifted from bead to bead. Her companion occupied herself with a Harlequin Paperback.

She considered trying to reach Paul again, but she doubted he'd answer. Eventually, he would see he missed her, call her, and she would tell him about the emergency then.

Haylee felt a prickle on her neck as if someone was looking at her. The nun who met her when she arrived watched from the doorway. She wore the same serene smile as before, gentle yet revealing nothing. Haylee walked over to the woman.

"I've spoken to Doctor Osmani," said the nun, "And he thinks it best if you leave and get some rest. Your mother was very frantic with you here. He is worried if you stay, it will only aggravate her more. Perhaps, tomorrow will be better."

Haylee tried to keep her expression stoic, though she felt overjoyed to be leaving this place.

"Will you be staying in town overnight?" the nun asked, "With a relative, or a friend?"

"I don't have any other relatives in Mobile," Haylee said. "It's always been me and my mother."

"I can give you the name of a motel, it's only a few blocks away," said the nun, "The rates are very reasonable. Many of the people visiting patients at Charity stay there."

Ignoring Haylee's insistence that it was not necessary, the nun jotted the motel's name and directions on a sheet of stationary. "I'll see someone contacts you if there are any changes in your mother's condition," said the nun, passing the paper to Haylee.

Haylee thanked her. After the nun disappeared, Haylee tossed the paper in the trash and crossed the room to a bank of phones. A phone book in a plastic cover dangled from a chain. Haylee flipped through the pages until she found the number and punched it in on her cell phone.

After a couple of rings, a heavily-accented voice answered sleepily, "Carlos."

"Mr. Garza, this is Haylee Woods."

"Haylee!" The voice exclaimed, "I tried to call you but your roommate said you were gone. Did someone tell you? Your momma is in the hospital."

"I'm here with her, Mr. Garza, but I need a favor."

"Sure, if I can."

"I need to stay in Momma's apartment, just for tonight. That is, if she doesn't have a boyfriend there."

"Honey, your momma hasn't had a boyfriend since you left. The day you got on the bus, she kicked the last one out. She's lived alone ever since."

"Are you serious? She was never without a man when I was there."

"I promise you, Honey, your momma's lived alone for some time, but it's late. If you don't mind, I'll leave the key under the mat for you." Mr. Garza continued, "Then you stop by tomorrow and we'll talk, okay?"

"Thank you, Mr. Garza, I will."

***

The sun had set for several hours when Haylee followed the sidewalk to the small parking lot. Only a handful of cars remained scattered across the lot. The Camry sat alone. She wished Paul was with her. Two men stood by a pickup some distance away, both of them smoking cigarettes. They paid her no mind as she checked the doors and peeped into the back seat of the Camry before slipping behind the wheel.

As she drove along, she noticed the city had grown. *Everything changes* she thought, and was immediately reminded of her mother--how unrecognizable she'd become. Forcing her mind back to the task of steering, she drove on.

\*\*\*

Haylee angled the Toyota into an empty slot near the steps that led to her mother's apartment. Glancing up, she saw the dark windows.

*What did you expect?* she thought, *It's almost midnight. The whole town is asleep.*

Haylee slipped out of the car, locked it, and climbed the stairs. The key was waiting for her under the mat as promised. The lock turned easily and she let herself in.

The apartment was freezing. She remembered her mother never let the temperature climb above 60. Apparently, Mr. Garza left the thermostat unchecked and now the place was like the Arctic Circle.

Haylee switched the lights on and the air off, then walked around the living room rubbing her bare arms with her hands. The place was pretty much as she remembered it: The same battered furniture, the coffee table with the loose leg that threatened to topple whenever too much weight was placed on it; and the sink filled with dirty dishes.

Wandering into the back of the apartment, she found her room just as she left it.

*You can take the girl out of the apartment, but you can't take the apartment out of the girl.* She laughed mentally at her joke.

The rumble in her stomach reminded her that she'd left her lunch uneaten on the cafeteria table. She angled toward the kitchen that shared space with the living room, to raid the refrigerator. She found bologna, sour milk, and wilted lettuce in the refrigerator. There was bread in the breadbox and even though bologna was not her favorite lunch meat, she was hungry and it was food. She settled for tap water rather than bad milk, and carried her supper to the sofa, stopping on the way to switch on the television.

On top of the set stood a photograph of her during her senior year, a week before she learned she'd been awarded the scholarship to Tulane. The photo stirred bittersweet memories.

In the picture, she wore her favorite purple blouse with her hair loose. Her long, brown tresses framed her face. She was smiling. She couldn't remember if the smile was sincere or just for the camera.

She turned away to focus on her meal. Carefully setting her plate on the coffee table to avoid disturbing the wobbly leg, her foot bumped something underneath. Reaching under the table, she slid out a shoebox. She placed the box beside her on the sofa and rifled through the contents.

Mixed in with several dozen receipts and a battered checkbook were several old photographs and a letter stuffed into a faded envelope.

Haylee removed the letter and photos, arranging them side-by-side on the coffee table. In one photograph, a younger version of her mother held an infant. A man stood beside her, his arm encircling her shoulders. He was smiling. A large, antique car was parked behind them. In another photo, her mother posed next to a girl about her age. The girl held a basket of eggs and an old hound lay by their feet. The other photos consisted of the man posing with other men. In one, he and a bearded man sat on porch steps with a clay jug resting between them. Another showed a man in a law uniform beside him, the antique car that appeared in the earlier photo was behind them. A note penned on the reverse side read, *Sheriff Lawrence.*

Haylee swept the photos aside and lifted out the letter. The paper was yellowed and brittle, so she unfolded it slowly for fear it might crumble in her hands. The faded ink forced her to place it under the table lamp to read the cramped script covering the page:

*Dear Claudette,*

*I am relieved to learn you are safely away and settled. Your departure caused a stir as we knew it would. Claude is fit to be tied, both worried and angry. No one suspects me. No one can know it was me that took you to the bus and gave you the money. They think it was the Stubs's doing, though*

*that reasoning makes little sense to me. The Stubses
have always been allies, as they have benefitted
themselves, from the union with the Woodards.*

*A word of caution, wait until you have word
from me again to reply. I have it on good
information that the incoming mail is being
monitored on the chance you will write.*

> *As always,*
> *X*

Haylee, slid the letter back into its envelope,
then replaced it back in the box, along with the
photos. She scooted the box back under the coffee
table. Whoever wrote the letter did not sign his or
her name. She thought about what the letter might
mean as chewed on her sandwich.

She knew the letter referred to her mother's
leaving. She'd always believed her mother left
home openly. Who were the Stubses? She decided
if her mother recovered, she would ask.

After she ate, Haylee washed the plate and
glass, along with the other dirty dishes in the sink,
and dried her hands on a dishrag. The idea of
sleeping in her old room made her uncomfortable,
so she opted to sleep on the couch instead. Taking a
clean sheet out of the linen closet and a pillow from
her mother's bed, she converted the sofa into a sort
of cot.

Haylee switched off the lights but left the
television on. She slipped out of her shoes and

jeans, then under the thin sheets to find her improvised bed was surprisingly comfortable. In a few minutes, despite the blare of the television, she drifted into a deep sleep.

***

*She was ten and they were at the beach. She wore her pink bathing suit decorated with bright yellow fish--the one she picked out all by herself when they were shopping at Kmart.*

*There weren't many people at the beach. It was early spring and the water too cold to swim.*

*Haylee wasn't concerned about the water temperature; she amused herself by splashing through shallow tide pools that chilled her feet and chasing tiny spider crabs, sending the tiny creatures scurrying into the surf.*

*As she played, she tried not to think of the Wolf who watched a little distance away. The Wolf was her mother's newest lover. Had you asked her why she called him Wolf, she would have said it was because she couldn't pronounce his real name (His name was Vaclav Hnedy, a Czechoslovakian National), but the real reason Haylee thought of him as the Wolf had to do with his sharp features, dark eyes, and black hair, which he greased straight back. When you added his thick sideburns that extended to his heavy jaw, he resembled the wolf in her Little Golden Book about Little Red Riding Hood.*

*She didn't understand the relationship between Wolf and her mother: They spent a lot of*

31

*time in her mother's bedroom. Wolf also could be mean. Sometimes, he hurt her mother and made her cry. Haylee didn't know why her mother let Wolf hurt her. After one episode when Wolf hit her mother with his fists and blackened her eyes, Haylee suggested they move to some place Wolf couldn't find them, but the suggestion made her mother mad. She scolded Haylee and warned her to never say anything bad about Wolf again.*

*Wolf could also be nice, like today. He drove them to the beach in his big car with the soft, cushy seats. When they arrived, he took Haylee to the little store across from the parking lot and let her order a strawberry soda and bought her a box of Crackerjacks. After she finished her Crackerjacks and soda, they walked to the water's edge so Haylee could play in the tide pools and chase the tiny crabs.*

*Haylee was having so much fun that she didn't notice the storm clouds slip over the horizon and fill the sky. The clouds continued to grow until they blocked out all the blue and extinguished all the light. The waves changed from bobbing triangular bits with soft edges into sharp, jagged points: Vicious teeth with sharp, white edges.*

*The sudden changes frightened her. Forgetting the crabs and the tide pools, she ran back to her mother. Claudette sat on a blanket talking and laughing and paid no attention to Haylee. She tugged her mother's sleeve, pointing to the approaching tempest, but her mother ignored her.*

*Haylee searched the beach, seeking something she might use to get her mother's attention, when she noticed a dark figure peering at her from the dunes. She approached the figure until she realized it was causing the dark sky and scary water.*

*"You're too late," it said, "I have your mother and soon, I'll have you."*

*Haylee raced back to the spot where her mother had been, but only the Wolf was there.*

*"That was tasty," he said, smacking bloody, red lips.*

*The Wolf's shape changed until he became the same dark figure on the dunes.*

*Haylee screamed.*

\*\*\*

The ringtone on her cell phone snapped her out of the dream. On the television, a pitch man fired off words like an auctioneer citing incredible ways to use a miracle cloth that removed scratches and polished at the same time. The phone rang again. Stretching an arm, she fumbled it out of her pants pocket and held it to her ear.

"Hello?" she said.

"Miss Woods," said a detached voice on the other end "My name is Laura Lee Sanders. I'm the ranking nurse of I.C.U. second shift. It is my unfortunate duty to inform you your mother died sometime around midnight tonight. We think she was trying to summon a nurse and accidently tangled the signal cord around her neck and strangled. I am so very sorry to be the one to break the news to you…"

The voice droned on, explaining that she needed to come to the hospital and sign release papers for the body tomorrow morning if possible. Haylee wasn't listening. Instead, a single thought filled her mind: *The Wolf ate her. Somehow, the wolf in my dream ate my mother.*

***

On the way back from the hospital the following morning, Haylee was grateful for Mr. Garza's company. He insisted on going along after making a few phones calls to business associates and helped arrange all the details of caring for Claudette's body, as well as paying the costs.

Haylee asked if the body could be cremated and they could have a memorial service sometime in the future.

"Would you like me to put the furniture in storage for you?" he asked as they bumped along in the old truck Haylee remembered from her childhood.

"You can sell it or give it all to charity," Haylee said, "I really don't see myself keeping any of it." She had gathered the few photographs and memorabilia earlier that morning and put them in a small cardboard box, sealed it and placed it in the back of Jen's car.

"As you wish," the old man said.

"Mr. Garza," Haylee began, "I want to thank you for helping with the cost of everything. I'll pay you back as soon as…"

The old man waved a hand. "You don't owe me nothin'," he said, "Your momma had her demons, but she was a friend. I wanted to do this."

He paused, considering how to continue, "Don't take this wrong," he said, "You bein' so pretty, and me a widower, but I consider you a friend as well. Actually, more like the daughter I never had."

A smile lit his face.

"What I'm trying to say, is if you need help with money, I mean with your momma gone and all, or a place to stay, the rent's paid up for a couple of months. Or you could work for me and get the place free of rent. I'd pay you, of course, beside the apartment. I need someone young to help run things and keep the books."

"Thank you, Mr. Garza, but I don't know…"

Garza waved his hand again, stopping her midsentence for a second time. "I don't expect you to decide right now. Just think about it."

Haylee smiled, "Ok, I'll think about it."

Garza gave a satisfied grunt and said nothing more.

Haylee sat with her hand on the door handle as the old Mexican eased the worn pickup into the slot marked *Apartment Manager*. The old truck chugged for a moment after the ignition was switched off before giving a final wheeze.

"Thank you again, Mr. Garza," Haylee said, easing herself out of the truck to the ground.

"Need help loading your car?" he asked.

"I'm only taking a few things back with me," she said, "Some photos and stuff. I put it in the car earlier this morning."

She started toward the Camry a few spaces away from the truck when Mr. Garza called after her.

"Remember my offer. I'll be here if you need me."

## -2-
## Letter

Paul Carter poked at the remains of what was once a fat, healthy, Maine lobster. Watching him from across the table, Haylee thought he looked like a child unable to accept he'd eaten all his candy. She turned her attention away from her boyfriend and let her eyes sweep the dining room. Elegant chandeliers sparkled above white, linen tablecloths. Waiters in black pants and maroon vests with matching bow ties scurried around, filling water glasses and attending to the diners' every need.

*This might be the finest restaurant in a city famous for fine dining,* she thought.

Tonight, Paul had traded his worn houndstooth jacket and Dockers for a dark suit and a wine-colored tie. She wore her little black dress with the spaghetti straps that Paul enjoyed seeing her in so much.

All of this pampering should have made Haylee feel like Cinderella, but even with the lushness of the night, the careful attention of the waiters, and the sophisticated menu, her spirits were less than buoyant.

"A penny for your thoughts?"

The unexpected question snapped Haylee away from her musings. Paul was leaning forward, peering at her with a mix of curiosity and concern.

"Oh," she said, feeling her cheeks flush. "I was admiring how wonderful everything is here. Are you sure you can afford this?"

Paul's position as assistant professor of Anthropology did not pay well, as the ragged Volvo he drove, testified.

"Let me worry about that," he said. "Your job is to enjoy yourself, tonight."

Haylee smiled, took a last tasteless bite of her own lobster, then pushed her plate aside.

"I'm stuffed," she lied.

"No, no," Paul said, moving his index finger back and forth, "We still have the cake, Birthday Girl."

He motioned to one of the waiters, and the man scurried off. The waiter returned a minute later with a pastry cart and another waiter carrying a silver bucket with a bottle of Champagne protruding above the rim.

The first waiter produced two glasses from beneath the cart, while the other presented the bottle to Paul for his approval. Paul nodded and the waiter popped the cork, pouring a measure of the bubbly liquid into each glass.

The second waiter served the couple two generous slices of cake.

Paul lifted his glass, nodding at Haylee to do the same. They touched the glasses together producing a delicate ping.

"A toast to being twenty-one," he said, "And to all the privileges it brings."

Haylee forced a smile, and took a quick sip of champagne. A moment of silence passed. Paul leaned forward, elbows on the table, hands cradling his chin.

Haylee studied his soft brown eyes. She had fallen in love with those eyes last fall after Jen convinced her to come to a party hosted by a faculty member new to the university. Jen said the thing was hush-hush and only the St. Charles campus students were invited. The new guy taught at the other Tulane campus. Because the administration had strict rules about faculty interacting socially with students, he only invited students he didn't teach. The whole idea seemed sinfully covert to Haylee, so she agreed to go.

The party was in the French Quarters, and when Haylee arrived, she saw the host was young, barely older than herself. She immediately fell in love with his unruly tangle of auburn hair, boyish features and those large, soft brown, eyes.

He introduced himself as Paul Carter and this was his first year at Tulane as an assistant professor of Anthropology. His concentration centered on American sub-groups, particularly the surviving cultures of Appalachia. Haylee found his easy style and sense of humor irresistible. She hung on to every word as he recounted the more quaint practices encountered among the hill folk.

Paul and Haylee spent the night together. They'd dated ever since.

"Ready for your present?" he asked.

"Really, Paul, just the meal is eno--"

He shushed her with an upraised palm.

"The present," he repeated, shifting in his chair so he could reach into his pants pocket. He withdrew a small box topped with a tiny bow and handed it to Haylee.

"Open it," he said, his eyes twinkling. Holding her breath, she lifted the lid. A ring crowned with a cluster of diamonds was nestled inside.

"It's a promise ring." Paul said, "It belonged to my grandmother."

"It's beautiful, Paul," Haylee said, lifting the ring from the box and turning it so the light lit the diamonds, bringing them to life.

Haylee took a breath.

"Paul," she said, replacing the ring in the box, and closing the lid.

"Something the matter?" Paul asked.

"Yeah," she said, placing the box on the table between them, "Something is. I'm dropping out of school. I'm thinking of going home and working for a while. Mr. Garza needs help running the apartments. He needs someone to keep books."

"Haylee, you can't be serious. Leaving school to work with some old Mexican? You're the most talented photographer I've ever met. I could probably get you a position here at the university instead. I had a student assistantship lined up for you next year when you started the master's program. But not just that, what happens to us as a couple?"

"Nothing's changing, Paul, except I'm moving back to Mobile. We can still see each other. It's not that far. You're making it sound like we're breaking up."

"Haylee, it's only been a week since your mother died. I think you need to take a step back and let things settle into some kind of normalcy before you make a life changing decision."

"My mother's death has nothing to do with this. I've lost my passion for photography. It's become a chore."

None of this was accurate. The truth was, her mother's death proved to be the final nail in the coffin she'd assembled over the last year. Though she couldn't completely explain why, but a part of her world died with Claudette. The hospital visit changed the way she viewed her mother and left questions: Questions that, with her mother's passing, would never be answered. Now, she just wanted to go home.

"If that's all it is," Paul continued, refusing to be put off by her explanation, "Accept my ring and move in with me. This way, you could take as much time as you need to sort things out and you wouldn't have to leave the city."

Haylee sighed.

"Paul, I love you, but right now, I just don't know if I can make a commitment. You deserve more."

41

Paul took a breath. "We'll talk about this later."

"Fine," Haylee shot back, wanting the last word.

Paul signaled the waiter and paid in cash when the check arrived.

They left the restaurant, waiting in an awkward silence while the valet took an impossibly long time to bring the Volvo around. Paul gave the man a small tip, then opened Haylee's door for her to slide in. His face was tight when he took his place behind the wheel.

Though Haylee wanted to explain her real reasons for postponing the next step in their relationship, it probably wouldn't make any difference. When Paul shut down, there was no talking to him. She tentatively placed a hand on his leg and felt it stiffen. After a moment, she withdrew her hand and turned away to watch passing buildings through the window.

When she first arrived in New Orleans, she found herself taken with the Old World architecture, spending long days with her camera, photographing many of the antique buildings. Her lens found other subjects as well in the form of street mimes, fortunetellers, and even the multitude of homeless that settled here. Now, it all seemed pointless. It would have been easy to blame her depression on her mother's death, but losing her mother played only a small part in something bigger. A growing restlessness inside her was the real catalyst. She needed to talk to Jen. Haylee decided she would suggest they skip class tomorrow, and have a long lunch at Copland's, on St. Charles.

Paul, still ignoring her, stayed focused on his driving, but his demeanor lost some of its hardness by the time they arrived. Paul walked Haylee to her apartment. Pausing outside the door, she squeezed his hand.

"Thanks for a wonderful birthday," she said, rising on her toes to kiss him.

His lips were stiff, punishing.

"We'll talk later," he said, pulling away.

Through the window, she watched Paul, his shoulders slumped, make his way back to the Volvo.

"Whatcha' doing?"

The voice caused Haylee to jump.

Jen stood, grinning, behind the bar that divided the living area from the kitchenette. "How was your birthday?"

"Lousy. Paul offered me a ring and I turned it down."

"You what?"

"I'm not ready, Jen. Too much has happened in the last week. Then we got into a fight over me dropping out of school for a while. He thinks I'm trying to break up with him. He's so damned sensitive."

"And you're not?" Jen laughed. "You're ready to quit school just because one art professor didn't go all googley over those photos of the park.

What I can't believe is that you turned down a ring."

"There's more to it than that," Haylee said.

"Whatever. Here." Jen held out a white envelope "It came in this afternoon's mail."

Haylee saw her name and address scrawled across the front. There was no return address. Carrying the letter to the kitchen counter, she slit the top open with a knife and removed a folded sheet of notebook paper. She smoothed it out and began reading.

*Dear Haylee,*

*(I hope I spelled your name right. Grandpa said that's how he thought you spelled it.) Anyway, you don't remember me. You was little when you and your momma left. I'm your cousin, Cynthie. I'm not writing for me, though it's good to talk to you. Grandpa is having me write as he is ailing.*

*We heard about Aunt Claudette. We was all sorry to hear she passed. Grandpa was especially sorry to have missed the funeral, not seeing his granddaughter before she died.*

*Grandpa says this is the year you come of age and so it's time to receive your inheritance. Did I mention he is very ill and not expected to live past this year? You need to be here at end of April, which is Homecoming at our church. We are all hoping you will come. We've missed you and Aunt Claudette since you all left and not a day goes by that we don't think about you and pray for your souls.*

*Anybody in Slaughter County can tell you how to get to Grandpa Woodard's place. We'll have a room ready for you.*

      *Your cousin,*
      *Cynthie Woodard*

              ***

After she finished reading, Haylee stared at the single page not knowing if she should take it seriously or toss it in the trash. She couldn't remember having any contact with relatives before. Her mother only referred to them in vague terms on rare occasions, yet somehow, they found her address.

The mention of an inheritance intrigued her. She decided to put the letter away until her thoughts were less muddled. She tucked it in the top drawer of the computer desk in her bedroom for safekeeping.

              ***

Haylee and Jen arrived at Copland's the next morning just as the lunch crowd reached its peak. The hostess handed Haylee a pager, promising no more than a ten minute wait. Though most of the diners were in jeans or shorts and flip-flops, Haylee and Jen, feeling adventurous, wore colorful summer dresses and white sandals they purchased at Macy's on Canal Street. The dresses, with their bright patterns of wild flowers earned several admiring glances from the male students waiting their turn for a table. She and Jen pretended not to notice, keeping an easy banter between them.

Ten minutes later, the pager vibrated. The hostess led them to a small booth near the kitchen where a waitress stood ready to take drink orders. Both girls ordered sweet tea. While they waited for their drinks, Haylee asked Jen, "Do you think I'm making the right decision? I mean, dropping out for a semester?"

"You want the truth?" Jen asked.

"Of course I want the truth. I wouldn't have asked otherwise."

"I think you're crazy."

Haylee pouted. "Thanks."

"Look, you're here on a four year scholarship with all expenses paid. I mean, how lucky is that?"

"Lucky? I worked hard to get that scholarship."

Jen held up her hand. "I didn't mean lucky in that way, just, scholarships are impossible to come by. I think it's silly to throw it away with one semester left before you graduate. What if you don't find a job? What then? And then there's Paul: He's a great guy and he really loves you, Haylee. He worships the ground you walk on. I can't believe you didn't accept the ring."

Haylee shook her head. "I know Paul cares about me. He spent a fortune last night on the dinner and the ring, and I threw it all back in his face. It's just hard to explain. Lately, I've been restless, like I don't know who I am anymore. I can't concentrate; everything is so…so… strange."

"I went through a phase like that with my painting," Jen said. "Nothing looked good to me. All my colors were off. It happens to all artists. It means you're having growing pains, reaching for something bigger. It's a good thing. Plus, you just lost your mom."

Haylee wanted to ask how any of this could be good, but Jen was busy poring over the menu.

The waitress arrived with their tea, ready to take their orders. Jen ordered blackened chicken. Haylee settled for a salad. When the food arrived, the conversation turned to dating, the change in the weather and what they might wear to the beach.

After lunch, Haylee helped Jen pack for her weekend trip to Baton Rouge to visit her parents. After seeing her friend off, she spent the rest of the afternoon flipping through the portfolios that earned the scholarship to Tulane. The work lacked discipline, consisting mostly of portraits of dilapidated houses and faces without hope, taken near the apartment she grew up in. They were meant to be social statements aimed at an audience of the well-to-do. Her goal was to stir their lack of compassion, but in truth, the photos were more a statement of how she saw herself: Lost and powerless in a world of unfairness and inequality.

For all their crudeness, there was no denying the raw power and beauty in their honesty. Ironically, the scholarship, intended to help her surmount the poverty of her childhood, to give her the educational tools and the techniques to improve her art, had robbed her of the driving force that brought her here. The pampered lifestyle she now lived, effectively killed her ability to capture images of value. She'd become a rebel without a cause.

Her first experience with cameras came about in junior high. With few friends and a dysfunctional home life, Haylee decided to join the photography club. The cameras the club provided were simple box cameras with a fixed aperture, but they served as a channel of escape from the parade of men, and her mother's constant drinking. Mr. Harmon, the club's sponsor, taught her how to develop film in the dark room. It wasn't until later, in high school, that she refined her skills, taking four years of photography as electives. The cameras were now 35 millimeter, allowing her to adjust depth of field, shutter speed, and attach filters. The instructor, a retired professional photographer named Louise Fortune, noticed Haylee's talent immediately, and encouraged her to begin building a portfolio. Mrs. Fortune took the completed portfolio and submitted it to several Southern universities offering scholarships in fine art. When the letter arrived stating Haylee was one of the applicants selected, both she and Mrs. Fortune cried.

It was Mrs. Fortune who drove her to the Greyhound Station, bound for New Orleans and college, secretly slipping a hundred dollars into her suitcase along with a note that Haylee found later, saying how proud the old lady was. Haylee continued to correspond with her, writing her once or twice a week until last winter when her former teacher was diagnosed with inoperable cancer and moved to a hospice in Virginia.

Losing contact with Mrs. Fortune was hard. The woman filled a part of Haylee's life her mother should have. Thinking of Mrs. Fortune now, Haylee found herself overcome with sadness. She put the photographs away, unable to look at them any longer.

\*\*\*

The next day, Haylee stopped by the registrar's office for the necessary withdrawal forms.

"It's too late for a refund, Dear," said the middle-aged woman behind the glass as she slid Haylee the paperwork. "You'll have to get signatures from the professors of each class and the Dean of Arts and Sciences to complete withdrawal."

She thanked the woman and exited the building into the sunlight. Not a single cloud marred the China-blue sky. Crossing the campus to her apartment, she felt freer than she had in months. Things looked brighter. Maybe she would be okay after all. The feeling was short lived. Paul stood waiting for her at the front door, hands jammed into his coat pockets.

Paul looked up at the sound of Haylee's approach. "I haven't seen you around the last day or so," he said.

"I've been busy."

"I guess you're going through with this, then," he said.

"Yeah."

Haylee looked down at the ground, pretending to study a candy bar wrapper someone dropped. "I guess I am."

Paul pulled his hands free of the pockets, wrung them together, then jammed them in his coat again. He opened his mouth, closed it, and cleared his throat.

"I was hoping we could talk," he said.

"Sure." Haylee said, unlocking the door. Stepping inside, she left it open for Paul to follow. She heard the scuff of his Hushpuppies against the carpet behind her.

"Would you like something to drink?" she asked, aiming toward the kitchenette.

"Iced tea if you have it," Paul said.

Haylee took a pitcher of tea from the refrigerator, dropped ice cubes into a couple of blue plastic tumblers, and filled them with tea. She crossed to Paul, handed him a glass, then took her place on the sofa opposite him, keeping an empty space between them.

Paul took a long swallow. He was about to place his glass on the coffee table when Haylee stopped him.

"Wait," she said, leaping to her feet, "I forgot coasters. If you leave a ring on Jen's table, she'll have a fit."

Haylee hurried to the drawer where Jen kept the coasters under the counter. Reaching for the drawer holding the coasters, she froze. On the counter lay another white envelope addressed in the same scrawl as the previous letter. She carried it back to the couch, unopened, the coasters forgotten.

"What's wrong?" Paul asked.

She sat down heavily, this time beside him.

"This letter is the second one from my relatives in Alabama. I don't know how they got my address."

"I didn't know you had any relatives. I thought it was just you and your mother. You've never talked about them."

"I've never *met* them. Mother hated them. When I was small, we lived with my grandparents, but Mother left before I was three. I don't remember anything about them."

"So anyway, what's so bad about a letter?"

"For one thing, why did they wait until now to write? Why didn't they write or call years ago?"

Paul's smile carried a touch of condescension. "Ever think they only now found out where you live? Or, maybe your mother did receive letters, but hid them from you, maybe tore them up, when they arrived? You said she never talked about them, so obviously, she wanted to keep you ignorant of your family for whatever reason."

"I supposed she might have. She got angry when I asked questions about family. Once, she beat me. After that, I didn't ask anymore."

Haylee balanced the unopened envelope in her palm, testing its weight.

"Aren't you going to open it?" Paul asked.

"Huh?" Haylee only heard a part of Paul's question.

"The letter...you might want to see what they have to say."

Haylee tore the edge of the envelope open and slid out a folded sheet of lined paper similar to the first, but this one was folded around a piece of red flannel. She fingered the flannel and felt something long and hard within its wraps. She set the cloth on the coffee table without opening it and unfolded the letter. She held it out so both she and Paul could read what was written.

*Dear Cousin Haylee,*

*I know this is my second letter, but you did not answer the first, so I am writing again in case the first one was lost in the mail. That happens sometimes.*

*Anyway, as I said in my first letter, I'm your cousin, Cynthie. Your mother and mine were sisters. When we heard about Aunt Claudette passing everyone was real sad and cried. We all loved her so much even though we hadn't seen her in so long.*

*We wish you would come back home. Grandpa has a room all made up for you. Mildred cleans it every week cause she says one day you will be back to stay. Grandpa says when you do we are going to have a big get-together . Grandpa says he is going to butcher a fat pig and we will celebrate.*

*Please come soon, we want to know about Aunt Claudette and to see you all grown and everything.*

*I made you a charm for good luck and have a safe journey home to us.*

> *7 blest be the day*
> *77 blest be the hour*
> *7777 blest be the day*
> *77 that Jesus Christ was born*
> *7 that Jesus Christ was born*

*Say the words three times a day holding the charm in your left hand when you do. Say them in the morning, at noon time, and before bed. It will keep you safe and help you find your way back to us.*

*I know I said in my first letter, anyone in Slaughter County can tell you how to get to Grandpa Woodard's place. You don't need to write ahead, just come. We're expecting you by the end of the month. That's when the land is passed down to us grandkids at homecoming.*

*Cynthie*

"Land!" Paul shook his head. "They're offering you land, Haylee?"

"That was the part I didn't understand," Haylee said, laying the letter aside. Her mother always told her there's no such thing as something for nothing.

She plucked the felt-wrapped object off the table, and pinched it between her fingers, exploring its shape.

"It doesn't add up," she said. "They don't even know me. Why would they want to give me property?"

"That's where you're wrong." Paul countered. "They seem to know you pretty well. Remember, this is your mother's family. These people are her mother, father and sister. They're your family too. Don't you realize what a treasure this is? They're offering you a chance to reunite."

Paul took a breath. His features settled into a study of concern.

"Haylee, this is the only family you are ever going to have. I think you should take them up on their offer."

"I don't even know where Slaughter County is," Haylee said, "It sounds weird."

"In case you've forgotten, I teach anthropology." Paul said. "I know exactly where Slaughter County is. It's on the border between Alabama and Tennessee in the foothills of the Appalachians."

"So how am I supposed to get there? I don't have a car. I'm not going to take a bus into the boonies."

"I have a car. Actually, this is what I came to talk to you about. I want you to be the photographer for my book."

"Are you serious?" Haylee wanted to pinch herself. "Paul, this book is your life's work. Your professional reputation is riding on it. Are you sure you want my photographs and not someone with more credibility?"

"I want *you*, Haylee, and not because you're my girl. Your work is amazing. We can start by visiting your relatives in Slaughter County. It will give me a chance to interview people who would turn me away otherwise."

"I don't know, Paul, going back where Mom grew up seems awkward."

"What's awkward? They want you to come. It says so in the letter. Look, I'll arrange for you to get an incomplete in your directed studies class. That way you won't have to withdraw and lose your scholarship. You can arrange for me to interview some of your kinfolk while we're there and you'll take pictures. The best photographs can go in your portfolio."

"You make it sound so simple." Haylee said.

"It is simple," Paul beamed. "I still want you to wear this ring."

Somehow, without her noticing, he had pulled the velvet covered box from his pocket, or his coat, and now held it in his hand.

"Paul, we've gone through this before," Haylee protested.

"I'm not asking you to make a commitment," Paul said, "I just want you to wear something of mine. Let's call it a friendship ring. If anytime you decide you don't want to see me anymore, you're free to give it back."

Haylee studied the boyish face with his brown eyes imploring her.

Her resistance wavered and she gave in. "Give it here, you big Bozo," she laughed.

As Paul slipped the ring on her finger, she felt the first stirring of tears.

## Chapter Three
## Cards

The pain in her hand began during the night, a thin thread of irritation, which grew into a fiery throb by daybreak. Sitting on the edge of the bed, she studied the dime-sized scar on the side of her left palm. She'd carried the disfigurement since childhood. Now, the scar glared back at her like an angry, red eye. It ached with a steady throb.

Stumbling into the bathroom, she swung the hinged mirror of the medicine cabinet aside and picked through the amber bottles until she found the Lortab. She shook out three tablets and tossed them into her mouth, washing them down with a gulp of water. While she waited for the pills to take effect, her moodiness returned, souring her desire to help with Paul's project. As fantastic an opportunity as it was, she decided she wasn't up to the task. She would have to tell him she changed her mind. The news would crush him.

How had her life become such a tangle of confusion? Depression hovered over her like a dark cloud, making it impossible to see the slightest glimmer of light in her future. Then, a thought occurred. Jen kept enough bottles of painkillers and sleeping pills on hand, Haylee could easily overdose. She could check out like her mother. It would certainly be a solution. A lot of famous people opted out that way for various reasons. She imagined a television screen displaying a professional looking gentleman dressed from the waist up in a white medical coat.

"Problems getting you down?" he asks. "Have you lost your zest for living?" He holds up a prescription bottle in his right hand and turns the label toward the camera. "When life becomes too much of a hassle, check out with Lortab; it's the easy way." he says with a wink.

*What in the hell am I thinking?* She asked herself, catching the direction of her thoughts. She forced her mind back to Paul. Still, the pills, so close at hand, so available, worried her.

*It would be so easy.*

She needed to get out of the house and away from temptation. She carried her cell phone to the couch and dialed Paul's number. After the tenth ring, she gave up. Why didn't he answer?

He might be sleeping in, but she doubted that. Paul was an early riser. He could be working on the book: He often cut the phone off when he was working.

Haylee tried the number again, but still no answer. Where in the hell was he when she needed him?

She couldn't stay in the apartment alone with her mind playing chicken with suicide. She had to get out, she had to find Paul.

Haylee pulled on a pair of jeans, jammed her feet into a pair of tennis shoes, then grabbed her wallet and keys. She locked the door and hurried across the commons to St. Charles Avenue. The streetcar was just making an appearance when she reached the street. She waved it to a stop, experiencing the first effects of the pills as she climbed aboard. Her mind was filled with cotton, causing her to fumble in her purse, confused about what she was looking for. She remembered she needed to put coins in the token machine. Haylee managed to drop the money into the slot, then wobbled to an empty seat behind the operator. As she settled, she stole a suspicious glance at the other passengers. Five matronly ladies, dressed for mass, gathered in a cluster. A solitary figure hunched in the back. The rest of the streetcar was empty.

"You all right, Lady?" the car operator, a black man wearing a gray uniform and cap, frowned.

"I'm fine," Haylee managed. The words were difficult to form; her mouth was dry from the Lortab.

The driver studied her, then turned his attention back to the controls. As the streetcar started along the well-worn tracks, Haylee watched the stately mansions of the Garden District fall away, replaced simpler Victorians converted into commercial properties. Colorful signs attached to their facades advertised every type of service.

A humming, like bees, filled her ears, making it difficult to keep anything in focus. The buildings lining the avenue rose and fell, swelling then deflating, as if breathing. She had taken too many pills; she was losing control, heading toward full-fledged panic. She had to find Paul. He would know what to do. She'd taken the streetcar numerous times to Paul's apartment, but never had a trip been such a nightmare.

Paul lived in the Pontalba Apartments on the corner of Jackson Square. He told her on her first visit how fortunate he was to have secured a vacancy two years back.

The oldest apartment buildings in the United States, the Pontalba, with their trademark wrought-iron balconies and superfluity of potted plants dangling in hanging baskets, made it a tourist mecca with its image gracing hundreds of postcards along St. Louis Cathedral and the French Market.

When Paul moved to the Pontalba, he immediately went to the nursery and bought half a dozen baskets of Begonias and Holly Ferns, which he displayed alongside the other tenants' offerings. She clung to the memories like a shipwrecked sailor might cling to a plank off a doomed ship.

The streetcar neared Canal Street, the end of its route, and Haylee relaxed a little. Only a little longer and the ordeal would be over. She still had to keep the fog at bay until she reached his apartment several blocks past Canal Street. Once there and beside Paul, she would be safe.

Haylee got off at the turnaround at Canal Street. Rising to exit, from the corner of her eye, she saw the man in the back rise as well. Something about the way he moved, with the look of a hunter in his eyes, reminded her of the men who visited her mother when Haylee was a child. The thought distracted her; causing her to misjudge the distance to the ground as she stepped off the streetcar, and lose her footing. Instinctively, she put a hand out, forgetting about her injury, to catch her fall. A wave of pain shot through her as her hand impacted the rough pavement. Her eyes stung with tears. She managed to keep enough presence of mind to glance behind her. The man was descending the two steps to the ground behind her.

Haylee struggled to her feet and hurried on.

The morning breeze off the Mississippi chilled the air, and Haylee hugged herself for warmth. Behind her, the sound of footsteps on pavement and heavy breathing warned her that someone followed. She dared not look to see if it was the stranger. A few merchants stood outside their doors hosing debris from entrances. They paid her scant attention as she hurried by. Their hooded eyes told her they would be of no help; she might as well be alone.

The quickest way to the Pontalba was Decatur Street. She took comfort in the fact it was heavily traveled. Haylee crossed Iberville, then Bienville, counting down the blocks to Jackson Square. If she was being followed by the man from the streetcar, he wasn't trying to overtake her. Still afraid to look behind her, she stumbled across Conti Street, barely avoiding stepping in front of a truck hauling produce to the French Market. The driver laid on the horn and yelled something in Creole.

Ronald Polizzi

At St. Louis Street with only three blocks left, Haylee stole a glance over her shoulder. The man she'd seen in the back of the streetcar stood at the other end of the block, his stare filled with menace. The sight of the man spurred her into action. Half running, half stumbling, she fought off the Lortab haze, desperate to cover the distance to the square.

She reached Wilkinson Street, angling left toward St. Peters Street where Paul's apartment was located.

*Only a little distance to go,* she told herself. Then, she was there. She hurried to the bank of buttons that rang the various apartments. Locating Paul's, she pushed the button twice and heard a faint buzz inside.

"Hurry," she whispered.

Impatiently, she tried the door, but it held fast, provoking her to do another round of buzzes. This time, she held each button several seconds.

Still, there was no response.

"He ain't there; he left a half hour ago," said a voice behind her.

Haylee turned to find a thin, middle-aged redhead dressed in shabby clothes, sitting behind a small table. The cardboard sign leaning against the table proclaimed the woman a psychic and card reader.

"Where'd you come from?" Haylee asked. "There was a man...the man following me, where did he go?"

"One question at a time, Darling," the woman said, "That fellow was up to no good, so I sent him away. As for me, I been here all morning."

Haylee blinked. "But the square was empty. Are you even real?"

The woman laughed. It was a healthy sound; joyous and full of life.

"I was real last time I checked," she said. "Why? Did the world end an' nobody tell me?" She laughed again.

"No, I...just didn't see you sitting there, that's all. I haven't been feeling well," she explained.

"I bet you're a college student."

"Yes." Haylee said, her eyes widening slightly in surprise. "I go to Tulane."

"I didn't think you was from around here. New Orleans folks have a certain way about them. You don't have it. Now me, my name's Rosalie Rollins and I hail from Texarkana.

"I been reading fortunes in this spot since my Studebaker died on the old Ponchartrain Causeway in 1957. It was only a two lane back then, not the nice road it is now. I caught a ride into town with a black fellow who sold shoes door to door. We lived together for a week, then he was off to Houston, but I had business here, so I stayed."

Haylee smiled at Rosalie's candor. "That's all very nice but..."

"I told you, that college professor stepped out just before you arrived."

"How do you know who I'm looking for?"

The woman paused to light a cigarette. Drawing smoke deep into her lungs, she blew it out in a long stream.

"I'm a seer," she said. "That means I know things. How 'bout a reading?"

"I don't have any money." Haylee said as an excuse to get away. A cold tingle had begun to crawl up her spine.

"I'll do it for nothing. It'll help pass the time. That professor might be back before we're done."

Rosalie indicated an empty folding chair. Not knowing what else to do, Haylee took the seat.

Rosalie produced a deck of tattered cards from somewhere beneath the table and dovetailed them smoothly several times.

"Ask your question," the woman said.

Haylee squirmed in the chair. "I don't know what to ask."

"How 'bout how things are between you and your boyfriend...no that ain't right," said Rosalie, "It's got to do with something else. Let's see..." She raised a finger as if testing the air. "You want to know about your momma, why she left home."

Haylee opened her mouth, but before she could reply, Rosalie placed the deck in front of her.

"Cut the cards into three piles," she instructed. "Then stack 'em back together."

Haylee cut the cards and restacked them.

Rosalie laid the cards in a star-like pattern and studied them, then rearranged them into two rows. Her expression changed as she worked.

"Girl, I've never seen a fortune like yours." She shook her head. "There's a message here, but I don't fully understand it."

Haylee stared at the cards. "What's the message?"

"It's a warning that trouble and travail are waitin' ahead, Darlin'. See this card?" She pointed to a card depicting a demonic creature. A naked man and woman stood with iron collars around their necks. Chains were attached to the collars. The creature held the man's chain in one hand and the woman's in the other. "The Devil" was printed on the bottom of the card.

"This beast is at the heart of it all. It has blood on its lips, and in its eyes. It knows your name."

"It knows my name? What do you mean it knows my name?"

"Haylee," a voice from the balcony called.

Haylee leaped from the chair and spun around.

Standing above her, Paul was watering his gardenias.

"Paul!" she cried, forgetting her question to Rosalie.

"I phoned you, but you didn't answer," he yelled back. "Wait right there. I'm coming down." He disappeared inside.

Haylee turned to face the woman.

"Why did you lie to…" her voice dropped off.

The woman was gone, along with the table and chairs. Haylee swept the square with her gaze, but it was empty. *How could she vanish?* she asked herself, but then Paul stepped out into the street.

"I'm so glad to see you," he said, his face all smiles. "I was afraid something happened to you."

Haylee fought to keep her head clear, but the buzzing was rising in her ears again.

"Where did she go?" she asked.

"What?" Paul asked, following Haylee's gaze around the square.

"There was a woman reading my fortune when you called from the balcony. But she's not here now. How could she have disappeared so fast? Even the table and chairs are gone."

"Haylee, when I called to you, you were by yourself."

"No, she was here." Haylee demanded, diverting her attention away from Paul toward the place where St. Peters intersected the square, a possible exit route.

"Are you all right?" Paul asked. His gaze searched her face.

"Why would you think I wasn't?" she asked, trying to mask the fog filling her vision.

"I don't know. I had this feeling something was wrong. When I called and no one picked up…What's going on? Your pupils are huge. Are you stoned?"

"I took some Lortab for pain," Haylee confessed, "I think I took too many." Suddenly, the words poured out. "I got scared and came looking for you and this lady--"

"The woman that was reading your fortune but vanished when I came out on the balcony?" Paul suggested for her.

"There *was* a woman. She was right here where we're standing. She was a fortune teller. She said her name was Rosalie something or other."

"Rosalie Rollins?"

"Yes," Haylee said, "So you know her? I told you she was here."

Paul sighed. "Haylee, Rosalie Rollins is an urban legend. She died in a wreck on the old Ponchartrain Bridge in 1957. They say she haunts the city looking for the person who struck her down. It was a hit and run. Apparently, her car stalled on the bridge. When she got out to look under the hood, she was hit by an oncoming car. They never found the other driver. The locals call her Bloody Rose because of what little was left of her on the road."

"So you think I imagined it," Haylee said.

Paul studied his girlfriend. "What am I supposed to think? Your pupils are like two black puddles. At least she cleaned herself up for you: Usually, she's covered with blood."

"That's not funny."

"What's not funny is you taking so many pills. That was really irresponsible, Haylee."

"I told you, I took them because my hand hurt so bad."

She offered her hand for Paul to examine. He took it and frowned.

"What the hell did you do?" he asked, "This thing is infected."

"It gets like that." Haylee said, "It happened when I was little, and we were living with my grandparents. Momma said I burned it on one of those cast irons, the kind you heat on a stove. Anyway, Mother never took me to the doctor for it; instead, they brought a faith healer, the kind that claim to pull fire out of a burn.

"It just does this every so often," Haylee added as Paul continued to study the infected area. "It's never been this bad."

"How often?" Paul asked.

"I guess the last time was around my fourteenth birthday. Mother always treated it with this nasty tasting medicine. She'd mix it in a liver mush and make me a sandwich with it so I'd take it."

"Liver mush?"

"Yeah, it's like potted meat, but you make it yourself. Everybody in the hills eats the stuff. Anyway, the infection would be gone the next day."

"Do you remember what the medicine was called?"

"No, I never paid much attention back then. The Wolf always went out for it."

"The Wolf?" Paul laughed.

"My mother's boyfriend. I called him The Wolf because of the way he looked. He reminded me of a wolf."

"Let's get some breakfast. I think food will help." Paul said.

Easing his arm around her waist, he guided her toward the apartment. They climbed the narrow stairwell leading to the upper floor with Haylee first and Paul behind her, his hands steadying her up the risers.

Paul's apartment was orderly. *It's so unlike his outward appearance*, Haylee thought. A leather covered recliner and matching sofa, flanked by end tables, each bearing a neat stack of magazines, sat in the center of the small living area. A ceiling-high book shelf, stuffed with paperbacks, stood against the wall opposite a kitchenette containing an apartment-sized stove, a single door refrigerator and dinette straight from the 1950s. A narrow hallway led to a tiny bathroom and cramped bedroom.

Paul steered Haylee to the double French doors that opened onto the balcony. He had set up the card table they used for board games near his Begonias, still dripping from their recent watering. The table reminded her of the one Bloody Rose sat behind. She shivered at the thought.

"What's wrong?" Paul asked.

"Nothing," she smiled, "Are we eating out here?"

"That's all right, isn't it? If you're not comfortable, we can go back in."

"No...no," she said quickly. "Actually, I think it would be nice to sit out here."

The balcony afforded a view across low rooftops to the slow moving river traffic on the Mississippi.

Paul seated Haylee, then went inside. He returned with a thermos of coffee and a paper bag filled with Beignets. He poured coffee for Haylee and himself, then spilled the square doughnuts covered with powdered sugar, onto a plate that he placed between them. After being forced to drink a cup of strong coffee and consume most of the beignets, Haylee managed to shake off the worst of the pills' effects.

The sound of live jazz, provided by a pair of street performers, filled the air. She still felt disembodied enough to let the music carry her along like a cushy cloud. The feeling was nice, not threatening. The soft murmur of tourists voices beneath them, coupled with the whistles and honks of the traffic along the river accented the music like a perfect seasoning.

They sat without talking, each deep in thought. Finally, Paul broke the silence with a question.

"What's going on, Haylee?" he asked, his eyes two question marks. "You haven't been yourself since your mother died."

Haylee took a breath. The air was filled with the Mississippi and she felt as if she was drinking in a part of the old, slow moving river.

"Paul, when I got up this morning, I tried to call you. I wanted to tell you I decided not to work with you on your book, but that was an excuse. I didn't want to meet my family. If we worked on the book together, I'd have to. But now, I think this is exactly what I need. I need to reach some kind of closure to Mother's death."

"This isn't the pills talking is it?" Paul asked, frowning. He searched her face with his eyes. "You're not going to tell me an hour from now you've changed your mind again?"

"No," she smiled weakly. "This time, I'm sure."

"Paul?" she asked after a moment.

"Yeah?"

"Can I stay at your place tonight? I don't want to be alone."

"What kind of crazy question is that?" Paul asked, "When did you have to ask permission?"

"Thanks," she said.

That night, they made love, not the fiery kind they usually shared, but slow and gentle. When they were done, Haylee snuggled next to him, and soon drifted into a sleep, where she dreamed she was walking in an endless field of wildflowers and butterflies.

She was sad when it ended.

*\*\*\**

The next morning, Haylee slipped out of bed, careful not to wake Paul. Creeping quietly to the narrow bathroom, she dressed in Paul's pajama top that fit her like an oversized dress, and removed the dressing from her hand that Paul had applied the night before. The wound glowed an angry red, pulsing as it softly throbbed. She rewrapped it with half a roll of gauze before taping it again. The gauze created a cushion, easing the pain.

Haylee padded into the kitchen to make coffee and soon, the apartment filled with the aroma of the freshly perked brew.

"Smells good," Paul said, appearing around the corner. He was dressed in the bottom half of the pajamas and a t-shirt.

Haylee gathered two cups and saucers. Placing them on the table, she poured the coffee.

Paul sipped his coffee experimentally, then set the cup down. "That's good stuff. How'd you learn to make coffee like that?"

Haylee frowned. "When your primary job is to sober your mother up in the mornings, you get a lot of practice."

"Sorry," Paul said, "That was thoughtless of me."

"I'm fine with it." The bitterness in her voice implied she wasn't.

"How's the hand?" Paul asked, changing the subject.

"It's about the same."

They sat in silence, the magic of the night a faded memory, replaced by the mundane concerns of the day.

"I guess I need to be getting home," Haylee said, "Jen will be back today and if the apartment isn't ship-shape, I'll never hear the end of it."

"You really need to move in with me," Paul said, "Then you wouldn't have to worry about Jen's fixation on cleanliness."

"I'd simply be replacing one neatnik with another," she laughed. Paul grinned back in that lopsided way she loved.

They finished their coffee and dressed. After cleaning up, Paul locked the apartment door and he and Haylee descended narrow steps to the street. While she waited at the curb for Paul to bring the car around, she thought about how her relatives might receive her in Slaughter County. Would they be receptive, welcoming her with open arms? Would they greet her with suspicion?

The letters spoke of an invitation to reunite, but her mother's last words painted a different picture. Something had driven Claudette away and caused her to drive Haylee away as well. She was about to return to the place from which her mother fled.

*Get a grip, Haylee*, she told herself. *The whole idea for this trip is to bury these ghosts once and for all, not conjure up more.* She was thankful when she spotted Paul rounding the corner with the Volvo. He pulled up to the curb beside her, leaned over to open her door, then straightened as she climbed inside.

He waited for her to fasten her seatbelt, before he nosed into the morning traffic. Haylee decided not to mention her misgivings about the planned trip to Slaughter County. She'd been ambivalent enough, narrowly avoiding a nasty break-up with the man she adored. Besides, Paul would be with her and that would be enough.

## Chapter Four
## Road Trip

On Thursday, with Paul's recording equipment and Haylee's cameras balanced atop suitcases covering the Volvo's back seat, they left. Jen stood on the sidewalk and waved them off.

The days leading up to their departure blew by in a whirlwind, leaving Haylee both aggravated and relieved. The Dean of Arts and Sciences proved to be the biggest obstacle. He refused to sign Haylee's application to withdraw for the semester. Without the dean's permission, she would either have to attend class and complete her assignments or receive a failing grade. Near tears, she called Paul hoping he could use his position on the faculty to help.

"Just go about collecting the things you'll need for the trip," he said, "I can deal with this. I'll have it taken care of by this afternoon."

"Are you sure?" she asked. The dean was not overly friendly. A thin man with pinched features and a mouth that appeared to have never experienced a smile, he'd listened to Haylee's request, all the while tapping his fingertips together. He glanced at the paper Haylee presented him, then pushed it back at her in a swift, dismissive motion, bidding her good day.

True to his word, Paul stopped by that afternoon with the withdrawal application signed in a shaky hand over the line marked *Dean of Arts and Sciences*.

"You can drop it off at the bursar's office tomorrow, and we're good to go."

Paul passed the sheet of paper to Haylee.

"How?" Haylee asked, staring at the dean's signature.

"Let's just say, I called in a favor." Paul grinned. "Look, I'd love to stay and talk, but if we're planning to be on the road tomorrow morning, I need to finish getting my things together. You need to finish packing too."

"I'm almost done," she said. She stood on tiptoe and kissed him lightly on the lips. "Thanks," she said, waving the withdrawal form.

"That's what boyfriends are for," he laughed.

*\*\*\**

Jen stepped out of the shower moments after Paul left. She wore a lavender terry cloth robe.

"You're in a good mood," she said, drying her hair with a thick towel. "You practically danced away from the door."

"Paul got the dean to sign my withdrawal form." Haylee said. "I'm a free woman."

"So, you're planning to make the trip after all."

"We're leaving tomorrow morning," Haylee said. "I thought you knew."

"I was hoping you'd change your mind," Jen replied. She took Haylee's hand and led her to the couch. "Haylee, I got a bad feeling about this. I mean, what you told me about what happened in the hospital and then the letters. Something's not right."

"What? You think my family has some kind of conspiracy cooked up like in the movies?" she laughed. Jen was always getting "bad" feelings and they never amounted to anything.

"It's not funny, Haylee, I'm serious."

"Paul will be with me the entire trip, Jen. I'll be fine. Besides, if I am inheriting land, I could use the money from the sale to pay Mr. Garza back for the funeral expenses."

She looked at Jen, her face serious.

"I know this sounds crazy. Mother and I didn't have much of a relationship over the last few years, but with her death, I feel like an orphan. Connecting with my cousins and grandfather might help that."

Jen smiled. "You're right. It was a silly thought. You know I get overly paranoid sometimes. Chalk it up to being a crazy artist. Promise you'll call me though, every day?"

Haylee grinned at her friend. "I promise."

***

As Paul maneuvered through the morning traffic, Haylee thought back on her decision to make the trip and the promise she made to Jen. She still felt butterflies about reuniting with her relatives. They would want to know everything about the past twenty years since Claudette caught the bus to Mobile.

She didn't know why her mother made the decision to break off relations with her family, changing her name from Woodard to Woods.

The last night of her mother's life, Claudette's babble hadn't made sense, though two things her mother said stood out: The name Petweenus, and the admission her mother treated her as she did to drive her away. Haylee vowed she would not leave Slaughter County until she knew why.

Paul turned onto Tulane Avenue, angling easily through the congested traffic-filled street to the far right that led to the I-10, East-Slidell onramp. This section of highway rose rapidly, offering an elevated view of the city. Below them, rooftops stretched in a line, all the way to the Mississippi. *It's almost like flying,* she thought. She wished her cameras were handy and not in the back seat of the car.

"So, are you excited?" Paul asked. They were out of city traffic and Lake Ponchartrain loomed just ahead.

"I'm a little scared," Haylee admitted. "I mean, what if Mother did something criminal and that's why she left? What if she stole money? Are they going to expect to be paid back?"

Paul laughed. "I doubt it was anything serious. More likely, it was a young girl wanting a life away from the farm; city lights and all that."

"You think?" Haylee asked, knowing it was nothing as simple as the letter in the apartment testified.

"I'm pretty sure your mother wasn't a thief," Paul continued. "She may have been misguided and irresponsible...how old did you say she was when you were born? Seventeen?"

"Sixteen." Haylee said.

"She was just a child herself."

"At least I've managed not to make that mistake."     "Don't be too hard on her." Paul said, "She grew up in a world where the values are different. You'll see for yourself in a few hours."

"That's what I'm afraid of," Haylee said, only half joking.

"Look, Haylee, Appalachian people are the friendliest, most trustworthy people you'll ever meet. New Orleans is a more dangerous place. I bet they don't even lock their doors at night in Slaughter County. Try that in NOLA."

They rode a little way in silence.

"I wonder if we should have wrote them we were coming." Haylee mused.

"Taken care of," said Paul, grinning.

"What?" Haylee looked at her boyfriend.

"I wrote them a week ago and told them we were coming."

"Paul, I didn't know if I was going a week ago! How did you get their address anyway? I was the one with the letter."

"In answer to your first question, I knew you'd come around, and to your second question, I called the county seat, a little town name Acedia. Your cousin works there as the county clerk. She was ecstatic about seeing you after all these years."

Haylee turned away. Arms crossed, she stared out the window, her right foot tapping an angry staccato on the floorboard.

"What's the matter now?" Paul asked.

"I don't know whether to be mad at you or not," Haylee muttered.

Paul rolled his eyes and sighed. "I can't win. I try to help out a little and this is the thanks I get."

"Help me out?" Haylee felt rage building. "And just how is making personal decisions for *me,* without even asking, *helping me out*?"

"Look, Haylee, I was just trying to take some of the pressure off of you. You were depressed, you were talking about dropping out of school--possibly ruining any chance you would have in the future as a serious, professional photographer. So, I took the initiative to create an avenue for you to pull yourself out of your slump, and give you an opportunity to put yourself on the map in the world of academia and photography at the same time."

"What you did was to guarantee a way to finish your book by using me."

Paul slammed on the brakes. Haylee, thrown forward, found herself on a collision course with the windshield. The seatbelt locked at the last minute.

She felt the strap cut into her shoulder as the car fishtailed to a stop. The sound of cars breaking hard, filled the air. A semi blew its horn as it raced past, barely missing them.

"Are you crazy?" Haylee shouted. "You almost got us killed!"

"I'm going to turn this car around and take you home, Haylee. I don't give a fuck right now if you ruin your future or not. Play 'poor me' the rest of your damn life if you want, but I'm through trying to help you."

Drivers behind them laid on their horns. Some shouted curses and gave the finger as they steered around Paul's car.

"At least pull over to the shoulder," Haylee said, forcing herself to keep her voice level.

Paul checked the mirror and angled off the road.

"Haylee," Paul said, loosening his seat belt so he could lean close to her. "How many times do I have to tell you that I love you? Anything I do...that I've ever done, was for you." His back rigid, he looked away. "I don't know why you can't accept that."

Haylee wiped at her eyes. "It's just that I want to make my own decisions, Paul. When you decide things without telling me, it hurts. Look, I want to make this trip. I want to illustrate your book, but I also want to be asked, not told."

Paul tensed as if slapped, his mouth twisted into a near snarl, his hands bone white as they gripped the steering wheel. Haylee feared he might snap it from the column. She watched as he closed his eyes and took a deep breath. Then his hands and face began to relax.

"I'm sorry," he said, the words sounding forced at first. "You're right. It wasn't my place to make that decision for you. I'll take you back to New Orleans if you want, but we've come this far..."

Haylee put a hand on his shoulder. She could still feel a tension inside him like a coiled spring that threatened to explode. The tension subsided so quickly she wondered if it had been imagination. Paul faced her with eyes pleading for another chance.

"We better get moving," she said if we're going to get to Acedia before dark."

\*\*\*

They stopped in Meridian, Mississippi, for lunch at a Denny's. A middle-aged waitress showed them to their table. After handing each of them a laminated menu, she hovered behind them, pad in hand, until they ordered.

The tiny tables and open grill reminded Haylee of her girlhood. On one of the rare occasions her mother left the house, the Wolf insisted Haylee experience dining in a restaurant and drove them to the edge of the city to a Denny's. Haylee remembered the parking lot contained more trucks than cars, and the crowd inside looked rough and uneducated, hardly a fine dining experience. Still, it was exciting, having people come to her table and ask her what she wanted to eat. The selection seemed vast and rich with choices, even though it seemed limited now. Of all the strange men in her mother's life, the Wolf was probably the kindest. Why her mother cut off her relationship with him, she didn't know.

She remembered the last time she saw the Wolf. He came home from work with a brown bag in his hand. He'd brought things home in brown bags before, but as usual, Haylee was not allowed to peek inside. Claudette took the bag and went into the kitchen. When she returned, she was frowning and she sent Haylee out to play.

Later, when her mother called her to dinner, the Wolf wasn't there. She asked her mother why he wasn't eating with them and her mother simply said the Wolf had made other plans and would not be coming over anymore. She then warned Haylee not to mention the Wolf or the brown bag to anyone. There was so much she didn't understand back then, not only her mother's relationship with the Wolf, but all of it, really.

While Paul polished off the last of his lunch, Haylee excused herself to go to the restroom. Two women stood before mirrors repairing their makeup. Haylee waited in an empty stall until they left.

With the restroom to herself, she unwrapped the gauze around her left hand and examined the infection. Thin, red lines spider webbed away from an ugly, gray, puss-filled mound. Using a tube of antibiotic ointment she purchased from Eckerd's the day before, she slathered the salve on the wound, then rewrapped her hand.

When she returned to the table, Paul was studying the ticket. He did a few quick notations on a napkin, then counted out several ones and laid them on the table.

"Ready?" he asked.

Haylee nodded.

"How's the hand?" He asked on their way to the car. It was the first time he'd referred to it today.

"Better," she lied, keeping her hand by her side, making it unobtrusive as possible.

\*\*\*

The first of the hills appeared outside of Birmingham. They jutted up from flat ground like pine-studded breasts. Some of the hillocks stood by themselves like lone sentries. Haylee remembered her Geology 101 professor talking about a process called *orogeny*. He said the area known as Appalachia was once at the bottom of a vast ocean. Sometime after the waters abated, but the land was still soft and damp, there was a shifting of the tectonic plates and large sections of land that slammed together, causing a buckle where they hit, creating what are now mountains.

He'd gone into more detail, but at the time, she paid scant attention to the lecture. She'd only taken the course because she needed the credit. Now, she wished she'd listened more closely.

The further north they traveled, the more numerous the hillocks became, until finally, they began to overlap. The road mimicked the terrain, rising and falling in a seesaw fashion. She was either going up or down. The flat land was behind them to the south. They were officially in the hills.

"Most people don't realize the Appalachians extend this far south," Paul said. "When you think of hill country you usually think of Tennessee and Kentucky, but the northern tips of Alabama and Mississippi are also part of the mountain region. What you're seeing here is the foothills of the Appalachian range."

Haylee was amazed to find some of the interstate cut through sections of the taller hillocks. Granite walls towered on each side of the road. All of this was a new experience for her. It emphasized how limited her world was. In her entire life, she'd traveled less than two hundred miles. She promised herself after she and Paul got married, they would vacation somewhere new every year until there was no part of the world she hadn't visited.

Actually, after Paul's book was published, she might even land a position as a photographer with a magazine like National Geographic, then travel would be a prerequisite.

"Whatcha' thinking?" Paul asked.

"I was thinking how different all of this is from home. I never realized how flat New Orleans is."

"This is just the tip of the iceberg," Paul said, "Though we won't see any *real* mountains, some of the ridges in Slaughter County come pretty close."

An hour later, Haylee saw first-hand what Paul meant. The hillocks—Paul referred to them as *ridges*--reached respectable heights, extending far into the distance. She found her earlier apprehension replaced by curiosity and awe for this beautiful place that stretched before her like a gift.

"I could learn to love it here," she said.

"Lovely, isn't it?" Paul said.

"It is." Haylee bit her fist to control the emotion welling inside her. "Paul, can we stop for a minute on the next rise?" she blurted.

"Sure. Any particular reason?"

"I want to get pictures."

Paul eased over to the shoulder of the road and cut off the engine. Haylee slipped out of the car and opened the rear door, going directly for her pink Cannon.

Camera in hand, she panned the instrument around in a circle, snapping at every facet of landscape that offered itself up as a compositional sacrifice. A raven perched itself on the limb of a deadfall, the forest behind it carpeted with a low mist the somehow had escaped the day's sun.

To her left, some hidden cabin's chimney pocketed in a valley, leaked a thin stream of smoke, creating a gray trail across the robin's-egg-blue sky. To her right, a hawk glided just above the treetops.

Haylee captured them all. Her camera buzzed and clicked happily, doing what it was meant to do, what she was meant to do. Once again, she was in her element, away from the sorrows and disappointment in her life.

After she'd exhausted every possible angle, she put the camera back into its bag. Her head swam as if she just made passionate love.

"Looks like your muse is back." Paul said, smiling.

"Yeah, I guess so." Haylee said, still feeling the excitement.

She opened the car's rear door and replaced the camera. When she slipped into the front seat, Paul had an Alabama map spread across his lap.

"We'll have to get off on US 72 when we reach Huntsville." Paul said. "From there, we'll pick up 79 and bingo! We're there."

"Where?" Haylee asked.

"Acedia, the county seat, if you can call Slaughter a county. It's about the size of New Orleans, excluding the West Bank, Metairie, and the other suburbs."

"Why's it so small?" Haylee asked.

"According to the Internet," Paul said, handing her a sheet of paper. "In 1869, William Slaughter bought up a large tract of land on the border of two counties, purchasing an equal portion from each. Then, he hired a surveyor to divide it into tracts. The tracts were divvied between his followers and their families.

Before moving to Alabama, he served as a Catholic priest in a parish in North Carolina. It was a closed off affair where everyone lived together in a kind of community. His followers believed he possessed powers, like the ability to tell the future and heal the sick. He preached the value of traditional living and following an Old Testament diet."

"So was it a commune? I didn't think those revisited until the sixties with the hippies."

"Back at the founding of the country. Protestantism mostly the Church of England was the only accepted brand of Christianity allowed. Though Catholicism wasn't completely prohibited it was heavily suppressed and Catholics were not only not allowed to hold office, but they could be imprisoned for sending their children to Catholic schools abroad.

"After the revolution, many Catholics migrated to Pennsylvania, where though Catholicism was not welcomed, Catholics there were at least allowed to live in small segregated communities. It was this type of community that Joseph Slaughter led."

Haylee handed the paper back, stifling a laugh.

"What?" Paul asked, returning her snicker with a grin of his own.

"You can be so anal," she said.

"Why? Because I take time to research?"

"Just drive."

A few miles down the road Paul began to slow. "Here's our turn," he said.

They approached a tall, green sign spanning the northbound lane that announced US 72 Huntsville.

"This is our exit," Paul said, "It shouldn't be far now."

Easing onto the off ramp, Paul navigated the exit loop leading to a narrow, asphalt road.

"So, this Slaughter guy ran a sort of cult." Haylee said. She'd seen cults roaming the Tulane campus, Hari Krishnas selling flowers, and Children of God with guitars, passing out pamphlets with suggestive covers. "What made him come to Alabama?"

Paul shrugged his shoulders. "When word reached the Church Fathers, Slaughter was defrocked. At the same time, word of Slaughter's activities began to circulate the neighboring communities. It wasn't long before the tolerance the surrounding towns had extended to Slaughter and his followers, began to dissolve. Many of his disciples were physically attacked and some of their homes set aflame. Slaughter had no choice but to flee. They packed up their belongings and trekked southward, finally settling in Alabama. He obtained rights to a large tract of land, and then petitioned the state government, such as it was, to designate his holdings as a Shire and name him Reeve."

"Shire? Reeve? Translate please." Haylee said.

Paul grinned. "A shire is an old British word for what we would call a county. The Reeve runs the shire, sort of a governor, but with judicial powers thrown in for good measure.

"Anyway," Paul continued, "Slaughter had enough political pull to get his way. The colony lived in peace doing whatever it was they did until Slaughter's death some thirty years later. Then, like most cults, without Slaughter to lead them, the cult fell apart. His disciples sold their land one by one and moved elsewhere. The area was surveyed a second time and assigned independent county status."

"So, my family may have been a bunch of crazy, religious freaks." Haylee said.

Paul laughed at her angst. "I'd say that's doubtful. Chances are, they took advantage of cheap land when the Slaughterites began selling and moving away."

Haylee gazed out the window. The mention of her family made her anxious. What should she say when they met? Would there be aunts and uncles, cousins, possibly even nieces and nephews. She had no idea who her father was and thought of dealing with a possible extended family overwhelmed her. She was glad Paul was here, he was great at smoothing over awkward social situations and turning them around. She watched him do it countless times. She might get through this after all.

When they reached the junction of State Road 79, Haylee's heart began to flutter What had been miles of pristine forest was now pocketed with the litter of rusted trailers and ramshackle houses their wall covered with tarpaper . Stooped figures with worn faces stared from porches.

A little further along, two old women sat under a large oak with a bushel basket between them, shelling peas into bowls cradled in their laps. An old hound lay at their feet. Past the old women, three men attempted to plow a field with a skinny mule. One of the men had the mule by the harness and was tugging furiously to get the old animal moving. The other two stood with hands on their hips, watching.

Haylee tapped Paul's shoulder and pointed out the oddity. "Haven't these people heard of tractors and tillers ?" she asked.

"We're in the Appalachians," Paul said. "People here are slow to change. Most of them still use outhouses and pump water with hand pumps. And to tell the truth, I doubt any of them could afford tractors if they wanted to."

Haylee had to agree that the area showed little sign of prosperity. From the looks of things, the people here barely eked out a living. She wondered if her grandfather lived in a hovel like the ones they passed.

They followed the narrow road, thick with long-leaf pine, sweet gum, red maple and an occasional cottonwood, waving broad leaves.

Haylee played at identifying the various species of trees, when she noticed a police car behind them. The car was practically on their bumper, so close that Haylee could see the scowl on the driver's face.

She opened her mouth to alert Paul when the car swung out into the oncoming lane and roared past.

"He's in a hurry," Paul commented.

"He was tailgating us," Haylee said, "I was afraid he might run us off the road. You didn't notice?"

"Well, he's gone now," Paul said.

A faded, hand-painted sign along the road announced they reached Acedia township limits. Beneath the town's name was written "Let he who is without sin cast the first stone". Something had collided with the sign, bending one of the metal legs so the whole thing leaned. Tall grass covered much of the lower portion of the sign, giving it an abandoned appearance.

*It's like the shacks we passed a ways back. No one seems to care around here.*

The town came into view, a row of single-story brick buildings with a few clapboard houses mixed in. The rusty street sign proclaimed this stretch of road Acedia Avenue.

"What, not Main Street?" Haylee laughed. "That's what the streets passing through the center of town are named in the movies."

"I guess they wanted to be different." Paul said. "That must be the town hall there."

He pointed to a building taller than the rest. Two ionic columns, supporting a roofed porch, graced by a series of marble steps, bestowed a regal appearance. Painted diagonal lines marked a parking area in front of the building. Paul parked the Volvo between two of the painted lines.

Paul opened Haylee's door, then skipped up the steps ahead of her. Reaching the heavy, oak double doors first, in a gentlemanly fashion, he held one open for her. He followed her through a foyer into a cramped aisle between long desks. Wood slats divided glass windows, every one labeled with the service it provided. One was reserved for recording deeds, and another was for paying utility and phone bills. Others were for registering vehicles and various kinds of licenses.

Though the multiple windows gave the impression that half a dozen clerks were employed, only one, a woman with her back turned to the counter, was visible. She hovered over a magazine, unaware of Haylee and Paul.

Paul tapped on the glass.

"Excuse me," he called through a circular-shaped hole.

"I know," the woman said, not bothering to look around. "You missed the Huntsville turnoff and need directions. Go back two miles and take route 23. It'll be on your right. It'll take you to the interstate. Then follow the signs. You'll be in Huntsville in no time."

"Uh…actually we're here to meet someone." Paul said. "Can you tell me where we can find Cynthie Woodard? She said she worked here."

The woman turned around in her chair. Slightly overweight with curly brown hair, she wore a pair of green slacks and a shirt that read *Hillbillies do it better*.

"I'm Cynthie Wood…"

She stopped midsentence.

"Haylee? Haylee Woodard. Of course, it's you. I'd know you anywhere." Rushing around the counter, she grabbed Haylee in a massive hug. "Why, you look just like your momma," the woman said, stepping back, leaving Haylee dazed and struggling to catch her breath.

The woman rounded up a couple of chairs and motioned for Haylee and Paul to sit.

"Well, I can't believe you came. Aunt Claudette never answered my letters." She shook her head. "Now, she's passed."

"But you're here," she beamed.

Haylee searched for something to say. "It's nice to meet you," she managed.

"Ain't you gonna introduce me to the handsome fella with you?" Cynthie asked.

"Oh, I'm sorry," Haylee said, feeling her face flush. "This is my boyfriend, Paul."

"Well you're just going to tell me all about it." Cynthie said, leaning forward.

Before Haylee could say anything, the phone rang.

"Damn," Cynthie said, moving around the counter. "I'm coming."

The phone rang twice more.

Haylee and Paul watched through the glass as Cynthie talked into the receiver, waving her free hand wildly.

"Whoever it is, has put a bee in her bonnet," Paul said, keeping his voice low.

"Sorry about that," Cynthie said, returning to Haylee and Paul.

She sighed. "Can I ask y'all a favor? I'll be off work in…" She glanced at the wall clock, "In less than two hours. I've got some work to finish up before I go. It might be easier for you to wait at the diner across the street. It's more comfortable than these hard chairs."

"So you need us to leave." Paul said.

"Now don't say it like that, Honey," the chubby woman said, "I was thinking of y'all."

Haylee tugged Paul's hand. "Come on," she said, "So Cynthie can work."

Outside, the heat from the afternoon sun rose off the black asphalt like a hot stovetop. Haylee was glad when they reached the diner's overhang across the street and stepped inside. The diner had no air conditioning, but three large ceiling fans circulated the air, keeping the interior tolerable. A few customers sat around Formica tables.

"Sit anywhere that's empty, folks," a woman called from several tables away. She had blond, shoulder-length hair and wore a faded, pink t-shirt tucked into worn jeans. A folded apron was tied around her waist. Haylee judged her to be in her mid-twenties.

"I'll be with you in a minute," she said before turning back to two men dressed in overalls and scribbling something on her order pad.

While they waited, Haylee scanned the room. Two plate-glass windows framed the entrance, decorated with potted plants. Windowless walls on either side were papered with signs from floor to ceiling. Most quoted biblical verses or moral adages. The effect was sobering.

One of the signs read: *Just to be is a blessing, just to live is holy.*

Another proclaimed, *O Lord, thou knowest how busy I must be this day; if I forget thee, do not thou forget me,* in bright, red letters.

"What's the matter?" Paul asked, leaning forward and waving a hand in front of her face. She realized was staring at the papered walls.

"Those messages," she said, "They're so weird."

"They're proverbs," he said, "Lots of Mom and Pop diners have stuff like that on the walls. Look, here's our waitress."

Haylee saw the waitress weaving her way between tables toward them.

"Howdy, folks," she said, extracting two menus wedged between the napkin holder and the glass sugar dispenser. She handed them to Haylee and Paul.

"What'll you have?"

Haylee scanned the offering. They were similar to Denny's: Pot roast, meatloaf, and veggie plates--except for the addition of liver mush.

Haylee smiled, pointing at the liver mush. "I haven't seen this on a menu before," she said. "My mother used to make it all the time."

The waitress nodded toward a grubby fry cook flipping burgers. The meat hissed as it landed on the hot grill.

"Mitch makes the best fried liver mush in the state," she said. "It's a favorite around here."

A banging sound caught their attention.

"Excuse me for a moment," said the waitress, looking across the room. A large man sporting a heavy, black beard, and dressed in khakis and a grey work shirt, hovered over an antique jukebox, banging it with his fist.

The girl walked over to the man, her hands on her hips.

"What do you think you're doing, Harvey?" she asked.

"I'm trying to get this damn thing to work," the big man said.

"It ain't gonna work, Harvey. Mitch pulled the fuse. The lunch crowd don't want to hear no Hank Williams."

97

"Well, the thing's got three of my quarters in it, so Mitch owes me seventy-five cents."

"I'll get your seventy-five cents back for you, then you go home. You're drunk."

"Order me a cup of coffee," Paul told Haylee, rising to his feet. "I need to go to the little boy's room."

Haylee watched Paul make his way toward the back of the diner where a sign read: Restrooms.

The waitress returned. "Sorry 'bout that," she said, pen poised over the order pad. "Mitch bought that jukebox from some feller traveling through, for decoration. It's been nothing but trouble."

"I noticed a sign on the way into town." Haylee said.

"What about it?"

"I just thought it was odd, something about casting stones?"

"Acedia is a place where the bible is respected," said the waitress, her voice flat. "We like to let people know where we stand when they come to visit. We don't take kindly to worldly attitudes and fast ways."

Paul returned from the restroom.

"What's going on?" he asked, glancing at the two women.

"I was about to take your order," the waitress said.

"Two coffees," Paul said.

The waitress shot Haylee a hard look before spinning on her heel and stalking off.

Paul looked at Haylee, his eyes puzzled. "Did I miss something?"

"I asked about the quote on the sign."

"Well, that went over like a lead balloon," Paul said.

"I don't understand," Haylee questioned Paul with her eyes, "I was only curious."

"Curiosity killed the cat or in this case, our welcome."

Haylee looked around. The people at the other tables frowned back. A few muttered what she thought might be threats, though she wasn't sure.

"Maybe we should go," she said.

"No, they'd think we were weak. We need to stand our ground." He raised his hand, signaling the waitress.

The waitress strutted to the table and thrust out a hip where she planted a hand.

"Yeah?"

"We want to add two liver mush plates to our order, please," Paul said.

"Be back in a few," said the waitress. She carried the ticket to the cook.

"Why'd you do that?" Haylee whispered, "We just ate a couple of hours ago. Besides, I hate liver mush."

"When in Rome..." Paul replied, "When our order comes, just bite the bullet and let me do the talking."

99

The liver mush arrived on a plate accompanied by mashed sweet potatoes, fried okra and a square of cornbread.

Paul dug into his with an abandon that surprised Haylee.

"This liver stuff is good," he said.

Haylee took a tentative bite. The taste flooded her with memories from when she was young. The stuff wasn't as bad as she remembered. Apparently, her aversion to it had faded, at least, a little.

When the waitress returned, Haylee noticed some of the stoniness missing in the woman's face.

"How's the grub?" she asked.

Paul beamed a smile. "Damn good," he said.

The compliment worked like magic on the woman, and the last bits of disapproval melted away.

"I told you Mitch was the best," she said, "Let me get you some more coffee. Oh, I'm Blanche," she said, extending a hand to Paul.

He took it and smiled. "I'm Paul and this is my girlfriend, Haylee." Blanche tossed Haylee a curt nod, beamed at Paul, then hurried off.

"Works every time," Paul said, grinning.

Haylee felt something, a prickle at the back of her neck. She turned to see the bearded man who'd fought with the jukebox, staring at her from across the room. Haylee took in the cold eyes, and chiseled features, as hard as the granite ridges surrounding them. She quickly looked away.

"That man is looking at us," she whispered to Paul.

Paul glanced at Harvey, then turned to Haylee, "Everybody's been looking at us. We're strangers."

Haylee wasn't sure about that. This was different. She heard the rasp of a chair scraping the wood floor and turned to see the big man, now on his feet striding toward her like a revved up steamroller, his face boiling.

"I thought I know'd you," he growled.

Blanche returned with a fresh pot of coffee just as the man shoved his way over.

"Harvey, I told you to leave." Blanche said, wedging between the bearded man and the table.

"I got a score to settle with this one," said Harvey in a slur. "I know who she is and that feller with her too."

"There's no way, Harvey. They ain't even from around here, so you can't know them."

"Why don't you just run along, Blanche," said the big man. "And let me deal with this."

Harvey leaned across the table until his face was inches from Haylee's. She wrinkled her nose at the stench of alcohol and bad breath.

"You got some nerve coming here," he hissed, "Either that, or you're a fool."

"Harvey, I'm telling you to shut your mouth and either go back to your table, or leave." Blanche said.

"And I'm telling *you* to get the hell out of my face," Harvey bellowed. Straightening up, he thrust his hands forward and shoved Blanche hard. She toppled backward into the table behind her, collapsing in an heap of table and chairs.

"That's enough!" Paul shouted, springing to his feet.

Before he could react, the man grabbed Paul's shirt and drove a massive fist into his stomach. Paul dropped to the floor with a groan.

Mitch, the cook, vaulted over the counter and raced toward the scuffle. Other customers left their tables, backing as far away from the commotion as possible.

Harvey snatched one of the toppled chairs and brought it down across Mitch's back. Mitch cried out and dropped to the ground.

Haylee scrambled to her feet as the scene played out in a bizarre slow motion. First, she watched Paul fold under the powerful man's punch and then Mitch, the sound of the chair striking his back like the crack of a whip. She worried the cook's back might be broken.

Not knowing what else to do, Haylee launched herself onto Harvey's back. Harvey threw himself from side to side, his breath raspy, his strength frightening. Haylee hung on as he whipped her around like a ragdoll.

"You fucking witch," he cried. "You took my wife and now I'm gonna make you pay!"

Grasping the arm she clung to him with, he flung her to the side.

Haylee landed hard. Dazed, she struggled to focus The big man filled her vision as he stalked toward her.

"I'm gonna crush you like a bug," he spat, lifting one massive boot above her.

"Hold it right there, Harvey," said a voice, low and gravelly, like someone who smoked for decades.

Haylee turned toward the voice. A man, even more gigantic than Harvey, stood in the doorway. She recognized him immediately as the man in the police car coming into town. He wore a neatly-pressed khaki uniform. His thin lips curved down in a frown.

"Back away from her, Harvey," he barked.

Harvey placed the foot back on the floor and stepped back, his face taking on a weary look.

An elderly man, tall and toothpick thin, pushed past the officer and into the diner. His plaid shirt was buttoned to the neck and the tails were tucked into denim pants. His large, gnarled hands were balled into fists.

"What's going on here?" Something about the way he barked the question told Haylee he, and not the officer, was in charge.

Blanche slowly got to her feet, using a chair for support. She rubbed her back with one hand, jabbing a finger at Harvey with the other.

"Harvey's drunk," she said. "He started messing with these two tourists and when I told him to back off, he pushed me down, then he tore into that feller there." She indicated Paul, who sat, bent over in a chair, still recovering from the punch. "Then, he hit Mitch with a chair and nearly broke his back."

"They was trying to protect the witch," Harvey said.

"What the hell are you talking about?" the thin man asked.

"Petweenus," said Harvey. "There she is, right there. Why'nt you let me finish her?"

"You fool, if that was the witch, you'd already be dead. Nobody's ever seen her and lived."

"I seen her," Harvey protested, "At the creek. I swear that's her."

The thin man knotted his hands. "Get him out of here, Riddle. I'll deal with him later."

"Yes, sir." The officer moved toward Harvey, "You heard the Reeve," Riddle grabbed Harvey's arm, jerking him toward the door, "Let's go."

The old man walked over to Haylee and helped her to her feet. A smile crossed his lips.

"Well, I'll be," he said. "My little Haylee. You're as pretty as your mother, maybe prettier. I wondered if God would allow me to see you before he called me home."

"You know me?" Haylee's head spun.

"'Course I know you. I'm your grandpa, Claude."

He guided Haylee to a chair and pulled another up for himself, folding his long legs to fit under the table.

"Who's the boy?" He nodded to Paul, who joined them, his face still pale.

"This is Paul, we're engaged."

The unbidden words surprised Haylee. Paul lifted his head, his eyes questioning. She nodded.

If Woodard noticed the exchange, he didn't let on.

"So I see," he said, taking Haylee's bandaged hand.

He studied the ring on her finger. "You was almost a widder before you was even married," he said, inclining his head toward the overturned chairs.

"That man," Haylee said, "He called me a witch. He called me Petweenus."

"Harvey ain't too bright. He's what you call slow. When he gets drunk, he imagines all kinds of things."

"I had it under control, sir," Paul said. "He took me by surprise, that's all."

"I'm sure you did, young feller." He extended a hand to Paul. "I'm Claude Woodard."

"Nice to meet you, Mr. Woodard."

"Most folks just call me, Reeve," said Woodard. "Blanche, how 'bout some coffee for my granddaughter and her beau?"

105

"Yes, sir," the waitress answered, limping away.

"I reckon we'll wait here till Cynthie gets off work, if that's all right. I pick her up in the afternoons. She ain't got no car since her deadbeat husband run off with it. That was three years ago this coming May."

Blanche brought clean cups and collected the dirty ones off the floor.

Woodard took a sip of coffee, then set his cup down solemnly.

"So, Claudette's dead," he said, matter of fact. "How did it happen, Hon?"

"She had a stroke, then a massive heart attack."

"I hope she didn't suffer. I wouldn't have wanted her to suffer."

They sat in silence while Woodard finished his coffee. "This sitting around is making me antsy," he said after he finished. "How about you two riding back home with me, and let Cynthie drive your car back when she gets off. That way we won't have to wait?"

"All our stuff is in the Volvo." Haylee said, unsure if she trusted this man. Though he claimed to be her grandfather he was still a stranger and the thought made her uneasy.

"Well, unless you need it immediately, I guess it'll be fine," said Woodard. "If it's the car you're worried about, Cynthie is a safe driver. In all her years of driving, she hasn't got one ticket."

Paul fished his keys out of his pocket and handed them to Woodard. "It's the gray Volvo parked in the front."

Woodard laughed. "I figured it was. It's only car I don't recognize."

Woodard inched himself slowly out of the chair. "I'm just gonna carry these keys across the street to Cynthie," he said, "I'm in the black Packard right outside."

After Woodard left, Haylee and Paul exchanged glances. "What do you think?" Paul asked.

"He seems nice," Haylee said, "But I'm wondering about the rest of the family."

"I'm sure they're all nice too." Paul said. He signaled Blanche for the ticket. She came over and waved away the bills he held toward her.

"No charge," she said. She looked at Haylee and smiled. "You should have said who you were; Mitch would have given you the V.I.P treatment."

Haylee and Paul rose together.

"Don't be a stranger, now," Blanche called after them.

Woodard waited outside and led them to an ancient Packard.

"I've only seen these in antique car shows," Paul whispered. "That thing must be seventy years old!"

Haylee motioned for him to be quiet. Woodard reached the car first and opened the door for them.

"I think we can all fit in the front," he said. "One thing about a Packard is they have lots of room."

Woodard slipped behind the wheel, with Haylee in the middle and Paul by the passenger door.

"I wish the others was alive to see how the family's continued," Woodard said, glancing at Haylee.

"The others?" Haylee didn't fully understand what he meant.

"It's just me and Cynthie now. The rest have passed on to the other side, including your poor mother."

"Grandmother, too?"

"Child, she died right after your momma was born."

"I'm sorry," Haylee said, "I didn't know. Momma never said much about the family."

"Did she tell you how you came to be named?" Woodard asked.

"No."

"Your momma was always taken with the stars. Seemed there wasn't a night she wasn't out in the yard looking up at the heavens. I should have had an inkling then, that she'd be a roamer. She named you after a comet. I think it was."

After several miles of cramped, twisting road, Woodard slowed and turned onto a slender, dirt track. "We're almost there," he said.

The track began to taper until the Packard threatened to scrape the clay banks on either side. As Haylee wondered if the car would be trapped by the narrow passage, a roof appeared above the trees. A moment later, the trees parted to reveal a rambling two story Victorian with gables and turrets protruding at odd angles as if a madman had designed the place. Woodard pulled beside the house and the three got out.

"Come on," he said, leading the way inside.

They passed through a simple foyer into a high-ceilinged room the size of a small apartment. Overstuffed chairs and settees from a century before, were scattered randomly around the room. Several large paintings, done in dark colors, hung on walls that were dressed in faded wallpaper. A staircase angled up to the second floor from the center of the room in a gentle curve. Bits of hardwood floor peeked around thick, oriental rugs that were scattered about like a patchwork quilt.

*This is where Mother grew up*, Haylee thought, searching the room for any clues that might shed light on why a teenaged girl would want to leave home.

Woodard motioned them to an archway through which Haylee could see a long table and eight chairs. A glass chandelier hung over the center of the table. This room seemed brighter than the others. In contrast to the living room, the walls were covered with a colorful pattern of daisies and brambles laden with dewberries. Honey bees circled the dark berries.

Woodard led them through the dining room to a door that opened into a large kitchen where an ample-sized black woman, wearing a white uniform and red bandana, stirred a pot on the stove. The room smelled of roasting meat.

"How's supper coming, Mildred?" Woodard asked.

"It'll be ready shortly, Mr. Reeve," the black woman said, her back to the three. "You home early. Miss Cynthie done already?"

"No, she'll be a while. I have someone I want you to meet," he said.

The black woman turned around, and her features changed from puzzlement to surprise. The large woman rushed forward and grabbed Haylee in a bear hug, lifting the girl off the floor.

"Lordy sakes alive! I never thought I'd live to see this day. I ain't seen you since you was a baby, Miss Haylee, but I'd know you anywhere. You the spittin' image of your momma."

The big woman stepped back, wringing her hands. She shook her head. "Praise God, but I never thought I'd see this day," she wiped away a tear.

"Do me a favor, Mildred, and show these two young folks to their rooms. I figure we'd give them a chance to rest a little 'afore supper."

Mildred set the stove to simmer, then took a rag from the counter and wiped her hands.

Her eyes narrowed. "Why's that hand bandaged?"

Haylee stiffened a little as Mildred took her hand, expecting the examination to be painful. To her surprise, Mildred's touch was gentle as she unwrapped the thick layers of gauze.

The black woman frowned when she saw the infection.

"Lordy, Child, was you trying to lose this hand? You ain't but a day or two away from gangrene."

Woodard looked worriedly from the doorway until Mildred shooed him away. "Get out of here, Mr. Claude. You know I can't work with people buzzin' around, and take this boy with you." She nodded toward where Paul stood.

"Miss Haylee's gonna be just fine. I caught it in time. Take Mr. Paul to the extra bedroom upstairs. We'll be along in a minute."

After the men left, Mildred took a jar off the top shelf of a double-door cupboard. She unscrewed the jar lid and dipped out a thick salve with her fingers, smearing it liberally on the wound. Haylee winced.

"I know it hurts, Honey, but this will take the fever out of it, along with the pain. Come on young 'un," she said, "Let's find you a bed."

-5-

**Dinner and some questions**

Haylee was gazing out the window, when she heard a knock on the bedroom door.

"It's open," she called.

Paul poked his head in. "Suitcases, and the ever-important cameras."

He carried the bags over to the bed. Haylee took the camera bag to the low vanity near the window and set it on top. Opening the bag, she checked each of her cameras, removing the lens caps, then replacing them. Satisfied, she zipped the bag closed.

"Have you noticed this place is like a museum?" Paul asked. "There's a Victrola in my room that could have belonged to Edison. I don't think there's anything in this house less than a hundred years old."

"Mildred said this was my mom's room." Haylee placed her camera bag on the top shelf of the closet. "She grew up in this house."

"Duh…" Paul laughed. "Where else would she grow up? This *was* her house."

"Paul, stop. This is important to me."

"I don't understand this sudden change in attitude. I mean, six months ago, you wanted nothing to do with your mother and now…well, now, you're obsessed."

112

Haylee didn't reply. Instead, she crossed to the bed and her suitcase. Flicking the clasps open, she reached under the neatly-folded clothes and extracted the faded envelope from the shoe box. She handed the envelope to Paul. He scanned it, then passed it back.

"Wow."

"Something happened here, Paul, something bad."

"Haylee, why don't you just ask your grandfather? I'm sure he could answer all your questions."

"What if she were abused, forced to have sex? Do you think anyone would admit to that?"

"That's a little dramatic, isn't it? I doubt if it was anything like that."

"I don't know, but for now, I'm going to keep this to myself," she said, sliding the letter beneath a layer of clothes. "Promise you won't say anything."

"Mum's the word," Paul said, crossing his heart. "Oh, Mr. Woodar...er, the Reeve said supper's ready. They're waiting for us."

"Well," Haylee sighed, "I guess this is it."

\*\*\*

They sat around the long table with Paul and Haylee on one side, Cynthie on the other, and Woodard at the head. After Woodard said grace, Mildred carried in a fare of fresh green beans, cornbread, creamed corn and a platter of roasted

113

meat. The Reeve served up each plate from a stack and passed them around.

"Mildred's the best cook in Alabama," he said, "Maybe in the whole country."

Paul took a bite of the roast. As he chewed, his eyes lit up. "This is good, but I can't place the taste," he said, "What kind of meat is this?"

"Possum." Claude said.

Snatching a napkin, Paul clamped it over his mouth half retching.

"Possum!" he gasped.

Woodard chuckled. "Easy, young feller, I was just ribbin' you. It's pig. Nothing you ain't had before, just cooked up a little different, that's all."

"Well, you got me good, Mr. Woodard." Paul said, wiping his mouth.

"Call me Reeve. No need for all that now that we are familiar."

Woodard looked at Haylee. "How long you plan to stay?" he asked.

"We were hoping a week," she said, "If that's not an inconvenience."

"Stay a year if you want, or move in. It's your house."

"My house?"

"This house goes to you when I die, and the land too. I'll make it official at Homecoming."

"But why?" Haylee looked at Paul, then back to her grandfather.

The old man smiled. "Because I can," he said, "For now, I'm adding your name to the deed.

Then, when I join the rest of the family on the other side, it'll go to you."

"Grandfather, I'm flattered, but what about Cynthie?" Haylee glanced across the table at her cousin, who'd not said anything.

"Don't worry 'bout Cynthie, she's got plenty. Ain't that right, Girl?"

"Yes, sir," Cynthie said.

No one said anything else; there was only the sound of silverware tinkling against the china plates. Haylee found the lack of conversation uncomfortable, and she was glad when Woodard spoke up again.

"So, what you two planning to do with your time here in Acedia?" he asked.

"Paul's finishing a book." Haylee said.

"A book, you say?" Woodard's eyebrows rose. "What kind, like a detective story or something?"

"It's non-fiction. It's about people who've kept old customs, like here."

Woodard frowned. "That's a peculiar thing to write about."

"I'm an anthropologist, Reeve." Paul said. "The book is part of my job requirement at the university where I teach. We're expected to publish in our fields every so often.

"Actually, I was hoping you could help me." Paul continued. "I need to interview some of the residents of Slaughter County. I thought you could introduce me."

"I hate to disappoint you, Son, but the folks around here like their privacy. I wouldn't know where to begin, asking them to let a stranger ask a bunch of questions. Maybe you should do your interviews on the other side of Bitter Ridge, in Tennessee. I hear they're friendlier over there."

The conversation dwindled into small talk, with Cynthie providing the momentum via a string of anecdotes and gossip about the local goings-on.

While she chattered, Mildred collected the supper dishes, then returned to serve cake and coffee all around. Haylee felt fuller than she remembered being in a very long time. She had to admit, Mildred was a fantastic cook. Woodard excused himself, citing bed time.

"Go on and take your time with dessert," he said, "I don't expect you young folks to go to bed as early as us older people."

Cynthie followed after Woodard saying she had to be at the Municipal Building early the next morning.

Left alone, Haylee and Paul went outside where a big, full moon cast a soft light. Perched on the steps, they sat holding hands. Around them, the night was alive with different sounds than they were used to in New Orleans. The call of night birds, mixed with the chirps of crickets and croaking frogs, replaced the unending roar of traffic.

"So, glad you came?" Paul asked.

"Yeah, I guess." Haylee said, looking into the darkness that covered the world like black velvet. "Grandfather seems really nice."

"He wasn't keen on getting me any interviews though." Paul said.

Haylee didn't answer. Somewhere in the distance, an owl asked *who...who*.

*Who*, Haylee echoed, *or what*? Somehow, she would find the key to the puzzle that was her mother.

*\*\*\**

At the breakfast table, Cynthie and Woodard were curiously absent. Mildred brought Paul and Haylee each a plate of eggs, grits, and fried liver mush. Paul eyed the meat patties with delight.

"I'm going to miss this liver mess when it's time to go," he said.

"Mush," Haylee corrected. "Not mess, Mr. PhD."

"An honest mistake," Paul said, gobbling up the patties.

Mildred reappeared with a coffee pot and refilled their cups. Haylee took the opportunity to ask where her grandfather and cousin might be.

"Folks get an early start around here," the black woman laughed. "Miss Cynthie's gone to town to finish up some work and Boss Reeve took her. I suspect he'll be back 'afore long. How that hand today?"

"It doesn't hurt at all. I forgot it was even infected."

"Good," Mildred smiled. "After you eat, I'll dress it with a clean bandage. In a couple of days, you'll be good as new."

After breakfast, Mildred inspected the sore. The redness had disappeared. The black woman applied more salve and wrapped it in a fresh dressing.

"You ought to be good as new in a couple of days," she said, smiling. "Now, go on. I got work to do." Her voice was playful.

Haylee went upstairs to pick through her cameras, choosing the Olympus with its wide field of view. When she returned downstairs, she discovered Paul peeping through the window.

"The sheriff's here," he said, "His car's parked outside."

Haylee grabbed his arm, tugging him away from the window. "It's not polite to spy," she said. "Besides, we have plans, remember?"

"Any place you want to start?" Paul asked, holding the front door open for Haylee.

"I thought we could drive around. We passed some interesting subjects yesterday."

Outside, Woodard and the chisel-faced man in the tan uniform stood under the big elm. Across from them, the familiar black and white sedan, Slaughter County Sheriff painted in gold on the side, sat next to Paul's Volvo.

Woodard motioned them over.

"This is my granddaughter, Haylee," Woodard said when the pair reached him. "And the young feller is her--"

"Fiancé," Paul said, extending a hand to the uniformed man, "Paul Carter."

The khaki clad man gripped Paul's hand.

"Pleased to meet you, Mr. Carter, I'm Lawrence Riddle. I want to apologize for yesterday. I hope you don't judge us by the actions of one man."

"Consider it forgotten," Paul said.

Riddle switched his attention to Haylee. "I'm sorry to hear about your momma. I don't know if the Reeve told you, but we dated for a time."

"No, I didn't know."

"She was a fine woman," he said, "I hoped she'd come home one day so we could pick up where we left off. I guess that won't happen now."

They stood for a moment as if each waited for the other to turn the conversation.

"Why the camera?" Woodard asked, nodding at the Olympus in Haylee's hand.

"I'm illustrating Paul's book," she said. "I thought we'd visit some of the places we passed yesterday so I could get photographs."

"Which places would that be?" Woodard asked.

"We passed some farms yesterday. Some men were plowing a field with a mule. Stuff like that."

119

"Well, I guess taking a few pictures can't hurt, long as you don't *disturb* nobody."

"Grandfather thinks we're interfering, because Paul wants to interview people about life here," Haylee told Riddle.

"I'm a cultural anthropologist." Paul said. "I record the way people live, how they interact with each other, their beliefs and fears."

"I saw a show on TV once, on the National Geographic channel, about a *anthro*-whatever you said, feller in Mexico," Riddle said. "He weren't Mexican, but the man with him was. The Mexican took the *anthro*-feller to a place where some witches had bottles hid. They was using the bottles to put spells on people."

"What happened?" Paul asked.

"The anthro-feller broke the bottles and sprinkled powder around the spot."

"To rob the witches of their power," Paul said.

"Yeah!" Riddle looked at Paul with renewed interest. "How'd you know?"

"My specialty is subcultures resistant to time. That includes folk magic and superstition."

"How 'bout that," Riddle said.

"If you're done jawin'," Woodard cut in, "We need to get to the business at hand."

Riddle ambled to his car and opened the back door.

"Let's go, Harvey." Riddle said to the man occupying the back seat. "The Reeve wants you."

Riddle led the man who attacked them yesterday toward the others. The man's wrists were handcuffed.

"What kind of Goddamn shit is this?" he muttered, "Holding damn court under a tree."

"I'll thank you not to blaspheme," said Woodard. He eyed the other man with a scowl.

"I don't know why you're so concerned about my language, consorting with a damned witch and all."

Woodard thrust his jaw forward, his hands clenched at his side.

"That's enough of your mouth, Harvey. As Reeve of Slaughter County, former shire of the same name, I declare court is in session. Sheriff Riddle, is the accused present?"

"You crazy bastard, I'm standing in front of you."

"Another word and I'll cite you with contempt, Mr. Cravat. We have to follow court protocol.

"I'll try once more: Is the accused present, Sheriff?"

"Yes sir," said Riddle.

"What's the charges, Officer?"

"Tearing up the diner, hitting Mitch Crockett with a chair, knocking Blanche over and punching that feller there in the stomach," he paused for a moment, scratching his head. "Oh yeah...trying to stomp on your granddaughter's head."

"Hot damn, that makes me mad," said Woodard.

"Don't I get a lawyer?" Harvey protested.

"Nope," Woodard said, "You know that's not how it works."

Woodard looked over to Haylee and Paul some distance away, where they had retreated when Riddle led Cravat from the car.

"I need you two over here to witness the sentencing."

"Sentencing?" Haylee whispered to Paul. "What's he talking about?"

"Your grandfather's a Reeve, Haylee. That's like a judge."

"Come on," Woodard called, "Stop all that muttering and get over here."

Paul put his arm around Haylee's waist and guided her to Woodard.

Woodard indicated where he wanted Paul and Haylee to stand, then turned back to Cravat.

"Harvey Cravat, I find you guilty of causing a disturbance in a peaceful diner, using a chair as a weapon, punching a man in the stomach, and trying to stomp on my granddaughter. Because of these infractions you committed of your own free will, I sentence you to be expatriated."

He struck his palm with a fist.

"Riddle will take you back to your place and take the cuffs off you."

"Let's go, Harvey," the sheriff said, taking him by the arm. Cravat slumped so much, Haylee thought he might not make it to the car.

Riddle opened the rear door. Placing a hand on Cravat's head, he guided the man into the car, then hopped in the front and closed the door. Haylee followed the car with her eyes as it spun around and roared away down the dirt lane.

Before Haylee could ask what she'd witnessed, Woodard pulled Paul to the side.

"'Afore you go running off, young feller, could I get your help for a bit?"

"Sure Mr. Wood..." Paul caught himself. "Reeve," he corrected.

"You don't mind, do you, Darling?" Woodard asked Haylee.

"Uh...no," Haylee said "I guess not."

"I appreciate the help." Woodard said. "I want to put up some signs I bought at the dry goods, I guess four years ago, along the road. I got this sickness and they've just been lyin' in the tool shed. But, since they found that Stein boy drowned in the creek, I figured it's time to put them to use. Sometimes, I think this place is becoming as dangerous as them big cities."

Woodard fished a set of keys from his pocket. Flipping through them, he grasped one between his thumb and forefinger, letting the others dangle, and passed them to Paul.

"This is the key to the tool shed behind the house," he said. "The signs are leanin' near the door

123

and the hammer and nails is on the shelf above 'em. Put the signs, hammer, and nails in my car trunk."

Paul took the keys and hurried off.

"Should you be doing this, Grandfather?" Haylee asked. "I mean, you're not well."

"What should I do? Sit around and wait to die?" Woodard asked. "Cynthie don't want me driving either, but hell, I ain't no worse for it. If I'm supposed to just lay down, I might as well go now. I know them doctors say I got a year at best, but until the pain gets the better of me, I'm gonna keep right on doing what I always have."

"Everything's in the trunk, Mr. Woodard," said Paul. He stood at the rear of the Packard, one hand on the raised trunk.

"I'll be back in a while and we'll talk." Woodard said.

He leaned down and placed a kiss on Haylee's forehead, then hobbled toward the car. She watched him climb inside, then back the big black sedan around. In a moment, the Packard kicked up its own cloud of dust and was gone.

Mildred was in the dining room, polishing the long, dinner table, when Haylee let herself back into the house. She took a chair and watched the black woman as she worked the soft rag in a circular motion to coax a deep gleam from the dark wood.

"I guess I've polished this table more times than I could find numbers for," Mildred said, adding polish to the rag. "But I still take pleasure in it. I suppose part of it is all the memories it holds. There was a time each of these chairs was filled at dinner every night. They all passed now, crossed over into God's hands."

"How long have you worked for my grandfather, Mildred?" Haylee asked, "If that's not too personal a question."

"If'n you askin' if I mind talking about my time here, the answer is I don't mind at all," she laughed. "I guess, in a way, I always worked for him. I grew up here, Miss Haylee. My momma worked for the family. When I was small, I played with your uncles and your momma, though I was a little older than them. Then, when my own momma got too old, I took over the chores around the place. This is much my home as anybody's."

"Then you knew my momma," Haylee said.

"Sure I know'd her. I always hoped she'd come home, but she never did. Never wrote neither, though we sent her a hundred letters."

"Can I ask another question, Mildred?"

"If you want, Miss Haylee."

"Why did my mother leave?"

"I can't tell you why, Miss Haylee," she said, looking away. Haylee thought she glimpsed a furtive glint in the woman's eye.

"You were here," Haylee continued, hoping to force more information from the black woman. "You must have some idea of why."

"All I know is I woke up one morning and she was gone. She didn't say nothing, she just left."

Mildred's hand, holding the cloth, began to circle faster, losing its slow, controlled movement. Mildred kept her focus on the table.

"I asked," Haylee continued, "Because she said something before she died. She mentioned a name."

"Did she?" Mildred said, "I reckon that's not so odd. Dying people lots of times think they is talkin' to folks already crossed over. I wonder sometimes if'n they are."

"I don't think this person was dead." Haylee said.

"And what makes you think that?" Mildred asked. The cloth whipped across the table now.

"It was the way she talked," Haylee said. "But what I found odd was the name itself: Petweenus. Does that name mean anything to you?"

Mildred stiffened. The cloth stopped, sitting idle. Mildred replaced the cap on the bottle of polish and gathered up her cloth.

"I don't mean to be rude, Miss Haylee, but if you'll excuse me, all this idle talk's takin' up too much time. I got work to do." Turning her back to Haylee, the black woman left the room. Haylee heard a door close somewhere in the back.

Stunned by Mildred's reaction, Haylee hurried after her, intending to apologize. When she reached the closed door, she found it locked. Raising a fist to knock, she paused. It might be better to leave things as they were for now. She would apologize later.

126

With time to kill until Paul and her grandfather finished posting the signs, she returned to her room. She put the Olympus back in the bag with the others and placed the bag on the closet shelf.

Seated on the bed, she pulled her cell phone from her pocket and punched Jen's number. Waiting for Jen to answer, she wandered to the tall window and looked out across her grandfather's property, toward the distant ridges, blue and misty.

After half a dozen rings, a voice recording asked Haylee to leave a message.

"Jen, this is Haylee, I just wanted you to know we made it. Talk later. Bye."

She flipped the cover shut, breaking the connection. "So what do I do now?" she muttered.

Shoving the phone in her pocket, she gazed out the window. It was a beautiful view. She formed a frame with her hands and panned across the opening, searching for a perfect picture, when a movement below caught her eye. A figure moved stealthily toward the stand of trees that bordered the back of the property.

As the figure crossed into a sunlit area, Haylee recognized Mildred, carrying a bulging burlap sack. Swinging her head right and then left, she crept across the clearing, disappearing into the trees. Haylee raced out of the room and down the back stairs. When she reached the bottom, she slipped out the back door in the direction Mildred went. A footpath led into the trees. After a little distance, it curved into a blind corner. Haylee danced around nervously for a moment, then decided to chance following the path. If Mildred happened around the bend, she could always claim she got bored and decided to take a walk in the woods.

When Haylee reached the turn, she saw the way was clear and began to think Mildred had not followed the path after all.

The trail angled down and bottomed out before it began to climb again. Unused to walking up an incline, Haylee found herself huffing for breath. She continued along until she saw the roof of a structure. Soon, the entire building, a small windowless cabin constructed of split logs, came into view. The burlap sack rested against the cabin wall.

Mildred was nowhere around.

A flock of large, black birds foraged nearby. A rustling in the brush to her left caused the birds to take flight. Haylee snapped her head toward the birds, then froze at the sight. A misshapen figure, thick as the tree trunks surrounding her, stepped into the clearing and ambled toward the cabin.

Another figure, deformed as the first, followed. Both wore tattered overalls and were barefoot. Haylee thought they might be twins. They grunted and squealed like a pair of excited hogs, moving surprisingly fast for the odd way they hobbled on stunted legs.

Backing away from the creatures, Haylee stepped on a twig, it snapped with a crack. The two deformed heads swung toward the sound. Afraid, Haylee began to whimper, when a hand clamped across her mouth. She struggled, but the hand remained firm.

"Don't say nothin', just be still. They ain't dangerous unless you get 'em excited," Mildred cautioned, "Just let 'em get what they came for and they'll go."

Mildred removed her hand and moved beside her. She held a finger to her lips.

The women watched the two deformed men stumble to the sack. They sniffed it, then one of the pair snatched it up and tossed it over his shoulder as they lumbered back into the woods.

After the creatures departed, Mildred led Haylee back into the clearing.

"What were those...those things?" Haylee asked, struggling to control her trembling.

"Their names is Sodom and Gomorrah," Mildred said. "And if'n you're smart, you'll stay away from here. These woods is dangerous. There's worse stuff than what you saw just then. If I was you, I'd run on back to the house 'afore you're missed. I'll be along directly. You never saw me today, you hear?"

Haylee nodded.

"Then get along."

Haylee needed no further urging. She hurried back the way she'd come.

Relieved when she reached the house, she burst inside, raced up the stairs, then closed and locked the door. She huddled on the bed, trembling, until finally, she was able to sit upright. She tried to puzzle out what she'd witnessed.

The appearance of Sodom and Gomorrah changed her perception of her surroundings: No longer did the woods seem to be a simple playground for squirrels and deer. There were monstrous things hidden in the trees. She'd seen them herself.

Paul and Woodard returned just before dark. Hearing sound of their voices, Haylee rushed down the stairs, relieved not to be alone.

"I'm so glad you're back," she gushed, "I was beginning to worry."

"Hey, what's the matter?" Paul asked.

"I…uh…missed you, that's all." Haylee said. Pulling Paul to her, she wrinkled her nose, "Ugh. You need a shower."

"Mending fences is sweaty work," Paul laughed.

Woodard stood, looking on. "Don't I get a hug?" he asked, grinning.

"Yes, Grandfather," Haylee embraced the elderly man.

"I'm sorry I kept him so long." Woodard said. "But I wanted to repair some barbed wire while I had the help. He's handier than you'd guess by looking at him."

"That's why I love him." Haylee smiled.

"Your grandfather suggested some places I might get interviews." Paul said. "I thought we'd go tomorrow and check them out. Are you up to taking some photos?"

"I was up to it today," Haylee said, "Until you two decided to have a stag party."

"It wasn't a party," Paul said, "I worked the entire time and have the blisters to prove it."

He held his palms toward Haylee. The pads beneath his fingers were bright red.

"Go on and wash up," Woodard said to Paul. "Then we'll get Mildred to dress those sores."

Paul gave Haylee a final peck on the cheek, then trotted up the stairs for a bath and a change of clothes.

Woodard looked at Haylee. "Speaking of sores, how's that hand? Any better?"

Haylee lifted the bandaged hand.

"Much better," she said, "Mildred said to keep it wrapped for a few more days, but it's almost well now. What made you change your mind about the interviews? You were against it last night."

"The feller grows on you." Woodard said, "After I thought about it, I realized it couldn't do no harm to ask a few questions. He might be doing us a favor. The old way of doing things is dyin'. Soon, it'll be lost. Maybe his book will keep some of it alive."

"Thanks, Grandfather. It means a lot to Paul."

"You're welcome, Darling." he said. "Now you and I need to talk."

**-6-**
**The incredible shrinking man**

Harvey Cravat watched a thin ribbon of light stream across his living room floor, stretching from the vertical gap between the window curtains. No matter how cleverly he adjusted them, the curtains never completely closed. This morning, the mismatched drapes were the least of his worries. It was the wasting disease on his mind; it was inside him.

He'd camped in the lazy boy with the lights off, allowing the night to embrace him. When darkness fell, he sat in blackness, sipping from the jar of moonshine, only leaving his chair to make a foray to the bathroom and back when the urge became too great.

The beam of light grew stronger. He saw tiny bits of dust floating within it like a billion tiny white stars. He'd forgotten how interesting something as simple as light through a window could be. Of course, all of this musing served as a means of procrastination; one more attempt to put off the inevitable.

Still focused on the light, he groped blindly with his right hand for the Mason jar on the side table. His face collapsed like a leaky balloon when he found it empty. He returned it lovingly to its resting place, wishing it contained one more swallow. The sixteen ounces of high-octane moonshine that normally would have put him in an alcoholic coma, only left him slightly befuddled. The forgetfulness he sought, eluded him. Instead, the liquid fire increased his discomfort, expanding his fear until he felt ready to burst.

Yesterday, the Reeve pronounced him expatriated. The expatriated of Slaughter County were treated like lepers, or worse, as if they didn't exist. Once the proclamation was posted around town, he wouldn't be allowed into the dry goods to buy hardware or groceries anymore. The diner would be closed to him. No more jukebox.

He was a dead man.

"It was that damn witch," he cursed, "She was the cause."

Riddle dropped Harvey off at his trailer, unlocked the cuffs and drove away without saying a word. Not even a good-bye, though the two of them had once been friends.

"Fuck you!" he yelled, shaking an angry fist at the departing sheriff.

Once Riddle was out of sight, Harvey went inside, got the keys to his old pickup and roared out of the yard as fast as the old truck could manage. Driving several miles, he turned off Route 6 onto a rough, dirt track that required him to cover half as much distance, over washouts and rutted stretches where he risked a broken axle.

Thirty minutes later, he reached a small, battered trailer. Plates of sheet metal and plywood covered the front with cardboard replacing missing windows. A plastic tarp hung in the open rectangle of a doorway.

Cravat parked as near to the washed out edge of the road as he dared, and laid on the horn, emitting several long blasts that echoed against the bank of trees stretching out on either side of him.

A rifle barrel poked though the trailer door at the sound of the horn, the owner hidden behind the tarp.

"Hey, Skunk," Harvey yelled out his lowered window. "You ain't gonna shoot me, are you?"

"Depends on why you're here," replied a high pitched voice, reminiscent of a door hinge in need of grease.

"I just came for a jar if you got one," said Cravat.

The tarp shifted to one side and a man so thin he could have been made of twigs, appeared in the doorway. He wore grimy overalls and a tattered flannel shirt. Ragged locks of hair hung from beneath a dirty baseball cap. A .22 rifle drooped from the crook of his left arm. He stepped forward smiling, revealing large gaps of missing teeth. He didn't offer his hand.

"Didn't I just see'd you the other day?"

"That was me. I need a refill, Skunk."

"You came at a good time," said Skunk, leading Cravat through the junk-strewn yard and to the back of the trailer. "I only got a few jars left.

Everybody wants a little for the fires. That what brought you here?"

"I ain't thinking that far ahead," Cravat said, "Let's say I'm just thirsty."

Skunk stopped at a low lean-to covered with another tarp. He pulled it aside and lifted a jar of clear liquid from stack of half a dozen others.

"Just one?" he asked.

"One'll do it," said Cravat.

Reaching into his pocket, he pulled out a few crumpled bills and handed them to Skunk. The man snatched the bills, counted them carefully, then passed the jar to Cravat.

Back in his car, Harvey pulled a brown paper lunch bag from under the seat. He dropped the Mason jar inside, then tucked it under the passenger seat.

With the jar of white lightning safely hidden, he began the long trip back.

The drive home was filled with strangeness, as if he passed through some alien place.

"I'm going nuts," he muttered, "It's the witch. She's working her spell on me."

For the second time, he cursed the bad luck that brought misfortune down on him. Woodard was the one who should have had to suffer; it was his doing, after all.

He pulled into the yard and went straight in, the brown bag of moonshine in his hand. Steering himself to the Lazyboy, he placed the jar beside him, and planted himself in the chair. When darkness settled in, he hadn't moved. The only motion he'd made was lifting the jar of liquor to his lips, relishing in the burning as the stuff made its passage down his gut.

Some time during the night, whether because of the alcohol or because the last of his energy dwindled away, he lost consciousness. He awoke to the feeling of being watched. At first, he saw nothing. He hadn't bothered to switch on the light, nor had he bothered with the television when it was time for the evening news.

As his eyes adjusted to the dark, he saw a form across from him, large and vaguely human. Still buzzed from the liquor, he wasn't sure if he saw something or not, but then it shifted. A ray of moonlight trickled through the gap in the curtains and fell across the figure.

Cravat froze.

A demonic face peered down at him, outlined by the moonlight. The broad forehead was crowned with bony ridge that protruded where eyebrows should have been. The sharply bent nose mimicked a vulture's and drooped above the slash of mouth. Large, pointed ears jutted from the sides of its head.

The demon lifted one claw-like hand. A finger, tipped with a ragged nail, jabbed at Cravat's chest. Cravat cringed, forcing himself away from the touch. The demon withdrew its hand. Looking past Cravat, it motioned at something unseen.

137

Cravat heard the sound of muffled footsteps. Another demon appeared with something he recognized immediately: The witch.

Cravat had seen her one other time, three summers ago. He had just taken a bride, a girl from another county he met at the diner. She had been just passing through and stopped for lunch.

One thing led to another and before the week was over, they'd slipped away across the county line to a justice of the peace and tied the knot. The marriage was short-lived.

He took her to Mantel Creek for a picnic not long after and left her by the water while he went back to the truck for the basket of food and a blanket. When he returned, his arms weighed down with the goodies, everything tumbled to the ground. Before him, face down in the shallow water, was his bride. The witch stood on the opposite bank.

He screamed and rushed into the water. Grasping the body of his wife, he carried her to shore, but it was too late. He remembered crying out in rage at the witch, and she melted into the woods, but not until he'd gotten a look at her. Her features were burned in his mind.

Harvey realized now, he'd been wrong in the diner. Though the resemblance between the witch and the other woman was remarkable--to the point they could almost be twins--one shocking feature made the witch unique. It was something so bizarre, Cravat forgot for a moment the perilous position that surrounded him.

The witch had no eyes, only bulges of white where her eyes should have been.

In a sudden moment of clarity understood the purpose of the demons, they served as the witches eyes. The first demon nodded at the second, who disappeared then reappeared with a rectangular box. Cravat had seen dozens of these over the years. They were snake boxes.

"What are you going to do to me?" Cravat croaked, eying the box.

At the sound of Cravat's voice, the witch cocked her head. The demon carrying the snake box sat it on the floor The demon wore a bag over his shoulder. He slipped it off and began to remove items from inside.

Cravat paled when he saw the contents. Bread, salt and water, were used by the Sin Eater of old at funerals to absolve sin from the dead.

*My funeral,* he realized, *my sins.*

The demon set the contents on the floor, and led the witch to them, helping her to her knees. Cravat watched her grope with her hand until she located each item. She took the bread and touched it lightly to the salt, then lifted it to her mouth, humming softly. Cravat's nerve broke. He tried to launch himself from the chair, but the demon thrust him back.

"No...please no," he begged, watching the demon with the snake box lift the lid.

The second demon forced Cravat's hand inside the box. For a moment, nothing happened, and Cravat thought it was all a joke. Then, he felt a stabbing pain, followed by an intense burning.

He must have passed out after that, because he had no memory of what happened next.

*** 

Harvey awoke the next morning in the Lazyboy, with sunlight streaming through the window. The dream--and it was a dream wasn't it--had been very real, more real than any he remembered. Then, he noticed the punctures just above the knuckles on the back of his hand. The skin around the punctures was brittle, with deep crevices spreading out like ripples in still water. The wasting process had begun.

## Stones and Bones

"Now, you and I need to talk." Woodard said.

He picked his way to the worn, overstuffed chair he favored, and eased into it. Stretching a hand toward a companion chair across from it, he motioned Haylee to take a seat. She sat, the worn cushion forming around her like a giant hand.

Woodard watched her settle into the chair, pursing his lips, as if he needed to time his words just right before speaking.

"It's sad you and your mother are not here together." he said, weaving his fingers together, separating them, then lacing them again. "She wouldn't have nothing to do with me after she learned she was pregnant."

Haylee said nothing. She studied her grandfather's face. His eyes filled with pain as if he was experiencing some unbearable memory.

"It's a hard thing for a parent to lose a child," he said, "Harder still, when they're just out of reach. I made overtures over the years, but I never heard nothin' out of her. It was like she was dead, like I was speaking into to empty air."

Haylee thought of her mother's own attempted communication: Calls Haylee refused to answer and letters Claudette sent, Christmas and birthday cards. Funny how there was never acknowledgment of those special days when she lived at home. It was only after she left and severed all ties that the letters and cards began to arrive. She never answered any of them, although she did call once to leave her cell number with Mr. Garza.

She would have said her mother brought any suffering she incurred on herself, but now, Haylee wasn't sure.

"Now that she's gone," Woodard continued. "I'd like to bring her home. She was unwilling when she lived, but now, I'd like to have her here."

"I'm sorry, Grandfather, but they cremated her. I don't even have her ashes. The hospital provided the cremation. It's what she wanted. Mr. Garza, the man that looked after her, showed me her will."

Woodard's face hardened.

"There's a cemetery toward the back of the property. Every Woodard that ever walked since we settled in Slaughter County is buried there. Until now, our family has remained complete: All of us joined as one on this land. Now, there's one missing, a rift in the cloth."

"I'm sorry, Grandfather," Haylee said.

The old man's features softened. "But you're here, Darlin'," he said, hinting a smile. "And it does my heart good that you'll take your momma's place."

Something about the words *take your momma's place* stirred an uneasy feeling inside her. The feeling lasted only a moment and then it was gone.

Still, Woodard noticed Haylee's expression change. "Look's like something's bothering you," he said, "Want to tell me?"

Haylee paused, lips pressed together. She should say something. She decided on something that bothered her since the restaurant.

"Just before Mother died, she was delirious; I guess from whatever she was suffering. She was unconscious when I arrived, but awoke while I was there. Anyway, she saw me and thought I was someone else. Someone she called the witch. It terrified her. She said this witch had come to bring her back here.

"Then, that man, Cravat, called me the same thing--the witch. Why?"

Woodard listened, one hand scratching at the bit of gray stubble that covered his chin. Hoisting himself out of his chair, he turned his back to Haylee, facing away from her.

"I reckon if I don't say something, you'll hear it from someone else," he said, "When William Slaughter moved his band of folks here, this land belonged to the Indians. Now, when most folks think of Indians, they think Choctaw or Cherokee, but there's one group few know about: the Alibamos."

"Alibamos," Haylee repeated. "That name sounds almost like Alabama."

"Exactly," said Woodard, "That's where the state got its name. The Alibamos came from Mexico. They was part of the Aztec people. When the Spaniards came looking for gold, the Alibamos were driven off their land. They tried to settle a little distance away, but the Comanche and Apache were too vicious. They had no choice but to keep moving.

"They became nomads, wandering further and further east, looking for a place of their own. Finally, they settled here. During their travels, the band had dwindled and they found it easy to hide their existence in the ridges that surround us. They did it well. No one, not even the other tribes, suspected this tribe of exiles dwelt here.

"Though their true home was a thousand of miles away, they kept their ways, including sacrificing humans to strange gods. Anyone unfortunate enough to wander too close to their camp was strung up, their hearts ripped out and offered to their demon gods. By the time William Slaughter arrived with his followers, the Alibamos were trading with the whites and had adopted civilized ways, though they still practiced in secret, deep in the woods.

"The chief had a beautiful daughter named Petweenus. The moment Slaughter saw her, he fell in love and wanted her for a wife. He met with the tribal elders and a long courtship was arranged, according to Alibamos culture.

"One night, Slaughter decided to surprise his future bride with a gift he'd bartered from a traveling merchant, a shiny gold bracelet. Slipping through the woods, he spotted the glow of a fire though the trees near Mantel Creek, too far from the Alibamos settlement to be their campfire. Curious to whom it belonged, Slaughter worked his way silently in the direction of the blaze. When he arrived at its source, he was shocked by what he saw. Reflected in the harsh light, the same merchant he'd traded with for the bracelet, hung on a wooden cross. The tribe, stripped naked, their bodies painted in barbaric symbols, surrounded him. At a word from the chief, they circled the cross while the merchant twisted above them in pain.

"If this were not enough of a blasphemous act, what happened next caused Slaughter's blood, already cold, to turn to ice. The circle parted, exposing Petweenus with a knife raised in her hand. In one swift motion, she ripped open the merchant's chest and pulled his beating heart from his body, holding it like a trophy for the others to see. The band of heathens cheered at the bloody trophy.

"Slaughter drew back into the brush. Hurrying back to the settlement, he rounded up the men and directed them to arm themselves. He led them back to where the demonic rite continued. On Slaughter's command, the men burst out of the brush, firing their weapons. The tribe was taken by surprise and fell beneath the hail of bullets. Only the High Priest and Petweenus survived.

"They were bound and placed at Slaughter's feet. He commanded an iron be heated in the fire and he blinded them with the hot poker, burning out their eyes. Even after this, his anger still raged. As a final punishment, he directed the merchant's body be removed from the cross and be given a Christian burial. Then he commanded the Petweenus and her father be hung back to back on the cross until death claimed them.

"As the troop of men grouped together to leave, Petweenus shouted a dire pronouncement that she would return and have her revenge on any white person that ever again dared to venture onto land held by the Alibamos.

"The next morning, Slaughter returned to the place of the crucifixion. The High Priest was dead, his body stiff, flies buzzing around him, but Petweenus's body was gone. Slaughter searched the surrounding area for days, confident he would find her body rotting nearby, but no trace of her was ever found."

Riddle cleared his throat, then continued.

"Not long afterward, several hunting dogs escaped the pen where they were kept. The owner of the dogs, one of Slaughter's followers, sent his two sons to find the dogs and bring them back. When night fell and the boys had not returned, a search party formed to look for the missing boys. They found the youngest one trembling in the brush.

"He told a strange tale: He and his brother heard the barking of the dogs. Following the sound, they found themselves at Mantle Creek, where they were ambushed by a wild woman with only holes where eyes should have been. She attacked them with a ferocity that overcame them. Grabbing each of them by the coat (it was winter with snow on the ground), she drug them into the creek, plunging their heads beneath the water. The one boy managed to break from her grasp and make his way to the bank where he ran into the woods and hid, but he feared his brother was not so fortunate and drowned by the mad woman.

"The others hurried to the creek. As they feared, the second boy lay face down, floating on the water. Several more drownings occurred afterwards. People said Petweenus had done it, that she was avenging the murder of her people. Some started avoiding that section of creek and wise folks still do."

"What would make Mother think Petweenus was after her? She was over three hundred miles away."

"I can't answer that, Darlin'," said Woodard, "Maybe she saw something that scared her so bad she had to run away."

Haylee mused over this. It might be possible; though the letter in her mother's apartment made her think differently.

Paul appeared. He'd changed into tan slacks and a green knit shirt with the Tulane emblem embroidered over the pocket. His damp hair lay flat, making him look nerdish.

"I'm not interrupting anything, am I?" he asked.

"We were just getting reacquainted," said Woodard. "I think we're done for now, though. Mildred ought to have supper ready any time now. I expect I should wash up." Woodard edged past Paul, hauling himself up the stairs.

"So, care to tell me what you talked about?" Paul asked. "Or was it top secret?"

He grinned.

"Paul, have you ever heard of an Indian tribe called the Alibamos?"

"Sure," said Paul, "Though not much is known about them."

Haylee repeated what Woodard told her about Petweenus and William Slaughter.

"That's a new twist," Paul said. "Though some Creek claim Alibamos as one of their nations, no one proved they made it this far east. Actually, I think it fairly unlikely they did. It's my guess they were assimilated among other western tribes."

"But what if they did?" Haylee argued, "What if they continued human sacrifice? Aren't you even curious?"

Paul pursed his lips and shoved his hands in his back pockets, a pose he assumed whenever he felt challenged, "First, I think there would be more evidence."

"Like what?"

"For one thing, the absence of mounds around here. The Aztecs sacrificed atop pyramids, not crosses."

"Fine," Haylee said, "I'll go to Mantle Creek on my own."

"You wouldn't know what to look for," Paul said. "But you're not interested in the Alibamos, are you? This has to do with your mother."

"I want to know what killed her."

"She experienced a massive heart attack and tried to signal the nurse. Somehow, she wrapped the signal cord around her neck and strangled. I know you don't want to believe that, but it's true."

Haylee dropped back into the chair and crossed her arms, staring away from Paul. She felt like a kettle about to boil over.

"You weren't there," she said, "You don't know."

"Haylee, you weren't there either. All you have to go on is what the hospital told you."

Haylee continued to glare.

Paul fidgeted for a moment. "I tell you what: Tomorrow, we'll take a look at the area you want to examine, but if we find no evidence, then we drop the subject. Fair enough?"

"Thanks," she said, rising to her feet, taking his hand, "It means a lot to me."

Paul smiled. "You mean a lot to me."

\*\*\*

At breakfast, Haylee watched as her grandfather crept to his chair. His thin hair looked grayer than before. His body stooped over; he inched along, sliding his feet as if lifting them required more effort than he could summon.

Gripping the table for support, he lowered himself into his seat. He managed a smile.

"Grandfather, are you all right?" Haylee asked.

"Bad night," he said. "The doctor said to expect them as the disease progresses. I have one from time to time, but I always come through."

"He needs to take his treatment," Mildred said, passing out plates and coffee cups.

"I'll get to it," Woodard said, "In my own good time."

"What you're gonna do is put yourself in the grave," said Mildred, ladling grits onto Woodard's plate.

"I'll bring the breakfast meat in a moment." she said, aiming toward the kitchen.

Woodard tasted his grits, then waved his spoon at Haylee.

"I hate to ask this," he said, "But can I borrow Paul once more? I have some chores needin' to be done and I just don't seem up to it today. I know you two had some plans, but this damn condition has just about got me whipped."

"Grandfather, maybe you should see a doctor," said Haylee.

"Don't you start with me, too. I'll be fine. I just need a little help, that's all."

"I'll be happy to help, Mr. Woodard." Paul volunteered.

"I appreciate it, young feller."

Something pricked at the back of Haylee's mind. "Paul, if you're helping Grandfather today, I need to use the Volvo."

"The Volvo?" Paul hesitated. "Any particular reason?"

"I just feel like getting out." Haylee said. She felt her face flush with anger. "Why? You don't trust me to go off on my own? I can take care of myself."

Woodard glanced at Paul, a grin cracking the lower portion of his face.

"The keys are upstairs on the dresser," Paul said. "Just don't adjust anything."

Woodard took a last bite of grits, then pushed himself up from the table. He managed to straighten himself partially. Paul crossed over to assist the elderly man, but Woodard brushed him away.

"I'm fine. If you'll follow me out to the barn, there's some feed bags and a bucket. Louise and Mabel are ready for breakfast."

"Louise and Mabel?" Paul repeated.

Woodard laughed. "That's my hogs. I did away with the cows some time ago, but I still have a taste for fresh pork. Funny, when you take time to raise a critter, you find yourself naming them. It makes the butchering more difficult, though."

Woodard tottered toward the back. "Come on," he said to Paul. "I'll introduce you to the girls."

Mildred came to collect the breakfast dishes.

"So, they left you to yourself, did they?"

151

"It's fine," Haylee said, handing the black woman Paul's and her plates. Mildred took them and placed them on top of the meat platter.

"I haven't seen Cynthie this morning," Haylee said, "She didn't come home last night?"

"Oh, she's got her own place," Said Mildred, "She just came over the other night 'cause you was here."

"Oh."

"So what have you got planned today?" asked the black woman.

"I thought I'd go into town," Haylee said, "And maybe take some pictures."

"I figured you'd visit the creek," Mildred said.

"What?" Haylee searched the black woman's face. "Is there something there? What are you saying?"

Mildred gazed calmly back at the girl. "I heard you and Mister Claude talkin' last night is all."

Haylee felt a short flash of anger. The woman was toying with her. She pushed down the rage, forcing herself to be calm.

"Paul is taking me there later, after he finishes up with Grandfather," she smiled.

"Well, I hope you two have a nice time. It's a pretty place."

"So, you've been there?" Haylee said, hoping to extract more information from the woman.

"Once, long ago," Mildred said. She ejected each word like shots from a gun. Haylee tasted the bitterness in them. Deciding it best not to question the woman further, she rose from the table.

"I should be back by noon," she said, feeling she needed to say something. Electricity filled the space between them.

Mildred turned, the plates rattling.

"Take your time," the woman said, "Ain't nothing goin' on here to concern you."

As Mildred disappeared into the kitchen, Haylee mounted the stairs for the Volvo's keys. Bounding back down, she sped out the door and to the car.

The driver's seat was positioned too far back for her to operate the pedals or reach the steering wheel without leaning forward. She reached down to the control lever and released the seat that allowed it to slide back and forth on the rails. When her hand touched the lever, she hesitated. Paul was a stickler about the driver's seat being just right. If she changed its position, he'd raise hell. Leaving the lever untouched, she scooted forward so she balanced on the edge of the car seat. In this position, she could reach the pedals and her arms weren't so extended. Being forced to drive in such uncomfortable position all the way to town would be almost impossible.

*To hell with it.* She pressed the lever and slid the seat forward. *Paul will just have to get over it,* she thought, switching on the ignition. She steered the car down the long drive, and toward town.

She was irritated Woodard ruined the plans she and Paul made to visit the creek.

The traffic on the way to town was nonexistent and the fresh air and deep blue sky melted away the sour mood she felt toward Woodard for spoiling the plans she made with Paul. Besides, she had formed a new plan, something she needed to do in private.

When she reached Acedia Avenue, she studied each building, seeking clues that might give insight to Acedia, itself. The structures were disappointingly alike: Single story rectangles of brick with plate glass windows. Only the messages written on the glass differed and even these were done in a uniform style, as if the same hand was responsible for the lettering.

She read the titles identifying the nature of the businesses; *Acedia Hardware*, *Slaughter County Veterinary*, *The Coffee Pot Diner*, *Acedia Dry Goods*.

Haylee turned onto the side street that marked the corner of the Municipal Building. The street sign identified it as Pride Road. Riddle's Black and White, parked to the side of the Municipal Building, clued her to the location of the sheriff's office. A girl's bicycle leaned near the door-- the first indication of children since she and Paul arrived.

Haylee drove past the bicycle and slipped the in a space between a ancient pickup and a battered Studebaker. She switched off the engine, careful to lock the door before advancing toward the municipal building's entrance. She looked back once to satisfy herself the Volvo would not be noticed. She wanted this visit to be a private one.

When she reached the corner where Pride Road intersected Acedia Avenue, she stopped to watch the activity across the street. A dozen workmen were busy detailing the façade of a church. She hadn't noticed the building before, though it was sizable enough to rival the Municipal building. She watched the men work a moment more before skipping up the steps to the tall, double doors.

Nobody was seated at any of the windows. Haylee peeped through the glass, searching until she spotted Cynthie in a far corner. Her cousin sat in a straight-back chair, dutifully copying from a sheet of paper into a large ledger.

Haylee rapped on the glass. The sound caused the woman to start and the ledger clattered to the floor.

"What the hell?" Cynthie spun around, then relaxed when she saw Haylee peeping through the glass. She reached down and picked up the fallen ledger, replacing it on the desk. \

"Whatcha need, Cousin?" she asked cheerfully, levering herself to her feet. She crossed to Haylee's window.

155

Haylee hesitated. Her questions to Mildred had pushed the wrong buttons, and she did not want to make this mistake with Cynthie. She needed to proceed carefully.

Cynthie gave her an opening. "Where's your beau?"

"Beau? Oh, you mean Paul." Haylee said. "He had to help Grandfather today. They left me with nothing to do so I decided to drive to town."

Cynthie nodded. The glass separated them like visiting arrangements in a prison. *But which of us is the prisoner?*

She wanted to suggest Cynthie come around the partition so they could talk face-to-face, but Cynthie stayed rooted on her side of the glass, making intimate conversation impossible.

"Well, you ought to take some time and look around town," Cynthie said. She seemed detached. The warmth she'd greeted Haylee with the day they arrived was now missing. "You could meet some of the folks that live here. Most all of them remember you as a baby."

"Maybe I will," Haylee said.

"Good." Cynthie turned toward the ledger.

"Cynthie," Haylee called.

The woman stopped and slowly faced Haylee again. "Yeah?" Her eyes were lidded, filled with caution.

"I came here because I wanted to ask you something."

Her eyes narrowed more. "What's that?"

"Did my mother ever visit Mantel Creek?"

"You need to avoid that place." Cynthie said.

"That's not what I asked," Haylee said, growing bolder. "Did my mother ever go there? Is that why she ran away, because something happened there?"

The woman stiffened. Haylee caught the tiniest twitch at the corner of Cynthie's mouth.

"I ain't the one you want to ask," she said.

"Who then?"

"Uncle Woodard."

"He said to see you," Haylee lied, "That you would tell me everything."

Cynthie studied Haylee's face. "That don't sound right. Are you sure that's what he said?"

"He wasn't feeling well, so he sent me here to see you."

"Come back in an hour. Maybe we'll talk then. Right now, I got work to do."

She turned on her heel and walked back to the ledger.

Haylee left without saying goodbye. She wondered if an hour would make a difference in Cynthie's willingness to talk. All she could do was try.

Haylee pushed open the large double doors and stepped out into the bright, morning light. The sun floated high above the rooftops of the low buildings, climbing steadily toward its zenith. With time to kill, Haylee decided to follow her cousin's suggestion and look around. Across the street, the workmen sat in groups of twos and threes, taking a midmorning break. Redirecting her gaze away from the men, to the church, she saw the wooden structure now wore a fresh coat of white paint, trimmed in green. Several tall windows, arched at the top and fitted with colored glass panes, lined the side of the church. A covered porch sheltered the front entrance. A steeple with an open section, exposing a large, brass bell, crowned the affair. A two-story brick building sat directly behind the church, connected by covered walkway. The building, square in shape, was unadorned. Two rows of tiny, barred windows lined the building. Haylee wondered what the purpose of the building might be. The bars suggested a jail or prison, but it was connected to the church. She thought of crossing the street for a better look, but the bold stares of the workmen scared her. She hurried to the Volvo and slipped inside.

She backed out into the street so the car was aimed away from the courthouse. She had no idea where the road would take her; only that she would not pass the church and the workmen. She felt their eyes boring into her, even through the body of the car. Now, she only wanted to get away.

A few houses lined the road, all of them clapboard affairs, with windows not quite square, and yards littered with rusted appliances and threadbare tires. Further down, a cemetery caught her attention. She drove the short distance and pulled onto the strip of grass between the road and the cast-iron fence that surrounded it.

A gate, suspended beneath a graceful and ornate arch, gave entrance into the cemetery. Haylee lifted the latch and the gate swung open.

The cemetery was very old. Many of the dates spanned back a century and a half. Haylee searched the names. There was a possibility William Slaughter's followers might be interred here, or even Slaughter himself. The article Paul showed her said Slaughter died in Acedia. It seemed reasonable his grave should be among these.

Haylee picked her way among the headstones. Many were nothing more than crude chunks of granite, the names and dates cut into the rock face by someone with little skill. The majority of these markers were for infants, all around the same period.

Moving on, she reached a section of more refined grave markers. These were marble with perfect lettering. Judging from the dates these burials were more recent, beginning around nineteen hundred. These would have been the families that bought land from the original owners, Slaughter's followers.

She was about to read the name on one in particular, when a voice spoke behind her.

"They're not real."

Haylee spun around, her breath caught in her chest. A young girl, about ten or eleven years old, stood a few feet away. The girl's long, blonde hair hung loose, cascading over her shoulders to the small of her back. She had large, blue eyes, a tiny nose and small, perfect lips. She wore a sack dress that hung past her knees. The pink bike Haylee noticed earlier at the Sheriff's office, leaned against the fence.

"You scared me," Haylee said, her hand over her pounding heart.

"The graves," said the girl. "They're pretty, but there's nobody buried here." She squatted next to a worn marble slab and traced the thin gray veins running through it with the tip of her index finger. "It's all a lie." Haylee moved nearer to the girl and dropped to her knees beside her.

"What do you mean it's all a lie?"

"They want people to think there's people buried here, but no one is." The girl replied.

She turned to face Haylee, her eyes focused on something a distance away. "I watch them sometimes. They don't know, but I do. They put up these," she indicated the tombstone with the gray veins. "But they don't dig a hole. They just put these up and then they leave."

"Are you sure?"

Why would someone go through the trouble and expense to build a fake graveyard?

"At first, I thought they would come back and dig a hole," said the girl. "You know, get it ready first, but they never did. They never came back."

"I think they might have while you were gone, at home or playing with your friends."

"I don't have any friends," said the girl. "There's no one but me. My friends are somewhere else."

"Well, maybe you were home when they came back."

"I live just down the road. I can see this place from my house. They never came back to dig the hole. They never do."

"Virginia!"

The voice caused Haylee to start. She turned to see Riddle standing just outside the gate, his eyes narrow, his mouth a thin, hard edge.

"Brother Boone said to get home, now, 'afore he comes here with a switch."

Virginia leapt to her feet.

"Bye," she whispered.

Haylee watched the girl hurry to her bike. Placing a foot on the pedal, she kicked off, then steered the bike down the road.

Riddle rested his large frame on the gate, his expression unchanged.

"Mind if I have a word with you?" he asked.

Haylee realized she was still on her knees. She stood up. Stooping, she brushed off her pants with her hands. Riddle continued to lean on the gate, blocking her exit. Feeling she had no choice, she picked her way through the headstones to the sheriff.

"I hate to disturb your er…meditation."

161

"I saw the cemetery and I thought it was the one Grandfather told me about. I wanted to see where the Woodards are buried."

"Sure," Riddle said, "No crime in that."

"Did you need me for something else?" The man made her nervous. Something about him warned her he was dangerous.

"I need you to follow me to my office," Riddle said. "It'd be better if we talked there."

"Can you at least tell me what this is about?" Haylee asked. The idea of the two of them in his office, alone, made her uneasy.

"Like I said, we'll talk in the office."

"I'm supposed to meet Cynthie in a half-hour. If I'm late, she'll worry." Haylee said looking for a way out.

"We wouldn't want that," Riddle said, smiling, "I'll do my best to keep it short."

Riddle held the gate open for Haylee, shutting it behind her. She climbed into the Volvo. It took two tries before she managed to swing the car around. Riddle waited until the Volvo was behind him, then drove slowly to his office with Haylee following behind. She expected him to flash his blue lights along the way, but he put on no show today. When they reached the sheriff's office, Riddle pulled into the slot marked *Official*, leaving her to park in the space next to it.

Riddle exited the car, and waited on the curb for Haylee. When she came up beside him, he swung the door to his office and motioned her to enter.

Haylee stepped into a space larger than the exterior led her to believe. A hidden cooling unit pumped out air cold enough to make her shiver under the pale fluorescent lights. Riddle walked around her to the oversized desk in the center of the room. Dropping onto an equally oversized leather chair, he motioned for Haylee to take a seat in an armless straight-back chair with a padded back and seat.

Haylee sat, pushing the chair back with her feet, giving herself a little distance from the sheriff.

Riddle continued to smile his benign smile, the cat about to dine on the canary. He leaned forward and resting his forearms on the desk he faced Haylee.

"We got a problem," he said.

Haylee waited for Riddle to say more. The man only frowned.

"I'm sorry," she said at last, "I don't understand."

"'Course you don't," Riddle said, shaking his head, "That's why you're here: For me to explain it to you."

"Sheriff, I really need to get going. I still have to meet my cousin and-"

"Hold up, young lady," he said. "What I got to say involves your cousin. Matter of fact, it was her that decided me to go get you."

"I don't-" Haylee began, puzzled as to where this was going.

Riddle held up a hand. "Just sit and listen," he said. Haylee stiffened, but managed to keep smiling.

"Cynthie told me you was asking questions about Mantel Creek. She also said that you said the Reeve sent you to her, 'cause she knew something that went on there. Is that so?"

To deny it would only make her look foolish. "Yes, I guess I did."

"Well, Cynthie is upset about it. Of course, I know the Reeve never told you to ask Cynthie those questions, did he?"

"No." Haylee said.

"Good. I'm glad we got that straight."

He pursed his lips, pressing the palms of his hands together. Then he touched them to his lips as if he was praying.

"I could charge you with a felony."

"What?" Haylee's eyes widened, her mouth frozen in an "O".

"I ain't going to. I'm gonna let you off with a warning, but using the Reeve's name, lying on him like you did, is the same as perjury around here. Next Sunday is homecoming. Homecoming is the most important day of the year and this year is special. It's the year of Jubilee." He nodded his head toward window. "That's the reason for all the fuss around the church."

Riddle kicked the chair back, rising to his feet. Haylee leaned forward to get up, but he motioned her to stay seated. He edged closer until he towered over her.

"Here's the deal. I want you to stop asking about Mantel Creek. You ain't gonna find nothing there. All you're doing is upsetting the folks around here. Whatever reason caused Claudette to leave, died with her. I'm asking you to let her spirit rest as well.

"Do that for me and I won't say nothing to the Reeve about you lying on him."

"I guess I don't have a choice," Haylee said.

"No, Ma'am, you don't." Riddle crossed his arms. "And it'd be best if you stayed away from Virginia as well. She's had a rough time of it. I would think poorly if someone upset her."

"Sheriff Riddle," Haylee said, rising to her feet. "I'm not feeling very welcomed. I came here simply to take some photographs for Paul's book. I'm not interested in local politics, but if my presence in this town is an inconvenience, then I promise, I'll be gone by tomorrow morning."

"Now, don't go getting all bent out of shape," Riddle said. "I guess I'm just overprotective of Virginia. She lost her folks a few years ago. She's been living with our pastor, Luther Boone. Luther's a single man. Virginia cooks and keeps the house. Sometimes, she comes here to watch the portable television."

Haylee followed his glance to the tiny television resting on a litter of papers like an electronic paper weight.

"She likes the cartoons," he said. "I use it to keep an eye on the news; you know, jailbreaks, terrorists, stuff like that. It gets the signal from Huntsville when the weather's good. On rainy days, it just gets fuzz.

"Anyway, when she has free time, I let her come watch the set. I guess, over time, she's grown on me. Now, I think of myself as an uncle or something."

Haylee had to smile at this. Some of the edge came off the mood building inside her.

"Well, I've taken up enough of your time." Riddle said. "You can see yourself out."

Sitting in the Volvo, Haylee tried to peer inside Riddle's office through the window. She squinted her eyes, shading them with her hand, but found it impossible to tell if Riddle was peeking back. If he was, he would see if she left in the direction she wanted. The thought someone could exert such control over her.

"Fuck you," she said.

She backed into the street so the car was facing the graveyard with Acedia Avenue behind her. Then she gunned the engine so the tires squealed loudly as she raced away.

When she reached the cemetery, the road behind her was still empty. Virginia said she lived in close proximity to the cemetery, close enough she could see it from her house. Haylee slowed when she reached the end of the road, the wrought-iron fence marking the back of the cemetery. Through the windshield, she saw three houses, any of which could be Virginia's. She hoped to see the girl's bike parked in the yard, but the yards were empty.

Haylee rolled forward, parking the car in the shadows beneath the low hanging branches of an ancient elm. She shut off the engine, wondering what to do next. She could try door-to-door, but tossed the idea immediately. Being a stranger, she doubted Virginia would be paraded out for her, so she would have to discover Virginia's address some other way.

Out of the corner of her eye, Haylee caught movement in the mirror. Her first impulse was to crank the car and race off. Riddle would recognize her snooping and not be happy about it.

To her relief, a battered pick-up, and not the Sheriff's car, came clanking down the road. As the truck rattled past, Haylee lowered her head, pretending to look at something in her lap. She watched it turn into the yard of the second house on the opposite side of the street. The doors opened, and a lanky man emerged from the driver's side. He walked around to the back of the truck and lowered the tailgate. A moment later, the passenger door opened and Virginia slipped out. She joined the man and he handed her a paper bag. She carried it to the house. The man hoisted a sack from the truck bed onto his shoulder and followed Virginia into the house. Virginia and the man came back out and returned to the truck, where he handed the girl another paper sack, then gathered the last two for himself. He said something to Virginia, then struggled across the yard to the house. Virginia set her sack on the ground and wrestled the tailgate closed. Once she had it latched, she brushed her hand off on her dress. She bent down for the sack, then stopped and turned her head toward Haylee. The girl stood for a long moment, staring, then, raising a tentative hand, she waved.

Haylee waved back hoping, the girl could see her, despite the shadows.

A voice, deep and male, rang out.

"Virginia, what the hell is taking you so long?"

"Coming, Papa Boone," the girl cried.

Snatching up the bag, Virginia hurried to the house without looking back.

As Haylee steered the car back to Acedia Avenue, she congratulated herself on her good fortune of stumbling onto Luther Boone's place. She wanted an opportunity to talk to Virginia again and knowing where the girl lived solved half the problem. Now, she needed to find a way to meet Virginia alone. If the girl was telling the truth about the graves, Haylee might have the first piece of the puzzle to why her mother left.

*What else did Virginia know?*

Haylee intended to find out.

**-8-**

## A Witch in the Armoire

She was still pondering the question of the graveyard and Virginia when she turned into the long driveway marking Woodard's property. As the house came into view, she saw Paul and Woodard under the large oak. They were seated in chairs passing a clay jug back and forth. Haylee parked next to the black Packard. Stepping out of the Volvo, she shoved the keys into the pocket of her jeans.

"Hi there, Darlin'," Woodard called.

Paul lifted his head. He looked as if he might topple any moment.

"Hi Darlin'," he repeated, mocking Woodard.

"Well, you two are getting along." Haylee said.

"Ah, honey, we're just having a little drink." Woodard said.

"Paul doesn't drink. Not like this," she swept her hand toward Paul.

"He's too stiff," Woodard said, "I'm just loosening him up a bit."

"He doesn't need to be picking up bad habits, Grandfather. We plan on getting married."

"Darlin', you're just like your mother. You always worryin' about nothing. A little shine ain't gonna turn him into a drunk. But I'll tell you this: You keep him on too tight of a leash and you're gonna end up squeezing all the life out of him. A man's got to run once in a while or he quits being a man."

He turned toward Paul and rubbed his hands together.

"I guess we need to get this feller to his bed so he can sleep it off. Think you can get him to his feet?"

Haylee leaned down and grasped Paul's arms.

"Paul, can you stand?" Haylee asked, her anger now concern.

Paul muttered a string of nonsense and giggled as if he'd told a joke. Tugging hard along with Woodard's feeble pokes, they managed to get the intoxicated man upright. Together, they walked him to the house. By the time they reached the staircase, Paul managed to find his legs. They got him to the bed, where Haylee undressed him down to his underwear. She pulled the covers over Paul and kissed his forehead before following Woodard out of the room.

Downstairs, Woodard paused at the bottom step.

"Darlin'," he said, "I reckon while you're here, you're gonna hear lots of stuff about me, much of it because me and your mother had a falling out. You're gonna have to decide what to believe: Them or me. You'll have to make the choice."

"No one has said anything about you, Grandfather."

"Maybe not, but they will. When they do, I'd appreciate if you didn't put me on the defense."

He pulled her close and kissed her on the forehead.

"I'm taking Mildred to the dry goods for a few things. We'll be back shortly. Keep an eye on your betrothed."

Woodard walked toward the back of the house. A moment later, Haylee heard Mildred's voice, followed by the back door closing. Looking out the side window, she saw Woodard and Mildred come around the side of the house. They got into the Packard and backed out of view.

With Woodard and Mildred gone, and Paul asleep upstairs, Haylee found herself alone. She rummaged around the living room, searching for something to occupy her.

The house was laid out with the entrance opening into the great room. From there, an archway led to the dining room. A door at the far end opened into the kitchen. Some time in the past, someone had built an add-on off the back that served as Mildred's quarters. Mildred was careful to keep the door closed.

Suddenly, she wanted to know what was in there. Mildred was hiding something. The woman's behavior attested to that, and Mildred's room might be the place to find the answers she sought. One thing was certain: Her mother had not left Acedia as

171

the rebellious teen that Riddle and Mildred wanted her to believe. Claudette fled because she was afraid of something. That something had to do with Mantel Creek.

She approached the door. Part of her wished it was locked. She had no key and, unlike the detectives on television, no lock picking skills. A locked door would end this foolishness. The room would keep its secrets and save her the consequences if her snooping was discovered.

She touched the knob, feeling the cold metal. This was the point of no return. Once done, it could not be undone. Her mind raced. What if the door was rigged so Mildred would know if she opened it? She'd read stories of people fixing a piece of thread to a door, then checking later to see if the thread was broken. If Mildred set such a trap, the woman would know someone entered uninvited.

Shoving the paranoid thoughts aside, she turned the knob. It held fast. Relief flooded over her until she noticed a key beside the door. It was dangling from a chain, the kind they issued soldiers for dog tags, made of metal balls.

Haylee stood on tiptoe to slip the chain off the nail it hung from. She carried it to the door and slid it in the lock. The key turned easily, and a moment later, Haylee found herself looking into a small hallway with two closed doors. One stood at the opposite end of the hall. The other door, the one closest to her, stood at a right angle to the first. She tried the knob of the first door and was surprised to find it unlocked. It opened into a room the size of a small pantry. The strong odor of mothballs permeated the air.

Cardboard boxes, stacked one on another and crowded against shelves, ran up both walls. Dust covered everything. This room had gone undisturbed for a long time, and it would be obvious if she tampered with any of the boxes. Then again, because this room had gone undisturbed for so long, would anyone bother with it now? Her trespassing only needed to go unnoticed for the few remaining days she would be here.

Confident she wouldn't be found out, she entered the room. She checked smaller boxes on the shelf first. All of them were unsealed; the flaps were woven one under another to secure them. She worked the flaps loose and looked inside. The first box disappointed her. It was filled with ostrich feathers, dyed for decorating women's hats. She folded the flaps into their original position, then opened the box beside it. This box contained five pairs of shoes of various shapes and sizes. One pair belonged to an adult male, another pair, an adult female. The three remaining pairs were all sized for children.

Another box contained dozens of gloves, every pair the same size. After working though more boxes, all of them filled with clothing odds and ends, she turned her attention to the larger boxes on the floor. Starting with a stack of three, she lifted the top box, placing it on the floor. The flaps were folded at the corners like the others. Haylee worked the flaps loose and peered inside. The box contained ankle-length dresses with cinched waists. The cloth smelled musty and made her sneeze.

Haylee refolded the flaps and wrestled the box back into place, disappointed she'd found nothing more sinister than old clothes. She turned toward the door when she noticed a heavy canvas sack in the corner. The sack was fitted with drawstrings wrapped around the opening and tied with a knot. It must have once been white, but now was a discolored gray. The sides bulged with whatever was stuffed inside.

She hefted it, surprised at its lightness. Curious, she began untying the knot. By the time she got the rope loose, her fingers ached. She massaged her hands, then pulled the top open. Looking into the sack, she noticed a tangle of wigs. The hair colors varied from platinum blond to raven black. She fished out a rich, auburn hairpiece. The hair was long and luscious, begging to be touched. She thrust her fingers into the piece to smooth out the tangles and brushed against something stiff and leathery. Haylee turned the hairpiece, pushing the stray hair aside. Attached to the hair by the roots was a human scalp. The tangle of hair fell from her hands.

Trembling, she struggled to calm her breathing. She raised the hair again, holding it between finger and thumb, so she could study the grisly thing. The scalp was ancient, older than the clothes and shoes. The question was, whose hair was it, and how did it end up here in her grandfather's house?

She carried the hair to the sack and dropped it inside, then pulled the drawstrings and retied them. Replacing the sack in its corner, Haylee retraced her steps to the hall. She still had not searched Mildred's room. She closed the door to the closet and moved to the other door. Like the room she'd just investigated, the door was unlocked and she let herself in easily.

The room smelled musky, but beneath the smell of musk, Haylee detected a more delicate odor she thought might be nutmeg. She remembered catching a hint of nutmeg about her grandfather as well.

A quick scan revealed a twin-sized brass bed in the center of the room. A tall armoire and low vanity, fitted with drawers, stood against the wall on the left. A cheap, rectangular mirror in a plain frame, hung above the vanity. Below the mirror, two photographs in stand-up frames sat on top of the vanity beside a ceramic basin and pitcher. Haylee skirted the bed to get to the two photographs.

Both were ancient, sepia colored daguerreotypes. The first depicted a black woman. She was young and beautiful, dressed in an expensive gown. A parasol dangled from her hands in front of her. The woman's face radiated an exquisite smile. A tall, white man with thick, curly locks, dressed in gentlemen's clothes, stood beside her. He held a white Stetson in one hand. He clutched black woman's waist. Haylee recognized the man as her grandfather.

The second photograph gave her pause. Surprised, she snatched it off the vanity and held it at eye level, studying the image. In the photograph, her mother looked back at her. Claudette, with her grandfather's house behind her, stood in a brilliant pool of sunlight. She'd never seen her mother look as beautiful as she did in this picture. She was wearing a gingham dress, hemmed just above her knees. She held an infant in her arms that she proudly displayed to the camera. Haylee thought the photograph must have been taken shortly before Claudette fled in the night, away from Acedia.

Haylee allowed herself to linger on the photograph a moment more, then replaced it beside the other on the vanity. There was still the armoire to explore and the window of time to do it was shrinking.

The armoire crowded the corner of the left wall. A pair of tall doors, fitted with brass knobs, stood above a wide drawer at its base.

Haylee held her breath as she opened the doors. Several solid colored shifts hung from hangers on a wooden dowel. Beneath the dresses was a pair of highly polished leather shoes with black laces. She lifted the shoes and turned them in her hand. She could see her reflection in the polished surface. She was carefully replacing them as they were when her hand grazed something hidden by the dresses. She located the object and removed a small, square, wooden box fitted with a hinged lid and brass clasp.

Haylee hefted the thing, wondering if she dared open it. She shook it, listening for a rattle but there was none. She carried the box to the bed and placed it on the worn bedspread. Unhooking the clasp, she lifted the lid. The box tumbled from her hand and a small, wrinkled, human head rolled across the sheet. Haylee stumbled back. The room winked out, replaced by another room, this one vast and dimly lit. She was someone else. She smelled wood smoke, though she could not find its source. Low voices murmured around her, faces, all a blur, peeked out of the haze. Someone placed something in her hands that began to twist and writhe, coiling itself around her. She opened her mouth to scream.

The lights flashed back on. She was standing beside the bed, the horrible withered head lying face down so its wretched features were hidden. Using the bedspread as a makeshift glove, she lifted the head and dropped it back into the box, then snapped the lid shut. The box went into the armoire and she shut the doors with a firm thrust. Her head swam from the strange dream, or vision, or whatever it was. She realized her hand was throbbing.

Haylee closed the door to Mildred's room, then rushed out of the tiny hallway. She shut the door to the add-on and withdrew the key from her pocket. Her hand shook so badly, she made several attempts before she could fit the key in the keyhole.

"What the hell are you doing?" said a voice.

Startled, Haylee barely managed to stifle a scream. She turned to face Paul. He was dressed in the same clothes as that morning. His face was creased, his eyes were two red orbs, and his unruly hair was more tangled than usual. Somehow, he missed a button so his now-rumpled shirt collar was an inch higher on the left than the right. His pants were creased with horizontal lines. His shoes were untied so the shoestrings trailed behind him.

"You scared me half to death." Haylee said. Turning the key, she was rewarded with a satisfying click. "What are you doing up? You look terrible."

"Never mind about me, I'll live. I don't think you should be snooping."

"Who said I was snooping?" Haylee said. "I'm just…looking around a little."

"That door was locked," Paul said. "Locked doors usually mean keep out."

Woodward and Mildred's voices outside the back door caught their attention. Haylee slipped the key and chain onto the nail. Taking Paul by the hand, she hurried him through the kitchen and up the stairs, her upraised finger signaling him to stay quiet.

Leading him into her bedroom, she motioned him to the bed, then closed the door. Haylee crossed to the bed and sat beside Paul.

"Okay, Nancy Drew," Paul said, "How many dead bodies did you find?"

"Paul, the first room was filled with boxes of women's clothes. There was a sack stuffed with human hair."

"Haylee, lots of people in areas like this keep hair from their mother and grandmother. Some have relatives' hair going back three and four generations. It's a macabre custom, I admit, but they see it as a way of remembering the departed."

"Paul, this hair had part of the person's scalp attached."

"Are you sure that's what it was? You're sure you didn't find a pile of wigs?"

"I've never seen any wigs like that."

Paul stood, absently running a hand one hand through his tangled hair.

"Since we got here, all you've done is look for reasons to convict your grandfather of…of some kind of strange conspiracy. It's like you want to find something wrong."

"Paul, I found things. A head…"

"And a body in the closet. Let me guess, Sheriff Riddle."

"You don't believe me."

Paul walked to the door. He placed one hand on the knob, then turned to face Haylee. "It's obvious you won't be satisfied until you find a way to convict innocent people whose only crime is to try to heal the wound your mother inflicted on this family. I'm going downstairs to see if Claude needs my help." He left, slamming the door behind him.

Haylee looked around, her vision blurred by tears. The blank walls stared back, mute and stoic. Her camera bag sat untouched on the dresser. She hadn't taken one photograph since arriving in Acedia, not that it mattered. Photography was not at the top of her to-do list at the moment.

Something was happening. Whatever it was had snared Paul, blinding him to things that should be obvious. Why couldn't he see how they were being manipulated?

Are was all of this in her head? Had she imagined the sack filled with human hair and the shrunken head? What if she found a way to slip the hair and withered head from their hiding places and present them to Paul? Would that be proof? Although unlikely, the substance the hair was attached to might be something other than someone's scalp, she supposed. Age did things. It certainly looked like skin, but how did she know for sure? She'd never seen severed human flesh. The same was true with the thing in the box. It certainly looked like shriveled human head, but could she be sure?

*Come on Haylee*, she quizzed herself, *Do you really think any of that was just stuff Mildred kept around for Halloween?* She doubted Acedia, with its fervent religious zeal, allowed trick or treat. Come to think of it, other than Virginia, she hadn't seen one child in the entire town. If there were children here, they were well hidden.

The problem was, she couldn't ask her grandfather about any of this without admitting she'd invaded Mildred's privacy.

She left the bed and walked to the door. Stepping into the hall, she heard Woodard's voice ring out like a bell, then Paul's less obtrusive voice. The two were in an animated conversation. An occasional laugh punctuated the exchange. Haylee was struck by the oddness of it all, how Paul, from a different world, settled in so easily with these people, while she, the granddaughter, was the stranger.

Woodard looked across the table to where Haylee sat. Mildred, off to the side, sliced a thick roast with quick, even strokes from a butcher knife. She made each cut with a single, smooth motion, her eyes focused on the task. Haylee watched the black woman work, following the knife as it cleaved the thin slabs of meat, dropping one-by-one onto the plate.

"You kinda kept hidden away this afternoon, Darlin'," Woodard said. "You don't feel good?"

"I guess I was tired after my trip to town." Haylee said. "I decided to lay down for a while."

"I hope you're feeling better." Woodard said. He took the platter Mildred passed him and stabbed several slices of meat, laying them on his plate.

"These taters came straight from the garden," he said, spooning a small mountain of mashed potatoes. He nabbed the gravy boat and poured a flood of gravy on the potato mound, creating a volcano, expulsing brown lava.

"I grew the collards too," he added, pointing his fork toward the bowl filled with cooked greens. "I could use some help if you got a little time. It'd give us a chance to get to know one another better."

Haylee pondered how to answer. Her plans did not include working in a garden.

"I'd love to," she said, "But Paul and I only have a limited amount of time here before we have to return to New Orleans. We still haven't collected anything for his book."

"That book," Woodard said, "I plumb forgot about it."

He scratched his head, then his face came alive, his eyes gleaming like two bright-blue sapphires. "I bet you I got enough stories to fill a book by myself."

"Thanks, Grandfather, but I think Paul needs several viewpoints, not just one."

"Actually, Claude, I think it would be great to hear what you have to say. Building the last chapters around someone of your experience might be just the thing I need."

"Paul, we *need more* than just Grandfather's experiences. I agree we should include him but...remember what we talked about." She nudged his leg with her foot under the table.

He had promised to take her to Mantel Creek and she intended he keep it.

Woodard continued to smile. "Well, you two decide. Right now, we got all this food that needs to be ate. Dig in."

Haylee nibbled at her supper with little appetite. Across from her, Paul shoveled food into his mouth like a man about to face famine and wanting to take in as much nutrition as possible.

"You know," Woodard said, "It probably would be good for you folks to get out a little, meet some people and get an idea about life around here. The garden can wait a day. I just don't want to lose the moon phase. That's what's important."

"So you follow the moon for planting?" Paul asked.

"For everything," Woodard said, "Not just the crops. To everything a season, same as the good book says.

"Take these taters," he lifted a forkful and panned them from Haylee to Paul, "They was planted during the time of waning. You don't want to plant taters when the light is increasing or they'll rot. Then there is some things that must be planted when the light is increasing. Everything has a time, whether you're setting a pole or butchering an animal."

The words "butchering an animal" sent Haylee's mind reeling. Scenes rose before her, foreign and wicked. A fire blazed, the same as earlier in Mildred's room when she stumbled on the shriveled head. This time, she saw its reflection against a wall made of woven branches and grass. Something moved behind her. Then, as suddenly as it appeared, the image vanished and her head cleared. Both Woodard and Paul were leaning toward her, their faces filled with concerned.

"Are you all right, Darlin'?" Woodard asked. "You passed out for a minute. Your eyes rolled up and you swayed like you was gonna topple off your chair."

"I feel a little sick," Haylee said. "I probably need to lie down. If you'll excuse me."

"Sure," Woodard said, "You do whatever you need to do to make yourself feel better."

Paul pushed his chair back and helped Haylee to her feet. "I'll see her to bed," he said. He slipped an arm around her and led her out of the dining room. Her head still swam and she was thankful for Paul's assistance. Paul steered her up the stairs and into her room. He helped her on to the bed.

"You need to get some rest," he said, "I'll be back to check on you in a little while."

Haylee grabbed his arm as he turned to go. "Paul, what's happening to me?" she asked. She felt tremors inside her.

"You got a little excited from the day." Paul said, "Your blood sugar is probably low from skipping meals. You've got to take better care of yourself."

"I saw something." she said, "No, that's not right. I was someone else. There was a fire and something else, something I didn't want to see."

"Get some rest," Paul said. He leaned down and kissed her forehead. "Do you want me to shut off the light?"

"No. I think I'd prefer to keep it on." The fear the images might return in the dark, scared her.

Paul stepped into the hall. He looked in once more. "I'll check on you in a little while," he promised, then closed the door.

Haylee huddled under the covers, shivering, waiting for morning and the safety of the day.

**Church of God with Signs**

Haylee woke with a sense of dislocation, unsure of where she was. Sunlight beamed though the window, lighting the far wall. She saw her camera bag resting on the dresser, bathed in a pool of sunlight. She was in her mother's room, of course. Everything had been a dream. A knock on the door caught her attention.

"You awake?" a voice asked. Paul opened the door and peeped in.

She managed a smile. "Hey."

"How are you feeling?" Paul asked.

"Better," she said.

"Do you feel up to eating? Mildred has breakfast ready."

The smell of fried sasuage and freshly baked biscuits drifted through the open door. She felt ravenous.

"Let me put on fresh clothes," she laughed. "I seemed to have slept in mine last night."

"Meet you downstairs," said Paul.

Haylee swung her legs off the bed, ambling to the dresser. She selected a fresh pair of jeans and a knit shirt. Slipping into the fresh clothes buoyed her spirits as if she'd cast off yesterday's worries and fears with the old duds.

Paul waited for her at the bottom of the stairs and they walked into the dining room together. Woodard, at the head of the table, smiled as they pulled up chairs.

"Mildred's made her sausage and gravy today. It's customary for Sundays. Make's the day special."

"Sounds delicious," said Paul, holding his knife and fork at the ready.

"So, how'd you sleep?" Woodard asked Haylee.

"Good, Grandfather," she said.

"You kind of scared me last night," he said, "You look better today."

Haylee couldn't say the same for Woodard. He looked as if he'd lost weight overnight. His face was skeletal, like death might be only a few hours away.

Mildred came into the room carrying a large platter of sausages and placed it in the center of the table. Woodard wasted no time stabbing several with his fork, levering them over to his plate. Whatever was wasting him away did not affect his appetite.

The black woman went back into the kitchen and returned with an equally large platter of biscuits. She placed them beside the sausages, along with a large bowl of white gravy dotted with pepper.

Woodard collected several biscuits and spooned a liberal helping of gravy over them.

"Dig in," he told the other two, waving at the waiting food.

Haylee picked a couple of the sausages and a biscuit. Following her grandfather's example, she spooned a small amount of gravy over them. The gravy and biscuits complemented each other. The sausage was good, though spicy. Paul, who'd piled his plate nearly as high as Woodard, tore into his food, chewing vigorously. He wore a look of pure bliss on his face.

"I'm going to miss this home cooking," he said to Woodard as he reached for another biscuit and spooned gravy over it.

"Mildred's the best," Woodard said, "It's a wonder I don't weigh a thousand pounds the way she feeds me."

Haylee said nothing, content to let the men converse.

"I was wondering," said Woodard, "If you two would accompany me to church? I could introduce you to some folks, for your book and all."

Haylee remembered the signs in the diner, full of admonitions and warnings. The thought of sitting in a pew, surrounded by fanatics, disturbed her. Besides, she planned to visit Mantel Creek today.

"I don't know, Grandfather," she said, "All I brought to visit were jeans. That's not really appropriate for church, is it?"

The old man shook his head. "No, it ain't. You can't go in jeans. But I imagine Mildred can scare you something up. I think we still have some of your momma's dresses stored away. She was about your size." He paused. "That's okay, ain't it? You went quiet on me."

Haylee realized she was holding her breath.

"Yes, that would be fine, Grandfather."

Woodard looked over at Paul. "How 'bout you, Son? You up for a Sunday service?"

Paul laughed. "Bring it on."

"Good," Woodard said, "I'll get Mildred to search for that dress."

*** 

Woodard said the service began at 10:00 and usually ran one to two hours depending on "how the spirit moved."

"Don't be surprised if they bring out snakes," he warned. "It's a demonstration of faith. The Bible says you'll take up serpents and not be harmed."

As Haylee slipped on the dark blue dress Mildred laid out on the bed while she'd taken a morning bath, she thought about the snakes. She'd seen a National Geographic documentary last year about snake handlers. The practitioners seemed to her to be just a mob of eccentrics. The handlers took up snakes and whirling and dipping they and did a sort of stomp dance known as clogging, amidst a circle of onlookers, while the congregation cheered them on with "Amens" and "hallelujahs", then the snake would be passed to another and the routine would begin again.

At the time, she hadn't thought much about it, just a novelty show for television. If her grandfather was correct, then today, she might be witness to something that wasn't electrons in a vacuum tube, but actual men and women taking up dangerous reptiles in a demonstration of faith in imitation of the Acts of the Apostles.

Haylee mentioned her unease to Paul.

"There's nothing to worry about," he said, " Though I admit most people, even southerners would file this kind of stuff on the lunatic fringe of religious behavior it's standard fare around here. These people do it all the time. Besides, even if someone gets bitten, it's usually not fatal. Many of these people have built up immunity to the poison."

Paul's confidence did little to alleviate her trepidation. Seeing that voicing her fears would do little good, she surrendered to what would be. When everyone was dressed, they met downstairs. Woodard surprised them by suggesting they take separate cars.

"I've got a couple of stops I want to make after church, some business to finish up that would only bore you two. You can meet me at the church and when service is over, you can come back here, or take a drive."

Though separate cars meant she and Paul would be free to leave as soon as the service ended, she worried about her grandfather.

"Are you sure you're up to driving?" she asked Woodard.

"I'm fine, Darlin'," Woodard said. "The day I can't do for myself is the day I'll just crawl in my grave and pull the dirt over myself."

In the car, as Haylee strapped on her seat belt, she asked Paul a question she'd tossed around since yesterday.

"Paul, have you noticed Grandfather seems to control where we go?"

"What are you talking about?" he asked, switching on the ignition.

"Take today," she said "He suddenly decided we should go to church."

"So?" He shifted into reverse, jerking the car so Haylee had to brace herself with a hand on the dashboard to keep from being thrown forward. "I thought it was a nice gesture, inviting us to church. Besides, he's giving me an excuse to talk to people." Paul shoved the lever into drive and the car gave another lurch. "You're just grabbing for straws again, Haylee, to feed this fantasy of yours."

"Am I, Paul? Answer this: How much have you gotten done on your book?"

"Well, not anything. I've been busy."

"That's my point. We've been here almost a week, we only have a few days left and you've got nothing done. Worse, I don't think you noticed."

"I plan on starting tonight. I'll interview some of the congregation after the service. I should have plenty of material then."

They reached the end of the drive. Paul swung the car onto the asphalt road.

"Since you're so concerned about my deadline, do you mind telling me what you've been doing? I've been busy helping Claude, but you've been free to do whatever."

"Well, since you asked, I visited the cemetery. It dates back to William Slaughter."

"Let me guess, you found scalp hunters hiding among the tombstones?"

Haylee opened her mouth to fire something back, then saw Paul smiling, his eyes twinkling.

"You can be a real asshole sometimes," she said, finding herself smiling as well.

"I try."

As they drove along, Haylee turned things over in her mind. Paul was changing; his book was on the back burner. He seemed unconcerned about finishing it at all. Always a doer, always focused on a goal, he'd now become an idyllic dreamer, content to spend afternoons drinking with Woodard.

The road curved ahead. This was where she'd encountered the workers with the blatant stares, eyes that seemed to penetrate her flesh; questioning eyes that followed her as she sped away. She stiffened, expecting to be confronted by them again, but the yards were empty, the doors and windows closed. No one looked out today. Even so, she felt an unholy creepiness filling the air like the radiation left from a bomb blast.

She wondered if the gawkers would be at church. She imagined they would. Acedia made plain their zeal for religion.

*What else do these people have to cling to?* she reasoned, reflecting on the tumbled shacks. Religion gave them hope of a better place someday.

They reached the bottom of the ridge and the woods thinned. High grass replaced trees. As they crested the second ridge, Haylee saw the town ahead. The stores lay dark behind wooden doors. Like the houses, the shades were pulled tight. She saw the church, its steeple pointing at a sky of pale gray. Claude's massive black Packard was parked to the side with a few other vehicles, scattered around it. Nothing moved. Haylee hugged herself tight. Paul seemed not to notice.

There was enough space for Paul to fit the Volvo next to Woodard's sedan. Paul got out and hurried around to open Haylee's door, extending a hand to help her out. Woodard, dressed in a black suit that might have been fashionable in the thirties, tottered over to the pair.

"I swear if you ain't the spittin' image of your momma," he said, his eyes moist, "She was beautiful, just like you." Woodard wiped his eyes with a handkerchief. "I'm sorry, but seeing you in that dress was like seeing Claudette."

"You must have loved your daughter very much," Paul said.

"Love, not loved," Woodard corrected, "I ain't never stopped loving her. I don't see where I ever will."

Haylee stood there, feeling awkward and confused. Woodard's comment about her mother

193

made her uncomfortable. Suddenly, the dress felt very foreign and she wanted it off.

The three stood in silence.

"I reckon we need to get inside." Woodard suggested, "Church'll be startin' in a moment."

They followed Woodard's stooped form to the front of the church where a series of wooden steps led to a covered porch with a peaked roof. Two tall, wooden doors, inlayed with colored glass, were propped open with door stops. Haylee peered inside. A foyer ended with a second set of closed doors.

Woodard led them up the steps. Each step the old man took was slow and unsure. When they passed from the porch into the foyer, Paul rushed ahead so he could hold the door open for the old man. Woodard shuffled inside and Haylee and Paul followed.

The interior of the church consisted of three rows of pews divided by aisles. The pews were crowded with middle-aged or older people, making her and Paul the youngest present.

They followed Woodard past the congregation to the front. The people, who earlier met her with sharp looks and suspicion, greeted her civilly. A few even smiled and she smiled back. Though she would have preferred to sit in the back of the church, she dutifully took her place beside the old man, and Paul took up the end of the first pew.

While they waited for the service to start, Haylee studied her surroundings. The walls of the church, even the windows were draped with black cloth. A simple pulpit, flanked by five straight-backed chairs, sat on a low platform ten feet from the front pews. A crudely-painted sign on the wall behind the pulpit said "Faith without Works is dead".

A door next to the sign opened and three men, dressed in white shirts and black trousers, crossed to the side of the platform. One man, with a particularly sour face, carried a violin. The two others carried a guitar and mandolin. They huddled together, pinging strings, tuning their instruments.

After several minutes, the sour-faced man played a slow, haunting melody that reminded Haylee of a lonesome mountaintop or windblown prairie. The two other musicians joined in, and she heard the rustle of starched shirts and dresses as the congregation shifted erect. Woodard also straightened in his pew. While the music played, the door on the platform opened and Luther Boone stepped out, followed by four men she didn't recognize. Each man carried a long, rectangular box, fitted with handles. The boxes were screened on the ends. The men took their seats in the circle of chairs, placing the boxes at their feet. Haylee guessed the unoccupied chair in the center was reserved for Boone.

As Boone approached the pulpit, the tempo of the music changed. Now, the melody became a rapid staccato that climbed, paused, then climbed higher. Boone swayed with the tune, rocking his body back and forth, his arms raised above his head like a groupie at a rock concert. This continued for a few minutes, then he brought his hand down in a slashing motion and the music slammed to a halt.

"Hallelujah," he said.

"Hallelujah," answered scattered voices in the congregation.

"Welcome, good and faithful of Acedia," he said, "Today is the Sunday before the Fullness of the Bride, a time of promise, when we demonstrate the power of the Almighty to all who have eyes to see and ears to hear. Today, we have guests to witness the power of the Spirit, for it will surely manifest as a witness to them."

Someone shouted "Amen!" and was echoed by several others.

"Though we may be a twig, we shall grow into a branch," Boone's voice boomed. "Though we may be a trickle, we will be a river."

"Yes, Lord," shouted one woman.

"Though now we are few, we shall soon be many. We shall prevail!"

The congregation jumped from their seats and burst into an incoherent babble that sounded like a flock of excited turkeys.

The musicians played a series of plaintive measures mixed with banshee-like shrieks from the fiddle and scathing runs from the mandolin. The result was like a mix of Hank Williams and Metallica.

The men and women worked their way to the space between the pews and to the low stage in a curious line dance, moving their feet with quick steps to the beat of the music. Not to be outdone, Luther Boone was also in motion, doing a complicated shuffle across the stage with moves equal to Michael Jackson's. It seemed like everyone but Haylee and Paul were in motion. Even Woodard slapped his knee with the palm of his hand in time to the music.

The dancers reached a place near the pulpit and formed a semicircle. Haylee watched as one at a time, they stepped into the center where they did a sort of clog step, performing for the others. Their fellows urged them on, clapping their hands and shouting encouragement.

After letting the congregation move and bob for a few minutes, Boone nodded to the sour-faced man with the violin. The music slowed and the people returned to their seats.

Boone, his back to the congregation, conversed with the men seated in the straight-back chairs. One by one, they reached down and lifted the boxes at their feet, then carried them and placed them at the pulpit.

"As we always do," Boone said, who now returned to the pulpit, "We'll take a minute to get ourselves right and wait for the Spirit. Let's all pray."

Haylee bowed her head and waited for Boone to lead them in the prayer. Instead, everyone in the church prayed aloud, each praying for something different. The result was an incoherent babble.

Fearing a migraine, she glanced around, seeking the best way to exit, when Virginia walked through the doorway and took a seat in the last pew in the back. The girl wore a long, white shift and a matching ribbon in her hair. Haylee tapped Paul's arm, motioning toward the back. He nodded absently, his attention locked on the scattered boxes on the platform. Haylee shifted, rising partially out of the pew, then Woodard placed a hand on her wrist. The old man frowned, shaking his head. She eased back down, but twisted around so she could keep an eye on Virginia. The girl had drawn her knees up and wrapped her arms around them in a fetal position. The congregation ended their prayers. Haylee fixed her eyes on Boone wondering what would come next.

"The Bible says 'They shall pick up serpents and not be harmed'." Boone shouted.

"That's what it says, for sure," cried a man.

"That poison will have no power, nor fire. Am I lying?"

"It's the truth," shouted a woman.

"Once the Spirit comes," said Boone.

"He's come," cried the man.

"What?" asked Boone. The sour-faced man drew his bow across the violin strings, up then down, mimicking Boone's question.

"The Spirit's already come," several people cried together.

"When?" Boone cupped a hand to his ear.

"At Jerusalem." answered the crowd. "On Pentecost."

"He's come?" Boone mimicked surprise.

"Yes, Lord," screamed the crowd.

"Then signs should follow," yelled Boone.

Stepping back, Boone spun around. That same moment, the sour-faced man played a flurry of notes on the fiddle, the mandolin and guitar players joined in a rock-bluegrass melody. Boone danced as if his feet were independent of his body. Haylee watched beside Woodard, who continued to grip her wrist as if he expected her to bolt.

Boone danced over to the rectangular boxes. Haylee realized what she thought was a random placement of the things, was not random at all. Scattering the boxes allowed Boone to move between them. The man searched for something as he danced, narrowing the area to between two of the four boxes, and then, just one.

Boone circled the box several times, then lifted the lid and reached in to pick up the largest copperhead Haylee had ever seen. He raised it high above his head, allowing it to move and twist, its scales sparkling. The snake looked around leisurely through lazy eyes as if puzzled by the hubbub.

"Behold the servant of the, Lord." Boone cried holding the snake like a trophy.

Boone lowered his arms, draping the copperhead around his neck so it drooped on either side, its long body almost brushing the ground. He strutted around the stage with the snake dangling around him like a golden mantle.

"Faith can move mountains." Boone said. The snake swayed with each step the preacher took. "Faith is visible. It don't hide under a bushel basket. The godly man and woman fears nothing. Neither poison, or fire, or serpents put them off. They can walk through a carpet of venom and not be harmed. That's where God'll get his 144,000, those set aside without sin who never bowed to the world. He'll get it right here in Acedia, in this church."

"You can see my faith." Boone began to pace. "Is it hidden?"

"No!" someone shouted.

"That's right, it's hanging around my neck like I might wear scarf or where a rope might hang." He paused, his eyes searching the faces of the congregation, "But it ain't me that needs to demonstrate faith today. There's another here who needs to step out just as I have stepped out."

The musicians fell silent. Now, the sour-faced man played a haunting sound, as if he channeled every lonely emotion from the surrounding hills into it.

One of the men behind Boone left his seat to retrieve a tray that was resting on the floor against the far wall.

He carried the tray, holding a cloth and a small vial, to Boone. Boone lifted the snake over his head and lowered it back into the snake box, then shut the lid.

"You can carry these other boxes back, boys," Boone said, reaching for the cloth and bottle of oil. "We only need the one."

The men collected the snake boxes and returned to their seats, setting the boxes at their feet. Only the box holding the giant copperhead remained.

"The word says 'anoint the sick with oil' and they will recover," Boone said. "We have one here tonight that is not sick in the physical, but is in need of having their spiritual eyes opened. I'm going to ask that person to come to the altar now."

The man standing at Boone's side stepped down from the platform. Walking over to where Haylee sat, he took her by the hand and led her to in front of the platform. Before she could draw back in protest, others rose from their pews, crowding around her. Together, they pressed her forward toward the preacher. Haylee twisted, looking to Paul for help, but the multitude blocked her view. Two older ladies with their hair twisted into tight gray buns, flanked Haylee on either side, smartly marching her to Boone.

Boone tipped the bottle of oil, wetting his fingertips. While the women gripped Haylee's arms, he pressed his fingers to her forehead. The oil burned where his fingers touched her skin. Her

201

eyelids felt too heavy to keep open. She closed them, listening to the cluster of people around her burst into another fit of individual prayer. Boone's voice rode above the others, a mixture of unintelligible sounds sprinkled with "Amens" and "hallelujahs. Then the preacher relaxed his fingers and Haylee opened her eyes. Boone's face filled her vision

"Sister, are you ready to demonstrate your faith in the Lord?" he asked.

She shook her head. "I…I don't know," She felt disembodied, as if she floated just above the floor.

"There is nothing to fear if you believe," Boone whispered. The his voice breathy reminding her of the hiss of a snake.

Boone held the copperhead again. Somehow, he'd gotten the snake out of the box without her noticing. He offered it to her, holding it in outstretched arms.

A beam of light broke through the black curtains like a thin, gold ribbon. It fell across the moccasin's scales, creating a spectrum of color and transforming the snake into a living rainbow.

The sour-faced man played softly. She recognized the tune as one her mother hummed to her when she was little.

She tried to focus on Boone, but his eyes burned so fiercely, she was forced to look away.

"You must do this," a voice whispered.

She wasn't sure if the voice was Boone's or someone else's.

The old women who flanked her each took one of her wrists, positioned her, arms out with her palms turned up, to match Boone's.

"Have faith, Sister," he said, placing the snake across her open palms. "God will watch over you. There's nothing to fear."

She braced herself for the weight of the thing, her heart pounding. She smelled fear oozing from her pores and wondered if the snake smelled it too. Around her, the sound of a million angry wasps buzzed. She floated higher. She thought if she could float high enough, she might be safe from Boone and the snake, that neither would be able to reach her.

Somewhere below, she felt something heavy placed in her arms. She looked down to see a girl bearing a great serpent in her arms. People in deep prayer surrounded the girl. Some had their hands on the girl's shoulder, or were touching her back with the tips of their fingers. Boone stood in front of the girl, watching.

Haylee floated higher until she was only inches from the ceiling. The girl below stood immobile while the snake twisted in her arms.

The buzz grew into a roar that muddled her mind. The sound made it hard to concentrate on the girl with the snake.

She pressed her palms hard against her ears to block out the roar. Something inside her shifted and she found herself tumbling toward the floor.

She braced herself for the impact, but there was none. Everything blinked out: *She was in the room with the flickering fire. Acrid smells of smoke and sizzling fat stung her nose. The weight on her arms (they were her arms again, not the girl she watched from the ceiling) increased. She held a monstrous serpent. Though she couldn't say exactly why, this was a serpent and not a snake, a fact that seemed important. It snapped its massive head back and forth, flicking its tongue, testing the temperature of the room, while its unblinking reptilian eyes sized up the occupants. Unlike before, she was able to see the others. Faces of both men and women watched with anticipation. Their eyes, catching the fire's light, sparkled like dozens of jewels. All of them waited for her to give them a sign.*

*She turned her attention back to the snake. The creature also seemed to be waiting for her signal. She felt confident; she had performed this ritual many times. Both she and the serpent knew what was expected.*

*Her eyes traveled the length of the fire pit, spanning its long, rectangular shape. An empty, ornate chair sat at the far end. Like the others, she waited for the chair's occupant to appear. Only then could she begin the rite. She shifted, uneasy, anxious to get about with the business at hand.*

204

*There was a movement in the back of the room. A figure crept in the shadows just outside of the fire's glow so it appeared only as a dark shape. Here was the trigger that would make everything plain. She knew just as sunlight melts away shadow to reveals thee things formally hidden by the darkness, the identity of the figure would sweep away the mystery of why she was here.*

*The figure moved closer to the ornate chair. The fire flickered, highlighting one hand bearing a great book. The figure moved to the edge of the shadows. She held her breath. A few more steps and she would see the face...*

The heaviness was snatched away and the vision vanished with it. For a moment, she felt a wave of dizziness and stumbled. Someone caught her, helping her stand. She realized her eyes were closed. When she opened them, Boone was lifting the snake from her.

Boone lowered the snake into the its box, then turned back to Haylee.

"You had a vision, Sister," he said. "What was it?"

*He knows.* The realization made her both cautious and afraid.

"You can tell me," Boone said. He spoke the words softly, his lips inches from her ear.

Suddenly, nausea rose in Haylee's throat. She gagged, barely able to suppress the urge to empty her stomach on Boone's highly-polished, white shoes. Sensing what was about to happen, the preacher took a step back. Haylee turned toward the door, the press of people opening for her to stumble to the exit.

She lurched past the congregation, through the foyer and managed to stumble down the church steps before she spewed her partially-digested breakfast across the sidewalk. When she was done, Haylee sat on the steps gasping for breath. The fresh air cleared her head a little.

"Are you okay?" asked a small voice.

Haylee, still hunched, turned to the sound. Virginia stood on the step above her; the girl's face was creased with worry.

"I'm better," Haylee croaked, her throat raw from vomiting. "I just needed some air."

Virginia tucked her dress beneath her and sat down on the step next to Haylee.

"It's gonna storm tonight," she said.

"Why do you say that?" Haylee asked. The faded sky, now a rich blue, was devoid of clouds.

"My momma told me," said the girl, matter-of-factly.

"Sheriff Riddle told me your parents were dead."

"They are, but they still talk to me. They tell me things."

"How did it happen? Were they in a car wreck?"

"Them in the church. They did it."

"How did the people kill them?" Haylee asked. She hadn't decided if the girl was simply imaginative or a pathological liar. Still, something about Virginia seemed genuine.

"They drowned them in the creek," said the girl. "I hid in the woods, but they had dogs. The dogs found me. Then the people took me to Brother Boone."

For a brief moment, Haylee felt a chill run up her spine. But this was too fantastic an explanation for even Reverend Boone to be a part of. Besides, questions would have been asked and someone would have come and found the girl and taken her away.

"Honey, if someone killed your parents, there would have been an investigation. Police would have come and asked questions. I'm sure whatever happened was an accident. Brother Boone was kind enough to take you in because there was no one to take care of you."

"There's people that would take care of me." Virginia protested, "But they don't know I'm here, and if they came, they'd get drowned too, so I don't tell no one about them."

The girl paused for a minute, then continued.

"My momma told me something else when she told me about the storm," said the girl. "Momma said to go with you when you leave here. She said you would keep me safe."

Haylee stared at Virginia.

The declaration certainly explained why Virginia had taken to a stranger so quickly. Of course, the request was impossible. She couldn't take the girl with her even if she wanted to without risking a kidnapping charge. Even if she could, Haylee wasn't up to the responsibility of raising a girl she only just met.

Why would Virginia even make such a request? Obviously, the girl was confused. Losing both parents could certainly do it. Haylee remembered a classmate named Marilyn Hollingsworth in the sixth grade. Marilyn's parents died in a house fire while Marilyn was spending the summer with her grandparents. What she remembered most about Marilyn was what a liar she'd been. The girl was famous for the whoppers she told. Haylee thought she made up the fantastic tales for lack of family. It was sad, really. Virginia was doing the same thing.

Before Haylee could decide the best way to explain to Virginia what she wanted was impossible, a voice spoke from behind.

"So, there you are."

Haylee turned to see Paul standing on the step above her.

"You rushed out of the church so fast I was afraid of what might have happened."

"I wasn't feeling well." Haylee said, struggling to her feet. "By the way, thanks for the rescue."

"She's sick," Virginia said, her voice sarcastic, as she worked her way between Haylee and Paul.

Paul ignored the girl, aiming his question at Haylee.

"Rescue?" He looked down at his feet, then his eyes lit with comprehension. "Oh, you mean the snake thing. It looked to me like you handled that fine."

"Thanks." Haylee said. "It's nice to know you were sitting back cheering for me."

Virginia watched the two adults, her mouth pulled down at the corners.

The service ended and people trickled out of the church. Woodard, bent slightly at the waist, hobbled down the steps, gripping the metal handrail for support. Virginia slipped behind Haylee as the old man neared.

"Looks like you lost your breakfast," Woodard said nodding his head at the lumpy puddle of vomit on the sidewalk. "I wondered why you ran out. I guess the service was a little too much excitement for you. How're you feeling?"

"Better, Grandfather," Haylee said. Several people glanced at the mess as they passed. One man looked back at Haylee and shook his head.

Boone exited with the last of the congregation and produced a ring of keys. Selecting one, he locked the church doors.

"I don't usually lock the doors to God's House," he said, "But we're doing some things for Homecoming I want to be a surprise." He pocketed the keys before descending the steps to join the others. "Girl, I wondered where you were," he said sharply to Virginia. "Didn't I tell you to stay put in that back pew?"

"Yes, Sir," Virginia replied in a timid voice.

"I'll deal with that later."

"Don't blame her," Haylee said, noticing the girl visibly tremble, "She was worried about me. She was trying to help."

"That might be," said Boone, "But it don't excuse what she done. I thought she was off on that bike again. I ought to get rid of the thing. That would put a stop to her wandering off."

He paused to adjust his collar and smooth his shirtfront. When he finished, the tension was gone from his face.

"I'm sorry," he said, "I worry about the girl. She's wild. I don't blame her. The sins of the fathers are passed on to the children."

He looked at Haylee, his eyes penetrating as they'd done during the service. "I was hoping you'd do me the honor of visiting a bit. You made an impression at the church. The Widow's League made up a lunch of fried chicken and 'tater salad for us, along with sweet tea and dewberry cobbler."

"I think we got time," Woodard volunteered before Haylee could decline.

"Good. I'll see all of you there, in say, half an hour?"

Boone grabbed Virginia's hand. "Come on, Girl," he growled. Half leading, half dragging, he pulled the girl toward the battered pickup.

"Grandfather, I'm not sure I'm up to lunch. I still don't feel well."

"Then just have a glass of tea." Woodard said, brushing off Haylee's excuse. "Boone don't live far," Woodard told Paul. "You can follow. I'll see you there."

The old man hobbled to the Packard. Haylee and Paul followed. On the way Haylee, had the unshakable feeling Virginia was right. A storm was coming, a very bad storm.

**-10-**
**Fried Chicken**

Brother Boone must have watched as they walked up the flagstone path, because he swung the door open before Paul could knock. The preacher ushered them in, and Haylee found herself in a comfortable room, with several large over-stuffed chairs. Woodard occupied one facing a small stone fireplace, swept free of ashes. A china cabinet, displaying hand-painted plates, stood near a door leading to the back of the house. Primitive paintings, all depicting religious themes, hung side-by-side, circling the room like a parade.

Haylee heard the tinkling of plates and the murmur of voices from behind another door.

"Have a seat, folks," said Boone, extending a hand, toward the chairs. Haylee chose the chair at the far end so Paul was between her and the two older men.

"The Widow's League is working on our lunch. How 'bout a nice, cold glass of sweet tea while we wait?" Not waiting for an answer, the preacher disappeared through the door where the activity was.

The busy sounds stopped and Boone returned, followed by a woman Haylee recognized as one of the two that stood beside her at the church service. She offered a glass to each person, serving Boone last.

"Thank you, Ida." The reverend said, taking his glass.

Without replying, the woman turned, and went back the way she came.

"Is Virginia around?" Haylee asked. "She was worried about me earlier. I thought I'd tell her I'm feeling better." Haylee thought seeing Virginia might take the edge off the unease she felt.

"I doubt she's up to talking." said Boone. "I gave her a good switching a while ago."

Haylee felt herself tense. Her fists clenched. "You whipped her?"

"Darn straight I did," Boone said. "And I gave her a whoppin' she'll remember, too. When I tell her to do something, I expect to be obeyed. Damned headstrong girl, always running off on that bike so I have to hunt for her half the afternoon," he shook his head. "Well, after today, she won't be my problem anymore. The Widow's League will see after her from now on. They're taking her to the Cloister." he laughed, "I'd like to see her slip off from there."

"The Cloister? Is that like an orphanage?"

"I expect you'll find out soon enough," Boone said.

Was the preacher expecting her to visit Virginia there?

*Fine. Grandfather will tell me.*

It was probably for the best that he pass the girl to someone else. Anyone who would beat a

213

child for having compassion needed to have that child removed.

*How many other times has he beaten her?* She wondered.

No one said anything for a moment, then Woodard spoke.

"So, what are we waiting for?" he asked, shifting in his chair as if he had bugs in his pants. "You invited us for lunch and here we are."

Boone laughed, easing the mood. "Claude sure gets to the heart of things where food is concerned, don't he?" He grinned at the old man. "I declare, I was just trying to be sociable. You don't have folks over and strap a feed bag to 'em first thing. You have conversation, then you bring out the food."

Woodard scoffed. "Damn, if you don't sound like an old woman. We can talk while we eat."

"The widows ain't finished," Boone chided. "They'll call us when they're done."

"Well, they need to hurry," said Woodard, "'Afore I waste away."

"Your granddaddy is something, ain't he?" Boone said to Haylee. "You'd think as much as he puts away, he'd be big as a barrel."

Haylee smiled in way of a reply.

"You impressed me at the church." Boone continued, unfazed by her reticence. "Not many would have been up to the challenge. You're a Woodard, no doubt about it."

214

"Actually, my mother changed my name to Woods," Haylee said, hoping to bring a little humor into the conversation.

"That ain't what I meant," said Boone, missing the joke. "I mean you got the gift."

Woodard, who until now, sipped his tea and listened, slammed his glass on the low table. Paul's head snapped around at the sound. Boone froze in midsentence.

"Sorry about that," Woodard said. "The darn thing slipped out of my hand. You know what though, Luther, Haylee don't want to hear about Woodards and a bunch of superstition. They're here to collect some stories for this feller's book he's writing. So, why don't we talk about something he can use?"

"All right," Boone conceded, "What are you interested in?"

"Actually," Haylee said, "Grandfather was telling me about Mantel Creek. That's it's supposed to be haunted by an Indian spirit."

"Ain't no 'supposed' to it," Boone said, "That's a place you want to avoid."

"Isn't that where Virginia's parents died?" Haylee asked. "That's what she told me this morning."

"You can't believe anything that girl says." Boone warned, "She's a liar and a thief. But to answer your question, they did die in the creek. Nobody knows what they was doing there, or even where they came from. I helped pull their bodies to shore. They was all swollen when we found them, like a dozen snakes had bit them. We found the girl a little ways away in the bushes. To this day, she's never told us what happened. None of 'em had an ID. The sheriff contacted the state police, and even the FBI, but we never found out who they were. The girl was no help. I named her Virginia."

Ida came out of the kitchen wiping her fingers on a dish rag. "We're ready for you, Brother Boone. The table's set."

"Good, Good," Boone said. "Virginia is in her room. She should be packed and ready to go."

Ida tucked the dishrag in her apron pocket, then strode to the back of the house with long, determined steps. *That's a woman not to be taken lightly*, Haylee thought. Virginia might not fare much better with this woman than with Boone.

Ida returned a moment later. "Reverend Boone," she said, her voice anxious and shrill, "She's not in her room."

"What?" Boone rose to his feet, "She's got to be. She must be hiding, damn girl. Just trying to stay here. Check under the bed, that's got to be where she's at."

Boone followed the woman to the back. A moment later, an angry cry shattered the air.

Boone came stomping back. "That little bitch climbed out the window, while we was talking. If she thought I whooped her before, wait till I catch her. I promise she won't be able to stand when I'm finished whoopin' her this time."

"She's probably scared," said Haylee. "You can't punish her for being afraid. She's only a child."

Boone turned to Haylee, his eyes burning like embers. "I think you should stay out of affairs that don't concern you," he said.

"Defenseless children are everyone's affair," she said, her cheeks hot, her own eyes fiery.

Boone took a step back as if he'd been struck. "You got a sharp tongue, girl. Best you get it under control before you lose it."

Haylee turned to Paul. "I've had enough of this nonsense. I'm leaving. Are you coming?"

Paul looked at Boone, then Woodard, as if at a loss of what he should do. The old man gave a slight nod.

Paul got to his feet. "Let's go," he said.

"What an awful man," Haylee said once they were inside the Volvo.

"It really wasn't any of your business," Paul said, backing the car around.

"Paul, I can't believe you're siding with them. We're talking about child abuse."

"We're talking about a hypothetical situation that might or might not have materialized. You should have let it go, Haylee. You've put your grandfather in an embarrassing position with the town's minister."

"I talked to the girl, Paul. She's scared. She needs help. She wanted to go with me when we left for home."

Paul became quiet the way he did when he was considering something.

"I wouldn't say anything to Claude," he warned.

"Don't worry," she said, "I have no intentions of saying anything at all. Actually, I can't wait to say good-bye to Acedia. I'm beginning to see why mother left."

"So you realize now all your theories about fake graves and shrunken heads were imagination."

"I know what I saw, but whatever secrets this town has buried can stay that way."

"So, we're done with snooping." Paul said.

"Almost." Haylee smiled.

"What almost?"

"I have one more thing I want to do and then I'll quit."

Paul groaned. "I'm afraid to ask what it is."

"I still want to visit Mantel Creek," she said.

\*\*\*

Lawrence Riddle pulled into the yard that belonged to one Harvey Cravat, now deceased. He stood beside his car for a moment, studying the silent house, now deep in shadows cast by several tall Magnolias. The trees must be fifty years old, Riddle calculated. Cravat was partial to their large, white flowers. It wasn't quite time for them to bloom, but they would before long. It was a shame Harvey wasn't around anymore to appreciate them.

Hitching up his belt, Riddle straightened and strode toward the house. He had business there and he intended to see it through.

As he approached the door, he wondered if he should have brought the crowbar from the trunk, but when he turned the knob, it swung open easily. Apparently, Harvey had not locked it.

Peering in, Riddle saw the house was filled with gloom. The blinds were shut so only a trickle of light worked its way in. He wondered where he would find Harvey. The man could be anywhere. There was no guarantee he was even in the house, though Riddle was pretty sure he was. He doubted Harvey would have tried to make it out the door. Sunlight only increased the pain of the wasting disease.

Riddle hitched up his gun belt and stepped inside. Harvey's Lazyboy faced the battered television with its back to Riddle. Harvey liked to sit in the worn chair and gawk at the thing, though all he got was mostly a fuzzy picture. Riddle noticed an empty mason jar on the end table next to the recliner. It was no secret Harvey was fond of liquor. The sight of the jar moved something inside of Riddle, bringing bitter memories of his former friend.

"You stupid bastard, why did you have to go and fuck up?" he muttered, shaking his head. "It didn't have to end this way."

Riddle wiped the moisture building in his eyes before pushing deeper into the room. Cravat was slumped in the Lazyboy. The chair's high back hid him from Riddle's initial search. The wasting had taken its toll. Cravat, who, in life was a big man, even by big men's standards, was little more than a shriveled husk, black and twisted. *Sort of like a pea pod left in the sun too long,* Riddle thought.

He opted to leave Cravat in the chair until he finished the other task. Back at the patrol car, he rummaged through the clutter of tools, selecting a medium sized axe, along with a coil of heavy cord. Armed with the two items, Riddle waded into the brush behind the house. It only took a short time for him to locate, and fell, half a dozen young oaks. He trimmed away the branches and dragged them, one by one, into the clearing he'd selected earlier. By mid-afternoon he'd constructed a pyre. The seasoned wood stacked in back of the house that Cravat collected for winter, served as fuel.

Riddle returned to the house to collect the husk of Cravat's body, surprised at the lack of weight. *It's like he's hollow, the wasting stole a part of him.*

He carried the body outside, and hoisted it onto the pyre. *Just in time,* he thought, *those are storm clouds coming from the south.*

He positioned the body as dictated by the old rites and covered it with a blanket of pine needles. Then, as an after-thought, he added some of the needles to the wood fueling the blaze. Satisfied all was correct, he took the acetylene torch, twisted the valve until he heard the hiss of gas, then struck a spark. The flame came to life with a whoosh. Riddle touched the flame to the pyre, watching the dry kindling birth fingers of flame that soon engulfed Cravat's body so it glowed like a single ember. Riddle said the prayers as it burned, watching the dark tentacles of smoke rise into the storm-gray sky.

**-11-**
**Stormy Weather**

"I think we should stay clear of Mantel Creek," said Paul. The first drops of rain splattered on the windshield.

"She said it would rain," Haylee said. "How did she know? The sky was cloudless. The storm came out of nowhere."

"What are you talking about?" Paul asked.

"Virginia said it was going to rain. I didn't believe her because today was too perfect, but it's raining."

"Not another conspiracy," Paul groaned. "She made a lucky guess. Gawd, Haylee, are you going to see a ghost behind every tree?" He took a breath. "This is the reason I don't want to take you to the creek."

"Fine, I'll find my own way."

"Haylee, why are you making such a big deal of this?"

"We've gone over this before, Paul. I really don't want to go over it again. I'll be so glad when we leave. We are leaving tomorrow, right?"

"Uh… I wanted to talk to you about that. I thought we'd stay another week."

"I hope you're not serious." Haylee fought to keep her voice level.

"I need more time for the book."

"Paul, we've spent close to a week here, and have nothing to show for it. What makes you think

222

another week will be different? Grandfather will find something to interfere with whatever we plan. I've had enough."

"Next Sunday is Homecoming," Paul said, "Claude wants us to stay until then."

"I hope you didn't tell him we would."

Paul's face reddened. "Actually, I did."

Too enraged to speak, Haylee turned away from Paul. Hot tears threatened to spill down her cheeks. *I am not going to let him see me cry.*

"He's an old man, Haylee, and he's dying. He was so happy that we were going to attend Homecoming Sunday with him."

Haylee felt some of the anger subside. Maybe Paul was right, maybe she should stay one more week. She did want to visit Mantel Creek. This would also give her a chance to talk to Virginia. Virginia was right about the rain. The storm was becoming more vicious by the minute. A true tempest was brewing.

"I'll stay for Homecoming on two conditions," she said facing Paul again. "One, you keep your promise to take me to Mantel Creek."

"And two?" Paul glanced from the road to Haylee. Their eyes met for an instant, and Haylee caught something furtive in the deep brown pools of Paul's eyes.

"I want use of the Volvo for at least one day. I have some things I want to do."

"And if I do this, you'll stay for Homecoming."

"Yes, I'll stay through next Sunday," Haylee said.

Paul thought for a moment.

"Deal."

They drove on. The rain began to fall in such heavy sheets, the windshield wipers were unable to keep up with the volume.

"Maybe you should pull over until the rain slacks off." Haylee said.

The road fell away along this stretch of road and the shoulder sloped rapidly to the valley below. She didn't want Paul driving over the edge.

"I'm fine," he said, but decreased his speed.

After a minute, Paul stifled a laugh.

"What's so funny?" Haylee asked.

"I never thought I'd watch you play with snakes," he said. "And a good sized one at that."

"I was a tomboy," Haylee said. "Playing with snakes is a prerequisite." This was partially true; she caught green snakes as a girl.

"So, what went through your mind? I mean, that snake was a monster. You looked like you were in another world, kind of in a zone. You looked…well…hypnotized."

"It was strange," Haylee confessed. "I guess I was in some kind of trance. It was like I was floating up around the ceiling. I could see the church below, and a girl who looked like me; she was the one with the snake. Then, I was falling toward the floor. I waited for the impact, but instead, I fell through the floor and into another world."

Haylee expected Paul to scoff, but he only said. "Wow."

"I'm pretty sure Reverend Boone suspected something happened to me, too. I think he expected it to happen. He made it happen somehow. I think something was in whatever he rubbed on my forehead, some kind of drug."

"Flying ointment." Paul said.

"Flying ointment?" Haylee looked at Paul with renewed interest. "What's that?"

"In the middle ages, witches were said to rub their bodies with a salve that enabled them to fly. The stuff was loaded with Henbane, Belladonna and other things that acted as hallucinogens. They didn't actually fly, but experienced a sort of hallucination that gave them the illusion they were flying. What you experienced sounded similar."

"*That's* why I was sick afterward."

"Probably."

"I'm sure of it. That son of a bitch."

"Look, Haylee, I wouldn't say anything."

"Why not?"

"I just think it would be best. You and Boone are already at odds. Let's make this last week as comfortable as possible for everyone."

"You mean for Grandfather?"

"Not just for Claude. We'll be at Homecoming too, along with Boone. It will be awkward enough after today."

225

Haylee took a breath. "I'll try," she said.

"That's my girl." Paul said, "I'll make it up to you, I promise."

"You better."

They reached the dirt track that served as the long driveway to the Woodard estate. The rain slackened into little more than sprinkle, though the sky remained angry and dark. The stands of trees, on either side, were little more than a thick, black curtain stretching into the distance. The dirt track ended, and the old Victorian stood directly ahead all angles and shadow in the overcast.

Overhead, a white scar of sky cut across purple- black clouds, the color of blood-filled blisters. For a fleeting moment, a darker shadow fell across them, then it was gone. Its passing left Haylee with a feeling of foreboding.

"What's the matter?" Paul asked, catching Haylee's expression.

"I got the strangest feeling just then. My mother would have said someone walked across my grave."

"Come on," Paul said, switching off the engine, "Let's get inside before the rain starts again."

Paul hurried around to Haylee's side of the car. Opening the door, he took her arm, and together, they crossed the yard to the house.

Mildred looked up from her dusting when they stepped inside. "Don't track no mud on the carpet," she warned. "Alabama mud is hard to get out once it's in the fibers."

"Yes, Ma'am," Paul said, in his most dutiful voice. He slipped off his shoes and helped Haylee slip out of hers. The two of them skipped across the carpet in bare feet, giggling as Mildred hurried them along.

"Get on up the stairs," she said, straining to keep a straight face. "I can't get work done with you two in the way."

At the top of the stairs, Paul gave Haylee a quick kiss, and left her to change while he went to do the same.

"See you in a few," he called, striding away.

Haylee shut the door, then crossed to the bed for her jeans and shirt. She wasted no time shedding her mother's clothes, though she was careful to replace the dress on the hanger. The dress made her uncomfortable, as if she wore her mother's ghost. Dressed in her own comfortable clothes again, she felt more like herself.

Outside, a heavy mist hovered just above the ground, as if the world had faded to a colorless gray filled with ghost trees and mountains made of gauze. Caught in the surreality of it all, she found herself in a reflective moment, where everything in her life was weighted against today. Even the prospect of marrying Paul, for the moment, filled her with apprehension.

At the university clinic, the doctor diagnosed her with mild depression. He prescribed pills, but they only numbed her feelings of depression. She was still depressed, but she didn't care that she was. After a week, she stopped taking the pills and flushed the remainder down the toilet. *It's just the blues,* she thought. *Like the song says, everybody gets the blues sometimes. It's my time.*

She realized for the week they'd been in Acedia, she and Paul spent very little time together. They slept in separate rooms, her grandfather insisted on that, and Mildred saw to it that they did.

*We need to take a day to ourselves and go somewhere,* she mused. *Perhaps, to a neighboring town where there's a nice restaurant.* She would suggest it to Paul when she saw him.

A knock on the door snapped her out of her musings.

"Miss Haylee, are you busy?" Mildred asked.

Haylee turned away from the window. "No, you can come in."

The door opened, and the woman filled the doorway.

"I was getting ready to do Mister Claude's laundry, and I thought you and Mister Paul might have some clothes that needs cleaning as well. I'd prefer to do all of them at one time."

"Why, thank you, Mildred. As a matter of fact, I do." She had wondered how she would get her clothes cleaned. She'd only brought enough for a few days, and she'd worn her current pair of jeans longer than was comfortable.

"Just bring 'em down to the back porch," Mildred said. "I'll wash 'em tonight, and hang 'em on the line tomorrow."

"Thank you, Mildred," Haylee said, as the woman turned to go.

"You already thanked me once," she called from down the hall, "Just make sure you have that stuff ready 'afore it gets too late."

Haylee was gathering clothes to wash when Paul came into the room. He held a cloth bag in his hand.

"Mildred's doing a wash," he said happily, "So I guess we won't have to go to the creek, and beat our clothes on a rock."

"I was thinking," Haylee said, "about us driving somewhere for the day and maybe having dinner at a nice place, maybe even catch a movie."

"Wouldn't that be rude?" Paul asked.

Haylee's heart sank. She expected Paul to jump at the suggestion, not question it.

"Going somewhere for a meal is rude? We're dating."

"We're Claude's guest. If we up and leave, he's going to think he's a bad host."

"Sorry I suggested anything. It's just we haven't spent time together since we…"

Haylee paused as Mildred stumbled into the room. The woman's eyes were large, her face creased.

"Sorry to bust in folks, but the Sheriff wants to see you, Mister Paul."

Paul followed the woman down the stairs with Haylee behind. Riddle was waiting at the bottom, frowning, his big hands on his hips, thumbs locked in the leather utility belt around his waist.

"The Reeve sent me," he said, "We're assembling a search party to hunt for Virginia. She needs to be found before dark. It gets dangerous then."

"Do I need to bring anything?" Paul asked.

"Yourself," said Riddle. "And you might want to wear something to keep off the rain."

"I'll get Mister Claude's extra rain coat," Mildred said, "I think it'll fit you, slim as you are." She hurried to the back and returned with a yellow rain jacket with a black border.

"I want to go too," said Haylee. "I'm sure the girl is frightened, and the sight of so many men is just going to scare her more. She trusts me."

"She didn't trust you enough not to run away," said Riddle. "The Reeve only sent for him." He pointed to Paul, "I'm afraid you're going to have to wait here." He motioned to Paul. "Let's go. The Reeve is waitin'."

Haylee watched the two men climb into the sheriff's cruiser. They drove away, the mist folding around them, erasing any traces they were even there.

The cell phone in her pocket pinged, signaling a text message. The sound made her jump. She'd stored it in her pocket thinking it useless as both she and Paul's phones had lost their signals when they reached the hills.

She extracted the phone and flipped open the cover. The message glowed brightly:

CALL ME

THERE IS SOMETHING YOU NEED TO KNOW

Haylee punched Jen's cell number and waited, then frowned at the screen. A new message glared at her.

NO SIGNAL DETECTED.

"Damn," she muttered, snapping the cover shut hard enough to make a whip-like crack.

*I had a signal. What happened?*

Holding the phone out in front of her so she could watch the signal bars, she turned to the right, then left. When a signal failed to appear, she stepped into the yard. The screen glowed dumbly back at her, but still failed to register a signal.

*I could take the Volvo, drive to the top of the next ridge and try there, but Paul has the keys.*

She studied the car hard as if simply wishing would start the engine. As she concentrated, the rear door on the right began to open.

Haylee's eyes felt as if they were going to bulge out of her head. She held her breath as the door opened completely. *I couldn't have done that. Could I?*

She saw a tiny foot attached to an equally small leg extend through the open door. The rest of the body followed as Virginia crawled out of the back seat.

"Virginia," Haylee barked, "What are...Do you know they have a search party looking for you? What in the world got into you, running off like that?"

"They were going to lock me up." She said, "I heard them talking. They want to make you one of them."

"Who does? One of what? If this is another..."

"Miss Haylee, are you talking to somebody?" Mildred stepped out the door.

"Vir-" Haylee stopped. The spot where Virginia stood moments before, was empty.

"Eh...no one," Haylee finished, "It's this damn phone," she held up the cell so Mildred could see. "I lost the signal again. I don't know why I try."

"Well, I can't help you with that. We ain't never had no phone here, but you need to come in out of all that dampness 'afore you catch your death of pneumonia. Come on now, and I'll make you a nice cup of tea to warm you."

Though she wanted to search for Virginia, Haylee followed the woman inside.

Haylee sat at the dining room table while she waited for Mildred to heat water and brew the tea. Studying the faded wallpaper covering the room, she debated telling Mildred the girl was here.

*If Virginia sees Mildred searching for her, she'll run again. It's probably best if I keep her whereabouts to myself.*

Haylee was sure Virginia would come out of hiding if she made herself available and alone. *She wanted to talk to me.*

*Later, I'll think of an excuse to go outside when Mildred goes to another part of the house. If she asks, I'll tell her I'm trying to find a place where I can get a signal on my cell.*

Mildred came into the dining room with a steaming cup in her hand. She set it beside Haylee. "Let it cool for a minute. It's hot," she warned. "I'm going after cream and sugar. I'll be back."

Mildred returned with the sugar and cream, along with a second cup in her other hand. She took a seat across from Haylee and slurped loudly from the cup. She finished with a satisfied sigh.

"It's a shame you couldn't get your phone to work. I hope it wasn't important. Who was you trying to call?"

"My roommate," Haylee said, "I wanted to tell her we would be staying another week. I didn't want her to worry."

"Well, I think she'll probably figure it out," Mildred said. "Don't you go worrying about things you have no control over." She took another loud sip of tea before leaning across the table toward Haylee. "I hope that little girl gets found 'afore it storms again. I was looking out the back door and them clouds is building fast. I swear I can feel the lightning in the air right here at the table. It makes my skin tingle, it does. It makes me want to hide under my bed until it's over." She laughed, "Ain't that just, plain silly, a grown woman hiding under a bed cause of a little noise and lightning?"

Haylee thought of Virginia outside in the storm. *I've got to find her and get her to a safe place.*

"Whatcha thinking, Honey?" Mildred asked.

"Thinking?" Haylee repeated the word.

"You was thinking about something. I saw your eyes wander. That's a sure sign." When Haylee didn't reply, Mildred continued. "You was thinking about that little girl, wasn't you? I knew it." A grin spread across the black woman's face; like a cat that cornered a mouse.

*She knows.* Haylee's heart rose, settling in her throat, choking off her ability to breathe.

"I-I need to go outside and see if I can get a signal." Haylee stammered. "My phone worked for a moment a while ago. I need to see if I can get it to work again."

"Suit yourself," Mildred said, watching Haylee stand. "But if you're thinking you're gonna see that girl, you're wasting your time."

Haylee hurried out of the room toward the door. Behind her, Mildred's voice rang out.

"I ain't your enemy, Haylee. It's just there are things you don't understand. Sometimes we have to do things where we don't have a choice."

Haylee threw the front door open only to be confronted by a wind gust so strong it nearly pushed the door closed again. She managed to fight her way outside where the wind whipped her hair and tore at her clothes. She ignored the gusts, more concerned about Virginia's safety.

*She's out here somewhere.*

The rain began again, the drops big and cold. Haylee's first instinct was to recheck the Volvo. Virginia might have sheltered there, though she doubted it. Fighting the wind, she wrenched the door open and scanned the back seat then the front. Virginia wasn't there.

"Virginia," she called, not caring if Mildred heard. It made no difference; the wind whipped her voice away, drowning it in the howl.

Haylee hugged the side of the house, seeking what shelter she could as she worked her way to the back.

When she reached the corner, the first flashes of lightning appeared over the ridges behind the barn. If Virginia wasn't in the car, Haylee thought she must be in the large outbuilding behind the house. The barn stood about fifty yards away. Haylee ducked her head and charged toward the double doors as the rain splattered her face and clothes, soaking her hair.

When she reached the barn, she jerked the doors open and eased into the gloom, glad to be out of the pelting rain and abrasive wind. She was assaulted by the smell of manure and chemicals.

Wooden crates rose above her head alongside bales of hay and stacks of bags with faded labels.

The barn doors blew open, then slammed shut.

Haylee jumped, her heart beating wildly. She stopped and took a breath, watching the door with a cautious eye. Her nerves settled, and she began working her way between the stacks.

"Virginia, where are you?" she called. "I know you're here."

The dimness of the place made it difficult to see more than large forms. The girl could be standing directly in front of Haylee, washed over by shadow, and she wouldn't know. She moved deeper into the gloom. Virginia, more than likely, sought a place in the back of the barn, away from the doors.

Something moved, making a soft scuffle across the floor. Haylee perked up at the sound. "Virginia, it's me, Haylee," she called.

She heard a series of footfalls. They were moving toward her, though she still could not see the girl. Then she saw a form too big to be Virginia. It moved toward her rapidly. She wanted to run, but the thing was on her in seconds.

Just then, a lighting flash lit the barn, illuminating her attacker. It was one of the deformed twins she watched from the woods.

The creature reached out for her and her scream shattered the night.

**-12-**
**Wolves in Sheep's Clothing**

Haylee awoke to Paul standing over her.

"Paul," she said. He helped her to her feet.

"Are you okay?" he asked, his eyes searching her face.

"I was so scared. There was this...this thing. It grabbed me and then you were here," she said, clutching Paul.

"Haylee, it's storming. What the hell are you doing out here in the barn?"

"If I tell you something, do you promise to keep it to yourself?"

Paul sighed. "Not another secret."

"Yes or no?"

"All right, I promise. Tell me."

"Virginia is here."

"What!"

"She's here, hiding somewhere."

"How do you know?"

"Because she hid in the Volvo and we brought her here. I caught her slipping out of the back seat after you left with the sheriff. We talked until Mildred scared her and she ran. I was looking for her when I ran into that creature."

Paul laughed. "Well I'll be damned. We tromped over half the county, knocked on about every door in town and she was here the whole time. So, where is she now?"

"I don't know, but I'm sure as soon as things quiet, she'll show herself to me. She seems to want to tell me something."

"Well, there's no point in worrying about it tonight." Paul said. "Wherever she is, she won't be going anywhere in this weather. I suggest we get into the house where it's dry."

They hurried across the yard, pelted by a rain that showed no sign of slacking anytime soon. Thunder rumbled across the ridges. Paul opened the back door, ushering Haylee inside where Mildred handed each a towel.

"Be quiet going inside," she warned, "Mister Claude's taken a bad turn. I don't want him disturbed."

"When did this happen?" Haylee asked. She looked at Paul. "Why didn't you say something?"

"He didn't know," Mildred said. "It was after Mister Paul went to find you. Master Claude collapsed in his chair. One minute, he was sitting there, asking me about supper and then he just fell over. All that worry about that girl did it to him. I told him he needed his treatments, but he's headstrong, same as Claudette was. Like father, like daughter."

"Is there anything we can do?" Haylee asked.

"No, Miss, there ain't. Best just to let him rest awhile, then I'll make him take his treatment. He'll be all right."

Though the news sobered Haylee, Mildred seemed confident, and she had no reason to doubt the woman's ability. Mildred had certainly cleared up the infection on her hand, though a thick callus-like knot remained. She rubbed it, remembering how frail he was.

The storm continued to pound away through late afternoon and the evening. Gazing through the windows facing the front porch, Haylee watched the trees across the yard sway like belly dancers as the wind ripped across the property. The wind was accompanied by a shrill whine like an eternal scream. Wherever Virginia might be, Haylee hoped she was safe. The idea she was probably alone and afraid tore at Haylee's heart. Still, there was nothing she could do. Virginia would have to do for herself for the moment.

***

Supper was a somber affair. Paul and Haylee sat at the table alone. Woodard remained in his room where Mildred made frequent checks on his condition.

"Master Claude ain't gonna join you tonight," she said, setting a platter of pork chops between the two, followed by a large bowl of mashed potatoes, gravy, collards and cornbread cut into squares.

"It's a shame, too. Pork chops and mashed 'taters is one of his favorites. I reckon I'll have to whip up some more when he's up to eatin' at the table again."

Woodard wasn't the only one not up to eating. Worry over her grandfather and Virginia robbed Haylee of any desire for food. The same couldn't be said of Paul. He shoveled food into his mouth with gusto equal to Woodard.

Dinner passed with little conversation. Haylee missed the constant banter Woodard brought to the table. Tonight, dinner seemed more a necessity than a social affair. The only sounds were the howl of the wind and the splatter of rain on the roof and windows. She rejoiced when Mildred came to gather the leftovers and dinner plates.

Paul leaned back in his chair and loosened his belt, sighing with satisfaction. "I'll bet I've put on ten pounds in the last week," he said. "You didn't eat very much."

"I wasn't hungry," Haylee said, "I guess I'm not over my queasiness from today."

Paul nodded.

"Well, I think I'll work on my book, unless you have something in mind?" He said, rising to his feet.

"No, you probably ought to get some work done. I think I'm going to check on Grandfather and then call it a night." She gave him a quick kiss. "Love you," she called as he disappeared up the stairs.

Mildred was washing dishes when Haylee entered the kitchen. The woman's hands were deep in sudsy water.

"I thought I'd check on Grandfather," Haylee said, "Before I go upstairs."

"Ain't nothin' to check on." Mildred said her back to the girl. "Best if he's not bothered. I told you I'd see him back to health and that's what I intend to do."

She turned to face Haylee, wiping the suds from her arms and hands with a dishtowel. "No disrespect, Miss Haylee, but I know what's best for Master Claude. I'd appreciate it if you didn't disturb him. He needs rest. Tomorrow, if you want to sit with him a while, then you can do so with my blessing. Ifn' I were you, I'd get some rest. If you'll pardon my saying so, you look a little peaked yourself."

Where she might have protested before, tonight, Haylee realized she had little fight left in her. She went without bothering to say good night. She did feel ill, but the illness was more spiritual than physical, a disease of the soul.

In her bedroom, a check of her watch showed it was ten minutes after eight. The rain pounded against the window like a sustained drum roll. She took her bedclothes out of the dresser drawer and laid them out. Before she changed into her nightgown, she dialed Jen once more.

This time, she managed a connection. The phone rang once, twice and then went dead.

"Damnit," she said, barely resisting the urge to sling the cell against the wall. She placed the phone on top of the dresser by her camera bag.

241

Whatever news Jen had would have to wait. The signal was sporadic at best.

She dressed for bed and then pulled back the covers, when she paused. Returning to the dresser, she reached into the top drawer and lifted out a small nylon case with a zippered top. She unzipped it and took out a bottle of Tylenol P.M. and shaking out two capsules, she carried them down the hall to the bathroom where she took them with a glass of water. She often used the Tylenol as a sleeping aid, though the side effects left her confused the next morning. She returned to her room and bed where the pills could do their work.

She awoke with the feeling of someone watching her. The storm now passed, silence filled the night as if time was frozen into a single moment. Haylee peered into surrounding dark. The blackness was absolute. Though she saw nothing, the feeling of another presence rang like a glass bell.

"Who's here?" she whispered. Then louder, with more confidence, "I know you're there."

A shuffle in the darkness answered her. Then the author of the sound revealed itself. The figure wore an ankle length dress. A row of large buttons stretched from the wide lapel collar to the hem in a fashion popular in the late fifties. A gray veil covered its face. Though the face was hidden, Haylee sensed something familiar about it.

"I know you, don't I?" Haylee asked. The figure nodded.

Haylee shifted to a sitting position. She saw more clearly, now that her eyes adjusted to the gloom. The dress was stained with large, dark splotches of dried blood. The figure's arms, extending from the short sleeves, were covered with similar dark blotches. Haylee studied the figure's hands: The ring finger on the left hand ended in exposed bone, the flesh cleaved away. Bone also protruded from the right wrist, and the right hand dangled uselessly.

"You're hurt," Haylee said.

The figure stepped closer and whipped away the veil to reveal a face more ghastly than the hands or arms. A section of scalp, a pink flap of skin, hung just above her left eye, exposing the skull, a portion of which was crushed. Brain dangled from the wound like cottage cheese gone rancid. One eye dropped from its socket partway down her cheek. Her opposite cheek was sliced so badly it resembled the opening to a bloody cave, exposing her upper jaw. Jagged bits of what had once been teeth gleamed in the moonlight that streamed through the window.

Even in her hideous condition, Haylee recognized the woman as Rosalie Rollins: Bloody Rose.

Rosalie smiled, if it could be called a smile.

"Why are you here?" Haylee asked.

"We never finished our business," Rosalie said. "I had one more card to turn over. She produced a deck of cards, plucking them out of the air with her good hand. "Take the top one," she said, holding the deck out to Haylee.

Haylee slid the card off the top of the deck, careful not to make contact with the woman's gruesome hand. She placed it face down on the bed beside her.

"Turn it over," Rosalie commanded.

Haylee flipped the card over. On the other side was a drawing from one of the books she owned as a child. A grinning wolf, dressed in an old woman's nightgown and sleeping cap, lay in a large, four-poster bed. One paw pointed forward as if pointing at Haylee. Beneath the drawing were the words THE BIG BAD WOLF. The card swelled, growing in size, until it filled the bed. Haylee backed away. The wolf moved. She saw its nose twitch as its eyes darted back and forth, sensing prey nearby. The wolf leapt from the card, flinging off its bedclothes as it did. It landed on all fours, pinning Haylee beneath it. A low growl escaped its throat. Hot drops of saliva splattered Haylee's chest. It opened its mouth, stretching its great jaws, then lunged.

Haylee screamed.

She woke trembling. Looking around, she realized she was alone. Soft moonlight poured through the window. Haylee threw off the covers and crawled out of bed. Shaken from the dream, she felt the need to diffuse the scream building inside her. She thought of going to Paul's room and waking him. Partway down the hall, she changed her mind, deciding to go downstairs instead. She needed a place she could sit and sort things out and there was tea in the kitchen. A cup might soothe her nerves enough that she could go back to bed. Rounding the bottom of the stairs, she noticed light spilling from under the partially-closed kitchen door. Voices drifted from behind the door.

She crept forward and identified the voices as Woodard's and Mildred's. They were locked in an animated conversation.

Reaching the door Haylee peered through the thin sliver of space. Mildred was seated in one of the kitchen chairs, cradling Woodard's head and shoulders in her lap. The rest of Woodard's body reclined across a second chair beside the woman.

"Daddy, you let yourself go too long this time," Mildred chided the old man.

"I had lots to do and still do," said the old man.

"If the wasting disease takes hold of you, all the chores in the world ain't gonna matter."

"Don't tell me my business, Girl," said Woodard.

"Ifn' you need straightening out, then I'm gonna do it," Mildred said.

She unbuttoned the top of her dress and opened it to the waist. Slipping a hand beneath the cloth, she lifted out one of her large, dark breasts and guided Woodard's head toward it.

"Come on, Daddy, that's good.," she said as Woodard's mouth closed around the waiting nipple.

Fascinated, Haylee watched Woodard suck on Mildred's breast like an oversized infant. While he fed, Mildred whispered encouragement.

"This will give you your strength back, Daddy. My sweet, sweet daddy, I take good care of you, I do."

Forced to crouch, Haylee's legs were beginning to numb. She shifted positions to relieve the pressure. As she did, a floorboard creaked under her. Mildred's half closed eyes snapped open wide and Woodard stopped suckling.

"Wha-?" the old man muttered.

"I heard something, Daddy." Mildred said.

Haylee backed away from the door. Ducking behind the table, she watched as Mildred's body filled the kitchen doorway. The woman swung her head around, her eyes searching for the intruder. *If she switches on the lights, I'm caught.* An eternity passed before the black woman turned back to the old man, pulling the door closed behind her.

Even after Mildred closed the door, Haylee dared not move for several minutes, her mind reeling from what she witnessed.

She crept up the stairs, feeling like a tornado passed through her mind, cutting a wide swath across what she thought she knew and what she'd seen. Exhausted, she fell into uneasy sleep.

\*\*\*

The next morning, Haylee awoke confused. She told Paul what she'd seen in the kitchen.

"It was all a dream, Haylee," he said. "You had a couple of nightmares from the Tylenol."

"Paul, I was awake when I saw Grandfather and Mildred in the kitchen. The dream with Bloody Rose scared me awake."

"You thought you were awake. Look, yesterday you had a bad scare. The dreams were your mind's way of dealing with it. Let it go. You were dreaming."

Haylee was surprised to see Woodard at breakfast. The old man carried himself with a vitality Haylee had not seen since her arrival.

"Morning all," he said, taking his seat at the head of the table.

"Grandfather, you look like you're feeling better. Mildred said you were sick and we missed you at supper."

"I got me some rest," he said, "Slept like a baby for once. It sure left me with an appetite. I feel like I haven't eat in days."

"Flapjacks and sausage," Woodard said as Mildred carried a platter stacked tall with golden-brown pancakes. She placed it in front of the old man, who stabbed half a dozen with his fork, then speared four links of sausage off a second platter. Mildred brought a tin of cane syrup and Woodard poured a generous amount on his plate and passed it to Haylee.

"Good cane syrup," he said, "Not that weak maple stuff Yankees use. That maple's got no bite."

Haylee spooned a little of the thick syrup on her own plate and passed the can to Paul, who imitated Woodard and soaked his flapjacks.

"So, what are you two up to today?" Woodard asked.

Haylee was taken by surprise by the question. She expected the conversation would center on Virginia, who, as far as Woodard knew, was still missing. Though she didn't know Virginia's exact whereabouts, she was confident the girl would find a way to contact her today. She planned to stay on the property to ensure this would happen. Paul would have to do any errands alone.

"Haylee wanted to see Mantel Creek," Paul said, "I know there's a lot of rumor about it--"

"Ain't rumor. But I guess you two ain't gonna rest till you go there. If you follow the road east, you'll cross it a mile or so from here. You can see it from the bridge. I caution against leaving the road and going down to the banks. The place is infested with snakes. Likely as not, you'll get bit."

"Actually, Grandfather, I thought I might hang around here today," Haylee said, "I still don't feel well."

"I'm sorry to hear that," said Woodard, "Suit yourself."

Woodard slid his chair back from the table and stood. "Well, I got a few things to take care of. Being Reeve is a full time job."

After the old man left, Paul turned to Haylee. "I thought you wanted to visit the creek," he said, "Yesterday, that's all you talked about."

Haylee motioned him to lower his voice. "I want to make sure Virginia is safe first," she said. "That was a vicious storm last night."

"So, you're going to sit around waiting for something that might not even happen. Haylee, she could be miles away by now. We have a chance to do what you wanted to do today and now you want to wait around and see if this kid shows up again?"

"I need to know she's okay."

"I understand that, but you're throwing away the only chance you'll have to visit Mantel Creek. If we don't go today, I don't want to hear any more about it."

Haylee paused. "Paul, why are you so determined to go all of a sudden? Yesterday, I had to twist your arm."

"You've gotten me curious about the place."

"Really…" Haylee smiled. She only half believed it was curiosity that prompted him now. Chances were, he didn't want her getting more involved with Virginia for fear it would jeopardize their relationship with Woodard.

"Once I'm sure Virginia is safe, I'll be ready to go. I'll want to take my camera."

"Want me to help?" Paul asked.

"I think if I'm not alone, she won't show herself. Best if it's just me. I'm pretty sure she's somewhere on the property."

Paul assumed a lopsided grin. "Well, since I'm not needed, I guess I'll just bumble around until M'Lady summons her humble servant."

Haylee laughed. "Don't be such a baby. I won't be long."

"Promise?"

"I promise," Haylee said. Standing on tiptoe, she gave Paul a quick kiss. "Be back in a flash," she called, and went out the door. Outside, the world seemed to shine from its recent bath. Droplets of water clung to the leaves of trees and dotted the tall grass like tiny crystals. There was a freshness in the air, a sense of cleanliness, a renewal that encouraged an optimism she recently lacked. Haylee looked around.

*Where do I begin?* she wondered.

She checked the barn the night before and it almost cost her life. *If Paul hadn't heard my scream,* she shuddered, cutting of the thought. She did not relish the idea of checking the barn again. The problem was, Virginia may have taken up shelter there sometime later. She would have to peep inside.

She approached the building with trepidation but the place seemed safe enough in the morning light. Haylee stepped inside, leaving the large double doors open wide to let the daylight in. Even as she searched through the stacks of crates and bales, she sensed Virginia was not here. After a few minutes, Haylee left.

Behind the barn stood a tool shed next to a hog pen. The hogs charged at Haylee, snarling against the wooden fence like guard dogs. The creatures were huge. How Woodard was able to think of them as pets, she couldn't fathom. There was nothing gentle about them. A heavy padlock held the door to the shed fast, eliminating a second hiding place. Haylee was beginning to think Paul was right, that Virginia was nowhere around.

*Or she's lying somewhere in the woods, injured or dead.*

She still needed to check the odd structure where she'd seen the half-human looking twins. Cutting back behind the barn, she picked up the path that led to the hollow. When she was far enough from the house that her voice would not be detected, she called Virginia's name, pausing to listen for a reply. The only sound she heard was her voice echoing in the trees.

She reached the bend in the trail and left the path, covering the last of the distance by cutting through the brush. She had no intention of being spotted by the half-human twins. She would survey the clearing around the building first, and if it looked like no one was around then she would check for Virginia.

*There's worse things than them*, Mildred said. Haylee did not intend to discover what those *worse* things were.

Haylee pushed her way to the edge of the trees. From her vantage point, she saw the building

251

clearly. The door stood open and she detected movement inside. In a moment, Woodard stepped into the open, followed by Sheriff Riddle. Woodard placed a lock on the door and snapped it shut. The two men stood, talking and waving their hands in wide gestures. Haylee suspected they were discussing Virginia. If Woodard had been alone, she might have stepped out of hiding and offered to help him search, but Riddle was with him. The man had given her a dressing down in his office once and she did not want to encourage a repeat.

She retraced her steps through woods and back to the path, hurrying to reach the house before the two men. She might say something to her grandfather later about Virginia.

At the house, she avoided the back door, entering the front so she would not pass Mildred. Happy to find the living room empty, she scampered up stairs.

Going past her room and on the way to Paul's, she heard a buzz. It took a moment for her to realize she'd left her phone on vibrate. It jiggled on the dresser like something alive.

Snatching it up, she answered.

"Hello?"

"Oh God, Haylee, I finally got through, I've been trying since last night."

"Jen, hey, what's happening?"

"Are you alone?" Jen's breath came in gasps.

"Jen, what's wrong?" Haylee asked concerned about the way her friend sounded.

"Haylee, you need to know something. It's about Paul. He's been lying to you."

"What? How?"

"Please, Haylee, just listen for a minute. Okay?"

"All right, I'm listening."

"You got a letter from admissions. I tried to call you and when I couldn't reach you, I opened it. I know I shouldn't have been going through your mail, but it looked important and…"

"Don't worry about it, Jen." Haylee said wanting to get to the crux of the matter. "Tell me what this has to do with Paul."

"Okay." Jen said taking a breath, then continued "The letter said you'd missed too many days of school and that they revoked your scholarship. I called them and pretended I was you. I said I'd gotten an incomplete, that Dr. Paul Carter arranged it. About an hour later, they called back and said they had no record of a Paul Carter on the faculty. They've never had a Paul Carter in the anthropology department. The only Paul Carter listed was a post graduate student that worked in the Anthropology Department as a student assistant."

"So he built himself up a little, he's an assistant and not a professor. I'm a little pissed he wasn't honest but…"

"Haylee, that's not all. Something still seemed wrong, the way he pressed you to make this

253

trip and all, so I went into your room and searched around until I found the two letters from your relatives."

"You know, you're becoming a pretty big snoop, Jen."

"Haylee, they weren't postmarked. I don't know how you...we missed it."

"Postmarked?"

"You know, when you mail a letter, the post office it's mailed from puts a mark over the stamp to cancel it. The stamps weren't canceled."

Jen was talking so fast Haylee was finding it difficult to follow.

"What are you saying?" she asked.

"Haylee--, I'm going to say this very, very, slowly. The letters didn't come from your relatives. They were never mailed. Someone here wrote them, and put them in our mailbox."

"Are you saying Paul did that?"

Jen took a breath. "He had too."

Haylee held the phone, saying nothing. Her head was spinning.

"Haylee, I'm worried. I know you don't want to believe what I'm saying, but it's true. I checked, Haylee. I checked myself; I know it hurts to hear this but..."

"He lied to me," Haylee said, the truth taking form in her mind. "Why did he fake those letters? Why couldn't he have just told me the truth?"

"Because he wanted you to take that trip, Haylee. For some reason he wants you there. Look, I'm coming to get you as soon as Michael gets here. I need to get you away from there, I think you're in danger. Look, Michael is pulling up now. Have your stuff packed. We should be there in a few hours."

Haylee hung up the phone, her vision blurred by tears. Paul lied since the beginning. Their entire relationship was built on lies.

Why? Was this his way of getting her away from Jen? Did he think he's have more influence over her if she were away from home and friends?

It made no difference, she reasoned. He'd been dishonest and that was enough. Relationships required two people to trust one another. Paul made a mockery of that. She slid her travel bag from under the bed and placed it on the mattress. Crossing to the dresser, she collected an armful of clothes and and began packing. As she worked, she debated whether to say anything to Paul.

*Let him find out on his own*, she thought, it would serve him right if she just got into the car when Jen arrived and left him to wonder where she'd gone.

She was placing the last of her things in the travel case when she heard Paul's voice behind her.

"What are you doing? Packing?"

Haylee spun around, locking her eyes on his. "I'm leaving."

"What do you mean?" Paul asked, his voice puzzled. "We agreed to stay another week."

"I'm leaving. Jen is coming to pick me up. I don't know what's going on, but whatever it is, it didn't work."

"Is this some of Jen's nonsense? Look, I can probably explain anything that's bothering you."

He put a hand on Haylee's shoulder. She knocked it away.

"Don't touch me, you bastard! You lied about teaching at Tulane. What else was a lie? I bet your real name's not even Paul."

"Haylee, let's be reasonable."

"Get away from me you fucking creep!" Haylee screamed the words. "And here's your damn ring."

Snatching the ring off her finger, she threw it at him. It hit the wall and fell behind the dresser.

"Damn it," he said, rushing to where it fell. "If you've lost that damn thing…"

He shoved the dresser aside and snatched the ring off the floor.

"Put it back on." he said, thrusting it at her.

"Are you crazy? We're through, I don't ever want to see you or that ring again."

"I said put the damn thing on your finger." Paul grabbed her hand and tried to force the ring on. Haylee clawed at his face with her free hand raking her fingernails down his cheek.

"Damn," he cried, jumping back. "I guess we do this the hard way," Paul said. He stepped into

256

the hall and slammed the door shut. Haylee rushed after him. Grabbing the knob, she tugged, managing to crack the door slightly before Paul pulled it shut again.

"You son of a bitch!" she cried, "Turn loose. Let me out."

"Claude, get up here." Paul yelled. "Bring the key, she's trying to leave."

Haylee tugged again, but Paul was too strong. The door stayed closed.

"Claude, get up here, pronto." Paul yelled.

"I'm coming," she heard her grandfather say. "What the hell's going on?"

"Grandfather, make him let me out." Haylee called.

"She trying to leave," said Paul. "Give me the key."

There was a click. Haylee tried the knob and this time it turned free but the door only rattled. She was locked inside.

"Grandfather," she called, "Grandfather, please."

There was no reply only the sounds of footsteps fading into nothingness. Haylee staggered to the bed where she sat elbows on her knees hands under her chin staring at nothing.

*They locked the door when they thought I was leaving. They want to keep me here.* If they were determined to keep her in Acedia, what might they do to Jen when she arrived? Suddenly, Haylee was terrified for her friend.

Ronald Polizzi

*I need to call her and warn her of what's happened.* She rushed to the dresser where she left her phone, and her heart sank. Her cell phone was missing. Tearing open her overnight bag, she slung clothes in every direction. The search through her bag proved futile as did searching under the bed and the dresser.

*Paul took it. Oh God, Paul took the phone because he knew I'd call for help.*

Dropping into a corner, she began to sob.

Haylee couldn't say how much time passed before the lock clicked and the door to the bedroom opened. Looking through red-rimmed eyes she saw the massive bulk of Sheriff Riddle fill the doorway. The sheriff stepped into the room with Woodard and Paul behind him. In his hand, the big man held a leather slapjack.

"Sorry about this, Darlin'," Woodard said, "But we're gonna have to move you for tonight."

"Why are you doing this?" Haylee asked, her voice a whisper.

Woodard didn't reply.

"Put your hands out, Girl," Riddle barked.

"No," Haylee said digging deep for what little resolve she had. "Not until you tell me what's going on."

"You'll extend your arms or I'll do it for you." Riddle said raising the slapjack.

"I don't want her bruised." Woodard said.

"I got ways to put a hurt on her and leave no bruise," said Riddle; moving with a speed that

258

belied the man's bulk. He snatched one of Haylee's hands, bending it backward until tears of pain spilled from her eyes. "Still want to play rough?" he growled.

"That's enough, Riddle," Woodard said. "Let her go."

Muttering under his breath, Riddle turned loose of Haylee's hand, leaving her to rub her injured wrist.

"Put your hands out, Darlin'," Woodard said, his voice not unkind. "Come on, we don't mean you no harm. It's for your protection."

Haylee extended her wrists and Riddle snapped handcuffs over each one. He took another pair and attached one cuff it to the center link of the pair Haylee wore, creating a tether.

"Let's go," Riddle said, tugging Haylee to her feet.

They led her downstairs and out the back through the kitchen. It became apparent they were taking her to the building in the hollow. After a brisk walk, the structure came into view. Riddle marched her to the door, where they waited while Woodard produced a key and opened the padlock. He slipped it off the hasp and swung the door open. Haylee had never been this close before. She noticed the walls were constructed of split log, a detail she'd missed before.

A glance inside showed a large fireplace. Slabs of meat hung from hooks against a far wall. The meat had an odd shape. Whatever the animal, it was large. The smell reminded her of butcher shops and hickory wood.

"Go on inside." Riddle ordered. "Stand by the door and stick your arms out and I'll unlock the cuffs."

Haylee stepped into the doorway and extended her arms. Riddle snapped the cuff open with a quick twist of the key.

Haylee rubbed her wrists.

"I hate to leave you here, Darlin', but it's necessary tonight." Woodard said. "Mildred left you some cold chicken for your supper and blankets and a pillow for a bed. There's a chamber pot in the corner so you don't soil the floor. I'll come for you tomorrow."

Without another word, he swung the door closed, and Haylee was plunged into darkness. She dropped to her knees. Feeling her way along, she found a sidewall and used it to navigate around. After a moment, she felt the soft texture of the blankets and pillow. She managed to spread them into a makeshift pallet, then went in search of the chamber pot. By the time she located everything, her eyes adjusted to the dark enough that she saw vague forms of the meat hanging on the hooks. Something about their shape was not right. Her inability to put her finger on why, irritated her. Finally, she pushed the question aside. Lying on the pile of blankets, she stared upward into the blackness.

Petweenus

*This is all a dream. I'll wake up in my bed in New Orleans in the morning and what a story I'll have to tell.*

There was nothing else to do but wait for the morning and the horrible dream to end.

### -13-
### A Lovely Pair of Coconuts

Jen was digging through drawers, tossing bits of clothing into a small overnight bag when Michael came through the door. He looked at Jen, his mouth open in surprise.

"What in hell are you doing?" he asked.

"Pack your things," Jen ordered, "We're going to Alabama."

Michael blinked. "What?

"Haylee needs me," Jen replied, continuing to stuff her overnight bag. "I'm going after her."

"Jen, you don't even know where she is. You said it was somewhere out in the boonies. How do you plan to find her?"

Jen turned to Michael, her face streaked with tears, her eyes flashing.

"The same way I know she's in trouble. I just will."

Michael studied his girlfriend, noting the way her hands trembled and the pain and fear reflected in her eyes. "We'll take my car," he said.

Something went off in his mind like the flash bulb of a camera. A body lay on a rough, wooden floor, covered with a linen cloth like his mother used to cover the dining room table during holidays. Though the face was hidden, he saw the shoes sticking out because the cloth was too short. They were black with crepe soles; the kind he wore for his part time job at Wal-mart.

*Those are my shoes; I'm the person under the cloth.*

It was a stupid thought and he brushed it aside, focusing on Jen, but the crepe sole shoes stayed in the back of his mind like a harbinger.

They packed the car and were on the road within the hour. When they reached Mississippi, they stopped at the Denny's in Picayune for lunch. Michael ordered a country fried steak meal and Jen, a large salad.

The spoke little while they ate.

When they finished, Michael signaled for the ticket. A thin-boned woman with disheveled hair and the beginnings of a stoop brought him the check. He peeled off several bills and handed them to the woman.

"Keep the change," he said.

This brought a smile from the woman. Clutching the wad of bills close to her breast, she hurried away.

Jen and Michael left the cool of the restaurant and stepped into the hot sun. Weaving through the mass of mostly pickup trucks, they angled toward Michael's Volvo , which stood out like a sore thumb among the redneck rides.

Michael opened Jen's door before letting himself in on the driver's side. A sign at the far end of the parking lot advertised gas at "rock bottom prices". Steering across the asphalt, he maneuvered up to the pump, and filled the tank.

Michael went inside to pay. When he returned, Jen had the tri-state map unfolded across her lap and was tracing their route.

"Here's Slaughter County," she said, stabbing the spot on the map with her finger. "But, where do we go when we get there? Haylee was vague about where her grandfather actually lives."

"We'll ask somebody," Michael suggested. "I mean, look how small the place is. Somebody's got to know."

"You're in charge of directions," he said as they pulled on to the highway.

The road weaved past herds of cows and the occasional goat. Oaks, their leafy branches spread like green umbrellas, dotted fields thick with tall grass.

The pastoral setting filled Michael with a sense of peace.

Glancing at Jen, his mood lost some of its buoyancy as he registered the stern set of her jaw and the sadness in her eyes. Her silent suffering tore at his heart. Focusing on the road, he blocked out the peaceful surroundings and willed the trip to end.

With Slaughter County several hours away, he turned on the radio and spun the tuner, avoiding the hard-core rock stations in favor of one that played what his friends referred to as elevator music. The music was tame, almost sleepy, but it filled the uneasy silence between them.

Michael was tempted to start a conversation, but thought better of the idea. What was there to talk about but Jen's feeling that Haylee needed help? He entertained himself by listening to the soft sounds coming from the radio and counting the mile markers as they cut across the Mississippi countryside.

They stopped at another Denny's for a restroom break in a town he missed the name of when they exited the highway. Michael ordered a hamburger to go. Jen unexpectedly requested chicken fingers and fries. Back in the car, she devoured them voraciously.

"You gobbled that up," he said.

"I wasn't really hungry," Jen said, her fingers tearing tiny strips of napkin in to bits of confetti.

"She's fine, Babe," Michael said. "Really, I can't even believe we're doing this. Both of us are going to look really stupid when we get to Acedia."

"I hope you're right," Jen said. "But it doesn't feel that way to me. Deep inside, it feels wrong. It felt wrong from the beginning. I should have never let her leave. I should have made her stay."

Steering with one hand, Michael fiddled with the radio dial. The easy listening station had faded into static. As he searched for another station, he caught Jen stealing a glance from the corner of his eye. During the last four hours, her silence had created an uneasy void between them.

\*\*\*

Jen gazed out the window at the passing scenery, though none of it registered. Instead, her mind drifted through pools of nothingness, leaving all her senses on lockdown. The dream that haunted her replayed itself in an endless loop.

She saw a dark place she thought might be a windowless room. Somewhere inside that blackness, Haylee called her name. Her friend's voice pleaded in peals of sharp pain, greased with fear. Since waking from the dream, the voice continued to call to her. She couldn't make it stop. It pounded in her ears, driving into her mind like a piston.

*I should never have let her go with him. The letter looked fishy and I should have said so. If I had, she wouldn't have left. It's my fault if anything happens to her.*

The thoughts added more layers of guilt to the weight she carried, pushing her mind deeper into the chasm of despair.

\*\*\*

The blue sky of day had given way to a purple twilight sprinkled with bits of carnation pink, when they crossed into Slaughter County. The flatness of central Mississippi a memory, the terrain here consisted of a rollercoaster of peaks and valleys. The apex of each ridge offered a spectacular view of more ridges extending into eternity.

"So this is the Appalachians," Michael said. "Where are the strip mines and shanties?"

It didn't look anything like his concept Appalachia, mountains stripped bare of trees and anything green, populated by half-starved men with chest length beards. This place was gorgeous. Even Jen was not immune to the beauty: Her eyes lost their vacant look. Michael smiled as he watched the beauty outside the car window draw her out of the dark place she'd taken refuge in.

"We should be coming up on Acedia before long," Michael said. "When we get there, we can ask directions, but, what then? Does Haylee even know we're coming?"

"I talked to her on the phone," Jen said, "She was going to pack when I lost the connection."

The flash of blue and red lights in the rearview mirror caught Michael's attention. He was traveling several miles below the posted 40 mile per hour limit. A siren wailed for an instant, then shut off.

"What's going on?" Jen asked.

"I'm not sure," Michael said, "We were under the speed limit."

He coasted to the shoulder of the road and cut the engine. Glancing into the side mirror, he watched as a giant of a man in khakis, strolled toward them.

"Why is he smiling like that?" Jen asked. She had twisted around to better see the big man approach.

"I don't know, but it can't be good," Michael replied.

Michael rolled down the driver's window as the cop neared.

The man reached Michael's door. Towering above the car, legs spread, hands on hips, the sheriff's face drew into a tight mask as he studied Michael though half-closed eyes.

"Did I do something wrong, Officer?" Michael asked.

The man continued to peer through half closed eyes.

Michael made another attempt to communicate. "Did I have a taillight out? Was that the reason you signaled me to pull over?"

"Where you headed?" the cop asked.

"Is that why you stopped us?" Anger tinted Michael's voice. "Officer...er..."

"Sheriff," said the man. "Sheriff Riddle. This is my county."

"Uh...excuse me...Sheriff. We're looking for a town called Acedia, but I'm not sure we're on the right road. According to the map, we should be there."

"Any particular reason you chose Acedia?"

"We're looking for my friend." Jen said, "Her name is Haylee Woods. She's visiting her grandfather."

The sheriff's broad face broke into a grin and he lost his rigid stance.

He shook his head, still grinning. "Why, you're Little Haylee's friends, how 'bout that."

Petweenus

"Haylee's all right, isn't she?" Jen asked, confusion dulling her face.

The sheriff removed his hat and scratched his head with a paw-like hand. "I reckon she is," he laughed, "I just saw her about an hour ago. She had a tiff with that boyfriend of hers, but he got in his car and drove off. Probably for the best, really. I didn't like that feller. There was something phony about him right from the start. Good thing he left. Little Haylee is special around here. Nobody would take kindly if she got hurt."

"Thank you," Jen said, "I was worried."

"Officer…" Michael started.

"Sheriff," Riddle corrected, tapping his badge.

"Er sorry…Sheriff," Michael corrected himself, "Could I ask one more favor?"

"Depends on what it is," Riddle said.

"Could you give us directions to where Haylee's staying with her grandfather? We've driven all this way and it would be nice to see her."

"I tell you what, you just follow me, and I'll escort you straight to old Claude's place," Riddle said. "You might not find it otherwise; it sits way off the road."

The sheriff walked back to his car and, with the lights still flashing, pulled onto the road, stopping a short distance ahead of Michael and Jen. He reached an arm out the window and motioned them to pull out behind. When they were in position, he started forward and they followed

269

behind. Michael made sure he kept a car length between them.

"Now, this is strange," Michael said. "This guy first looks like he wants to eat us alive and then you mention Haylee, and he's all smiles. At least we know she's okay."

"I'll feel better when I see her," Jen said. She watched through the windshield as the patrol car led them along. "You know, that guy gives me the creeps."

"He seems all right," Michael said, "A little territorial maybe, but small towns are like that."

"I just want to get Haylee and get out of here." Jen said.

"Babe, you and I are on the same page about that," Michael said, "The sooner, the better."

Riddle kept the pace steady, but not too fast. The patrol car lights blazed in a colorful spinning flame as night slowly cloaked the landscape.

With the absence of streetlights, the road was little more than a black tunnel. While Michael concentrated on driving, Jen gazed out the window, but the sides of the road were filled with such a deep gloom, they may as well have been draped with a heavy, black cloth.

After a couple of miles, Riddle's left tail light blinked, signaling a turn. Michael followed the sheriff onto a narrow road of hard packed dirt, then another turn and they were on asphalt again.

"Where the hell is he going?" Michael asked, "If he wanted to get us lost, he's done that."

The sheriff signaled another turn, this time onto a double track leading off the asphalt where they passed a battered mailbox leaning at a forty-five degree angle.

Bumping along behind the sheriff, they skirted low-hanging branches, pressing them on both sides until the narrow track opened into a wide clearing. Michael's headlights picked up a two-story house with a covered porch and a gothic upper story.

Riddle stopped in front and switched off the lights. Michael parked a little distance behind, then shut the engine off and waited to see what the law officer would do.

"This is where Haylee's grandfather lives?" Jen asked. "It looks like something out of the *Psycho* movies."

Riddle walked toward them.

"I guess we get out." Michael said, sliding from behind the wheel. He walked around to the passenger's side so he was between Jen and the giant when Riddle reached them.

The Sheriff displayed the wide grin he'd worn earlier. "This is the place," he said. "Come on, I'll introduce you to the Reeve." Taking long strides, Riddle marched them up to the door.

After a couple of hard raps, the door opened. A tall, thin man with creases lining his face, peered out at the visitors. A cloth napkin dangled from the man's shirt. He snatched it loose with a grin and laughed. "Damn it, Riddle, you caught me right at suppertime. Who's that with you?"

"Sorry, Reeve," Riddle said, "but I brung some friends of your granddaughter's. They come to visit."

"Well, come in, come in. Any friend of Haylee's is a friend of mine. I expect she should be back shortly. Care for some supper?"

"No, thank you," Jen said, following the tall man into the house. "You said she should be back soon. She's not here? She knew we were coming."

"Yeah, I believe she did say something about that, now that you mention it."

They followed Woodard into the house. Stepping through the door, Jen quickly scanned the living room. Worn, generously-stuffed chairs and a love seat, were positioned around a medium-sized area beneath a tall ceiling. Faded wallpaper covered the walls. A half-opened door exposed a large, black woman collecting dishes from a long, dining room table. The woman glanced through the door and her eyes locked onto Jen's for an instant before the woman looked away.

Her gaze was like ice against Jen's skin. She turned back to Woodard, who busied himself moving chairs into a semi-circle.

"Sit down," he said, sweeping toward his handiwork with an arm. "Mildred's gonna bring out some sweet tea. You two are up for that, ain't you?"

Jen nodded to be polite, though what she wanted most was to get back in the car and drive away. The vibes of the place screamed: *Leave as fast as you can.*

"May I ask where Haylee went?" Jen said. It seemed odd her friend would go anywhere, knowing they were on their way.

"Oh, she went to town with her cousin, Cynthie. Cynthie hates to go alone," Woodard said, seating himself.

"I'm Claude Woodard, by the way," he said, turning to Michael and extending a hand, "If you haven't guessed it already."

"Pleased to meet you, Mr. Woodard," Michael said, taking the offered hand.

"Call me Reeve," Woodard said, "That's the way folks around here do it."

The door leading to the dining room swung open, and the black woman ambled in with a tray of glasses filled with an amber colored liquid.

She offered glasses around, then took the empty tray back to the kitchen.

With Mildred gone, Woodard lifted his glass toward the others. "A toast," he said, "to the return of my granddaughter and new friends here with us now."

Michael lifted his glass and Riddle followed suit. Jen leaned forward, halfheartedly copying the men.

After the toast, both Michael and Jen took a long sip of the tea. From the corner of her eye, she noticed Woodard placing his glass on the table without tasting it. Something about this whole affair bothered her as if Woodard and Riddle were acting out a scene. Nervous, she took another sip of the tea.

"Haylee told you why we're here, didn't she? We came to take her home," she said, resting her glass on her knee.

Woodard rubbed his chin with a thumb and finger. "Does seem I heard something about that," he said.

Jen blinked. The room was swimming around her. Woodard's face moved in and out of focus.

Alarm bells went off in her head as images swam past her eyes, filling her head with fog. She fought them off, struggling to stay conscious. A blur of motion caught her attention. Someone was coming through the door.

*It must be Haylee*, she thought. *Thank God she's here*. Paul Carter strode in to the room with a smirk on his face.

"Such a lovely pair of coconuts," he said.

Paul's laughter rang in Jen's ears as the room faded to black. It was the last sound she remembered.

## -14-
## Petweenus

The rattle of metal, followed by the squeal of rusty hinges, snapped Haylee awake. She looked around. Thin streams of light from the morning sun filtered through cracks in the mortar between the rough-hewn planks of the smoke house. Someone outside was fooling with the door. Woodard, she told herself. He was probably bringing her breakfast.

The rattle continued.

*He must be having trouble with the lock,* she thought. *Good, maybe he'll give up and leave.* She looked around. Now that it was day, enough light filtered in that she saw the room clearly for the first time. The fireplace, composed of large stones, was held together with the same mortar used to seal the spaces between the log planks. The oversized hearth was wide and tall enough she could hide inside.

*And if I did, he'd find me easily enough.* She turned her attention to the slabs dangling from iron hooks. *I could disguise myself as a meat carcass, but, where would I stick the hook?*

She was locked in a single-room building, empty except for the fireplace and the slabs of meat. Her grandfather would work the lock open soon, and when he did, he would do whatever he planned. Her only hope was for Jen to become suspicious and contact the state police when she saw Haylee wasn't where she was supposed to be. She had no doubt Woodard would have some explanation for why she was not in the house. She prayed Jen would see through the lie.

While these thoughts passed through her mind, her eyes examined the slabs of meat across from her. The carcasses were composed of long trunks, some slim, others more muscular with broad chests. All were unusually wide across the chest for four-footed animals. The forelegs, chopped off where the paw should have been, were out of proportion when compared to the hind quarters that had been butchered below the ham. Haylee moved closer for a better look. When she did, she gasped. Now she knew why the slabs looked odd: These weren't the carcasses of pigs, cows or even deer. These were human cadavers.

She turned away, the bile rising in her throat. Dropping to her knees, she vomited the little her stomach held. She managed to gain her feet and stagger to the far wall, as far from the butchered bodies as the room allowed, when she heard the door open. Mildred stood in the doorway.

"Come on, Miss Haylee, while we got a little time. It won't be long before Master Claude knows I'm gone. I already wasted time with that damn lock 'cause I couldn't find the good key and had to use the bent one."

Haylee stumbled to the woman. "Those are bodies," she said. "Someone hung bodies in here." She said, her face pale with shock.

"We ain't got time to worry about that now," Mildred said, "We got to get you away from here. Once the Sheriff comes for you, it'll be too late. I can't have that happen."

"Why?" Haylee asked, letting the woman lead her out by the hand.

"I saved your momma," said Mildred, "When you were just a little thing. I thought then, it was over, but they lured you back. Now, I got to try once more. I can't let the abomination go on. It's a sin against God."

"You were the one that wrote the letter," Haylee said. "You were the friend that helped her leave."

"She was my sister and there were others that helped. You'll meet one of them. He's gonna get you away from here."

"Gomorrah," Mildred called toward the woods.

The freakish creature lumbered out from the trees still dressed in tattered overalls. Haylee shrank back from the thing.

"Don't be afraid," Mildred said, "He's gentle as a lamb; so's his brother. Most times, anyway, long as you don't try to confine 'em. They don't like walls."

Gomorrah lumbered up to Haylee. Extending his neck, he sniffed at the girl. Haylee steeled herself not to move.

"That's good," Mildred said, "Stay calm. He means you no harm."

"Take her to Hooch." Mildred said. "Understand? Nod if you do."

The creature nodded its massive head.

"Off with you then, both of you."

Haylee followed the creature toward the trees, then paused to look back at Mildred.

"Thank you," she said.

"Don't thank me," Mildred replied, "I'm doing this as much for me as you. Just beat it out of here."

With that, Mildred disappeared into the smokehouse.

Haylee followed Gomorrah through the woods. The creature showed a certain grace as it moved through the trees. In this element, Gomorrah lost the appearance of a freak. The wildness transformed him into a thing of wonder, and his lumbering gait fell away. Now, his movements were supple and sure. He moved without disturbing a leaf or blade of grass.

Gomorrah followed no path. Instead, some inner sense kept him on track, or so Haylee guessed. Since she did not know their destination, she was forced to trust Gomorrah's instinct.

Gomorrah traveled so swiftly, Haylee had to trot to keep up. Every so often, the creature would pause and wait for her to close the distance between them before moving on. Those times he would watch with gentle eyes that seemed to hover on a perpetual sadness. She saw there was intelligence behind them, though she suspected it was different than hers. Such a strange being, she wondered what his origins were. However he came to be, he was cursed with being a misfit. His deformed appearance camouflaged the gentle nature inside him.

They reached a place where the land angled down so steeply Haylee found herself grabbing the brush and large rocks for handholds. Gomorrah, his footing solid as ever, was not bothered with the steep pitch.

They reached the bottom of the ridge. Breaking through the dense brush, they found themselves on a creek bank. Though she was never introduced to it, she knew this was Mantle Creek, the place the witch lived, where the massacre of the Alibamos Indians occurred. Something about the place was hypnotic. She forgot everything else as she took in the ambiance around her. Gomorrah also seemed to be affected because he hesitated, turning his disfigured head in a long sweep around.

Though the creek was a brush-choked affair, a sandy bottom tinted the water a pale gold in the sunlight that filtered through the trees. It was a pretty place and she could see how Virginia's family decided to pick this place to stop. How ironic a place with such a bloody history could appear so tranquil.

*It's a trap,* she reasoned, *a beautiful trap.*

Gomorrah waited while she worked her way through the brush to the water's edge. Bending one knee and placing the other on the ground, she dipped the fingers of her right hand into the water. Ripples, shimmering with a rainbow of colors, moved across the surface in ever-widening circles. She lifted her hand and touched her wet fingers to her forehead so a tiny trail of liquid trickled down, past her nose to drip off her chin.

*I have been baptized in the waters of Mantel Creek. Now, I too, am a part of its history.*

A rustling in the brush across the stream jerked her out of her musings. Gomorrah, suddenly alert, rushed over, taking Haylee by the arm, motioning her to follow him into the thick leafy growth. Deep inside the foliage, she peeped out as a girl, whose face was framed by straight, black hair, broke through the tangle of green on other side. She appeared to be the same age as Haylee, though the shadows made it difficult to be sure. Even though she could not see the girl clearly, she sensed something familiar about her.

The girl turned her head to the side, aiming one ear toward Haylee as if listening. She lifted her head, sniffing at the air.

*What is she doing?*

As Haylee watched, the girl turned back toward Haylee. Sunlight caught her full in the face, and Haylee gasped. *She could be my twin, except for her eyes.* Her eyes were solid white with no iris or pupil.

*She's blind!*

"She's better'n a dog," said a gruff voice from across the water. "I don't know why you keep that old hound, when 'tweenus does just fine."

"She picked up on that revenuer the other day, I'll admit," said another.

"Hey, Girl, what you hear?" said the first voice. The owner, a grizzled character with a long beard and a narrow face, appeared behind the girl, who still cocked her head.

"Mhaaaa whaaa mhaa," she said, moving her hands wildly about.

A second man appeared, looking much like the first. "Why you asking her anything? You know she can't talk."

"Dhaaaa Mhaaa," said the girl.

"Somebody's around," said the first man, pushing past the girl, causing her to stumble. He charged to the creek and thrust a foot in the water, ready to cross to Haylee's side. Haylee held her breath.

*If he crosses, he'll see us.*

Then, the bushes rattled behind the two men. Both men and the girl turned at the sound.

"They's come up behind us, you stupid girl," the first man said to the blind girl. He raised his fist, ready strike her, when the second man stayed his hand.

"Don't waste time on her, Orville. They's trespassers, let's get 'em."

The men rushed off, leaving the girl to stumble behind them.

"If I was you, I'd make tracks while you have a chance," said a voice.

Hearing the voice, Gomorrah jumped up and down, clapping his hands like an excited child.

A small man stepped from between the trees. He wore a long beard like the men she'd seen moments before. His hair, the few strands he possessed, hung to his shoulders. A baseball cap covered the top of his head. He dressed in a white, long-sleeved shirt tucked neatly into dark, wool trousers.

"Sodom will lead the Stubses on a merry chase, but they won't be fooled for long. We need to be gone when they come back."

Haylee studied the man closely. Though this stranger looked less fierce than the Stubses, she wasn't sure who he was or if he could be trusted.

The man looked back at her with gentle eyes. "You needn't fear me," he said, "I'm here to rescue you. Gomorrah is my boy; Sodom too. They's brother's."

"You're Mildred's friend," said Haylee.

"In a manner of speaking, but there's no time now. We need to get to a safe harbor. Once there, we can talk. "Gomorrah, find your brother. I'll see you at the fort. Make sure them Stubses don't follow." Gomorrah nodded, then melted into the trees. The little man reached out a hand to Haylee. "Come on."

Haylee followed the man through the brush, amazed at how easily he negotiated the tangles of thick branches and briers. The foliage seemed to part magically around him, allowing him to pass effortlessly though the barrage of natural obstacles.

*Like father, like son. He's as at ease in these woods as Gomorrah.*

"One thing about them Stubses," the little man said as he broke trail. "They ain't no woodsmen. It's a wonder they can find their way home."

"Where are we going?" Haylee asked, "You have a fort?"

"You'll see," said the little man.

A few moments later, they broke out of the thick brush and angled toward a tall rock formation, near the top of the ridge they were climbing. The little man walked toward a large section of bare rock as if this section of mountain had gone bald. He went straight for a stand of saplings just below the bare rock. Suddenly, he disappeared into solid rock. As Haylee neared the spot where he vanished, she saw the rock was split, the fissure hidden by brush. She stepped through the crack and into in a cavern the size of a spacious bedroom.

The cave was furnished with handmade chairs constructed of stout branches and bound with thick cord. A cot stood in the back of the room covered with a coarse blanket. A propane camp stove, complete with a coffee pot on one of the burners, rested on a low table. An army footlocker was placed beside it. Lanterns cast a warm glow from various corners and filled the place with soft light. The effect of it all was surprisingly homey.

Virginia, who was sitting in one of the chairs, jumped to her feet when she saw Haylee. The girl threw her arms around Haylee, bursting into tiny sobs.

Haylee dabbed at the girl's eyes with her shirttail.

"What in the world are you doing here?" she asked, blinking in disbelief, "How did you find your way to this place?"

"Gomorrah brought me," Virginia said. "I was in the barn hiding from the storm when he saw me. I was scared at first until I saw he wasn't going to hurt me. He brought me here."

"Well, I'm glad you're safe," Haylee said. "I was worried about you. I looked everywhere after the storm and when I couldn't find you..." her voice dropped off when she saw the hurt in the girl's eyes.

"I'm sorry, Haylee, I didn't mean to make you worry."

Haylee smiled, "I know you didn't."

The little man, who'd been digging through the footlocker, produced a briarwood pipe and sack of tobacco. After stuffing the pipe and setting a match to it, he drew on the stem and sent a plume of smoke into the air, where it took the form of a miniature cloud. He pulled up a chair next to Haylee and placed a hand on her knee.

"Little Haylee," he said, between puffs. "I ain't seen you since you was a tiny thing, less than a year old. Your momma had you in one arm, wrapped in a pink blanket, and a suitcase in the other. That night, I wouldn't have given two cents for your chances or your momma's. I had Mildred write Claudette a letter. Oh, I guess it was maybe a month after she left. She sent it general mail. I never knew if she got it or not." He laughed, "I guess I should introduce myself. Folks call me Hooch."

"I guess I should thank you," Haylee said.

"Oh, I didn't do it solely for her. I had reasons of my own, though I did love that woman more than I can say."

"Hooch, if you knew my mother, then maybe you knew my father. Mother would never tell me who he was. I've always wondered...always wanted to know."

Hooch's face drew tight. "I know who he is," he said, "but it ain't my place to tell you about him, it's his. In my opinion, some things is best not known. I think this is one of them."

"My father is here? In Slaughter County?" Haylee asked, ignoring the caution.

Hooch stood up.

"Oh, he's around all right, but what's important is for you and Virginia to put Slaughter County as far distant from you as you can."

"I'm not going anywhere until I know what this is all about," Haylee said. "I've been lied to, drugged, and held captive by my grandfather and

285

now, I'm wondering if my mother died by accident or if she was murdered."

Haylee noticed Virginia, who was amusing herself by twining a pair of sticks with string into a vaguely human shape, watched them closely.

Hooch noticed too.

"I'd rather not speak of such things with the child present," he said, nodding at Virginia.

She looked at the adults and smiled. "I'm making a doll," she said. "Her name is Amy."

Haylee moved to where Virginia was binding the stick arms to her doll.

"She's going to be very pretty, Virginia." Haylee said. "But she needs some hair, don't you think."

"She needs long hair, like mine." Virginia agreed.

"I have an idea," Haylee piped up. "Why don't you go outside and see if you can find some long grass, then I'll help you with the hair."

"Thanks," Virginia said.

Clutching her doll, she hurried out.

Haylee turned back to Hooch. "She's gone. Now, I'd like to know what all this is about."

"Darling, you walked into a hornet's nest when you came to Slaughter County. Your momma should have been straight with you from the beginning. There's a reason they want you here. They need you to keep going."

"What do you mean keep going?" Haylee asked, suspicion tinting her words.

"It's a long story and I don't know if I have the strength to tell it in a way that will satisfy you."

"Try," Haylee said.

Hooch tugged on his pipe, then removed it from his mouth. Eyeing the bowl with a frown, he tapped it on his boot heel. Gray ash fell on the cavern floor.

The corners of Hooch's mouth turned up in a sad smile.

"How old would you say I am?" he asked.

"I don't know," Haylee said, her voice hinting irritation. "Why?"

"Guess," Hooch said. "It's important."

Haylee sighed.

"Okay," she said. "Sixty. You look to be about sixty years old."

"This year will be my two-hundred and twenty-first."

"What?" Haylee wanted to laugh. "You can't be serious."

Hooch drew up a little in his chair.

"I was born in 1788, in a settlement in Virginia on the great wagon road, where the city of Roanoke sits today. In 1813, I made the trip from Virginia to Alabama with a group of folks, led by Joseph Slaughter, looking for a place where we could practice our beliefs and be left alone. We settled here in the foothills of the Appalachians, our beloved mountains, where we still live today."

Haylee looked at Hooch, doubt coloring her features. "Joseph Slaughter didn't settle here until

1859. If you had been one of the original settlers you'd have known that."

Hooch allowed the tiniest of smiles to play across his lips. He shook his head.

"Joseph Slaughter is my brother. 1859 was when we came out of hiding. Too many people were being lured into the surrounding country by the promise of cheap land. We needed to keep ourselves separate, so Joseph and I made a trip to see the governor. We'd accumulated a substantial amount of wealth, mostly by robbing the unfortunate souls that wandered to near the colony. We stripped them of their belongings and then offered them as living sacrifices to the Ilhuicateotl, the great god.

"Joseph was very persuasive as he explained to the governor how as a religious colony we needed certain autonomy to ensure our ability to worship in our own fashion. The governor seemed more interested in the lavish amount of money Joseph was offering for the land than our explanation. Shortly thereafter, we left for home with papers in our possession proclaiming our settlement a shire and Joseph as Reeve. In essence we could legally institute our own laws within our boundaries."

"I'm sorry," Haylee shook her head, "This is too much. I can't accept this."

"If your momma was still alive, she'd tell you it's true," Hooch said. "If you was still around tomorrow, you would see it's so. This is why I have to get you and Virginia out of here tonight."

"Okay, let's say this is true, that you are *that* old, though I think it's impossible, what does any of it have to do with me?"

"They need you to produce the next Petweenus. Same as your momma produced you."

"Petweenus, I thought that was the witch's name." Haylee said.

Hooch held up his hand. "Just listen and I'll explain it all. It has to do with the cycle. Seven years of seven years and then the Jubilee. A girl child is born, a special child with a certain mark. It's timed, so's when the year of Jubilee arrives, the child is flowered. The old Petweenus is sacrificed and made into Teoctli, or sacred wine. The girl is impregnated with the sacred seed and bears the next special child."

\*\*\*

Hooch glanced over his shoulder toward the cave mouth, satisfied Virginia was out of earshot.

He went on.

"That's why they kept Virginia and didn't kill her with her parents. Claudette had carried you off and they was needing a girl child. She was gonna serve as an experiment to see if they could produce a Petweenus with an outsider. But when you arrived, they didn't need her anymore. I imagine they were going to use her in the fire ceremony when they create the Teoctli."

"This Teoctli, you're saying it keeps you alive?"

"That's what I'm saying, along with long pig. You have to eat a little long pig every so often. No other meat will do."

"Long pig? I've never heard of it."

"You saw some in the smokehouse. That's where they keep it."

"There were no pigs in there," Haylee said, her eyes wide. "They were the remains of human bodies."

Hooch drew up his legs, then leaned forward on his elbows. "Darlin', that's what long pig is–the flesh of humans."

"You said in order to be special, the person would have a special mark, right?"

"Yep, the special one has the mark."

"I don't have any marks on my body so I can't possibly be this special person," Haylee said.

"Sure you do." Hooch said.

"I ought to know about my own body," Haylee argued.

"Look at your left hand," Hooch said.

Haylee held the palm of her hand to her face. "I don't see anything," she said.

"Not the palm," Hooch corrected, "The side of your hand. There's a bump there, just below your little finger."

"It's a burn mark," Haylee said. "It wasn't something I was born with, it's just a scar."

"That's where you're wrong." Hooch said, "Matter of fact, you was born with six fingers on your left hand, or, I should say five fingers and a claw, same as all the others. That's the mark. When your momma left with you, Mildred tied a cord around the claw so it would die and fall off. Claudette made up the story of the burn so you would stay ignorant of the truth. You're the host and it's a fact."

Haylee stood, pushing the chair away from her with her calves.

"I need some time to think," she said, her voice strained. "All of this is just too over the top."

She walked to the cave entrance, then paused before going out. "One question," she said.

Hooch looked up. "What's that?"

"Let's say what you told me is the truth. What happens if I do leave so I don't produce another set of twins? What happens to everybody?"

Hooch smiled, though his expression was sad. "We all die."

291

**-15-**
**Escape**


Haylee struggled to keep her voice level. "Virginia, get away from her."

Virginia gave Haylee a puzzled look.

"She's my friend," the girl said. "She's nice and I like her. Besides, she looks like you."

The blind girl swung her head toward Haylee, her body twitching.

"I'm sure she's nice, Honey, but the men that were with her are not nice. They may come and hurt us. They may hurt her if she doesn't go back where you found her."

"What if she gets lost?" Virginia asked, "She can't see how to get back."

"I'll tell you what," Haylee said. "What if we take her back? Then she'll know how to get home."

Virginia thought about this for a moment. She smiled. "I guess that'll be okay."

The blind girl listened to them. Haylee didn't know if the girl understood, but her face became taut. She seemed nervous. Virginia kept a tight grip on the girl's hand.

"I'm going to take you back," said Virginia, "So you won't be lost. So you can go home."

The girl twisted, her face a landscape of terror. "Naaaaaww…naaawwww," she said, wringing her hands, looking sightlessly back and forth.

Reaching out, Haylee touched the girl's hand. The blind girl jumped.

"Don't be afraid," Haylee said in her softest voice. "I'm Virginia's friend. I won't hurt you."

"Frrrreeend?" the girl said.

"Yes, my name is Haylee."

"Hahhlee," the girl said, tracing Haylee's face with a hand. "Freeend."

"Friend," Haylee repeated. "What is your name?"

The girl's forehead creased, the pupiless eyes rolled upward as if trying to remember something.

"Pah...pah...tweenniiissss," she said.

"Petweenus? That's your name?"

"Mah name Pahtweenniiiisssss," the girl stretched out the last of the word.

Haylee's mind reeled. Was this the witch? The idea was ludicrous. She was no older than Haylee.

Could she have been named after the Indian witch because she was blind? Only the cruelest of families would have done something so crass. Then she remembered the two men who'd been with her. Neither struck her as being particularly kind. Haylee could easily imagine them mocking the girl's blindness by naming her after the witch.

*Well, I'm not sending her back to those horrible men. No matter what happens, I won't do that.*

293

She would take the blind girl with them. There were places in New Orleans that would care for the girl and where she would be safe. Haylee prayed Hooch would be willing to add one more person to the party he was taking to Skunk's.

Hooch stood outside the cave when they broke from the trees.

"I see you picked up the witch while you were out," he said, the corners of his mouth turned down. "That girl is trouble. You shouldn't have brought her."

"Virginia found her," Haylee said. "And when we tried to take her back to the creek, she acted so afraid I didn't have the heart. And she's not a witch. She's someone who is lonely and scared."

Hooch grunted something unintelligible. "Well, let's get her inside before the Stubses find her missing and come looking."

Hooch led the way into the cave. Petweenus lifted her head in that odd way, sensing the change in the environment. Virginia led her to back of the cavern. Sitting together on the floor, Virginia talked to the girl in a low voice, punctuated with an occasional giggle from one or the other.

"I think Virginia's found a friend," Haylee said. She and Hooch sat near the cave entrance on the homemade chairs.

"I imagine both of them could use one," Hooch mused.

"Do you know anything about her?" Haylee asked. "How did she end up with the Stubses? I can't believe she's related to them."

Hooch locked Haylee with his eyes. "She's not a Stub," he said, "She's a Woodard. Not just that, she's part of the reason your mother left. She's your sister."

Hooch's words rocked Haylee with such impact, that she almost tumbled from her seat.

"You and her are twins," Hooch continued, "Your mother had a twin. Hers was born blind and half-crazy, same as Petweenus here. They always are, like I told you before, it's how it works."

"When you helped me and Mother escape, why did you leave my sister behind? Why didn't all of us go?"

"Several reasons," said Hooch. "Firstly, your sister was already with the Stubses. One of their duties is to care for the *oocti,* the one that becomes the wine. Secondly, even though you and your momma was on the run, they still had the girl. She's what's needed to make the Teoctli to keep the colony alive for another cycle. If I helped her escape with the two of you, I would have set things off for sure. By leaving her with the Stubses, I bought you some time. What I didn't count on, was twenty years later, I'd be having to do it again."

Hooch hoisted himself out of his chair. "If you'll excuse me, I need to tend to some stuff. My boys are not back and I'm worried. I got to believe the Stubses forced them to go to ground. Either that, or they ran into a search party and can't get back till the searchers move on. They're skilled in the ways of the forest, but I still worry."

Hooch hesitated at the entrance of the cave.

"I won't be too long," he said, "Keep your eyes and ears open. If dark arrives, and I'm not back, believe the worst. Take the girls and follow the creek. It leads to the highway. You may get lucky and flag a trucker down. They're rare, but it happens." He nodded a goodbye, then disappeared into the trees without glancing back.

\*\*\*

The afternoon passed slowly so much had happen it felt like days had passed. As Haylee mused on the information Hooch provided she watched Virginia and Petweenus pass the homemade doll between them. The blind girl cradled the doll as if it was a baby, cooing softly as she rocked it in her arms. Here was a person capable giving and receiving love, even more reason she couldn't be left behind.

It was late afternoon when Hooch returned, his face grim. Sodom and Gomorrah were still missing.

He brushed past Haylee and strode to the back of the cave where he produced an antique double barrel shotgun and a faded box of shells. Taking the gun to a corner, he broke it down, oiled the various parts, and checked the trigger and hammer mechanism. He finished the job and propped the gun against the wall.

Noticing Haylee looking on, he leveled his gaze at her. "I'm hoping it won't be necessary," he said, "But you never know. One thing is for sure, if they have their ways, you won't be going anywhere except to where they need you. I'm figuring there might be a fight."

"Hooch, why are you doing this?" Haylee asked. "You said yourself, if you succeed in getting us away, you're signing your death sentence."

Hooch chuckled, though his face remained grim. "Oh, they'll be mad all right, madder than a nest of wet hornets. I suspect they'll take me apart bit by bit. Or maybe, they'll hang me on one of those crosses they love so much. Either way, my life won't be worth much."

"So why risk it?" Haylee asked.

"Let's just say, I've had enough," he replied. "I'm tired and ready for it to end."

Though this wasn't an answer, Haylee said nothing more. Instead, she toyed with her own thoughts; the enormity of their situation sinking into her mind like a stone. She realized she now accepted those things Hooch told her as truth. Never mind how preposterous it all sounded, she realized it was true.

She would have to make decisions when she reached New Orleans again. Her sister needed to be cared for, she needed to arrange to send Petweenus to the school for the deaf and blind, and there was Virginia, who also needed to be enrolled in school. She chuckled. For the short time she'd been in

Slaughter County, she had discovered a twin sister and been adopted by Virginia. *Won't Jen be surprised when I get home and she finds out I brought guests.*

*Jen!* She forgot Jen was on her way to rescue her. Paul had taken her cell so she couldn't warn her roommate of the danger waiting for her.

"Hooch, I have a friend that's coming to give me a ride home. At least she was," Haylee waved her arms, "Until all of this happened."

"You're worried about her, right?" Hooch said.

"Yeah, shouldn't I be?"

Hooch tugged at his beard. "I don't know, Darling. Sometimes they let people come and go, pretending they's regular folks living in a regular town. Especially if they think to do otherwise would cause trouble. The colony don't like attention. So maybe they'll just tell your friend you left with so-and-so and that'll be it."

This eased Haylee's angst a little.

"No sense in worrying," Hooch continued, "there's nothing you or me can do about it, anyway. You've got responsibilities now." Hooch nodded to Virginia and the blind girl playing with the doll. "Keeping them safe is gonna be job enough."

She knew he was right. She held the safety of the two girls in her hands and she intended to do everything in her power to see they stayed safe.

Outside, the fiery yellow blaze of sun mellowed into a swollen, red-orange ball. As the light faded, so did Haylee's resolve. Soon, it would be time to make the trek to Skunk's and from there…?

*I have every reason to be afraid. I know who these people are. They're murders and fanatics.* She promised herself she would try to put on a brave face for Virginia.

As night settled, Hooch pulled a large piece of oilcloth from the footlocker and hung it to cover the entrance to the cavern. He then circled the room, trimming the lantern wicks until each glowed with a bright flame.

"Guess you might be hungry," he said, returning to the footlocker. Reaching in, he lifted out several thin cardboard boxes.

"I got these several years ago." he said, "But they's still good. They call 'em MREs. They feed soldiers with 'em. I must have twelve dozen of 'em or more stashed around."

"How did you come by so many?" Haylee asked, feeling the need to talk.

"The army came around one day, tromping through the woods without even a by-your-leave. There must have been three or four truckloads of soldiers. I guess Claude didn't like 'em snooping around. It was just a matter of arming the traps and bam-o, all of 'em was gone. The Stubses hid the trucks in one of the old barns, on their land, but not 'afore me and my boys collected some of the cargo. The MREs was part of what we took."

299

"The Army must have investigated." Haylee said, "That many people can't disappear without setting off a massive search."

"Oh, they came." Hooch said arranging the MRE's into a neat stack. "They even had helicopters flying overhead, but they never found nothing. In the end, we convinced them the trucks had passed us by for somewhere else."

Carrying the MREs to the table, he read off the contents.

"We got Spaghetti and Meat Sauce, Chicken with Rice, and Mexican Chicken. What's your pleasure? The Mexican is good, but spicy."

"Do you like spaghetti, Virginia?" Haylee asked.

"Yeah," Virginia said, "And Petweenus wants spaghetti too."

"Well, that leaves Chicken with Rice for you and the Mexican for me." Hooch said, "Can you live with that?"

Haylee nodded.

Opening the boxes, he slipped each into its heating sleeve, then poured the solution provided with the meal into the plastic bag before setting each aside. Haylee watched as the packages began to smoke. She passed a hand over one and felt heat.

"That's something, ain't it?" Hooch said. "It's done through chemicals. We surely live in a world of wonders. That's the one thing I'll miss when I'm gone."

"You don't have to do this, Hooch," Haylee said, "I mean, risk your own safety for ours."

"We'll set out around midnight," he said, his voice firm. Noting the set of the man's jaw and the seriousness of his gaze, caused her to let any further protest die.

He passed out the meals. Virginia took the one for Petweenus and carried it to the girl. Sitting down beside her, Virginia removed the wrappings and placed the plastic fork supplied with the rations in the girl's hand. Then she guided the girl's hand to the food. Petweenus felt it with her fingers, tossed the fork to the side and began eating using her hands.

Haylee watched the girl gobble the food, leaving a coat of tomato sauce smeared across her chin and cheeks.

*She's starved!*

Haylee took her own meal and sat a few feet away from the others. She felt the need to be alone, to think. She noticed Hooch also sat by himself, chewing slowly, his eyes unfocused. She wondered what he was thinking.

She checked her watch. The dial showed six p.m. which left six hours to kill. Waiting was the hard part. Picking up her tray, she carried it to where Hooch sat in a corner, his face a study of hard lines.

"Do you mind?" she asked, folding her legs, dropping down beside him.

He smiled, "Help yourself."

Haylee glanced at the stone walls surrounding them.

"Can I ask you a question?"

"I reckon," Hooch said.

"Why do you live in a cave?"

"I had a house once." Hooch said, "A nice little cottage with a garden and a white fence to keep the critters out of my vegetables."

"So, why did you give it up?"

"It's a long story," Hooch said.

"I've got time," Haylee laughed. She had lots of time.

"I told you, sometimes the colony lets people what passes through alone." He leveled his gaze at her. "Sometimes they don't. On this occasion two men and a woman stopped at the diner. It turned out later, they'd robbed the bank in Florence that morning, but that's not why Riddle and the Stubses took 'em into the woods. The colony needed human flesh and these varmints were handy. Back then, I was part of things, and being Joseph Slaughter's brother, no one questioned what I had to say. That's when I did a foolish thing. I took the girl for myself. I told Riddle and the others I wanted a housekeeper, but in fact, I wanted what was between her legs.

"You may have noticed, other than Virginia, there are no children in Acedia. That's because the Teoctli does something to a man's insides so all he can produce is monsters. That's how Sodom and Gomorrah came to be."

"The girl's name was Sylvia. I suppose, thinking back now, she was average, but at the time I thought she was the most beautiful creature I'd ever laid eyes upon. I don't know what I was thinking, that I could take an outsider as a wife and all. Anyway, it wasn't long after I moved her in with me that Joseph found out I had the girl and she was pregnant, he waited for her to deliver. I think he wanted to see what kind of creature would be born. She had twins, both boys. I named them Sodom and Gomorrah, later.

"Anyway, she'd no sooner gave birth than he snatched her off the birthing chair and hung her on one of the crosses to die. He left lifeless body for to the crows eat denying her the dignity of a decent burial. He wanted to do the same with my boys, but I took 'em and we hid in the hills. Mildred slipped out at night and brought milk and helped me feed 'em. She still looks after them, God bless her.

"Anyways, like the Stubses, Joseph was no woodsman. He never found my little fort, nor has anyone. I don't expect they ever will.

"What I told you happened twenty years ago. Sunday will be the first time I won't drink the Teoctli for Jublilee. How long I'll live, I don't know, probably not more than a decade, I figure. I just want to be sure my boys will be all right when I'm gone."

"Where did this Teoctli come from?"

"The Indians, they taught Joseph how to make it when he took Petweenus as wife. The same place he learned about the crosses and how to snatch a man's still-beating heart out of his chest. They also taught him to eat human flesh and he brought the custom back to us, mixing it with what we already believed."

"Wait a minute," Haylee said. "Joseph never married Petweenus. He was going to but when he saw her involved with some kind of human sacrifice. He had her killed with the rest of the tribe."

"That's the story that's told to keep people away from the creek, but that's not what happened.

"Joseph did fall in love with Petweenus and the night he was gonna give her the ring, he stumbled on one of their rituals. He watched the rite play out and then questioned Petweenus about what it meant.

"He learned Petweenus's father was the Teopixqui, the one whose seed produced the means to make Teoctli. I told you the Teoctli changes people. If you drink it and then get a woman pregnant, she'll produce monsters and lots of time, die during the labor. The exception is the Teopixqui, who produces only girls and always twins. Because of this, Petweenus and Joseph could never consummate their marriage. They wanted each other passionately and needed a way to change things. Petweenus suggested Joseph become a Teopixqui, then he and she could mate safely. She told her father, Joseph wanted to become the Teopixqui of his own people. Joseph and the chief had discussed religion at length, and the chief respected Joseph as a man of God, a Tlamacazqui.

"The chief agreed to mix the *icoatzin*, the potion that changes a man into a Teopixqui, believing Slaughter intended to mate with one of the women in the colony. This would serve as a witness to the Ilhuicateotl, the great god who gave the Alibamos the sacred wine of eternal life, for it was prophesied one day all men would come to know Ilhuicateotl. What the chief did not know, was what Petweenus planned. That very night after Slaughter left, while her father slept, she placed a serpent in his bed and poked it with a stick so it struck her father several times. The chief woke confused and shocked to find he'd been snake bit.

"Petweenus, assuming the guise of the terrified daughter, ran through the village crying her father had been bitten. The Teoctli had changed him like it does all of us, so the poison caused his body to break down. By morning, the wasting disease had begun to consume him and by nightfall, he passed, his body a blackened shell.

"Petweenus brought Joseph before the tribe and declared him the Teopixqui. The tribe did not accept the news well. Instead, there were whispers Petweenus and Joseph had plotted to kill the chief.

"Several of the Indians called for a rebellion against the chief's daughter. Joseph, fearing for his life and the life of his new bride, had them executed. Others of the tribe stole off in the night until only a few Indians remained. These were

305

absorbed by the colony as brothers and sisters in the new faith Joseph now preached, a religion where men and women were like gods, who never died."

Haylee paused, then locked her eyes on the little man.

"So if you drink the Teoctli, you just keep living? I mean like, forever?"

"As far as I know, you will, unless you get eat by a bear or the like. At least, until Jesus the Savior returns and catches us up."

"Hooch, people must have noticed no one in Acedia grows older. Even if it was just census takers, somebody must have asked questions in the last two hundred years."

"Oh, some did in the beginning. When they came snooping, we made sure they got lost in the woods and were never found. Then, when the first Great War was fought we began to change our names. We had the clerk in the courthouse issue deeds to our new identities, tombstones were placed in the cemetery so's it would look like the colony had grown old and died. We've kept that practice still today."

"Virginia told me there were phony graves in the cemetery. I didn't believe her."

"Well, you needed to. She was speaking the truth." Hooch stretched his arms and opened his mouth in a wide yawn. "I suggest you get some rest. We have a long way to travel and you're gonna need to be rested. You can use the cot if you want."

Virginia was already asleep, curled against Petweenus. The blind girl's hands stroked the younger girl's hair.

*How strange*, Haylee considered, settling into a seated position against the cave wall, that *things should end here, surrounded by madmen and cannibals.*

Pushing the thought aside, she closed her eyes, and let the day's exhaustion carry her away.

*** 

*She found herself in the apartment on Michael Boulevard. The sound of the electric meat grinder whined from the kitchen, which meant her mother was preparing liver mush. The house smelled of it. It embarrassed her to have her few friends over because of the odor.*

*The whining stopped. Her mother peeped through the door.*

*"You're home," she said, stepping though the door, wiping bits of red tissue from her hands on the stained apron. "I was wondering when you'd get here.*

*Haylee stared at the apparition, gazing back at her through calm eyes. Her mother looked young, her skin glowing with health. Though she was forty, she could easily pass for someone in her late teens.*

*"Don't you have a hug for your momma?" the woman asked.*

*Haylee gave her a halfhearted hug. There was no warmth to the embrace; her mother's body felt cold like ice.*

*"Things are going to be different now that you're back," said the woman. "I know I haven't been a good mother to my girl, but I had my reasons. I intend to make up for those years of neglect."*

*As the woman talked, Haylee tried to remember something important. Then it came to her.*

*"Momma," she said, "You're dead. You died a month ago. They burned your body like you wanted."*

*The woman eyes flashed anger. She raised a hand against her. Haylee felt the sting of a slap across her cheek.*

*"Don't ever talk to me like that, Girl," the woman said. She raised her hand again, ready to deliver a second blow. "I won't have it."*

*"You're dead," Haylee said, "I saw your body."*

*Claudette rubbed her face with her hands.*

*"Lies," she said, "It's all lies. I can't be dead," she questioned Haylee, eyes filled with uncertainty and fear, "Can I?"*

*Claudette began to age. Deep crevasses appeared across her forehead her face folded into sagging wrinkles.*

*"You did this," the woman said, her voice fading, "It was all your fault, you killed us all."*

*"No!" Haylee cried, "No."*

\*\*\*

308

Something touched her, snapping her awake. Hooch hovered over her.

"It's okay," he said, "You was only dreaming. You need to get your things together. It's time to go."

Haylee rose to her feet, feeling stiffness in her joints. She flexed her knees and arms. As her head cleared, she saw Hooch carried the shotgun in the crook of his arm. Virginia stood behind him, holding Petweenus's hand.

"If you believe in God, I suggest you pray we'll make it through this alive." he said, "Let's go."

**-16-**
**Betrayed**

Outside, the air felt chilly for this time of year. A mist blanketed the ground. Hooch took everything in with a careful glance.

Facing the group, he spoke in a near whisper. "We'll be passing across Stubs land," he said, "It's an unpleasant place. When we reach it, make no sounds."

He motioned the group forward.

A pale moon floated above the trees, tinting the mist with a greenish glow as the stuff reached toward them like octopi tendrils.

Hooch kept a steady pace and the others followed in total silence. Even Petweenus, prone to noisemaking and incoherent babble, stayed quiet. Hooch positioned Haylee in the rear with himself at the head, sandwiching Petweenus and Virginia safely in the middle.

Hooch led them down the ridge and had them ford the creek in a shallow spot near where Haylee encountered the Stubses. They climbed onto the opposite bank where they were greeted by a wide path. Hooch halted. Facing the group, he placed a finger to his lips.

"We got to be quiet now," Virginia whispered to Petweenus.

The trail passed under a tall archway made of sheet metal and iron rods. Chains with every manner of hook, dangled beneath. The effect was

310

chilling, adding another dimension of ugliness to Woodard's brood.

Further along, they passed cars and trucks, some military, every vehicle wheel-less, rusting away. A cabin stood in the distance where a single light glowed in a window. The stink of burned rubber filled the air. Haylee heard moans drifting on the air. Hooch dropped back and whispered in her ear. "That's the hopeless you hear, crying out to God. Nothing can be done for them, best not to listen."

She wanted to ask him what he meant, but the little man was back in the front again, hurrying them along.

Haylee caught up to Hooch. She tapped his arm and pointed through the trees toward several small fires.

"That's gas fires, they been burning for fifty years or more." Hooch said, "This area is filled with tunnels and mines. Some of them collapsed and some are about to. You need to be careful where you step so you don't fall into one."

The fires became more numerous and Haylee thought she saw broken timbers jutting from the earth, their ragged ends pointing skyward.

Then, she saw the crosses.

They broke out of the woods into a barren place, its perimeter marked by a sagging barbed wire fence. The crosses stood on the other side.

The crosses were of various sizes, some tall, others the height of a man. All of them were weathered with splintered ends. Chains, ending in hooks, dangled from the cross arms. Haylee shuddered at the idea of what the hooks might be for.

Something was attached to two of the largest crosses, though she couldn't tell what from this distance. Hooch saw them and leapt over the barbed wire. He raced ahead, leaving Haylee and the others to catch up.

When he reached the first of the great crosses, he fell to his knees. Head thrown back, he gave a cry of anguish, before attempting to climb it. The cross proved too wide for him to reach around. He was only able to flail his arms and pump his knees.

When Haylee reached him, she saw why he had reacted as he had. Nailed above them was Sodom, and on a nearby cross, hung Gomorrah. Neither was dead. The twins writhed in pain, their mute throats forming silent cries.

"My boys," Hooch sobbed, "I got to help them."

Haylee could only stand beside the little man, helpless. The twins hung high above their heads. Thick spikes jutted from their wrists and feet, securing them to the crosses. It would require a unit with sophisticated rescue equipment to free them.

Suddenly, Petweenus froze. The girl began to twitch. Hooch, on guard, lifted the shotgun, swinging the barrel side to side.

Virginia whimpered.

"What's going on?" Haylee whispered.

Pinpoints of light appeared, growing larger. The lights circled the group.

"A trap," Hooch warned, "We've been betrayed. Scatter!"

Petweenus was the first to break away. Arms extended, she stumbled into the brush. Virginia ran after the blind girl, calling her name. Haylee stood frozen, then chased after Virginia.

She heard shouts behind her and the thunder of Hooch's double barrel.

The gunfire caused Virginia to run faster. Haylee called to her, but the girl continued on, ducking into a pocket of thick brush. Haylee reached the spot where Virginia disappeared when something moved to her right. Beams of light cut through the night. Haylee darted away from the beams, charging blindly through the trees as panic filled her mind. Suddenly, the ground broke away, swallowing her foot, then her leg. She found herself pitching forward before she crashed through something brittle, then she was falling.

\*\*\*

Haylee awoke to sunlight warming her face. Somewhere, she heard the sounds of birds. She opened her eyes and struggled to her feet, surprised to find herself in a tunnel. She saw a patch of blue sky through the ragged hole high above her head. Bits of rotten board lay scattered on the ground. She must have fallen into one of the mines Hooch warned her about. Her head ached. Exploring

313

around the pain, she found a large knot on the back of her head. She fingered it gingerly. Other than the bump, she seemed to be whole.

She brushed the dust off herself, then peered down the tunnel. All she could see was black. Unless she could devise a way to climb out of the hole, which was unlikely, she would have to follow the tunnel shaft to its end. If she was lucky, it would lead to the tunnel's entrance. If not, it could be blocked or take her in the wrong direction. It could also be just one of many shafts that formed some kind of complex network, where she ended up circling around and around, but never got any closer to escaping.

*I could die here and no one would ever know what happened to me.*

She had no idea which direction to go and the thought of feeling her way through the dark terrified her. Anything could be lurking in the blackness. However, not only did the lack of food and water make it unwise to stay where she was, but with the sun up, those looking for her would find her neatly trapped should they stumble upon the exposed shaft.

The last thought spurred her into action. Venturing into the shaft would be scary, but she couldn't wile away the time sitting here. Her pursuers might be scant minutes away.

First, she needed decide which way was out. She thought she knew the direction Hooch's cave lay unless the tumble into the shaft had turned her around. There was no guarantee that direction would lead to the shaft's beginning, but it felt right. Her decision made, all that was left to do was try.

The dark swallowed her like a black embrace, welcoming her into its cold, silent hall. The blackness felt as if it had substance. It filled her with its ugly color, clogging her nose and mouth. Her lungs filled with its dark nature, making it difficult to breathe. It tangled her legs, weighed down her arms and slowed her progress. A feeling of fear and desolation swept over her. She wanted to scream. Faces peered out of dark holes, taunting her like the children did in elementary school. She saw a movement from the corner of her eye.

Lauren Taylor, who'd bullied her in fifth grade blocked her way.

"They have a name for you," the ten-year-old said, her hands playing with her long, blond braids that were tied with blue ribbon to match her school uniform. Haylee glanced down. She was also dressed in a white blouse and blue skirt.

"They call people like you bastards because you don't know who your daddy is."

"Stop it," Haylee cried. The words still cut her the way they did that day on the playground at school. The taunts sent her crying to Mrs. Marshall, who was chaperoning the students that day. Mrs. Marshall took Haylee to the cafeteria and found her some milk and cookies. Haylee spent the rest of recess alone, watching the other children play through the cafeteria windows.

"You're not real," Haylee said. "You can't be. Nobody stays a child. We grow up."

Haylee charged the girl.

"You're still a bastard," Lauren repeated. Then, she vanished.

Haylee leaned against the rough wall of the tunnel, pressing her face against the cold stone. The encounter left her shaken and ashamed. Imagination or not, what Lauren said hurt as much now as it did when she was in elementary school. Several long minutes, perhaps hours passed before she moved again. In the blackness, time ceased.

*This must be what death is like,* she thought, her hand brushing the wall as she pushed on. With each step, she prayed for a speck of light, marking the end of this black journey. As she waded through the blackness, voices whispered to her, reminding her of every failing, every weakness.

"You'll never leave this place," they promised, "You'll die with us, become one of us."

"You're wrong," she told them, "I'm going to find my way out, and when I do, I'll walk in the light where your voices can't reach.

"I will," she whispered, "I know I will."

When she walked into the ladder, she thought she'd gone the wrong way and hit a dead end. She groped the rungs. The ladder was made of wood slats; her fingers traced the nail heads securing the rungs to the vertical posts.

She placed a foot on the lowest rung, and began to climb. Nearing the ladder's end, she saw a thin square of light. She reached up and felt the section outlined in sunshine move. Haylee pushed and it swung up and away. She crawled through the opening.

Rising to her feet, she saw she was in a barn. The smell of hay, mixed with the acrid smell of urine, stung her nose. Though the windows were shuttered, enough light filtered between the gaps in wall to tint the area she stood in gold. Caught up in the moment of freedom after her ordeal in the tunnel, Haylee didn't notice she was not alone in the barn. The pool of light was concentrated on the tiny area where she stood, leaving the back of the barn shrouded in the same blackness as the tunnel.

Needing to know where she was, she crossed to a particularly wide space between the boards of the structure and peeped out. A cabin she thought might be the one they'd passed stood 100 yards away. The horizon was blocked by a line of trees above which stood the ever-present ridges. If she was correct about her position, she could backtrack to the creek and follow it to the highway where she might flag a passing truck. Once safe and away, she would go to the state police and tell what she knew.

A gurgling from a corner of the barn caused her to turn. She inched toward the sound with cautious steps, though part of her screamed to run the other way. Something about the sound demanded investigation. The darkness parted and she saw a cage with something moving behind the

317

heavy gauge wire. A girl with her fingers entwined in the wire looked from the other side. Something about her was familiar.

The girl opened her mouth, attempting to speak but only produced another gurgle. When Haylee pressed forward, recognition struck her with such force she staggered back.

Jen, blood stains on her chin and blouse, stared back. She opened her mouth to reveal the swollen stump of a tongue that was no more. Michael's slumped form lay curled at the back of the cage. The putrid smell told Haylee he was dead.

"Jen!" Haylee cried "My God."

Jen, her fingers still entwined in the wire, rattled the door of the cage. A massive padlock held the door fast.

"I've got to get you out of here." Haylee said. She thought a pry bar might serve to separate the wooden frame of the cage, though the ends were banded with strips of metal. Her mind raced as she scoured the barn for anything that might free Jen.

Pockets of clutter: Frayed rope, hoes and rakes with broken handles, and rusted chain, lay scattered amongst rotted canvas and gunnysacks. Flinging away the rotted cloth, she dug through the heaps of broken garden tools beneath, but there was nothing here she could use.

"I'm going outside," she told Jen. "I might find something out there. I promise I'll be back."

The mute girl nodded.

Haylee walked toward the doors when they opened. A thin woman in a shapeless dress, a bucket dangling from one hand, stepped inside. Haylee shrank into the shadows, holding her breath.

The woman ran her free hand through limp hair, brushing the stray stands from her face. She might have been pretty at one time, but any beauty had faded.

"'Time to slop the pigs, Annie,'" she muttered. "Always, it's 'Annie to do the dirty work. Wipe up this mess, Annie. Cook our supper, Annie'."

Haylee watched from her hiding place as the woman approached the cage.

"Annie's got you some eats," she said. "Good corn mush."

Haylee felt for something to use as a weapon, settling on a short piece of wood that had once been part of an axe handle.

*I'll attack when she opens the cage. She doesn't look like much of a threat. We can lock her in the cage. What if there are others outside?* She would have to take that chance. She wouldn't have another opportunity to free Jen.

Annie put the bucket on the floor and thrust a hand into a pocket of her dress. The woman drew her hand back and frowned, staring off to the side. Haylee followed Annie's gaze, and an icy chill passed through her veins. Haylee forgot to shut the trap door she crawled through.

"Who's here?" asked the woman. "I see'd where you came in through the floor. Might was well come on out." Annie circled the barn as she spoke.

*She's circling to the door to block my way.*

Haylee rushed from the shadows, gripping the makeshift club in one hand.

Unfazed, Annie stood her ground. "Come on girl," she smiled, beckoning with her hand. "Come on and dance with Ol' Annie."

Haylee hesitated, stopped short by the look of anticipation in Annie's eyes.

Annie backed up and kicked the barn door open with her foot.

"Orville, Jasper, I got her trapped in the barn. Come on and get her." Annie yelled.

She blocked the door. "Now, that's a smart girl," Annie cooed. "You just stay right where you are and you won't get hurt.

"You might as well put that little piece of wood down. You ain't going nowhere, no how."

Defeated, Haylee dropped her weapon.

The two men she'd seen with Petweenus slipped past Annie, accompanied by another man the same height as Hooch. He wore dirty jeans, and a stained, flannel shirt. Thin strands of shoulder-length hair hung from beneath a grimy baseball cap.

"That's the last of 'em," the man said, "I expect my money."

"You'll get it, Skunk. The Reeve said to make sure you get everything you're owed."

"What about her?" Annie asked, nodding to Haylee. Should I lock her in the cage?"

"Naw," said Jasper, who appeared to be the one in charge. "The Reeve wants her taken to the cloister. The widows'll see to her. Fetch me some rope. I don't feel like chasing her again."

Orville plucked a soiled bit of rope off the floor, tested it, and moved toward Haylee.

She took a step back.

"Go on and run, little rabbit." He grinned, showing several missing teeth. Jasper slipped behind her and pinned her arms in a bear hug. Orville clasped her wrists together, quickly circling them with the rope.

The two men led her outside where a battered Chevy waited. They forced her into the truck between them. As they drove away, Haylee watched Annie pick up the bucket and walk back into the barn.

## -17-
## Paul

Paul sat on the edge of the bed. He held the ring he'd given Haylee in the palm of his hand. Woodard directed him to keep it for the time being. After a moment, he replaced it in the small box he used to present it to Haylee, remembering how casually she declined the ring. If she'd known its history, she might have reacted differently. She would learn soon enough.

He discovered the colony shortly after he and Haylee met, two years earlier. It was his second year at Tulane.

He'd earned his Master's in Anthropology at the University of Alabama and was accepted in the Tulane doctorate program. As part of the program, he was required to work as a student assistant.

Shortly after he arrived, he began passing himself off as a junior professor. It started as a joke, but he soon realized the masquerade had its perks. It was especially useful for meeting female students. The trick was to only date the girls from the St. Charles Avenue campuses. He used the excuse that the administration frowned on faculty-student dating and he was being cautious.

One of his duties as student assistant was to read the essay assignments by undergraduate students and grade them, freeing the professors who taught the classes from the chore. The essays came from both the Tulane and the St. Charles campuses.

322

Paul discovered he could glean valuable information from the assignments.

Because most of the essays centered on the students' families and customs, he knew which buttons to push should he happen to meet the girl who authored it. When Haylee's paper appeared in the stack, he was taken with the perky, individualized script. There was something about this girl's handwriting he found sexy.

He thought back to where he'd heard the name. His mind retrieved an image of a girl with soft, brown hair and large, brown eyes. She attended a faculty-student mixer with a blonde. The school held one each semester as a way to allow students to meet the faulty in a relaxed setting. The blonde introduced her as a roommate and someone new to the city. Several times during the night, he found himself studying the brunette as she circulated the room from group to group. He'd jotted her name on a piece of paper. Now, he had her essay in his hand.

When he read what she wrote, his eyes widened. The account she gave of her family was not what he expected. Instead of recording blissful memories of cheerful Thanksgivings and happy summers with family and friends, the flowing lines told a story of a childhood spent with an emotionally abusive mother. Haylee knew little of her family except she was born in Slaughter County Alabama, and that her mother had left home at an early age, shortly afterward. Her father's identity remained a mystery and her mother refused to tell her anything about him.

The account was fairly long, spilling over to the backside of the paper. When Paul finished, he had a seed of an idea. Googling Slaughter County, he learned that it occupied the northeastern tip of the state and had the distinction of being the smallest and least populated of Alabama's sixty-seven counties.

What if he paid Slaughter County a visit? By reading the essay, he knew the girl was frustrated that she knew so little about her father. She stated several times, as a child she was teased because of it by the other children.

There was a story here, he was sure. Something he might even be able to sell to one of the networks. Appalachia was a hot topic at the moment. Just the other night one of the networks had done an hour show during prime time on West Virginia high school students and their struggle to escape the poverty that surrounded them after graduation. Here was someone who had escaped but was still a captive of the mountains because of the mystery surrounding her birth. If he could develop this into a story now was the time to cash in. He knew from experience there was always someone willing to talk, some one that knew everyone's business. He only needed to find them. After all one man's misery was another man's fortune.

Paul placed the essay parallel with the computer screen. Checking the atlas, he calculated the distance to be more than six hours by car. Was he really considering driving that distance on the spur of the moment? He realized that was exactly what he planned. If he left now, he could be there by early afternoon. He was free until Monday, so there was nothing keeping him here.

Tossing a few items in an overnight bag, Paul grabbed his laptop. Soon, he was rolling down the road toward Slaughter County.

***

When he reached Slaughter County's borders, he noticed a car behind him. A quick check of his rearview mirror showed bubble lights on the roof. He thought the cop might be dogging him, though he did so at a distance.

The terrain rose and fell. Somewhere on one of the descents, the patrol car vanished. On the next rise, Paul checked his mirror. The road was clear of traffic. He relaxed. Police in small towns and rural counties could be a dangerous nuisance. They often ticketed people for trumped-up infractions.

A few minutes later, a small collection of buildings appeared as he approached a town farther down the road.

A bullet-riddled sign announced he was entering the township of Acedia. Below the town's name was written "Let he who is without sin cast the first stone".

*Well, it fits,* Paul thought. *If you're going to name a town after one of the seven deadly sins, why not make a case against judgment as well?* He

325

laughed. *These hicks are something else. Hardcore religious freaks on Sunday: moonshiners on Monday.*

Moments later, he found himself cruising down the main drag of Acedia, Alabama. Paul slowed the Volvo to better take in the buildings that composed the town. The south side of the street stretched in an unbroken line of buildings, while the north streets right-angled into the distance, creating short blocks. *This place is like a compound with the far side of main street serving as a balustrade.* He read the street names one-by-one as he passed: Lust, Avarice, Greed. Each street named a human failing.

He reached the last buildings before the town dissolved into pasture and wood. A large church and a courthouse stood across from each other, separated by a side street. The street sign read Despair. With no traffic behind him, Paul halted to better study the church. It needed major repairs. He noted missing shingles on the roof and that the steeple leaned dangerously, threatening to topple at any time. Vines crawled up the steps and across the porch where doors that once created a Turkish arch hung at opposite angles on broken hinges. A gap between them exposed the interior. The whole affair created a contrast to the building in good repair on the opposite corner.

As Paul rolled past the church, he caught a glimpse of a churchyard. A sagging chain link fence surrounded tall, marble monuments. He made a sharp turn onto Despair Street and pulled up beside its twisted gate. Graveyards could offer a wealth of information about a place. This one, he thought, should be a gold mine.

He swung the battered gate aside and waded through the high, weed-choked grass. The names on the markers were almost exclusively women, but what caught his attention were the dates. They were staggered about fifty years apart. Taking a seat on the ground, he pulled a notebook from his pocket and began jotting names and dates, when a shadow fell across him. A tall, grim faced man in a khaki uniform, towered over him. A wide brimmed hat cast shadows into the deep crevices of the man's face, creating a sinister effect. Paul gathered his feet under him, and stood.

"Hello, Officer," Paul said. "Is everything all right?"

"It's Sheriff Riddle, and you're trespassing, Son," said the man, nodding at a thin, metal sign tacked to one of the pines among the headstones that read *Private Property Keep Out*.

Paul shoved the note pad into his pocket. "I'm sorry, Sheriff, I don't know how I missed that. I'll leave."

"Well," said Riddle, "I guess I can overlook it this time without giving you a ticket. Go on and finish your business. I'll need you to stop by my office when you're done, though. I need to fill out a report."

"A report?" Paul eyed the lawman in an attempt to discern what the man really wanted.

"That's what I said, Son. My office is right there on the corner. You don't need to knock, just come inside when you're done. Don't think about trying to run out without checking in with me first. There's only one road in and out."

Riddle tipped his hat and walked back to his car. Paul watched it roll slowly down the street, where it parked on the corner.

Paul harbored the uneasy feeling it was Riddle's car he spotted in the rear view mirror on his way into town. For whatever reason, the man shadowed Paul from the time he entered Slaughter County until the sheriff made his presence known moments ago.

He decided it might be wisest to abandon the investigation and leave. Run-ins with rough lawmen in the past taught him to apologize and get out of dodge unless he wanted to find himself in a kangaroo court, robbed of every penny he possessed in trumped up fines.

Paul wanted no trouble. He decided if Riddle intended to fine him, he would pay whatever the amount without argument.

Slipping behind the wheel, Paul steered up the street and parked beside Riddle's patrol car. He strode to the green door set in a red, brick façade, with as much confidence as he could muster. *Never let 'em see you sweat.* The door opened easily and a gust of cool air brushed his face as he stepped into Riddle's office.

Riddle, reclining in an expensive, leather swivel chair, feet propped on a large desk, smiled when he saw Paul.

"Well, good," he said swinging the chair around and lowering his feet to the floor. "Saves me the trouble of tracking you down."

"I don't understand," Paul said.

"You got Louisiana plates on your car," said Riddle. "Why is a fellow from Louisiana so far from home?"

"I'm doing some field research," Paul answered, "I'm an anthropologist."

"Got some I.D., Mr. Anthropologist?" Riddle held out a hand. Paul removed his driver's license and passed it to Riddle.

Riddle looked it over then handed it back.

"Look, Sheriff, I'm sorry if I was someplace I wasn't supposed to be. If it's okay with you, I'd just like to be on my way."

"Well, it might not be that easy," said Riddle, "We don't get many visitors. Those that do visit, many times end up staying."

Paul felt a chill.

"Now, want to tell me why you're here?" Riddle asked, this time leveling his full gaze on Paul.

Paul recounted his position as student assistant and chancing on Haylee's essay. When he finished, he waited, prepared for the worse.

Instead, Riddle smiled. "Son, you may have just saved your life. Come with me. I've got

329

somebody who's going to be very interested in what you told me."

That person was Claude Woodard, and, during the next few hours, he learned about an elixir called *Teoctli* that could keep a man young forever, about the role of *Teopixqui* and Petweenus, but most of all, why a girl named Haylee Woods was so important to it all.

When he left, his head reeled with the wonder of it all, but more importantly, he possessed information that would turn science and the anthropological world on its head. Now, all that was left was to draw a certain fly into the spider's parlor and he was just the one to do it.

Shrugging his musings aside, he rubbed his hands together in anticipation. Only a few days left and it would be finished. Then, he would collect his reward. Hopping to his feet, he headed downstairs to see what Mildred was making for supper. Suddenly, he had developed a voracious appetite.

-18-
## Who's Your Daddy?

Haylee sat on the bed, staring at the unadorned walls. For three days, she'd been held prisoner in the cloisters. She noticed the building with the barred windows behind the church while she was at the cemetery. Now, she knew its name. The cloister consisted of three floors topped with a flat roof. Each floor was accessible by a stairwell. Her room, located on the second floor, contained two windows, both barred. One window looked across Despair Street, Riddle's office, and the jail. The other window looked over Acedia Avenue. She spent her time gazing out this window, counting the cars and trucks that passed. In the three days of her confinement, she only counted five cars.

*Even if I were to escape, the chance of catching a ride out of here is practically impossible. No one comes this way, fortunate for them.*

Several times during the day, women came and went, bringing her meals and ensuring her water pitcher stayed filled. She asked the women about Jen and Virginia, only to be met with silence. Though this infuriated her, it made little difference. No one was talking. Other than the visits for out of necessity, she was alone.

The room was comfortable enough, though scantly furnished, with a large bed (big enough to sleep three) and a small end table that held the pitcher of water. A small mirror hung above the table, though she had no comb, brush, or toiletries to have need of it.

The biggest obstacle was time. She passed the hours doing calisthenics and pacing the room. All the while, her mind sought some way of escape. She also worried about Virginia. What had happened to the girl? She listened whenever she heard voices outside her room, in the hopes one might be Virginia's. She tried not to think about Jen with the black stump of what was left of her tongue, locked in the cage in the barn.

*If only I hadn't let Paul talk me into coming. If I had only listened to Jen.* She could *if only* all day and nothing would change. The question remained what to do now. *I will find Virginia and we will leave this place. That's my goal.*

On the morning of the fourth day, Haylee was greeted by a woman she'd not seen before. The woman, same type of clothing as the others: An ankle length shift, decorated with a simple print pattern over high-top lace up shoes. Like the others, she wore her hair pulled back and twisted into a tight bun. She carried a bundle of white cloth in her arms.

"Good morning," said the woman.

Haylee turned. "You talked," she said.

"Of course," the woman replied.

"But the others, they--"

"The Silent Mothers. They do not speak."

Haylee leveled her gaze at the woman.

"I want out of here. I want to go home. I want Virginia brought to me, and I want to leave."

The woman smiled. "Of course you do, Dear. But sometimes, we don't get want we want. You have a duty, a destiny that must be fulfilled, much like our Blessed Savior had his duty."

"Fuck whatever you're talking about, I have rights."

"Don't be a petulant child. It doesn't become you." The woman carried the bundle to Haylee and began to unfold it. "Isn't this beautiful," she said, "Your mother wore it, and before that, your grandmother."

Despite herself, Haylee watched as the woman unrolled the cloth so it lay across the bed.

"It's a gown." Haylee said.

"A wedding gown, dear. Yours."

"I'm not getting married," Haylee said.

"Oh, but you are. It's an arranged wedding. It was arranged long ago, before you could walk or talk." The woman lifted the gown by the shoulders and held it to Haylee. "I think this will fit you fine. I'll make the final alterations tomorrow morning."

The woman scooped up the dress and disappeared out the door. She closed the door behind her and slid the bolt back into place.

\*\*\*

Woodard and Cynthie made their appearances early afternoon. Woodard had shed his customary jeans and work shirt for a dressy, starched white shirt, adorned with gold cufflinks and black sharply-creased pants. He wore wingtip shoes and his hair smelled of cream. He looked more vital than Haylee had ever seen him. Cynthie wore a sleeveless, knee-length print dress. She stayed by the door as Woodard strode into the room.

Haylee scowled when she saw them. "What do you want?"

"Why, I just came to check on my girl, that's all. Can't a grandfather check to see his grandchild is being treated properly?"

"Locking me away is treating me properly? As far as I'm concerned, you can go to hell."

"I declare," Woodard laughed. "If looks could kill I reckon I'd be lying dead on the floor right now."

"I want to see Virginia and my sister." Haylee demanded.

"What makes you think they're here?" Woodard asked, a smile playing around his lips.

"Don't play games with me," Haylee said, "You're holding them somewhere."

"The fact is, Petweenus ain't here," Woodard said, "She's back with the Stubses."

"And Virginia? I swear if you've harmed her, I'll--"

Before she could finish, Woodard crossed the room with surprising speed. Snatching Haylee by the hair, he jerked her head back, leaning over her, his face so close, it filled her vision.

"You'll what, little girl? Fact is, you won't do shit. You ain't got no power a'tall. You'll do as you're told."

He slung her backwards, nearly knocking her off the bed. Haylee sprang back, pushing herself erect with her arms.

"You can bully me all you want, old man. You can keep me locked away, but you can't make me follow you."

"No? Why, I think I can. Cynthie, have Virginia brought in here."

Cynthie grinned in a way that made Haylee shiver. She slipped into the hall, returning with Virginia, who was dressed in a white gown. Two men Haylee recognized from the church service, followed behind them.

One man kept his hand on Virginia's shoulder. The other handed Woodard a small, coffin-shaped box.

Woodard handed the box to Haylee.

"It's a little present," he said, "Open it."

Haylee fumbled with the tiny latch before lifting the lid. Inside, was a child's freshly-severed finger.

She gaped at Virginia, terrified by what she saw. The man standing beside Virginia held up the girl's left hand. It was wrapped in a blood-soaked bandage.

"You monster!" Haylee whispered.

"That's for the stunt the other day," said Woodard, "for that chase through the woods. Now,

Ronald Polizzi

here's the deal: You do as you're told and Virginia don't lose no more fingers. But hear me good, you get out of line even once and next time, I take two. And after that, I take the whole hand and so on until she's nothing but a stump."

"What do you want?" Haylee cried.

"Same thing as I've always wanted: You to take your dutiful place and bear a child. I know it's a hard pill to swallow," he said. "Claudette did you no favor, taking you from here into the world. But as fancy and exciting as that kind of life may seem, its end is death, while ours is life eternal."

"So, who beds me? Do you draw straws and the short straw wins, or roll dice? No wait! It's you, isn't it? You're going to be the father of the baby because you're Joseph Slaughter. You bedded my mother, your own daughter, didn't you? That makes you my father. It's like Hooch said, you're the only one allowed to have sex, so you screw all the girls." She dragged her hand down her face. "Oh God, that's why Mother would never tell me. She was ashamed to admit her father had sex with her and I was the result."

"Quiet, Child," Woodard warned. "There's some things not discussed in this holy place."

"Holy!" Haylee felt the blood rise in her cheeks. "There's nothing holy here. How many of these women have you had sex with?"

"Be careful," Woodard warned, "Or I'll have your tongue."

Haylee's anger boiled over.

336

"Go on, cut it out, Grandfather, or I guess I should say Daddy. Do me like you did Jen. I'll make it easy for you." She stuck out her tongue.

"Girl, I'm warning you for the last time."

"What's wrong?" Haylee cried, "It's not appetizing enough for you? I thought you liked the taste of human flesh."

"Silence!" the old man cried. "Or it won't be your tongue I take, but hers." He snatched Virginia by the arm and shoved her at Haylee. "One more blasphemous utterance and I take not only a tongue, but two fingers this time!"

Haylee bit back a reply. She turned her back to Woodard.

"Turn around, Girl, and face me," he said in a cold, hard voice. Haylee turned slowly, tensing herself so she wouldn't tremble. "We eat flesh because the Lord commands it. It's in the Book, plain for anyone to see. If I am anything, I am the Lord's servant, as are all here. I'll not let a child, one who grew up in perdition, judge my actions. Tomorrow is the wedding. You will clean both your body and your mind so you may stand in the presence of the Lord as a presentable vessel, of which no one need be ashamed. You will do all that Hazel directs you to do without complaint and to the fullest of your ability, else the child pays for the transgression. Understand?"

Haylee nodded, her face hard.

"Good," Woodard said.

He turned and left. The men followed him with Virginia between them.

Cynthie was the last to go.

"Best watch your mouth, Cousin," Cynthie said, "Unless you want to end up like the Silent Mothers."

"What do you mean?" Haylee asked.

"They don't talk cause they can't. It's hard to talk when your vocal cords been slit." She drew a finger across her throat.

Haylee could still hear Cynthie's insane cackle through the closed door. She was grateful when it faded down the hall.

Left alone, Haylee propped her elbows on her knees and cradled her head in her hands. She looked at the heavy bars fixed to the windows and the stout door made of hardwood that was bolted securely from the outside.

Rising, she walked to the window where she gazed across Acedia Avenue to the distant ridges and freedom. They looked back mockingly.

*You'll die here,* they whispered.

"Screw you," she muttered under her breath.

Hot tears spilled down her cheeks. She dropped onto the bed and clasped her hands behind her head. Lying on her back she stared at the ceiling.

"I'll never stop trying until I get out of here," she promised to herself. "I'll never stop until I win."

She repeated the words until she fell into a dreamless sleep. She awoke to a plethora of clangs and knocks, accompanied by voices. The door swung wide and the woman who had shown her the wedding dress came in, beaming a smile bright as the sunlight that was streaming through the barred windows.

"I brought you some breakfast," the woman said, carrying a tray with a bowl of steaming hot stew and a glass of cold milk.

"You can call me Hazel," she said, placing the tray on the small table. The stew's aroma filled the room. "I've been assigned to look after you."

Hazel waited a moment, an expectant look on her face, and a benign smile playing across her lips. When Haylee made no move toward the food, Hazel retreated to the door.

"Eat up," she said, her hand on the doorknob. "It'll be a long day and you'll need your strength."

She closed the door and threw the bolt.

Haylee circled the tray, expecting to find bits of human flesh floating on the surface of the stew. Lifting the spoon, she stirred the stew's contents. Vegetables with chunks of chicken bobbed to the top. Relieved to find nothing taboo, she devoured the meal. After she finished, she felt better, her resolve to escape renewed.

There was a knock on the door and Hazel entered again, followed by two men lugging a large, copper tub. They placed the tub in center of the room and left. Moments later, roughly a dozen women, each with a steaming bucket of water, began filling the tub.

Hazel took a basket from one of the women and tipped it over the tub. Rose petals spilled out into the water, filling the room with their scent.

"Get yourself cleaned up," Hazel ordered, "I'll be back in a half hour."

Haylee waited until she heard the lock snap into place to slip out of her jeans. The warm, soapy water transported her to a place where her mind felt at peace for the first time since Jen's call. She was still soaking when she heard the click of the bolt being retracted. The door opened and Hazel walked in carrying more clothes.

"Time to get ready," said the woman in a singsong voice. She placed the silky bundle on the bed. "I brought you clean underclothes. When Haylee didn't move, Hazel frowned. "The bath's over," she said.

"Are you going to stand there watching?" Haylee asked.

"Better me than the Stubses. Best hurry. Those boys don't know the meaning of patience."

"Would you at least turn your back?"

"How 'bout this," said the woman, taking a large bath towel and stretching her arms out so the towel blocked her view of the tub.

Haylee climbed out of the tub, her feet making a wet, slapping sound on the wood floor.

She took the towel from Hazel and wrapped it around herself.

"There's clean underclothes and a shift," Hazel said. "If you're embarrassed to dress in front of me, do it quick while I'm gone. But don't dally. I'll be back in a jiffy."

When Hazel left, Haylee sorted through the things on the bed. There was a pair of granny underpants, a plain, white bra and a shapeless cotton garment that reminded her of a nightgown. Though the style was foreign, the clothes were clean and a nice change from her own soiled things.

She was dressed and waiting when Hazel returned. This time, the woman carried a glass of milk.

"Nice and warm," she said, handing it to Haylee.

"Thank you, but I'm not thirsty," Haylee said.

"I'd drink it and be thankful for it," Hazel said, "The Reeve's orders. You don't want that little girl hurt."

Haylee sniffed the liquid. A nutty substance hovered around the rim.

"This is something besides milk," she told Hazel.

"Yes, there's a little something else in there, but it ain't poison or nothing like that, just something to help you relax. You ain't the first to get it, they all do."

Haylee put the glass to her lips and sipped. She found the taste bearable enough. She downed the contents and passed the glass to Hazel.

"I'll be back later with your dress," Hazel said.

Watching Hazel leave, Haylee felt the room shift. She felt very tired.

*It's whatever they put in the milk.* She stumbled to the bed. The world faded away just as her head hit the pillow.

She was shaken awake by one of the Silent Mothers. The mute woman motioned her to sit up. Another woman stood to the side with the wedding gown draped over her arms.

"Time to get ready," Hazel said. Hazel took the dress and held it against Haylee so it hung to its full length. "I worked on it most of the night," Hazel said, "so it would be perfect for you. It ain't every day a girl gets married. Oh, it will be a lovely, lovely day." Hazel mused. "I just love weddings. They come so seldom, you know, with no young people around. Perhaps, you'll be the one to change things, to mend the rift. One can only hope."

"Change things how?" Haylee asked. The Silent Mothers helped her to her feet. She swayed, still feeling the effect of the drug.

"No one's told you?" Hazel asked.

"No one's told me much of anything," Haylee said, fighting to keep her balance.

"There is a prophecy that one day a male child will be born and not the girl twins as has always been the case. He will sacrifice himself so we will no longer need the Teoctli, but eternal life will be ours. It will be then that we will convert the world and will rule as the 144,000."

Haylee laughed. "Hundred forty-four thousand? I doubt there are more than a hundred people in Acedia if that many."

"The promised one will heal us. We women will bear children again. The men's seed will again be without taint. It will be a glorious day, and you may be the one. Father Joseph believes you will be. But enough talk, I've got to get you ready."

Hazel helped her into the dress, fastening the tiny hooks in the back. She stepped back to look at her handiwork.

"Ain't you a sight, pretty as a picture. It was wrong for your momma to run like she did, but God's plan goes forward. You're back, just as you never left. " Haylee sat in a straight back chair while Hazel brushed her hair until it fell over her shoulders. "It's best you don't fight any of this. Just do as Father Joseph directs and it'll go well for you. All of them went through it and came out fine. God takes care of his children."

A silent mother brought the veil. Hazel pinned it in place, then took Haylee by the hand.

"Come on," she said, pulling Haylee to her feet. "Are you feeling all right?"

"I'm still dizzy from that drink," Haylee admitted.

Ronald Polizzi

"You'll be fine." Hazel led her to the door. "They're waiting for us."

Hazel held Haylee's hand, leading her like a little girl. Behind her, she heard the thud of the boots of the ever present Stubses who were never far away.

When they reached the bottom floor, Hazel threaded a maze of hallways to a set of stairs Haylee thought led to a basement. As they descended, the fear she'd experienced in the tunnel took hold of her and she began to shake.

"There ain't nothing to fear, Honey," Hazel said, feeling the girl's tremors. "We're taking a shortcut, nothing more."

At the bottom of the stairs, Haylee was relieved to see the glow of lanterns lighting a long corridor. A second set of stairs angled up at its end.

"This leads to the church," said Hazel. "It's bad luck for anyone to see the bride before the ceremony, so we take one of the old tunnels. There's I guess a dozen of 'em scattered around since the Indian days. Back then they hid the women and children in them when there was an attack. This one is still used."

The far stairway opened onto a narrow hall. Exposed studs lined the walls. Haylee realized they were between the walls of the church. Hazel worked her way to a section of wall she pressed with her hand. A panel swung open to a study furnished with a desk and a shelf of books. The woman pointed to a door.

"We go through there," she said.

Hazel pushed Haylee ahead, forcing her to lift the hem of her dress so she didn't trip. Haylee reached the door, and stopped. Her mind, pushing away the fog created by the drugged milk, flashed a warning.

*Run before it's too late.* She was here in the bridal gown just as she should be. This was why she'd been conceived and this was how it was supposed to end.

She turned the knob and walked through the door onto the raised platform where Boone preached and the sour-faced man played his fiddle. What waited for her beyond surprised her.

At first, she thought it was simply a trick of the shadows. Tiny pinpoints of light offered a scant bit of illumination. Thick cloth that still covered the walls and ceiling drank up most of the light, resulting in deep pockets of darkness.

Monstrous faces, grim with crooked noses, down-turned mouths and narrow eyes, peered through the blackness. They filled the pews and spilled across the back of the sanctuary, clothed in dark robes. Each person held a pencil-thin candle. More monsters stood grouped in a corner at the edge of the platform. Haylee shrank back until she realized the grotesque faces were masks, ugly caricatures in the style of Hieronymus Bosch. Hazel came up behind her and guided her to the center of the stage, where she positioned Haylee with her

345

back to the crowd. Behind her, a cheer rose, filling the sanctuary with a roar.

One of the masked figures stepped forward and faced Haylee from a distance. Another moved to stand beside her. The other two stood to either side.

Haylee studied the hooded figure that faced her. The mask it wore was twisted in an ambiguous expression.

*Was it smiling or frowning?*

"We are gathered here tonight in the presence of the Four Faces to declare the combining of *Teopixqui* and *Cihuatl* in sacred union as decreed by the All Father *Ilhuicateotl.*"

The figure finished speaking and nodded to the masked figure next to Haylee.

"And Adam gave names to all cattle," said the second one, his voice like the first, making it impossible to identify. "And to the fowl of the air, and to every beast of the field; but for Adam there was not found a help mate for him. And the Lord God caused a deep sleep to fall upon Adam, and as he slept: he took one of his ribs, and closed up the flesh instead thereof; And the rib, which the Lord God had taken from man, made he a woman, and brought her unto the man. And Adam said, This is now bone of my bones and flesh of my flesh: she shall be called Woman, because she was taken out of Man."

The words dissolved into meaningless waves of sound as the drug overcame her. Haylee

346

drifted in a sea of bliss under a colorless sky. In the distance, tiny stars twinkled.

*But it's not night, so why do I see stars?* A gentle wind carried her along. *The wind is chanting like a hundred voices.* She listened to hear what the wind was saying, but didn't recognize the words.

Haylee continued to drift when something tugged at her, something sought to pull her from her beloved sea. She fought, resisting this new current, but it persisted.

*Someone is tugging my hand.*

The sea faded, and with it, the blissfulness. She watched the ocean dissolve into the church sanctuary and the stars shrink to simple candle flames. The figure nearest her held her hand, spreading her fingers. He slipped a ring on Haylee's finger.

"Don't go throwing it away again, Girl," the muffled voice warned, "It stays on your finger, where I put it."

She was unsure if the voice was Woodard's, Boone's, or someone else's. Haylee glanced at the ring. It was the one she'd thrown at Paul.

A cup was thrust at her, pressed to her lips.

"Drink," whispered the voice. The hand holding the cup tilted it so liquid seeped between her lips. The bitter taste made her shiver.

"A little more, Darlin'," coaxed the voice, forcing more of the bitter stuff into her mouth.

"The union is complete," said the masked figure standing behind the pulpit, "The seed will continue."

The crowd shouted its approval at the words.

Haylee's mouth felt dry from the potion. Her head swam. Already dizzy from the milk, she had moments when she wasn't sure where she was. A vaguely familiar face peered at her. It took all her concentration to remember that the face belonged to Hazel.

"We're going to the fires now," said the woman. "We'll be there a while. That's where the real ceremony happens."

The woman took Haylee's hand and led her off the stage and past the now empty pews. Somehow the people had disappeared, along with the masked men.

Outside, the cool air eased the effects of the drugs. Haylee spotted Woodard's big Packard. A bearded man Haylee thought might be a Stubs, stood by the open rear door. Hazel steered them to the car and nudged Haylee inside, sliding onto the large bench seat beside her.

"What happens now?" Haylee asked.

Hazel smiled, "Why, darling, we drink the drink of life."

**-19-**
**Sacrament**

One of the bearded men drove the Packard. Woodard's absence only grazed Haylee's awareness. Hazel kept whatever thoughts she had to herself and Haylee did not press her with questions. The drink they'd given her dissolved her will. She rode along, content to allow the others to do with her what they would.

Even so, a small part of her remained untouched, watching from afar. Though its muted voice could not be heard with any clarity, this small part of her watched and waited. It noted they were traveling in a caravan. Headlights shown through the back window and cast her shadow across the ceiling of the Packard. Through the windshield, she counted a dozen taillights ahead. Together, they created a ribbon of light, threading its way through the night. The cars rolled along in somber fashion. *It's like a funeral procession,* the part of Haylee's mind that thought and feared, said. She passed time by peering out the window. Even in the dark, she could see the now-familiar live oaks and tall cedars marking the track that served as a drive to Woodard's Victorian.

She fully expected the caravan to slow and turn between the cedars. Instead, they plodded along past the drive and on to where the road angled down. At the foot of the ridge, they crossed a bridge constructed of crossties and logs. Here, they slowed.

Haylee watched as the cars ahead turned off the highway one by one. Moments later, the Packard turned off the smooth asphalt and bumped onto a rutted track badly in need of grading, and was bordered on both sides by high, clay walls. The car kicked and bucked along the track to end its journey in a barren field amongst the cars and trucks that had already arrived.

The figures exiting the vehicles still wore their robes and masks. Hazel led Haylee after the maskers into the field.

Haylee recognized the place immediately. The crosses were as she remembered them, stretching into the distance. Three of the largest crosses were marked by a ring of stones. A crude, four-foot pyramid, made of stones of various sizes, stood before the center cross. Four tall stacks of wood, arranged in a square, stood outside the stone circle. The congregation circled the wood piles. Some stood, others sat on the ground. The murmur of voices in casual conversation drifted in the air.

A robed figure, the man that officiated the union ceremony, stepped into the circle, positioning himself in front of the center cross. The figure raised his hands, hushing the crowd.

"We are blessed once again to celebrate the year of Jubilee. The old fires are extinguished and the new fire brought to life. As it burns, so do the fires of our hearts.

"Fire is the element given to man from the great one, Huitzilopochtli, who gave his life to become the sun. Because of this, the great fiery sphere rises each day and warms the Earth. Tonight, we rekindle the sacred flame so Huitzilopochtli will hear the pleas of his people and remember us once more. Our cries wake him. Our shouts cause him to climb the heavenly stairway each day. Therefore, we must be faithful to invoke him in the true way taught in the book and passed to us from the first *tlamacazqui*.

"Two truths, two nations, one of blood, the other of fire, joined together. Blood of the lost tribe come to America wearing skins of red. Fire come to America wearing skins of white and the branch grafted onto the true vine.

"God put our feet on the path that led us from our native state in the high mountains to the green paradise of these hills, for we are the chosen who cannot die. Why, you ask? Because it is God's will that we bring the word to the world and through the power of the teoctli, the wine of eternal life, we shall rule forever.

"Today, the prodigal child was returned to us and the union was performed. As I stand here in the name of Jehovah *Huitzilopochtli*, I proclaim this will be the time the one awaited will be born, the horned child of promise."

"How can you know?" cried someone from the crowd.

"I heard the words in prayer," said the masked one "The voice of God, *Ilhuicateotl*. And the voice said what was lost will be returned and she shall bear he for whom the people long. Brothers and Sisters, I believe it."

The crowd broke into excited chatter until the masked voice stilled them.

"We must sacrifice to gain *Ilhuicateotl's* attention. Only blood speaks strongly enough to be heard by Jehovah's ear. When Cain slew Abel, He heard. When Isaac slew the ram, He heard faintly, but when the sons and daughters were offered, He heard and spoke to the people. Even the last prophet, Jesus, found he must slay himself upon a cross in order to gain the attention of the most high. And so, we too use crosses, for they are the means to perfect sacrifice."

The sound of a drum, a soft, slow tapping at first, building into a loud sharp staccato, punctuated the night. A second drum joined the first with a counter rhythm. The figure by the cross moved in time with the drums. Bobbing and bowing, he weaved, graceful as any dancer. The crowd parted on the opposite side of the circle. Four men waded through those seated, carrying the limp figure of Petweenus between them. They carried their charge to the pyramid of stones and placed her body so her back was centered on the apex. While two men held her in place, the other two fastened her arms and legs to four thick stakes driven in the ground so that her body was locked into the unnatural position. Petweenus remained motionless, though her weight, supported on a single point--her back bent nearly in half--must have caused unbearable pain.

*I'm witnessing my sister's torture. Why am I so calm about it? And why isn't she fighting back? Because they drugged her like they did me.* The small bit of mind unaffected by the drugs whispered. *I could be tied to that rock and I wouldn't bat an eye.*

The drums beat faster now. Another dancer, a naked woman, appeared out of nowhere. Her long hair whipped as she swung her head, her hips rocking back and forth with sexual abandon. At first, she was only a movement in the shadows. She edged closer, spinning around, her arms raised above her head as if she was rejoicing just to be alive. There was an energy about the woman that charged the air. Something glinted in her right hand, black and jagged. Haylee forced herself to shake off some of the drug-induced stupor to focus on the object.

The dancer moved closer and Haylee saw the woman's face. Their eyes locked and a jolt shot through Haylee, momentarily parting the fog clouding her mind. The naked dancer was Jen. Her face was expressionless. Only her eyes burned with a terrible fierceness. The object she held was a blade made of what might have been polished black glass, though Haylee thought it might be some type of black rock. She opened her mouth to call to her friend, when Jen made another pirouette and Haylee made a shocking discovery. A three inch gap ran the length of Jen's backbone from her neck to her buttocks. The edges were bloody and ragged, and heavy, black stitches held the two halves together.

*That's not Jen. Someone is wearing her skin. I can see where they sewed it around themselves.* Nausea swept over her and she stumbled.

"Easy," Hazel whispered, turning the girl so Haylee faced away from the monster that was once her friend. "Take a breath. We've a little ways to go yet."

When Haylee did manage to face the goings-on again, a large cauldron rested near Petweenus. Two more men, each holding a torch, stood beside it.

The drums stopped. A woman wearing a mask that depicted a grinning cat placed a bundle of twigs on Peteewnus's naked chest, wedging them between her small breasts.

The masked figure raised his hands. His voice rang out as he slowly turned, his eyes scanning the entire circle of people. "It is time to light the new fire, the God fire that burns two score and ten plus two."

A torchbearer stepped forward and lit the small stack of wood on Petweenus's chest. The twigs caught, flames exploding with a crackle. The air filled with the stink of burnt flesh. The second man extinguished his torch, then jabbed it into Petweenus's burning body until it caught. He carried the torch to the first of the four stacks of wood placed around the circle and set it ablaze. He moved to the second, and third, lighting each one.

When he reached the fourth, he paused as Jen's imposter raised its knife. As the last stack of wood caught fire, the stone knife came down, slicing across Petweenus's abdomen. Then, the imposter shoved its hand into the gash and ripped out the girl's still- beating heart. As it raised the heart in triumph, the congregation broke into a cheer. A dozen members of the group produced butcher knives. Rushing forward, they swarmed on the dead girl. It only took a moment to hack the blind girl smoldering body to pieces. As each section of her body was cut free, it was tossed into the cauldron.

A dark pool stained the low pyramid and the ground around it. Steam drifted upward from the cauldron while its grisly contents bubbled merrily.

The horror continued. Haylee recognized the screams even before she saw Paul dragged across the field by two burly men. Unlike Petweenus, he was not given the benefit of being drugged before his hands and feet were staked to the ground and his back bent to the point of breaking.

"Where's Woodard?" he cried, "You can't do this. Woodard promised I'd be given the *teoctli* for bringing you the girl."

"You were promised eternal life," said the mask with the twisted mouth. "And that will be granted. Those who give themselves in sacrifice, live forever with Huitzilopochtli. Be safe on your journey."

The stone knife plunged into Paul's abdomen, ripping it open. Paul began a scream that became a gurgle as his heart was ripped away. After they removed Paul's body, Hooch was led to the little pyramid. Other than drawing a single, sharp breath when the pointed stone bit into his back, Hooch made no sound as they forced him over the pyramid. Like Paul's his body was carried away to hang on the cross.

The man Haylee recognized as Skunk came next. *So this is his reward for betraying Hooch,* she thought, watching the knife do its job, *the same as Paul's.* A parade of men and women she thought might have had the bad luck to wander into Acedia by mistake, followed. Now, the ground was a bloody carpet of dark mud, stinking of copper and death.

Haylee let the drugs carry her away. Her surroundings melted into a dreamscape and she watched from a faraway place. Some time during the night's atrocities, after the last of the blood sacrifices were done, she heard music. Flutelike sounds mixed with what might have been a harp, wafted to her ears. The pleasing sounds were in stark contrast to the hacked bodies dangling from the crosses. Someone took her hand and led her into a dance. Whoever her partner was, he was graceful. He glided her around and around, all the while whispering suggestively to her words that were both vile and shocking.

When the dance was over he bowed, then slipped into the crowd. Figures moved around her.

Someone passed her a silver cup that smelled of blood. She passed it on, declining to drink.

The fires, exhausted to hot coals, flickered in the waning dark. The congregants trickled toward their cars and trucks. Hazel and Haylee returned to the black Packard. Haylee kept her eyes forward, lest they graze the grisly scene behind them. She felt exhausted and dozed several times on the way back to the Cloister, dark nightmarish images stalking her dreams.

She slept though the next day. Even the troubling dreams that pricked her mind like needles could not rouse her. The second day after the ritual slayings, the Silent Mothers shook her awake.

Moving without speaking, they set the small table where they set a breakfast of sausage, eggs and biscuits, accompanied by a steaming mug of coffee. Then they filed out, leaving her alone.

Haylee devoured the eggs and biscuits, though she could not bring herself to touch the sausage. Images of the congregants conversing casually with each other as they nibbled chunks of flesh ladled from the large cauldron turned her stomach.

*I'll never eat meat again.*

After she finished breakfast, she sat on the bed facing the window that looked out over the ridges. Hawks circled lazily above the pines, gliding on wind currents. She imagined herself circling with them, free from her confines and the horror her life had become.

357

A rap on the door caused her to turn. The men that brought the large copper tub before, returned with it again. Like before, several women with buckets of steaming water followed and filled it. A young woman carried towels and fresh clothing and placed them on the small table after removing her breakfast. She followed the others out, locking the door behind her.

Haylee shed her old clothes and settled into the warm water. The Mothers left soap and she lathered her body until her skin burned. After her bath, she donned the long, shapeless shift and soft slippers. Then, she sat on the bed and resumed watching the hawks.

With her world reduced to a single room, even the hawks failed to amuse her after a time and she took to her bed. She left her meals untouched, not bothering to bathe when they brought the tub. Filled with despair, she felt the last remnants of hope begin to fade. She waited for death to rescue her.

She could not say how many days or weeks passed when Woodard walked through her door. Had she not recognized his voice he might have been a stranger, he was so changed.

"Well, you're a mess, ain't you?" he said.

At the sound of his voice, she turned to face him.

He stood tall, his once sunken cheeks now full and glowing with health. His hair was full and black.

A young woman stood by his side. Haylee was taken by her striking good looks.

"Howdy, Cousin," said the woman. The voice was Cynthie's. "Surprised?"

"You got to forgive Cynthie, she gets stuck on herself after the change," Woodard said, "You'd think after…how old are you, Darling?"

Cynthie laughed, "Grandfather you know a girl never tells her age."

"You're too young to be one of them," Haylee said.

"That's where you're wrong," Woodard said, "True, Cynthie was just a girl of twelve when she took the sacrament, but she was one of twenty or so children that made the trip from Virginia. She was the only one to survive the trip. Fever and disease got the others. Truth be told, I think she was a little jealous of you, wasn't you, Cynthie."

"I'll get my chance, Grandfather."

"It's my job to see that's not necessary by making sure this un' does her duty." Woodard chided, "Now, how 'bout giving us some privacy? I need to talk to this one alone."

Cynthie strutted to the door with an exaggerated swing of her hips. Woodard followed and closed the door, then he returned to Haylee.

"You need to haul your ass out of that bed. You been poutin' long enough. It needs to stop."

Haylee said nothing; she laid her head on the pillow and gazed at the gray ceiling.

"You need to get yourself fixed up," he said.

"Why?" Haylee asked.

"Cause it's time to consummate our marriage."

"Oh, is that what you want? Why didn't you say so."

Haylee tossed the covers aside and spread her legs. She tugged the shift up, exposing her thighs.

"What are you waiting for, Grandfather? I promise I won't fight you. Have your way with me."

Woodard's mouth twisted into a snarl, his hands clenched into fists. "Girl, I warned you about your blaspheming."

He took an angry step forward and jerked the shift back down so Haylee was covered. For a moment, he looked as if he was going to strike her. Then his hands relaxed.

"Remember the child," he said, "I'm gonna have a bath brought for you and a change of clothes. I expect you to wash. Then we'll get these bed sheets changed. You'll cooperate or the next time you see Virginia, she'll lacking an eye."

"You're a fucking monster, and I hate you."

"Hate me as you will. It makes no matter as long as you do as you're told." Woodard said. He turned on his heel and left.

***

He came during the night, after she extinguished the lantern (there was no electricity in the Cloister). Earlier, she'd bathed and dusted herself with the powder the Silent Mothers brought, along with a clean shift for her to change into. She wore no underclothes because they hadn't brought her any. It mattered little to her that they didn't.

She felt his presence before she saw him. Opening her eyes, but lying still to not show she was awake, she studied his silhouette. He appeared little more than a dark spot in a larger darkness. She thought he might be studying her he stood so still. She'd wondered how she would react when the time came, playing out scenarios in her mind.

In one, he came to her with kisses, his hands caressing her, exciting her as he mounted her. In another, he brought flowers and they initiated the act together. In all of her imaginings, she carefully hid her grandfather's face; the idea of her grandfather, also her father, having sex with her, was too repulsive to contemplate. In none of the scenarios did he come in the dark and stare. She dared not move, preferring him to think she still slept. She could only make out his form vaguely. Could he see her any clearer? She doubted he could in the pitch black room.

As he moved closer, she closed her eyes pretending to be asleep, She judged his approach by the sound of his boots on the floor. Soon he was close enough she could hear his rapid breathing accompanied by a rhythmic chant. She concentrated, the better to decipher what he said.

*"Nimitznotlatlauhtilia...onmochihuaz...ticm ochihuiliz,"*

*"Nimitznotlatlauhtilia...onmochihuaz...ticm ochihuiliz,"*

*"Nimitznotlatlauhtilia...onmochihuaz...ticm ochihuiliz."*

A rough hand snatched the covers away, allowing the night chill to sweep over her. She was shoved on her back while an arm snaked under her gown. Fingers probed her private parts. These weren't the explorations of a lover. They were hands seeking information about her body.

"You ain't no virgin." The voice carried the same muffled quality she heard in the church. Of course, he was masked again.

The fingers probed deeper.

"But you ain't been used all that much."

She squeezed her eyelids tight as he lifted her gown. In a moment, he mounted her, guiding his member inside her in an easy motion. His thrusts were deep and rhythmic. And then he was done. She heard his footsteps recede, then the click of the door closing behind him. She was out of bed before the bolt was thrown. Hiking up her gown, she squatted over the chamber pot so the seed he put in her might drain back out. She heard other girls say pregnancies could be prevented this way. She prayed they were right.

Three more night visits marked the next two weeks. Each time he left, she squatted over the chamber pot until she was sure she'd undone the foul deed put into her.

When she missed her period, she tried not to panic, telling herself she'd been late before and there was nothing to worry about, but days turned into weeks, then another month passed. She'd grown used to her confinement, though it took a toll on her mind. She whiled away her time holding conversations with imaginary visitors, including Jen's ghost. They talked about all sorts of things and nothing at all.

"I'm having a baby," she told Jen one day. Jen nodded her understanding. She never spoke. Haylee thought it was because the Stubses cut out her tongue.

"It's supposed to be twins, but it feels like just one. Grandfather put it in me."

Jen crossed the room and put a sympathetic arm over her friend's shoulder, then Haylee began to cry.

***

Woodard sat in the straight-backed chair across from where Haylee perched on the bed staring blankly at the wall.

"Hazel tells me you been sick in the mornings. They saw where you threw up in the chamber pot." He said, eyeing her carefully. She did not return his look but continued to stare straight ahead.

"I think it's time you left this place." He walked toward her. "They tell me you been acting odd, talking to the walls like there was somebody there. I'm gonna bring you home with me. That way, Mildred can look after you. We can't have nothin' happen to the baby."

When he left, Haylee went back to the window to watch the hawks circle over the pines.

**-20-**
**Reckoning**

Woodard drove her back to the old Victorian the next day. Mildred was waiting in the car. Haylee was only mildly surprised to see the woman appeared younger and thinner than when she'd last seen her.

"There's my baby girl," Mildred said.

Woodard seated her next to the black woman, then took his place behind the wheel. "You sure look poorly, Ms. Haylee," Mildred said. "That place did you no good. No good a'tall. Well, you're going home now. Things'll be better, I promise."

The sun shining through the windows warmed her skin, but it could not warm her spirit.

*Home. How can I go home? They took that from me when they locked me away and again, when Grandfather made me pregnant.*

"It sure is a beautiful day, ain't it." Mildred continued. "Lawd, yes. A day the Lord has made." Mildred continued her prattle as they rolled along past the tall pines and sweet gums. Woodard lowered his window, filling the car with the smell of honeysuckle. "I just love this time of year," the black woman said. "Everything is so alive in the spring time."

Mildred paused. "I see you not up to talking, Miss Haylee, and that's all right for now. You go ahead and be just as quiet as you want, but I bet when you see what's waiting for you at home, you're gonna jabber up a storm. Yes, Lord."

Woodard turned onto the long drive. Beneath the floorboard, the tires crunched as they ate up the last of the distance. In a moment, they broke through the trees, onto the lawn where the old house stood, tall and silent, against a blaze of blue sky. Woodard steered into a spot of shade on the side of the house and shut off the engine. Swinging open the driver's door, he stood with arms folded, a frown on his face, waiting for the two women to exit.

"You just go on about your business, Daddy." Mildred said, "I'll get Miss Haylee settled."

Woodard grumbled something under his breath, then stalked away.

"Don't you pay him no mind, Miss Haylee," Mildred said, her voice carefree as she climbed out of the car. "He's a grumpy old cuss, but he'll get over it soon enough." Reaching through the open door, she tugged Haylee out beside her. "Just wait till you see what's waiting for you," Mildred cooed, walking Haylee to the front door, "Now, Daddy Woodard's not happy about it, but I said 'Daddy this is for the best.'"

Mildred hurried her up the tall staircase, stopping outside her mother's room, where she'd stayed.

"Close your eyes," Mildred's eyes twinkled with mischief.

Haylee continued to stare from unfocused eyes.

"Well, if you ain't gonna close your eyes, then turn around." Mildred said, turning Haylee so her back was to the door. "Now, stand just like that until I say so."

Mildred swung the bedroom door open and stepped to the side.

"Now you can look," she said.

"Haylee!" cried a voice. Virginia raced out of the room. She wrapped her thin arms around Haylee's legs. "I prayed you would come back and you did."

Haylee looked down to where the girl clung, her brow creased as if she was trying to remember who this strange waif might be.

"It's me, Virginia," the girl said. "Don't you remember me?"

"Virginia," Haylee repeated, then she began to cry.

***

"I think we should go out," said Virginia.

She sat on the bed they shared next to Haylee. Virginia stayed at Haylee's side, seeing that she bathed and fixed her hair. She also carried the meals Mildred fixed upstairs to the bedroom where they ate. Haylee refused to leave the room.

"It'll be cold soon," Virginia pointed out the window where the distant trees blazed every shade of red and gold. "Mildred said if we start now, we can make a winter vegetable garden. She has seeds

367

and everything. Can we make a garden, Haylee?" Virginia pleaded. "I really want to, it would be fun and we could eat the vegetables when they're grown."

Haylee studied the closed door. What had once been her prison now served as fortification, a shield against those who hurt her. Though she loved Virginia, she wasn't sure she could pass through that door.

In here, she was safe from Woodard and the rest. Only Mildred made an occasional visit to check the progress of her pregnancy. She placed a hand on her stomach, tracing its rounded shape. Jen called them baby bumps. Most women would be excited about their pregnancies.

*I feel like Rosemary in the Gore Vidal novel.* Her pregnancy was her horror and shame.

"Come on, Haylee. It'll be fun," Virginia said. She wasn't giving up the idea easily.

Virginia grasped Haylee's hand in a pretend tug. Haylee looked at the small hand that gripped hers. It was the hand with the missing finger. Since their reunion, neither of them mentioned it. Virginia seemed to have gotten past what they did to her. Haylee wanted to forget her own abuse, but couldn't.

*I've been disfigured, a different way than Virginia, but it's damage just the same.*

Haylee let Virginia lead her to the door.

"We can get seeds from Mildred." The girl jabbered excitedly. "She said we can grow carrots and peas and some other stuff. We'll be like farmers."

*What if the door is locked?* A part of her hoped it would be, then the problem would be solved. It opened easily at her touch and she found herself in the hall with no one blocking her way.

Virginia hurried her down the stairs to the kitchen. Mildred stood in the familiar place by the stove, stirring a large pot. The smell of stew meat filled the room.

"Why, Miss Haylee, it's so nice to see you up and about. You need exercise. Exercise ensures a smooth delivery when the time comes."

"We want to make a garden," Virginia chimed excitedly.

"I think we can arrange that," Mildred said, grabbing a dishrag off the peg by the stove, wiping her hands. "But the first thing you got to do is find a sunny spot. Plants need lots of light."

They followed Mildred outside, where Virginia flittered back and forth from one sunny spot to another.

Mildred pulled Haylee to the side while the girl hunted for the perfect spot.

"I don't think you're having twins." Mildred said, "Though it's too early to tell for sure. The way it's growing so fast makes me think it's a male. If it is, then it's the one promised."

"I don't care what it is," Haylee said, "I want it gone."

"It'll be gone soon enough and if it's male, sooner still," said the black woman. "I've come to believe that what will be, will be. Twice, I've tried to end this abomination against nature and God. I thought it was over after I helped your mother get away but they brought you here to take her place. Now it's cost a good man his life. Curse the day Joseph Slaughter was born."

"Well, I see you come out of your hole."

Haylee turned to see Claude Woodard amble toward them. Again, she was struck by his youthfulness.

Virginia shrank back at his approach. She hid behind Haylee, her arms locked around Haylee's waist.

Woodard strolled up beside them and gazed down at Haylee's tiny bulge. He placed a hand on her stomach.

Haylee pulled away. "Don't touch me," she spat.

Woodard's bottom lip curled, his eyes narrowed. "Be careful how you speak, Girl," he said. "Father Joseph will be here later to see how his seed is thriving inside you. I suggest you show him more courtesy than you have me."

"Father Joseph...but you're Joseph Slaughter, Grandfather."

Woodard laughed. "Whatever gave you that idea? Because I'm the Reeve? Darlin', I'm not your grandfather or your daddy. Joseph is. I'm named Reeve because it helps keep strangers' eyes off him.

Only when the promised one is born will Joseph take his rightful place. Then, the rift will be mended and all men will know the truth of *Ilhuicateotl*. Don't do nothin' to hurt the baby," he warned, then stalked away.

Mildred, who'd slipped off, returned with stakes and string. With Woodard gone, the three of them staked out a rectangular plot and fenced it off with the string. Haylee tried to focus on the task, but one thought haunted her.

*If Woodard isn't my father, who is? Later, I'll see who he is, but what face will I see? Who is the true Joseph Slaughter?*

Slaughter did not come that night, the day after, or the day after that. Haylee and Virginia worked the little patch of ground, preparing their garden for planting, and at night, she watched the fires burn their savage dance, an echo left from a culture mostly forgotten. All the while, the thing in her belly grew.

With the garden staked out and divided into plots for the various vegetables they would grow, Haylee asked Woodard for shovels and hoes.

Woodard fished in his pocket, where he produced a key ring with a dozen keys. "I don't want you doing nothing to harm that child you're carryin'," he said, "Let the girl do the work."

They walked around to the back of the house where the tool shed stood, and Haylee slipped the key into the ancient padlock that secured the door. The shed door opened with a creak. Cobwebs

371

covered most of the shed's contents. A variety of garden tools leaned against the wall, wedged against a cardboard box. Virginia stepped into the shed and selected a shovel and hoe, then stopped in front of the box.

"Why is there a box of salt in here?" she asked, reaching down to scoop some into her hand.

"Salt?" Haylee asked, looking where Virginia reached with her free hand. Her eyes fell on a white skull and crossbones, the words *Strychnine Hydrochloride* were printed beneath it in bold red letters.

"Don't touch that," Haylee cried, jerking the girl back. "It's poison."

On their way back to back to the sunny spot, Virginia asked Haylee about the box.

"It's poison, honey, bad poison. It could kill you."

"Then why is it here?" the girl wanted to know.

"I don't know, Honey," she said, though she thought she did. "Touching that could have made you sick or killed you. Didn't you see it was marked *poison*?"

"Nobody ever taught me to read," Virginia said. "I've never been to school."

"What if I taught you?" Haylee asked, "Would you like that?"

"Would you?" Virginia asked, dancing with excitement.

"Sure."

Virginia grabbed Haylee and hugged her. "I love you so much," she said.

Haylee felt a tear in her eye. "And I love you."

Staying true to her promise, Haylee let Virginia do most of the work. Actually, her belly was becoming so swollen it was difficult to do much of anything. *I should barely be showing at all, but I look like I'm in my third trimester. What have they done to me?*

Virginia went straight to work. Jabbing the shovel into the soil, she created a line of shovel marks to act as a border. As the girl worked, Haylee noticed Woodard peeping through the window, wearing a look of distrust.

*Why won't he leave us alone? Why won't everyone leave us alone?*

Virginia turned over the last shovelful of dirt when a sleek, dark sedan rolled up the driveway. The doors opened and two men in suits got out. One of the men gave Haylee a friendly nod.

"Howdy, Ma'am," he said, "I'm looking for a Claude Woodard. I was told this was his address."

Haylee knew the drill; Woodard put her through it enough.

"Mr. Woodard doesn't live here anymore."

"Who might you be?" the other man asked. His eyes swept his surroundings as if memorizing the layout.

"I'm Deborah Marlborough," Haylee said, taking Virginia's hand. "This is my daughter."

The first man glanced at the house, then back at Haylee. "Anyone else live here besides you and your girl?"

The front door opened and Woodard stepped onto the porch. "Can I help you gentlemen with something?"

"Yes, sir," said the stern faced man, "We're agents Bradley and Summers," he nodded at his partner, "We're investigating a missing person, possibly a kidnapping across state lines. This was the last location the missing party was reported to be."

"Oh," Woodard glided down the steps toward the two men.

Haylee held her breath, wondering what he might do.

"I'm Thomas Marlborough," he said, extending his hand.

"Pleased to meet you Mr. Marlborough," said Summers, "Your wife tells me Mr. Woodard doesn't live here anymore."

Woodard shook his head in mock pity. "I'm afraid Claude died shortly after he sold this place to me. He was suffering from cancer. The doctors didn't give him much time. He said he wanted to spend his last days with family."

"You wouldn't happen have an address?"

"No, sir," Woodard said, "I don't. I didn't want to press him about personal things."

"I understand," Summers continued. "I guess we'll have to ask around."

"Maybe I can help you with your search," Woodard said.

The two men exchanged looks.

"We're looking for information on these two people." Summers said, producing two eight-by-ten glossies. He checked the back of the photos "A Jennifer Mason and a Michael Bullock, both residents of New Orleans. They told relatives they were driving to Acedia to visit a Haylee Woods who was staying with her grandfather. That was four months ago. They never returned home."

Haylee jumped at the mention Jen, then she caught Bradley eyeing her. Had he seen her reaction?

She took Virginia by the hand. "Come on, honey," she said to the girl. "Let these men finish their business. We need to get supper started."

"But we don't make supper, Mildred does." Virginia protested.

"Mildred's ill today so we have to do it." Haylee said, giving Virginia's arm a tug.

The two agents nodded as she passed. Haylee was careful not to look back as she guided Virginia into the house. She pushed the child up the stairs ahead of her, then slid the curtains aside on their rods and waved frantically. The men were looking at Woodard and didn't see her. Throwing away caution, she tapped on the window, hoping the agents would look up. If they heard her raps, they didn't respond. Her heart sank as she watched them climb into their car and drive away.

The bedroom door burst open, slamming against the wall with a crash. Woodard charged inside and grabbed Haylee by her shoulders, flinging her to the floor.

"Don't ever try that again," he stood over her, his hands balled into fists. He unbuckled his belt and jerked it through the belt loops. It dangled from his hand like a wide, flat whip. "I think you ought to be taught a lesson."

He brought the belt down across Haylee's legs. As hot pain shot up her shins, she screamed. The belt bit into the flesh again and she twisted in agony. Virginia threw herself on Woodard, but he tossed her halfway across the room.

The belt struck a third time and Haylee felt the trickle of blood. She screamed again. Then Mildred was there, staying Woodard's hand.

"Stop it, Daddy. You'll kill her."

Woodard lowered the belt. Breathing heavily, he stepped back, his eyes wild.

"Go on downstairs," she said, "I'll deal with this."

Woodard stumbled out the door, his footsteps disappearing down the hall.

"That was a foolish thing to do, Miss Haylee," Mildred said. "You could have got yourself kilt and then what would have happened to her?" She nodded toward Virginia, who was huddled in the corner.

She helped Haylee off the floor onto the bed. "I'll bring something to treat your legs. You're going to have some nasty bruises."

\*\*\*

The next morning, the pain in Haylee's legs was nearly unbearable. She hid it best she could as she and Virginia descended the stairs to work the garden. The garden was important to Virginia and Haylee intended that Virginia be allowed to continue working in it. She was surprised that when she asked Woodard for the key to the tool shed, he handed it to her as if nothing had happened.

Outside, Haylee sat against the side of the house, her legs too painful to stand on. She gave Virginia the keys to the shed, then waited for the girl to return with the tools. When Virginia did not reappear right away, Haylee became concerned. The shed contained a lot of dangerous things aside from the strychnine, and Virginia couldn't read. After an agonizing wait, Virginia came around the corner, struggling with the hoe and shovel.

"I had trouble with the lock," she said, smiling, "But I got it open." She handed the keys to Haylee.

Taking the hoe, Virginia went to work, her face pinched with concentration as she worked the ground in a chopping motion. Watching the girl, Haylee felt a sense of pride at Virginia's dedication to the plot.

*She's all that keeps me going. Without her, I would have found a way to end it.*

377

"Mildred is going to teach me how to cook," Virginia said, taking a break. Even though the weather was pleasantly cool, beads of perspiration gleamed against Virginia's skin in the bright sunlight. "Then I can cook the things we're growing when they're ready."

Despite the horrendous events in her life, Virginia still found something positive to hold to.

*She's amazing,* Haylee thought.

\*\*\*

Two weeks after Woodard's warning, Joseph Slaughter made his visit. Though all but the most severe of the bruises were now faded, Haylee's legs still pained her. Nights were especially bad. Mildred thought nerve damage was the cause.

The black woman shook her head. "There ain't much I can do, Miss Haylee, except give you something to help you sleep."

\*\*\*

Between her painful legs and her swollen belly, Haylee spent her time in her room gazing at the distant mountains through the window or down at Virginia who still faithfully worked the tiny patch of garden alone. It was too difficult for Haylee to make unnecessary trips down the stairs. At night, Virginia would present her with whatever dish Mildred taught her to cook that night and Haylee always made a grand showing of how good the food was.

Haylee was massaging her pained legs with her hands when Mildred peeped in.

"They want you downstairs," she said.

"They?"

"Sheriff Riddle brung Father Joseph. He wants to see you."

Immediately, she thought of Virginia alone in the kitchen. Riddle couldn't be trusted around her, none of them could.

She levered herself off the bed, bracing for the agony she felt each time she put weight on her legs. The pain came in a sharp, wicked wave, then settled to a bearable ache.

"I'll help you," Mildred said, "Put your arm on my shoulder. We'll take it slow. Easy, now. That's good."

They inched to the staircase one step at a time.

Riddle stood at the foot of the stairs, grinning.

"Hey there, pretty lady," he said, with a grin that split the bottom of his face. "Getting kinda of big around the waist, ain't you? 'Course, I always did think preggy women had a charm about 'em."

Haylee said nothing.

"Shut your mouth, Riddle," said a voice. "I won't have you disrespecting my wife."

*I know that voice. That's the voice I heard chanting in the bedroom.*

"Come here, Girl, so I can see how far along you are," the voice continued.

Riddle stepped back, averting his eyes. Mildred helped Haylee down the last steps.

"I can make it from here," Haylee said, "Virginia shouldn't be alone."

Father Joseph sat with his back to her. Woodard sat across from him, facing Haylee's approach. She thought she detected fear in his eyes as she stumbled along on her damaged legs.

*He's afraid Joseph will see what he did to me.* Some of the bruises were still visible below the hem of the shapeless shift Haylee wore.

*In a moment, I'll see the face of the man in the visions, the one in the shadows in the long house. I'll see the face of my father.*

These thoughts passed through her mind as she neared the man who, until tonight, wore a mask. She rounded the chair until she stood face to face with Joseph Slaughter.

The sour-faced man who'd played the violin at homecoming smiled at her.

Like Woodard, he looked younger than before. Many of the creases that gave his face a pinched look were now missing. His mouth still curved down in a permanent scowl, and his eyebrows arched as if he carried an undying anger against the world.

"Come to me, Darlin'," he said, reaching out a hand. His lips smiled but his eyes remained narrow slits, hard and unforgiving.

Haylee allowed him to draw her forward. He placed a hand on her belly, the fingers probing here and there.

"I was a doctor as well as a priest," he said as he examined the bulge. "You've done a good job carrying the baby. You got a healthy one inside you. I can feel him wiggle."

"Why did you kill Paul?" Haylee asked. "And Jen? She was my friend."

Slaughter glanced at Woodard, "You told me the girl had lost her spirit, Claudius. I think you misjudged her." He turned back to Haylee. "Claudius served me well from the beginning. He scouted ahead when we made the journey from Virginia. The passage was filled with danger, both beast and savages, but Claudius blazed the way, making the passage safe for us all, as the Archangel Michael might have done, with his fiery sword. As a reward, I made him Reeve, and he still serves in that post today.

\*\*\*

"But to your question: Who knows the mind of *Ilhuicateotl*? He provides who he will for sacrifice and we do not question his wisdom. We accept all he sends to us with thanksgiving and joy.

"As for the boy, Paul: True, he delivered you to us as promised, but it was a traitorous act and traitors cannot be trusted. If he would betray you, he would one day betray us."

"And your brother, Hooch?"

"Another turncoat, and so, received the same fate. *Ilhuicateotl* receives all offerings equally, no matter the color of their heart, be it purest white or darkest black.

"But there is one you have not asked about. The one that helped your mother escape and released you from the smokehouse. Oh yes, I know about Mildred's part in this." Slaughter said, his eyes twinkling with devious humor, "I've always known. Just as I knew where to find you."

"Then why didn't you…" Haylee glanced through the arch that opened to the dining room where Mildred set the table for Woodard's guests.

"Offer her at the fires as well?" Slaughter said, finishing her sentence. "She is special. She is a healer. She serves *Ilhuicateotl's* purpose even when she seeks to fight us. It matters not now, anyway. You will deliver the promised one soon, as *Ilhuicateotl* showed me in the vision."

"Was leading me to believe Woodard was my grandfather part of *Ilhuicateotl's* plan too?"

Slaughter stood. "I think Mildred has dinner ready," he said. He rose and took her hand, speaking as they went. "You see as a priest of the Holy Apostolic Church, in order to be faithful to my vows, I am not allowed to wed. Therefore I made Claudius surrogate in my place and like in all things, he brought honor to that role. Until today, I have never revealed myself to any of my brides. They assumed it was Claudius that bedded them, even your mother."

382

They reached the table and Slaughter took Woodard's place at the head.

"So why are you telling me?"

"Because you will give birth to the promise. It is only right you should know."

Woodard and Riddle joined them. The sheriff took his place to Slaughter's left, while Woodard sat on the right.

"Won't you join us?" Slaughter asked.

Haylee caught Virginia standing in the kitchen doorway out of the corner of her eye. The girl shook her head.

"I don't think so." she said "I don't feel that well."

"Father Joseph asked you to join us," Woodard growled at Haylee. "You do not refuse him."

Slaughter waved his hand. "Simmer down, Claudius. This is not a battlefield, where you issue orders. The table is a place where sustenance is shared, a place of peace. If she wishes to abstain, then she may."

Slaughter cast a kindly eye at Haylee. "You have permission to withdraw. Should you feel like eating later, Mildred will see to whatever you prefer."

Haylee made the painful climb up the stairs to her room. Her legs burned like two pillars of fire. It was a relief to reach the bed and shift the weight off her feet. She wished Virginia was here so she knew the girl was safe. Should something set

Woodard off, even Slaughter might not be able to hold him back.

The baby moved inside her. *He's ready to come out. And when he does, what will it mean?* She shuddered at the possibilities.

***

Virginia joined her an hour later, the girl's face drawn. Haylee jumped to her feet, ignoring the ache it caused as she rushed to the girla and swept her up in her arms.

"Mildred said I needed to come up here. They're drinking and arguing about you. That's why he came tonight. They have to decide what to do with you after the baby is born. I think they want to kill you like they did my parents."

Haylee felt her blood chill. Not for herself: she had nothing left, but for fear of what might happen to Virginia. She pulled the girl to her, clutching her tight.

"It's okay, Haylee," Virginia said. "You don't need to worry. Momma told me what to do."

### -21-
### Monsters

It was past midnight when the screams awakened her. At first, Haylee thought it was the dream.

She and Virginia were huddled inside the smokehouse and had barred the door. From outside, came the cries of those unlucky people who had not found shelter from the huge, horned creatures stalking the woods. The creatures were apelike, with sharp, jagged teeth. They moved with lightning speed, trapping their victims, and wrapping them with their long, muscular arms that ended with claws that they used to tear away flesh. They devoured the unfortunates alive.

Haylee jerked awake and looked around. She was in her bed alone. Even though the dream vanished, the screams continued. She slipped from under the covers, careful not to disturb Virginia, and crept to the door.

"Mildred, help me!" the voice cried, "My stomach's on fire. The damn girl poisoned me!" She heard bumps on the stairs. "I'll kill that little bitch!" Woodard roared "Gawd, my stomach's filled with hot lava."

Haylee's mind raced, trying to fathom exactly what happened.

*Somehow, Virginia did what I couldn't or was too afraid to do. But if he reaches her...He's already taken a finger. What will he do to her now?*

Woodard's voice rose in pitch. He was close. She needed to wake Virginia and hide the child before Woodard reached them. She spun away from the door, toward the bed. Virginia was awake. She sat upright with the covers piled around her, smiling.

"I put monsters in the bad people," she said. "So they couldn't hurt us anymore."

Something slammed against the door. Haylee screamed. She snatched Virginia from the bed. Thrusting the girl behind her, she scanned the room for a weapon. Failing to spot one, she placed herself between the girl and the door, and readied herself for when Woodard burst through. If necessary, she would use her fingernails and teeth as weapons to defend Virginia.

Minutes passed and Woodard failed to appear. Haylee waited and still the enraged man did not charge through the door. Her heart pounding in her chest, she crossed the room to the door, conscious of each step along the way. Her hand on the knob, she eased the door open, braced for the inevitable attack from the other side.

Woodard lay face down in the hallway. A thin ribbon of blood trickled across the threshold, away from the door.

"He's dead," Mildred said. The woman stood to the side wringing her hands. "You need to leave while you can, while it's dark. The keys to the Packard are in his pocket. Meet me downstairs when you're done."

Haylee knelt beside Woodard's body and shoved a hand into his pocket and felt for the keys. Her fingers located them, and she pulled them free, then stepped quickly away from the corpse.

She looked at Virginia. "How?"

Virginia smiled. "I put poison salt in his food," said the girl, "From that box in the shed. I took a little every day that I worked in the garden, and hid it in salt cellar in the cupboard. Then I put it in his food."

"Strychnine is poisonous to touch," Haylee said, "You should have gotten sick."

"Mildred gave me gloves to wear." The girl smiled. "I think she wanted me to put monsters in him."

***

At the foot of the stairs, Mildred handed Haylee a bottle of dark liquid. "Drink this when you stop to rest," she said.

Haylee eyed the bottle. "What is it?"

"It'll kill the thing growing inside you."

On the way to the car, they passed the twisted body of Joseph Slaughter on the lawn. Riddle's patrol car was missing.

*He's somewhere out there. We'll need to be careful.*

Haylee unlocked the door and shooed Virginia inside. "Come with us," she said to Mildred. "They'll blame you if you stay here."

She shook her head. "What will be will be. The people are without a shepherd. Someone needs to help them along. It's up to me to do that." She nudged Haylee into the car and closed the door. "You need to go while you can. See you take care of Virginia."

Before Haylee could say she would, Mildred was gone.

The Packard fired up easily, and the gas gauge showed a full tank. Haylee backed the car around, then steered it down the long drive toward freedom. As Haylee steered the sedan along, she watched for car lights behind them that would mean Riddle was on their trail. She remembered how easily he dogged them when she and Paul first crossed into Slaughter County.

They reached Acedia without incident and passed through the sleeping town without any sign of the sheriff.

*They're going to wake up tomorrow morning with their whole world changed,* she thought as the town fell behind them. *I hope they suffer as much as Jen did. As I did.*

A few minutes later, she spotted Riddle's car where it left the road and crashed through a barbed wire fence before smashing into a massive oak. She pulled over to the shoulder of the road. Leaving Virginia asleep on the passenger's side of the bench seat, she quietly opened her door and picked her way across the field, following the ruts the car made. When she reached the patrol car, she saw that the impact of the crash drove Riddle's upper body through the windshield so he lay partially on the hood.

Haylee gazed at the dead man with as much emotion as if he was a limp sack filled with sand. Any anger or fear she felt earlier had eroded away. After a moment, she walked back to the Packard and continued their journey.

Two miles outside of Huntsville, she found a clearing in a pocket of trees that hid car from the road. They slept until noon. When they awoke, Haylee felt better. She fixed herself as much as possible then drove into town. At the second pawnshop she visited, she was able to sell the ring.

"I'll be honest with you," said the broker, a stocky man with close-cropped hair. "I can't give you near what it's worth. Two-hundred is the best I can do. I'm crazy to offer that, but you look like you could use the bucks, being pregnant and all."

Haylee took the money and thanked him. Then the girls ate lunch at Denny's, and drove on to Birmingham where they stopped at a motel. She left Virginia in the car while she went inside to check in.

In the bathroom of the room she rented, she uncapped the dark liquid Mildred gave her. Lifting it to her lips, she hesitated.

*There's a life inside me, innocent of the sin that created it. It deserves a chance.*

She lowered the bottle and tipped the contents into the sink. When she finished, she turned on the faucet and let the water run while she carefully wiped the bowl of any trace of the stuff that might have clung to the porcelain. Virginia, who was delighted to find their room had a television, was watching cartoons when she returned.

The next morning, after breakfast, they climbed into the Packard and Haylee pulled onto the interstate. At the I-10 junction, she steered the car south. The morning sun poured through the windshield, warming her skin and promising a beautiful day.

### -Afterward-

Haylee completed her circle of the room after pausing to stop and speak to each of the clusters of the beautifully dressed people scattered about. Her most recent photographs, black and white portraits of runaway teens with haunted eyes, hung, neatly framed on the windowless, off-white gallery walls.

She caught snatches of conversation as she worked her way to where Mr. Garza waited with Adam, who was now four.

"They're so sensitive," said a woman pointing to a photograph of a boy and girl dressed in dirty jeans and t-shirts. The pair was huddled in a dark doorway. The girl's head lay on the boy's shoulder. Neither could have been older than fourteen.

"A tragedy," said the man. "The children, I mean. The photograph is superb."

Haylee smiled. Though she received a multitude of accolades for her work, she never tired of them. It validated what she did.

Another group composed of art students from a local university, scribbled notes, moving from one photo to another. Earlier, they interviewed Haylee about this particular series and what inspired her to focus on runaways. They explained she was to be featured in an article they were writing for the university newspaper.

The fifteen city tour promoting her book: *Forgotten Angels*: *Portraits of Children of the Streets,* was a huge success. Tonight, they were in Houston, the last stop of the tour. Tomorrow, she would fly to Chicago where she would appear as a guest on *Oprah.*

She'd arranged for Virginia to travel with her. Mr. Garza would watch Adam while they were gone. Adam called the old man grandpa, and Haylee had come to think of him as a surrogate father.

When Haylee showed up on the old man's doorstep, pregnant and with Virginia beside her, Garza welcomed her inside immediately. Though he must have wondered how she'd gotten into such dire straits, he asked no questions, seeking instead to make Haylee feel as safe and comfortable as possible.

After Adam was born, Garza encouraged Haylee to take up photography again. He also proved an able publicist, pitching her photographs to the Chamber of Commerce, local banks, anywhere he could find someone willing to hang them. He arranged interviews with two of the local television stations, resulting in her first show at one of the local universities.

Before she knew it, she was receiving offers from other universities wanting to display her work. Not long afterward, she was contacted by one of the New York publishing houses inquiring if she would be interested in publishing some of her portraits. They were thinking of her series of homeless children and were willing to offer her a five-figure advance.

She took a breath. It still seemed like a dream. *But it's all real,* she thought. *The people here are real and they came to see my work.*

Mr. Garza caught her attention with a wave, drawing her out of her musings. She covered the last of the distance between. Adam raised his arms to her as she neared. She lifted him off the floor, sounding an exaggerated grunt as she did.

"You're getting to be such a big boy," she said cradling him close to her breast. "Momma can hardly lift you anymore."

"I thought I'd take him back to the hotel," Mr. Garza said, holding out his own arms for the boy. "He's tired and needs a nap."

"I see you in an hour." Haylee said. "That's when the signing is over."

She kissed Adam and handed him to the old man.

"Say bye to Momma," Mr. Garza told the boy.

"Bye, Momma," Adam said obediently.

As Mr. Garza made his way through the crowd to the exit, Haylee saw Virginia weaving her way to her, towing a boy about her same age behind her. Virginia had grown into a beautiful teen and had her pick of any boy she wanted back home. Even so Virginia was far from conceited. She was popular with the other girls and was always getting invitations to parties and sleepovers.

"This is Cody," Virginia said, when she reached Haylee. "He invited me to have an ice cream across the street at the Dairy King. Is it all right if I go, Haylee? Please?"

Haylee smiled. Cody was cute, with curly brown hair and spray of freckles across the bridge of his nose. The boy kept his eyes on Virginia, as if in a trance.

"For an hour," Haylee said, "And don't go anywhere else. We still have to pack for Los Angeles."

"Thanks, Haylee," Virginia said. Still holding Cody's hand, she spun him around toward the exit. "Haylee is going to be on Oprah." The girl told him excitedly, leading him away.

Exhausted, Haylee found a chair by the table that the gallery provided for her to sign copies of her book. She dropped into it and let out a long sigh.

*I am so ready to be finished with all of this and get home. I feel like I haven't stopped moving since we started the book tour. Now I know how rock stars feel.*

Though the tour was hectic, she was grateful for the positive reception of her work. Book sales were phenomenal and she was told she earned a permanent place among the top photographers. Several agents solicited to represent her when the tour was over. Her photos considered instant classics; she would not lack for work.

*I really need to talk to Pawpaw about selling the apartment building and retiring. I'm making enough off the book sales we won't need to worry about money. We can buy a nice place in the country, where Adam can grow up without all the turmoil and violence of the city. We'll find a spot with lot of land and a pond. Pawpaw can take Adam fishing and maybe we'll even add a stable and horses.* The thought made her smile.

Lost in her future plans, she didn't notice the person approach her until he softly spoke her name.

"Ms. Woods?"

Haylee looked up at the young man standing over her. It was one of the catering staff.

"I'm sorry to disturb you, Ms. Woods," he said uneasily.

"No, it's all right," she said. "I was just resting for a moment."

"I was asked to give you this," the young man said, rushing the words. He handed her a sealed envelope and a tiny rectangular gift box.

She scanned the blank envelope. It was square like a greeting card.

"May I ask who these are from?"

"The lady didn't give a name," said the young man, "She said she was an old friend and someone you would recognize when you opened the gift."

"Thank you," she said, placing the envelope and tiny box on the table.

The young man nodded and left. Haylee toyed with the envelope for a moment, lifting it, testing its weight in her hand. Finally, her curiosity became too great. Turning it over, she worked the back flap loose and slid out a sheet of stiff paper. The message was written in black ink in tight, even characters.

*Dear Haylee,*

*How good to see you again. It's wonderful you've done so well for yourself. I thought the photographs were lovely. It's too bad there weren't any of us, but you can take some next time we get together.*

*I was also pleased to see how Adam has grown, and how healthy he is. We talked for a while. He's a regular little chatterbox.*

*Well, you're probably wondering who wrote this. The answer is in the box.*

Haylee laid the note on the table. Her hand trembled so badly, she had difficulty picking up the box and loosening its lid. Inside another, a folded piece of paper rested on top of white gauze. Haylee unfolded it:

*Remember the charm, Cousin? Did you ever wonder what that bit of cloth was wrapped around? Why, it was your finger, the extra one. Inside this box is another charm. Guess whose finger I made this one with?*

*Looking forward to seeing you soon,*

*Cynthie*

Haylee dropped the note like it was a hot sheet of metal. With a shaky hand, she lifted the gauze that covered whatever lay beneath. Nestled in the box cushioned by a pillow of cotton, was Virginia's mummified, finger.

20/07/2008

Ronald Polizzi hails from the Deep South. Early in his childhood, his parents suffered serious illnesses and he was sent to a rural part of Alabama to live with his grandparents. While there, his uncles entertained him with stories of Night Hags, Bog Witches and Devils at the Crossroads. These stories would later serve as a foundation for Mr. Polizzi's fictional South, filled with haunted bayous and creatures birthed in unholy swamps.

He earned his Bachelor of Fine Arts degree and a Masters in Art Education from the University of South Alabama. Mr. Polizzi worked as a musician, a portrait painter and a teacher before turning his full attention to fiction writing.

Mr. Polizzi lives in Mobile, Alabama with his wife, daughter, one brother, their dog and sixteen cats.

www.ingramcontent.com/pod-product-compliance
Lightning Source LLC
Chambersburg PA
CBHW070354260626
47161CB00001B/132